Ilya Ehrenburg

The Stormy Life of Lasik Roitschwantz

THE STORMY LIFE OF LASIK ROITSCHWANTZ

A novel by
Ilya Ehrenburg

THE POLYGLOT LIBRARY NEW YORK

Russian title:
BURNAYA ZHIZN' LAZIKA ROITSCHWANTZA
translated by Leonid Borochowicz and
Gertrude Flor.

224 West 20 Street, New York 11, N.Y.

Library of Congress Catal[illegible]ber: 60-11369

Printed in U.S.A.

A Selected List of Published Books by Ilya Ehrenburg:

Dreizehn Pfeifen, n.d.
Scènes de la revolution:
  Un événement bien curieux, Paris, 1923.
Michail Lykow, Berlin, 1927.
La vie de Gracchus Babeuf, Paris, 1929.
Visum der Zeit, Leipzig, 1929.
The Extraordinary Adventures of Julio Jurenito, New York, 1930.
The Love of Jeanne Ney, New York, 1930.
Das Leben der Autos, Berlin, 1930.
Die Traumfabrik, Berlin, 1931.
Die Heiligsten Güter, Berlin, 1931.
A Street in Moscow, New York, 1932.
España, Madrid, 1932.
Der Zweite Tag, Berlin, 1933.
Der Bürgerkrieg in Oesterreich, 1934.
Estampa de España, Madrid, 1937.
A spanyol hadszintérrol jeleuti, Braitslawa, 1938.
The Fall of Paris, New York, 1943.
The Fate of Europe, Sydney, 1944.
The Tempering of Russia, New York, 1944.
Cent lettres, Moscow, 1944.
We Will Not Forget, Washington, 1944.
We Come as Judges, London, 1945.
En Bulgarie, Sofia, 1945.
Wrocilem of USA, Warzawa, 1948.
The Storm, London, 1949.
Il leone della piazza, commedia in tre atti, Torino, 1949.
Wobronie pokoju, Warzawa, 1950.
Dem Frieden, Berlin, 1952.
The Thaw, Chicago, 1955.

The Stormy Life of Lasik Roitschwantz

1

It can be said that Lasik's life went to the dogs because of an involuntary sigh. It all might have been different had he not sighed!

But the reader does not know which Lasik we speak of. For, after all, there are many Lasiks. For instance, that fellow Lasik Rochenstein, who played the part of the Tsar Paul at the club "Red Awakening," grunted a bit unnaturally; or, Lasik Ilmanovitch, the committee's district secretary, the biggest glutton there ever was. Boldly he ate Mazzoth with eggs last year, without the slightest fear of being purged from the party.

And not only that, but the rascal even used the reputation of the Health Department, claiming the nutritional value of such foods. And besides, they do not create gases in your stomach! There is also someone in Odessa, called Lasik. I went there to give a lecture on French literature. As usual, there were many questions like: "To what class do you belong?" and "Why don't you tell us about Comrade Koslov's expedition?" and "Confess, you son of a bitch, for how many pounds were you bought?" There was also this remark: "Look here, Shapiro, Lasik has fallen asleep already." Even though my name is not Shapiro, I became curious. Meanwhile there were many people around and I did not succeed in finding that Lasik who was asleep. I do not even know who he is, but one thing I know: he is a good-for-nothing. Everyone is trying to learn but he is sleeping.

No, Lasik Roitschwantz has never sunk that low.

I know everyone will say: "But goodness, what a horrible family name he has." . . . I shall not deny it. There are better-sounding names even among the tailors of Homel, not to speak of the orthodox clergy. For instance, Rosenblum or Applebaum.

And who cares about family names, anyway? For, after all, in our day and age, it would have cost Lasik a mere trifle to become a Spartacus Rosaluxemburgsky. Just look at Onissim Afanasjewitch Kutchewod, the bookkeeper of the concern "Firewood." He transformed himself into an Apollo Entusiastow. It is only a matter of two rubles and the proper enlightenment. If Lasik Roitschwantz had not yet been tempted by such glorious possibilities, he naturally had his reasons. He held on firmly to his rather plain family name, even though many a young lady hearing it would cry out: "Ay-ay-ay."

His name was an integral part of his well-weighed, deliberate plan of life. Whose pictures adorned the wall above Lasik's small bed? The answer is not easy. I should rather ask —how many pictures. Well, surely not less than one hundred. Everyone knows that the tailors of Homel decorate their walls with all kinds of Spanish naked beauties. But Lasik was not dumb. He liked to admire the lovely beauties when visiting others; his walls, however, were covered with pictures cut out of a magazine called "The Fire."

That man, for instance, with crayfish eyes—do you know who he is? Well, he is the deputy delegate of Pensa for the union of "Production of Chemistry." And that youth in the swimming trunks, stretching his thighs toward the sun—that was the famous proletarian minstrel, Shurka Bezdomny. To the right were the international categories. Do you not recognize them? The hostage of Portugal's hangman, Miguel Trakanza. To the left? Sst! . . . A proven fighter, Comrade Shmurigin, the chairman of Homel's . . . You understand, don't you?

To be sure, among all these fascinating photographs, there was also that of Lasik's dead aunt, Chassya Roitschwantz, who used to deal in fresh eggs in Glukhow. The picture must have gotten there by mistake. Poor aunt Chassya, standing between marble pillars, looked frightened and tense, with her mouth slightly open, like a chicken ready to lay an egg. Nevertheless, once when Pfeifer, the official landsurveyor, visited him, Lasik pointed at her photograph, saying: "This is the leader of all the proletarian cells in Paris. She is one of the oldest party members. Just look at those eyes! Such inexorable determination!"

All these brave fighters protected Lasik during the day. At night, they frightened him. Even the hostage from Portugal meddled into Roitschwantz' private life in the dark, suspicious quiet of the night: "You concealed from the Finance Inspector Pfeifer's pants, his overcoat and Syomka's jacket, for which he gave you the material . . . But do you also know what the Solovetski Islands are? Could that mean perhaps that a small, insignificant tailor from Homel would like to spend his life in a monastery, among other things? You thought it was hot in Portugal, huh—eighty degrees! In reality it was a hundred. Terrific! But on the Solovetski Islands it is closer to a hundred and fifteen below zero. Yes, my dear Lasik Roitschwantz, there you can dream a long time about the heat in Portugal!" And the hostage smacked his tongue and laughed sarcastically.

Shurka Bezdomny screamed horrible words just like the small business people in the club "Red Awakening." No doubt he hinted at Pfeifer's pants as well as at the Solovetski Islands: "You think you can cover yourself with a fig-leaf, you dog? We will teach you, you crazy Pole."

Even the good aunt Chassya, who used to give little Lasik a nickel on the day of Chanukka, even she cackled reproachingly: "How could you? Oh! . . ." Lasik crawled under the blanket.

Nevertheless he did not take the pictures off the wall. He would remain firm to the very end, just like Comrade Shmurigin. As though he had not suffered enough for his principles, you might say. He had even memorized sixteen poems written by Shurka Bezdomny, telling of a certain abnormal Communist brigade, that rode into death with a "victorious smile on its forehead." Nor was he frightened by the hand of Lewka, the barber, who within one minute transformed his kind and nervous countenance into that of a hardened scoundrel. What could you do. They planned to perform a play by Comrade Lunacharsky at the club "Red Awakening." This much you can say for Lasik: he will not commit sabotage! A scoundrel? Well, maybe. Yet, he willingly performed his role for the club. Despite the fact that he was repelled by her, he pretended to attack Sonitchka Zwiebil, leaping and snapping like a mad dog. Well, wouldn't you agree, what has a tailor from Homel got to do with a mad dog? Not only that, but on top of everything came the fact that Sonitchka's husband served in the militia. To be sure, those dog leaps were strictly a matter of the state, but Lasik did not know how citizen Zwiebil would react to such a performance. However, Lasik would not remain behind his contemporaries. He barked bravely, showing his teeth; then he bowed deeply to all the little merchants, who were roaring with laughter: "Oh what a fool, that Roitschwantz!" He murmured softly: "Thank you, Comrades, merci from all my heart." He could endure anything.

Even his strange sounding family name . . . Why did Rayetchka send him away? Surely not because of a fever blister? Just ask Lasik, and he will tell you: "Fever blisters—nonsense. A blister opens up and disappears just like any commissar in Homel. However the family name . . . How could anybody walk arm in arm with someone who had such a stupid name?" "With whom is Rayetchka walking?" "With Roitschwantz, naturally" . . . "Ha-ha-ha."

It does not matter. Let them laugh. Lasik is smarter than all of them put together. When summoned to answer the forty-seventh questionnaire, the red-haired Comrade Gorbunov of the administration asked Lasik:

"Family name?"

"Roitschwantz."

"What did you say?"

"Roitschwantz. You will excuse me, please, but this is a name which shows certain attributes. Right now there are many people who add some 'red' to their name, pretending they have always owned it. Since you do not happen to be from this town, I can reveal to you that the eating-place "Red Shelter," was just plain "Shelter" before. And over there, the Red Flag Street shockingly enough was nothing but Vladimir Street. If you think that the "Red bath-house" was always red, you are mistaken if you please. It has only happened a year ago that it blushed so becomingly. It was the bath house with the worst reputation for certain "families." My name, however has been Roitschwantz ever since I was born. Our official Rabbi can prove it, too. In my last name alone, they gave me an unobtrusive hint to guide the path of my life. However, I can see that you do not understand what I am talking about, therefore I shall explain it to you: 'Roit'—means 'red.' "

Comrade Gorbunow laughed out loud and asked in a sneering tone of voice:

"Well, well . . . and what does 'schwantz' mean?"

Lasik shrugged his shoulders disdainfully:

"I should say it is quite sufficient if one half has some meaning. 'Schwantz' means nothing. It is just an empty sound."

2

Lasik's downfall did not come because of his name. It was only because of that sigh. Perhaps it was not even the sigh, but rather the economic situation, or the hot weather, or perhaps even certain other lofty problems. After all, who knows, why tailors from Homel must be annihilated? . . .

It was indeed unbearably hot that certain day. The river Sosch dried up before the very eyes of the inhabitants of Homel. On the other hand, Comrade Kugel, the examining magistrate, was soaking wet, as though he had just been dragged out of the water.

It was around seven o'clock in the evening when Lasik decided to pay a visit to Fenitchka Hershanowitch, the cantor's daughter.

Fenitchka sang international songs in the club "Red Awakening." Quite frankly, she became a member of the club in a very sneaky way. For indeed, what kind of small businessman was this fellow Hershanowitch? What did he manufacture? He circumcised innocent little boys for three rubles apiece. The "cell" could have easily found out that Fenitschka lived on the shameful income of her father. The old Hershanowitch had said to his daughter:

"This fellow Schatzman stares at me for ten minutes without batting an eyelash. There are two possibilities—either he wants to marry you, or he wants to send me away to the Northern Narym. I beg of you, sing them a hundred international songs. Perhaps you can make them forget that I sing, too. If Daniel knew how to tame real lions, why should you not know how to calm those Jews? You will see, they will kill me yet, and I am only sorry that I ever circumcised them." I do not know whether Fenitchka's trills softened the hearts of the government committee members, but anyway Lasik heard her and he fell in love, passionately and silently. His name did not disturb Fenitchka—she was modern and broadminded. But the one thing she could not get used to was Lasik's shortness. And anyway what else is there for a cantor's daughter to do nowadays? To dream of a career like Mary Pickford and to dance foxtrots with people who did not belong to the party? With Lasik? . . . I must admit, Lasik's head just about reached Fenitchka's armpit. To be sure, he tried to walk on tiptoe, but that merely gave him more corns. How could he express his ardent feelings under such circumstances? How could he kiss Fenitchka's cheek stealthily on a quiet lover's lane? Even with a leap, he could not have reached her.

If Homel was broiling hot that day Lasik was doubly so: his heart was on fire, too. He had just finished pressing Pfeifer's pants. He got ready to leave the house and in order not to arouse any suspicious thoughts, he said to his neighbors:

"I am going to attend the course of political studies. If you only knew what the Chinese Question is! It is even more difficult to understand than the Kabbala. If I were Schatzman, I would forbid the small business people to occupy their minds with such weighty problems. This should be a matter of consideration and thought for some very high committees, but not for tailors in Homel . . ." He sighed, but it was not that sigh that ruined him, nor even the next one which came from the thought of Fenitchka's being so unattainable. Today he would tell her everything. He would tell her that David was small and Goliath, on the other hand, a boorish strong fellow, just like Schatzman. He would say that the nightingale was much smaller than an Indian turkey. He would tell her that, keeping in mind present history, a small organized minority can become victorious. He would tell her . . .

He might have surely come up with something to convince even the frivolous Fenitchka, but suddenly his attention was drawn toward the one-eyed Natik, who was busy pasting an enormous poster on the garden fence of the former Episcopalian School.

Whatever could have happened in this big world? Perhaps an Operetta Theater from Moscow had arrived for guest performances in Homel? In that case, one could not help but spend all his money for the best seats: Fenitchka was a very musical person. Or, it could be that they have come up with some new editions in favor of that Chinese manslaughter? Or perhaps that rascal Dishkin wanted to get rid of his stupid, nineteenth century guide for writing love letters, under the pretext of a campaign for enlightenment?

The poster was intended for citizens of average height, and Lasik had to stand on his toes, just as though Fenitchka Hershanowitch would be right in front of him. As soon as he had read the first sentence, he started with a jolt and quickly looked around. Next to him stood a woman citizen unknown to him. A member of the Moscow Operetta? Or was she an income-tax collector? The more Lasik read, the more he became agitated. His polka-dotted necktie fluttered, his diminutive head sitting on top of the indestructible celluloid collar bobbed up and down, the marvelous American atomizer with its miraculous scent of orchids that Lasik intended to present to Fenitchka, danced in his trouser pocket. Even his trousers shook, these exceptional pants made of English cloth (a spendthrift had to leave them behind when he was arrested in a raid after the second fitting). The giant letters on the poster swayed back and forth. The garden fence reeled. The sky shook.

"The proven leader of the Proletarians of Homel, Comrade Shmurigin, is dead. For six long and glorious years, the Red sword in his calloused hands made all international bandits tremble. And even though great men pass away, their ideas remain with us forever. Instead of the one, ten new fighters will appear who will punish all the hidden enemies of the revolution, relentlessly. . . ."

And here it happened that Lasik heaved a deep sigh, loud and doleful, let us say freely, from the bottom of his heart. Was it pity he felt for Comrade Shmurigin, who had died of a twisting of the bowels? Or was he seized by panic because of the ten new fighters that were to follow? Where should he get hold of their portraits? And furthermore, what would their position be toward all these half class-conscious minor tradespeople like him? And the trousers he had failed to declare to the Inspector of Finance, Pfeifer's trousers . . .

After that sigh, Lasik proceeded on his way. But he was not to tell Fenitchka anything of Goliath's infamous demise, nor was he to spray her with orchid perfume from the American atomizer.

Comrade Kugel, the examining magistrate, said to him in a foreboding voice:

"You have reviled the shining memory of Comrade Shmurigin, in public."

"I only sighed," Lasik sighed humbly. "I sighed because it was very hot and also because his sword has fallen from his calloused hands. I always sigh like that. If you do not believe me, you may ask the Citizen, Miss Hershanowitch, and should the Citizen Hershanowitch not be the proper witness because she is the daughter of a synagogue employe, you can ask the messenger boy of the Inspectorate of Finance. He knows very well how loud I always sigh. I might even tell you that last year they were going to force me to quit the union because my sighs were so unbearable to everybody. At night I am preoccupied with the political course and naturally I sigh for myself, but the Pfeifer family insist that I disturb their hard-earned sleep."

Comrade Kugel interrupted him:

"First of all, you talk too much. The bourgeoisie has invented not only the Taylor system but at the same time also the notorious aphorism: '*Time is money.*' With this they express the admiration of the dying class for the miserable increase of material values. We, however, say just the opposite: 'Time is *not* money.' 'Time is more than money.' You have just robbed me, and consequently the entire Workers' state of five most valuable minutes. Therefore, let us get to the point! The Citizen Matilda Pukke stated that you, after reading the poster in question, broke out into triumphant laughter, using an expression that cannot even be repeated here."

Lasik smiled politely. "I do not know who this Citizen Pukke is. Perhaps she is deaf-and-dumb or completely out of her mind. I can tell you only one thing: I am not even capable of triumphant laughter. When I had to laugh triumphantly in the Comrade Lunatcharsky's comedy, I was completely dumbfounded at the sight of the duchess, even though Lewka, the prompter called out at me: 'Laugh, you idiot.' I assure you, Comrade

Kugel that if I could use certain expressions and laugh triumphantly in bright daylight on Main Street, I would certainly not be an unhappy, insignificant tailor. I would either lie in some unknown grave or else, I would sit in Moscow on the most important peoples' committee . . ."

"You are pretending that you have just fallen down from heaven into our classless society. But it will hardly help you. I am accusing you under paragraph 87 of the penal code, which provides for punishment for offense of the Flag and Coat of Arms." When he heard this, Lasik wanted to sigh, but he controlled himself in time.

3

A sigh, even when heaved from the very bottom of the soul, can be attributed to certain sad events. Lasik's behavior, however, in the course of that court procedure deserves to be reprimanded. Then it was that his hereditary defects revealed themselves! For, you must know, Lasik had not always dedicated himself to the Chinese Question or other such clear ideas. Until he was thirteen years old, he spent his time trying to figure out the absurdities of a certain Talmud, while his fingers twisted the scant hair in his chin. If two Jews find a *Talles* —to which of them does it belong? To the one who saw it first, or to the one who was first to pick it up? You try to solve this problem. Lasik's chin burned from his active fingers. The question is: What is more important, the head or the eyes? The invention or the manufacturing? Enlightenment or will power? If it were given to the one who saw it first, the head would be insulted: "I have ordered the hand to pick up the Talles." Were it given to the one who picked it up first, the heart would be hurt: "I have whispered it to the eyes that a treasure is waiting for them." Were the Talles left to lie on the way, a handsome Talles that any Jew could use when praying would be lost. Were the Talles cut into two, it would not be of use to anybody. If the two Jews were to take turns in using the Talles, one after the other, they would not be able to stand each other's smell. For, though the stomach of a fish could be big enough for a man, the most wonderful paradise is too small for two. So, what to do with that treacherous Talles? What to do with the two Jews? What to do with the Truth?

The best thing of course is not to find any Talles and not to be preoccupied with the Truth. But still, a Talles might just be there on your way. So, all one has to do is to stay by himself: whether it is in the far corner of a fancy-goods store or in a filthy latrine, as soon as man is alone he will begin to think about the truth.

It had been a long time since a curly growth of hair had covered Lasik's chin. Long since those curls were shaved off by the nimble hand of Lewka, the barber. And long, long since he had forgotten the teacher's stick and the story of the two Jews who found a Talles. However, the habit of meditating about things had remained.

It would be ridiculous to suspect that Lasik was superstitious. He had hardly been thirteen years old when he already understood that a Talles could not be of use to anyone, and it would be better to find two hundred thousand or at least three rubles in the street. He comprehended that man originated from the monkey and not from a debatable "image," that an operetta was far more interesting than any synagogue with all its choral chants, that Hershanowitch was a big rascal, that ham and peas tasted as good as meat with prunes, and in general, that this was the real twentieth century. Once, Lasik even had the opportunity to finish off the old Hershanowitch all by himself. Besides, he could have proven his great admiration for science. It happened one evening that Fenitchka was gazing at the starry sky. Lasik, bewitched by the pale face of the young girl, stood there not daring to breathe. It happened then that the old Hershanowitch had the idea to lure Lasik into a trap:

"I find it rather ridiculous to think that you claim to this day that the sun stands still and the earth is turning around. I am not telling you to look at the sky at the hour of the sunset: who knows, maybe you are as blind as a mole and incapable of seeing anything at all. I am not going to ask you how could Joshua let the sun stand still, if it does not move at all: for you will surely answer: 'I was not there', as all fools do. By the way, it might be interesting to know whether you were there when the monkey created man? But anyway, I will prove it to you that the earth stands still, and you shall not be able to contradict me. Even though you talk as though you were a naive Christian boor from Moscow, still you once studied the Talmud, and you know very well that a woman cannot be handed any divorce papers if she moves about. They cannot hand her divorce papers in a train or on a boat, not even when she simply walks in the street. If the earth would move around, all the women would be moving too. For, I should say, women live on the earth. Then, there could never be any divorces: therefore the earth is standing still."

It is true, Lasik was paralyzed by Fenitchka's nearness and by the beauty of the starry sky; nevertheless he answered Hershanowitch without fear:

"Your views, if you'll forgive me, are fit for a little boy.

If one looks out of a moving train and sees another moving train, it seems that both are standing still. Who divorces a woman? Her husband. Were he to move into the opposite direction he would notice that his wife is also moving. But since both are moving in the same direction, it naturally seems to the man that his wife is not moving at all. Besides, I might add, a divorce can be given on any American boat, as long as there is an official of the 'ZAGS'* there, and it does not cost more than sixty kopeks. The main thing, Citizen Hershanowitch, is, that there should be great love and the magnificent glitter of stars—everything else can be settled with a stamp."

Lasik had uttered all this with firmness, even though he knew, that from now on it might be harder for him to reach Fenitchka's cheeks, even when standing on his toes. But what can be done, Lasik was a man of the twentieth century! Yes indeed, it was his way of smoothing his chin, his cunning smile, his logic, above all this logic at any price—that brought about the downfall of this honest tailor. Instead of giving a short answer to the magistrate's first question, that he was of proletarian origin, and then to disprove the slander of the Citizen Pukke, Lasik answered ambiguously:

"Guilty? If I am guilty of anything, it is only of the fact that I am alive. But I am not even guilty of that. Certain ridiculous prejudices are to be blamed, and of course the cholera, too. Had there not been an epidemic of the cholera, there would not have been any Lasik Roitschwantz, and I might ask you, Comrade Magistrate, what would this crazy Citizen Pukke do then? I came into this world, because it was ridiculous to measure the cemetery with a measuring tape, for the misfortune was so great that it could not be measured at all. You do not know what I am talking about? It is very simple. At that time there was a great cholera epidemic, so terrible that almost all the Jews would have died and those who did not die, naturally did not

* Civil registrar's office.

want to die. Nowadays there is the Department of Health and even Comrade Semashko, in person, for such matters. But in those days the ignorant Jews believed that the cemetery would stop growing if it were measured with a measuring tape. And so, they measured and measured, but the cemetery kept growing. And they remembered that if one cannot outwit Death, at least one could cheer it up. They found the most miserable Jew, one Mottel Roitschwantz. He did not even have a copper coin in his sack. All he had was a sad sounding family name. He used to wash people's dirtiest wash, and on Purim he would deliver expensive gifts from house to house for five kopeks. In short, he might as well have died of cholera, and no one would have mourned him. But as it happened, he did not die. Some rich Jews got hold of this Mottel Roitschwantz, and they also found the unhappiest girl. They said: 'You two shall receive thirty rubles from us, you shall have chicken and fish, but you will celebrate your wedding on the cemetery so we can cheer up Death a little bit.' I do not know whether Death was cheered up, and whether the Jews were gladdened. The bridegroom had, besides his miserable name, also a big hump on his back, while the bride was lame. I do not even know whether the cholera ceased, but one thing I know and that is, that I, Lasik Roitschwantz was born, and this seems to be my only guilt."

"How about telling us what you did on the eleventh of July at seven in the evening?"

"I was on my way to see a member of the club 'Red Awakening,' Comrade Fenja Hershanowitch. Before that I pressed a pair of trousers, and after that I was put into jail like a real criminal."

"Meanwhile, after having read the proclamation to the working people, you expressed your counter-revolutionary feelings openly."

"How could I have expressed my feelings openly, when I

never express them at all? Do you think I expressed myself openly when the chains of autocracy fell, or when Bogdanow, the chief of the police, was hiding in our courtyard under the big barrel? No, even then I said to myself: let Lewka, the barber, yell out loud, he does not know any better. But I did not express anything, even though at that time the whole world expressed something: even Bogdanow came crawling out from under the barrel and expressed himself. I am an enigma, and neither the Citizen Pukke nor you, Comrade Magistrate, nor anyone else on this earth knows what feelings lie perhaps dormant in my soul. Whom could it interest anyway what goes on inside a little tailor? But should you insist, I will tell you this: the coat can be turned around but not the soul. I was on my way to Comrade Hershanowitch and I have not expressed anything. You might ask, why did I sigh when I read the proclamation to the working population? Why shouldn't I have sighed? After all, this was an appeal to sigh. On my wall hangs the picture of Comrade Shmurigin. I happen to be deeply absorbed in the course of political enlightenment. I could recite for you on the spot all of Comrade Shurka Besdomny's works. If, however, such misfortunes occur, and I, Lasik Roitschwantz, must sit on this black bench for the accused, I shall confess to you that I did not declare Pfeifer's pair of trousers to the Comrade Finance Inspector. I declared eighty, when in reality it should have been one hundred and fifteen. This is a difference of exactly thirty-five rubles. For that you may punish me, and I will sigh only softly. But you cannot sentence me for insult of the Flag and Coat of Arms, when there had not even been a Flag or a Coat of Arms; there was only the Citizen Pukke, and even so I have not insulted her in any way."

Meanwhile, Matilda Pukke, a woman with pale green melancholy eyes and a party member for nine months, repeated the statements she had made in the preliminary investigation: the accused had run over to the poster, read it and broke out into shameless laughter. The impudent expression he used could not even be repeated, in light of the campaign for combatting the increase of barbarism. Lasik listened to all that, then he winked to the presiding chairman:

"I told you she must either be abnormal or else she is deaf-and-dumb. Indeed, Natik had put up the poster. True, I stepped closer to read it. What are proclamations put up for anyway? To be read, isn't that right? Here is where I heaved a sigh. How do you know? Maybe I felt sorry for Comrade Shmurigin? As though it were a trivial thing, to die of obstruction of the bowels. And besides, I understand full well the meaning of an official funeral for a government-city of our size. If they could celebrate weddings on the cemetery, well, that happened two hundred years ago, and besides there was the cholera, while now there is no cholera, only the economic rebirth and the Chinese Question. In the old *Cheder* I studied the Talmud. That is, naturally, open deceit, and since then I have already read the entire *Communist Gospel.* But even in that indecent Talmud it says, you should laugh when everybody laughs, and cry when everybody cries; and if the whole world reads the Bible, do not get the notion to read the Talmud; on the other hand, if everyone reads the Talmud, forget there is a Bible in this world. Could you really believe that I, Lasik Roitschwantz, who has survived eight different governments, do not know such a simple truth? When the sewing machines had to be delivered, I delivered mine too. When there was joy about the awakened Turk's successes, I was happy too. They put up this poster, and I sighed. What do you want of me, with that crazy Pukke? . . ."

I repeat. Lasik rushed into his own destruction, and one could understand one of the people's judges growling morosely to his neighbor:

"He is dumb, but shrewd. He makes fun of us."

The speech of Comrade Gurewitch, the attorney general, was

short and impressive: "The Citizen Roitschwantz is the rotten product of the castration of the personality by the clergy. He attempts to pour new wine into old bottles with his empty words; but that is naturally the typical exploitation. The unexpected confession of an evil deceit against the state inspectorate throws a new light upon this wolf in disguise. His assertions that the proclamation was put up for purposes of sighs coincide completely with the insinuations of the white-guardist press, while the selfless statements of Citizen Pukke are dictated entirely by her class conscience. On these grounds I rule, without further cutting down this diseased branch and without bringing up the question whether we are dealing with a social menace in this case, that Citizen Roitschwantz be submitted to corrective punishment."

Comrade Landau, the counsel for the defense, distinguished himself on the other hand by a verbosity that knew no restraint. He spoke for a full hour. It seemed that Lasik was the only one listening to him.

"In our day and age, science knows about hallucinations of hearing, so-called acoustical mirages. The Arabs see imaginary oases. The imprisoned man hears the song of the nightingale. I do not wish to cast a shadow on Citizen Pukke. But I must submit her words to a strictly scientific analysis. Certainly, Lasik Roitschwantz is a degenerate type. I insist that a medical opinion be obtained. What he calls 'a sigh' is a purely pathological phenomenon. Perhaps we are dealing here with a serious hereditary taint. A marriage consummated in a cemetery can, according to eugenics, produce abnormal descendants. I am considering all the facts, and it is his origin that outweighs everything else. You may indict the Jewish bourgeoisie for having invented the Talmudic schools and other means of enslaving the Proletariat,—such as those infamous weddings in the midst of graves; but you, as the victorious class, must, in a fine show of magnanimity, acquit this miserable little merchant!"

Warily, the presiding chairman asked Lasik whether he had anything to add to what he had stated before. It was obvious that the chairman was worn out by Comrade Landau's discourse and dreaded the loquacity of the defendant. But Lasik understood that his case was lost. He no longer denied the statements made by Citizen Pukke.

"What could I add to so many clever speeches? When the lion speaks to the tiger, it is best for the rabbit to remain silent. I would only like to make a small suggestion. Comrade Gurewitch belongs to the party and so does Comrade Landau; it seems that there exists a minor disagreement between them, just as might happen in our Small Businessmen's Club. Therefore I propose a compromise. If, for instance, Comrade Gurewitch demands that I be imprisoned for six months, and Comrade Landau asks for my acquittal, I propose an even division: imprison me for three months. Then everybody will be satisfied, even Citizen Pukke. And if I personally will not be happy about it, I did conceal Pfeifer's pair of trousers from the authorities. And besides, as Comrade Gurewitch put it, I am a rotten product anyway. Naturally I would much prefer if you were to listen to Comrade Landau and send me home. I will even promise never to sigh again and spend all of my remaining years studying the Chinese Question. But on the other hand, I'm afraid, you might listen to Comrade Gurewitch's plea. I can only say that this is a lottery, like it says in the Scripture! In that case I will be in bad trouble. That is why I propose that you carefully examine the pros and cons, accept my compromise and sentence me for as few months as possible, since there surely must be several small orders awaiting me, besides the hope for sympathy from Comrade Fenja Hershanowitch. Without hope and with no orders I could easily die. But nobody wants to die, not even Comrade Gurewitch. For all citizens, except for a few cut-off branches, must live and thrive together in unity, like the irresponsible trees thrive on the high banks of our navigable Sosch."

4

Lasik had an unusually tender complexion. Only Lewka, the barber, knew how to shave him neatly. But Lewka was not a plain barber, he was a world-famous celebrity. The story went that once he had shaved the nape of a visiting lady from the Comintern so artistically that the aforesaid little lady burst into tears, crying: "What a great land this is." And she had given Lewka a dollar bill, with an American cow on it. Perhaps this was a lie, I do not know; but anyway, he shaved Lasik in a masterly way: neither cuts, nor any ugly redness or burning, only freshness, relaxation, triple spraying with toilet water, and to compound the ecstasy, he sang softly into his ear a new tune, just smuggled in: *Yes, we have no bananas* . . . While Ziperowitch, his rival, left nicks and cuts on everyone and to top it all used the cheapest yellow cotton.

But who would even mention Ziperowitch and Lewka in one breath! In prison, it was Lewka that Lasik missed most. He was a child of our agitated times and adapted himself quickly to all forms of life. Naturally, neither was there a Fenitchka Hershanowitch in prison, no starry skies, nor any guest performances of the Moscow Operetta. On the other hand there were no finance inspectors in prison either. If only Lewka were here! . . . Lasik just could not entrust himself to the prison barber: the result would be cuts and scratches and continual abusive language, and of course the pimples afterwards. What would Fenitchka Hershanowitch say to all this in six weeks? But on Lasik's chin tiny red curls began to sprawl. It did not matter how he looked. His appearance certainly did not bother him in the midst of eight unshaven scoundrels. What really mattered was the spiritual itching that the beard created.

Lasik understood very well what had brought about his downfall in court. He had solemnly promised himself to think as little as possible. Naturally, it is difficult not to meditate in prison. You have twenty-four hours daily in which you can philosophize free of charge. You can ponder at length upon various heartbreaking human destinies. It becomes even more difficult when tiny tufts of curly hair begin to make their appearance on your chin; how great the temptation to wind them around your finger and thus become absorbed in thought. There is nothing as influential on philosophy as a curly beard; and it is that little beard that has driven many a scholar of the Talmud to the craziest conclusions.

Imagine, for instance, a small pea lying on the ground. A little mouse swallows the pea. A cat eats the mouse. A dog bites the cat to pieces. A wolf eats the dog and a lion devours the wolf. A man appears, and what does he do? He kills the lion. One might think that man is master of the universe. But, the man goes home, and stumbles over a tiny pea. He falls and hits his head on a rock and is dead. The little mouse comes running, laughing at the man, and the mouse swallows the pea, and the cat eats the mouse, and so it could go on and on, endlessly. Now, you tell me, could beardless men ever have reached such conclusions? Lasik was sitting despondently on his bunk, picking at his beard and thinking, not about the tiny pea, but rather about our acquaintance, Citizen Pukke.

Suddenly, he chirped happily. Lewka, the barber, had entered the cell. This was no mirage in the desert, nor was it the song of the nightingalc, imagined by a prisoner. No, it was Lewka, the real Lewka standing right before him!

In spite of his great joy, Lasik, being a very judicious small businessman, heaved a sigh:

"Who else died, Lewka? Perhaps the Portuguese hostage?"

"What in the world has this to do with the Portuguese hostage when we live here in Homel? And nobody died besides old Schimanowitsch, who had to die anyway with his 82 years. And Chassin had a little girl, so he should know how to sell damp sugar. But I am here, neither because Schimanowitsch passed away, nor because of the fact that Chassin had a little girl. All this is unimportant family stuff. I am here because of an extraordinarily important case for the state. I got in because of . . ."

One can be the first barber in the world and still remain a hopeless braggart. Lewka swelled up solemnly, like a sparrow ruffling up his feathers: "I fell in here because of that damned barrel."

At this point I should explain that, regardless of our great achievements, the city of Homel does not yet have any decent plumbing. From the dark past, the inhabitants of Homel have inherited indecent, noisy barrels that go thundering through

Main Street. I beg you not to despise the city of Homel because of this. After all, there are a great many cultural institutions in Homel—two theaters, a circus, and a movie house. In its museum there hangs a fish from Holland of such splendor, that any Jew would thank God if he could have it for his Sabbath meal. In the park, named after Paskewitsch, they have a real wolf on a chain that frightens the poor innocent children with his shrill howling. And what about the club *Red Awakening*, the meeting place of the small business people? And the streetcar project, planned down to the smallest detail? And the posters of the local Department of Chemistry, with the friendly caricatures of Comrade Pinkes? No. Culturally, Homel was not too different from the capital. As to the plumbing, that is a secondary matter not worthy of that much attention. Surely, the city of Athens is quite famous; people from all over the world, even from America, go there. Well, Athens has no plumbing either, so why get excited about Homel with its shocking barrels?

It goes without saying that the local authorities protect the citizens' noses by all possible means. The barrels are permitted to drive through the streets only by night, and besides they must be tightly closed. Of course, not all people respect even the strictest law. I am not talking now of that scoundrel Hershanowitch—he knows all the regulations by heart, like the Ten Commandments: where one may spit and where it is not permitted, at what spot one may cross the market place, on what days one had to hang out the flag and even on which side one enters the streetcar, though that was only a project yet in Homel. However, there are citizens in this world of greater importance than Hershanowitch, and so, one day the barrel rolled through the street in broad daylight, and it wasn't even covered. What can one do? It happens, as they say in Homel, that one must show his respect sometimes even to his spittle.

On a hot summer day, one merely has to yell: "She's coming"—and the inhabitants of Homel do not stop to ask who. They know it right away, and immediately they close their windows, crawl into the farthest corners, and hold their noses tightly.

And it was just this barrel that got Lewka, the barber, into jail. The misfortune occurred in the street, and there was no time for him to find refuge in the nearest shop. He pressed his fingers tightly to his nose and complained angrily: "May they rot together with this insufferable stench!" Naturally, it is foolish to shout like that in the street. However, Lasik had not suspected Lewka without reason. Indeed, the barber had a glib tongue. During the time when the *Ungodly* undertook their campaign, he had screamed so loud that he had become hoarse. Also, he had once broken into the synagogue shouting: "Down with that rotten Sabbath! Long live, let us say, Monday!" At the movies he could not sit still: they had to throw him out innumerable times. For instance, they were showing an English Lord who wanted to make an innocent maiden accede to his wishes, and right away, Lewka loses his senses: "I'll show you, you insolent feudal!" . . .

In short, Lewka was famous in town for being loud and fresh, and therefore no one should have been surprised at his exclamation concerning the barrel. Lasik asked him suspiciously:

"If you did nothing but shout in the street, why did they put you in jail? That is nothing unusual, you always do that. Lewka, I do not believe it has anything to do with the barrel!"

Lewka squinted ironically.

"Who said that it had anything to do with the barrel? Naturally it had nothing to do with the barrel, the barrel passes by every single day. It has rather to do with a certain Citizen Pukke. She informed the authorities, saying I had delivered a rebellious speech."

Lasik started to think:

"I was also thrown in jail because of the Citizen Pukke. She must be a completely crazy wench. But I ask myself, if she is going to walk the streets of Homel a little longer, how in the world is anyone going to be able to move about? So far we are only nine, but who knows, tomorrow there might be one hundred and nine of us. I am going to think all night, to try to find out what this is all about, and what this Citizen Pukke is afraid of: Rumania's meddling or some more intrigues on the part of the moneylenders? Listen, Lewka, since you are here anyway, please shave me right away, so I will not think so much."

But oh, even though they had arrested Lewka with all his instruments—he happened to be on his way to the sick Osja Saitzew, whom he was supposed to shave—they had taken his razor away. Obviously they were afraid he might do himself harm. Ridiculous! Lewka would not cut his throat because of a female like Pukke!

"But if you care, Lasik, I can soap you, for they had nothing against my keeping the soap-brush. Naturally, your beard will remain as it is, but still you can imagine that you have no beard anymore."

For a long time, Lewka soaped Lazik's chin. Then he cursed frightfully, curses I would rather not repeat, and finally after this last exertion, he fell asleep. Lasik, however, could not sleep. He wound his tiny beard around his finger and kept on thinking. It was long past midnight, when he awakened Lewka, who was snoring shamelessly:

"Now I understand everything. Do you know what this is all about? It is because of the well-known *Economic Order.* She is not afraid of the Rumanians or the moneylenders; her only fear is that of losing her job, since all slow workers are being fired mercilessly. Naturally, this woman Pukke would also like to eat fowl and fish. That is quite understandable, and in my opinion, we should not be angry with her at all, but on the contrary, we should give her a blue ribbon like at an agricultural exhibition."

5

At the sight of one-eyed Natik, Lasik was overcome with emotion:

"It is simply wonderful that they have thrown you in jail, too, Natik. First of all, now they have no one out there to put up placards. Consequently, Citizen Pukke will have to think up a new trick. In the second place, we are now ten men in here, and should one of us die of longing for the real freedom, today, we could bury him according to all the backward rituals—for, we are exactly ten Jews. You might ask: 'How can we be ten, if one of us dies?' Well, the tenth would be the guard. Even though he swears he is a transcaucasian Georgian from a half-independent federation of states, I personally think he is most probably my nephew twice-removed from Mosyr and that his real name is Kapelewitch. By the way, if, because of longing for the real freedom and for Fenitchka Hershanowitch, I, Lasik Roitschwantz, should happen to be the one to die, I beg you not to say any sad prayers over me. I would rather have Lewka humming that song of the foreign bananas that was smuggled in. I have never tasted such fantastic fruit, but I do know what an ardent passion means. And I beg you, do not say *Kaddish* over me. I would rather you said: 'He was perhaps a rotten product, and he certainly didn't declare Pfeifer's pair of trousers. However, he loved true freedom, the rich blossoms of the trees on the banks of the river Sosch, the stars that whirl around somewhere on the empty horizon, and above all, he loved a maiden from Homel, whose name shall remain a deep secret forever.'

"I beg you to say all this—if I die. But naturally I am not even thinking of dying. I even intend to prove to you, Natik, that you are a castrated personality, to quote Comrade Gurewitsch. If I was able to talk down that shrewd rascal Hershanowitch, I shall prove to you in five minutes that the earth does not rest on three pillars and that it is much better to keep your mind on a nice Chinese Lecture than to repeat all your life the same sad phrases, which are known not only to all the cats of Homel, but also to all the dogs."

Lasik had hardly started with his enlightening lecture, when his attention was drawn to a new prisoner, or rather to a new suit of clothes. Lasik saw this world through the eyes of a conscientious self-employed tailor—the first thing he always noticed was the cut of a suit. With his eyes he touched the cloth of the newcomer's suit: that was contraband merchandise of the finest quality, perhaps eighty rubles the meter. Not too well cut, most probably by Zimach. But of course, he should have been a shoemaker, not a tailor. To spoil such a wonderful material! Well, all in all, it must have cost him forty tcherwontzes. Perhaps you think the saying "All is vanity" is foolish? Wait and you will see what will be left of that heavenly material after one week, with all those bristles sticking out of the bunks. But, anyway, who could be that scoundrel to afford such a suit? . . .

At long last, Lasik looked at the fellow's face. Right before him was the most notorious rascal of Homel, Mitjka Raikin: he sold typewriters, bought matches and licenses, he was the administrator of the railway station, he was building a Pavilion of Agriculture where they would serve lemonade to the village correspondents and distribute wicked pamphlets; with the greatest pleasure, he ate roast chicken every God-given day. As a matter of fact, Mitjka should not have been surprised to have landed in jail, though he was genuinely baffled. He shrugged his shoulders, sneezed naively, thus trying to express his indignation, and pulled his trousers up, so they would not touch the prison floor. Lasik was the first one he approached:

"Well, how do you like that?"

Lasik found Mitjka's question most rude. Let him ask Zimach, who had made that handsome suit for him. After all, Mitjka was not an examining magistrate. Why did Lasik owe him an answer to a stupid question?

"Me? I say nothing."

"Oh, sure, what is there to say? That's a real joke! To treat me like a bandit, putting me behind bars! And I have contributed all of five tcherwontzes for those Yellow Chinese. I should say, I am not about to build a nightclub, but rather a valuable cultural pavilion, that was already approved four times by the central authorities. If, for instance, they have put you in jail, I am sure you have in some way acted against the law."

Seeing Mitjka suffering such torture in his soul, Lasik condescended to reply: "Yes, indeed I have done something. I sighed in the presence of Citizen Pukke."

"See, I told you. That certainly is an absolute violation of good morals. You landed in jail because of your actions? But why me? In my case they thought up such a funny story that it would give me a good laugh, were I myself not here in this insufferable prison. Just listen to this: If I want the *Ukrain-Matches* to buy calculating machines from me, instead of from Schwarzberg, I have to give the manager twenty per cent. That is a simple business deal. But what happens? At first he wants forty per cent, as though this were not a government city, but rather a settlement somewhere outside the gates. When I say politely, 'No thank you,' he goes and buys those calculating machines from that miserable Schwarzberg. But then, they arrest me as though I had killed someone, and they throw me into this horrible dungeon. And I ask: 'Why such torture?' So they answer me: 'You, Raikin, are a corrupt individual.' Is it not foolish to call a plain business deal by such a punitive name? I am certainly not dumb and I know quite well what this is all about. The manager of *Ukrain-Matches* is a mad anti-Semite. That is the first thing. The examining magistrate is capable of eating all Jews alive, no matter what wonderful explanations they might give him. That is number two."

At this point, Lasik tried to protest.

"But Comrade Kugel is a Jew too, just like you and me, except that he is a party member of long standing."

But Mitjka was not satisfied:

"That does not matter. I am telling you, they are all anti-Semites. This is a replica of the Beilis Case. But at least, America was on Beilis' side. And who will take an interest in me? Nobody. And so I ask you: what is there for me to do? One thing only—to sit here and sigh."

"Naturally you may sit. But I would not advise you to sigh. If you must express your indignation, it might be better you sneezed, as you were sneezing right now; just so you don't sigh. Comrade Landau has explained it to me. He said that sighing is a purely pathological phenomenon. And at that, I assure you, if I am acquitted halfway, it will be only because of my exceptional origin. However, your unforgettable parents have surely not been wed in a cemetery, but probably under some luxuriant canopy; thus you may easily get another several endless months in prison for every sigh. No, Citizen Raikin, even if you were a second Beilis—you had better sit still and sneeze, and when you get tired of doing that, you may talk to me about the great Chinese Question."

About three days later Lasik made the acquaintance of a new inhabitant of cell number six, the manager of the Homel Branch of the *White Russian Timber Trust,* Comrade Tchebischew. The suit Tchebischew wore was shabby, perhaps twenty rubles the meter—an average price. To be sure, in Tchebischew's wardrobe there were four first-rate English suits and even a dinner-jacket, but very few knew about that. So as not to lead the lesser people of this world into temptation, Tchebischew would wear an English suit only at home, after having closed all the shutters tightly. As to the dinner jacket, he did not dare to appear in it even before his few close friends. With the dinner jacket he tempted only his phlegmatic wife at night. How then could such a cautious gentleman get into prison?

After having inspected the companions fate had destined for him, Tchebischew chose Lasik. He embraced him around his neck (Lasik hardly reached up to his waist) and began the conversation in lyric tribute:

"I am not talking of you. You happen to be a nice Jew. But they are not all like you. Some time ago, I personally fought for equality. But who could have known it then? I can even understand that the Jewish settlement district has been abolished. But what do we see? They take away our land and give it to people who come from somewhere else. But where do they confiscate it? In Siberia, where they are sending us now? No. They take it away in the Crimea where we used to travel, to delight in the view of the azure-blue sea. Perhaps even on the coast at Yalta. Now, just tell me, is that not revolting?"

Lasik felt pity for Tchebischew.

"So you owned a nice little farm on the banks of the azure-blue sea?"

Tchebischew was offended.

"My dear man, I am a university graduate. 'Farm,' indeed! I traveled to Yalta merely for the spring season. Before the revolution my sole occupation was the study of the Roman law. That is quite a different matter than planting cabbage. That is a culture you can't possibly understand . . ."

"Well yes, even though I am now interested in the *Chinese Question,* I'll admit it is . . ."

"Do not interrupt me! I will explain it all to you. This is no longer equality of rights; this is Jewish oppression. It is the annihilation of the native population by the immigrating elements. Judge for yourself: I was delegated by the Department of White-Russian Timber to purchase the necessary furniture. Naturally such a purchase involves expenses. It is no simple matter to keep in line with the estimates. Comes a shabby, miserable commissar and offers furniture three times its value. I try to make him understand: At such prices it would hardly be possible to carry through according to the estimates. What will the Department of Labor say? How many people have to be silenced? I say to him: forty per cent is the minimum. But he starts to bargain just like in the market. Forgive me, but they are a dirty race. I had to buy the furniture from his competitor. And now, the result—prison, a ruined existence, foregoing all remains of a cultural life, the devil knows what else. How can I, a simpleton, a naive Russian, survive in the midst of that mass of Jews. You tell me!"

"Very simple. While you were talking, I was thinking. A young man has to find a pretty girl, like Fenya Hershanowitch perhaps. A key has to find its lock, such is the beginning of happiness. When you have been here for a while, they will let you go, for sooner or later everybody will be sent home. If they would not let us out, where would they find room for the newly arrested prisoners? You will be set free, either because of a minor amnesty or by some order of evacuation, or simply because, forgive me, my ever-offended face will disgust you. And then you will be a manager somewhere, if not in the Timber Trust, then probably in the Sugar Syndicate. After all, there are not so many people, who are acquainted with the genuine Roman Law. You shall sit once again in a magnificent office. So now, I shall introduce you to Mitjka Raikin. He used to sell typewriters, but if you need furniture, I give you my word of honor, he can procure it quickly, too; he is the biggest rascal in Homel. I believe you have time enough on your hands—twenty-four hours a day, and you can talk to him about anything. Suppose you agree with him on thirty per cent. Then no one will be able to say to him that he gave, and by the same token, nobody can say to you that you took. It will be the simplest deal in the world, and you will both be completely satisfied. When the key has found its lock, one can drink some wine, two rubles a bottle, and laugh, like only angels laugh in Heaven. You will see, Citizen Tchebischew, that the real culture, unobtainable to me, will be awaiting you. Only I, forgive me, will remain unhappy, for I have not the key, and I may perhaps never again see the eyes of Fenitchka Hershanowitch, which are just as azure-blue as the sea at your unforgettable Yalta."

Lasik's prison term should have expired on the tenth of August. On the evening of the sixth, Lasik was called into the penitentiary office. He suppressed a sigh in time.

"They can't let me out yet, and they can't shoot me yet. Therefore they probably want me to fill out the forty-ninth questionnaire. But just tell me, how should I know how many cubic meters of air my poor father swallowed? . . ."

Lasik was mistaken. The chairman of the Commission for the Discharge of Penitentiaries, District Attorney Wassiljew, had summoned Lasik Roitschwantz out of most philanthropic motives:

"We want to let you go before your term expires."

Lasik became thoughtful.

"Now I really do not understand anything. Don't you think I have made my modest inquiries? My nephew twice-removed, the spotless party-candidate, Comrade Kapelewitch, has informed me that amnesties are given only at the anniversary of the October Revolution and on the First of May, the great workers' holiday. But unfortunately it happened to be in July when Citizen Pukke found out that they were going to give the axe to many officials in the civil service. That is an absolutely uneventful month. To be sure, occasionally women prisoners may be set free on the Eighth of March, on the occasion of Women's Day. However, it is not March, and besides I certainly am no woman citizen. Why, then, would you set me free?"

Comrade Wassiljew could hardly utter the first few words, "The commission for discharge . . . ," when Lasik interrupted him triumphantly:

"I told that rascal Raikin that there would not be enough space for everybody! Naturally I understand that it is not nice to be a guest for too long, and I am ready to relieve you immediately of my miserable presence."

Meanwhile, Comrade Wassiljew was a very honest District Attorney. He looked long at Lasik and said:

"Your jokes do not amuse me at all. This is nothing but idle bourgeois talk. Before I can let you go, I must convince myself that you have improved. Honest toil—that is the basis of our Free Society. If a money-lender rises against the flag and other symbols of our hardworking republic—that is quite understandable. However, a tailor, like you, should respect and idolize the emblem of peace and labor. Promise me never again to violate the laws given by the Government of the Workers and Peasants, and I shall immediately sign an order to release you before your term."

"Merci, no," Lasik replied firmly. "Today is the sixth of August.

Of course, I shall not deny it—four days make quite a difference. After all, we do not live to be two hundred years old, like the Patriarchs or the elephants, who could ignore perhaps four bright days of their life. Just to see the fluttering birds in the former Paskewitch Park, as well as Comrade Fenya Hershanowitch, four whole days earlier might be the most wonderful thing! But I cannot give you this solemn promise, since I have not read the laws of the Government of the Workers and Peasants, and furthermore because I do not know whether or not Citizen Pukke is still promenading through the streets of Homel. No, I would much rather sit another four days, in the midst of burning tears and century-old spiderwebs."

"You are not fooling me, Comrade Roitschwantz. I have brought to justice more than one faker. You might be of limited intellect. That I will admit. But you know very well the difference between honest labor and demonstrations against the law. Therefore I am asking you for the last time—do you repent for your behavior and have you decided to subordinate your individual conduct in favor of the common interest?"

"I certainly am sorry for not declaring Pfeifer's pair of trousers. That was my worst offense. I said the same thing in court to the presiding judge. Afterwards, to be honest, I did not think about it any more. I did think about the Citizen Pukke and the eyes of Comrade Fenya Hershanowitch. Thus you are quite wrong in assuming that I had any feelings of remorse when sitting behind bars together with Citizen Raikin. Once having stated it openly in court, that I was sorry, it should have sufficed. How long can one think about such a pair of trousers? You may make a little cross in your book: 'Roitschwantz has repented,' and we will not lose any more words about this past moment. However, as to the calamitous promise, you will not get it from me. Except for that incident with Pfeifer, I am an unconditionally honest tailor, and if I promise to finish an order by Friday, I keep my promise. How do I know what can happen to me tomorrow?

Man is nothing but a tiny sliver amidst the foaming waves of our Sosch. Why do you think I concealed thirty-five rubles to the Minister of Finance? Only because in the windows of the old-fashioned apartment of a synagogue-employee flashed the devilish eyes of an unapproachable female citizen. I am neither tempted by the most delicious meal nor by wine from Crimea, neither bright scarves nor diamonds. But when I saw those eyes, in one moment I lost all my class-consciousness. I went around sighing, and she just laughed. I cried to her: 'My heart is breaking into pieces,' and she just went on calmly singing her international songs. That was when I made up my mind to act drastically. I failed to declare the pair of trousers to the Finance Inspector and for those thirty-five rubles I purchased an American atomizer loaded with the scent of orchids. With it, as with the poetry of my heart, I intended to win that unapproachable Citizen. However, just then ensued the intervention by a person well-known to you, about whom I'd rather not talk right now. The atomizer was left behind in that terrible office, and I am sure its contents have evaporated by now. How can I face Comrade Fenya Hershanowitch now? I possess neither fragrant vapors, nor laughter, nor solemn speeches. Perhaps I will throw myself into the deep waves of the Sosch, or travel to distant Siberia to find some other kind of deceiving happiness. I cannot give you such a fatal promise. I am not a saint, but only a half-educated tailor. You do not believe me? I will tell you a good story. Naturally, you will lose time, which is more expensive than money, but on the other hand, you will hear the real truth; and truth, in my opinion, is even costlier than time. I am almost a Marxist like you, and I know quite well that this is all class-babble. But under the backward coat of two hundred years ago, there was still a real human heart beating, and even though we are both genuine Marxists, we are, besides, and I hope you will forgive me for saying it, also real human beings, and that is why I want to tell you that story now.

"It happened with the *Zadik* from Kotzk—the same one who had locked himself away to spend the rest of his life to discover the truth by subtle reasoning. He had spit on wealth, on his wife, and on his honor. He had spit on everything. He sat in a small chamber, eating dry bread. The books he read were horrible, of the kind like the Chinese Question, and he was absorbed twenty-four hours a day in those books. He must have been the strongest man you can imagine, and naturally the whole world said that the *Zadik* from Kotzk had no weakness whatsoever. Not only that, they said he was not even a man any more, but one great, exalted thought.

"However, before his death, the *Zadik* from Kotzk said to his favorite disciple: 'Do you know, my dear pupil, what I have done all through my dark life? I have spent it committing a great sin: I have been listening to women singing.'

"At this point I should like to explain, Citizen District Attorney, that a pious Jew is, under no circumstances, permitted to listen to women singing. That is naturally a deliberate prejudice, but as you know, all people like to think up different prohibitive rules: then they can live a little merrier. For instance, that scoundrel Raikin does not belong to the party and he may dance the fox-trot at home without any fear. We, however, Comrade District Attorney, are forbidden to do that, and that is why you can well understand that it is quite possible for certain backward Jews to be forbidden to hear women singing. Now imagine the saintly *Zadik* from Kotzk confessing to having spent his whole life in his tiny room filled with books and thoughts, listening to women singing, and revealing the following secret to his favorite disciple:

" 'In my room there was an old grandfather clock. It was made by a miserable watchmaker from Proskurow. Soon afterwards he went insane. The watchmaker's beautiful bride had died, and the stroke of that clock sounded like a woman's voice. It was so wonderful and so sad, it made me smile and cry whenever I heard it. I knew it was a sin. I was supposed to sit there and think about the truth, but instead I found all kinds of excuses to be near the clock: 'it is too slow,' or 'it's a little too fast.' I moved its hand and the clock struck once more, and it was as though a beautiful maiden were speaking to me of love and sorrow, of stars and flowers, and of the mad watchmaker's lively springtime, when birds were singing and the rain came rushing down.'

"The favorite disciple was overcome with fear because of his insignificant belief, and he protested to his teacher:

" 'What shall I do now, rabbi?'

"And the *Zadik* from Kotzk replied calmly:

" 'If you have no clock, you can hear the rains rushing down, for the books cannot take away the rain from you, and they cannot take away the smile, not even the sin, nor can they take away love.'

"Citizen District Attorney, you can see that even this backward *Zadik* had understood what this was all about. Now you tell me, how can I promise you anything? You may keep me here not only four days, but even four years, and I will still not confess openly. I have listened to this clock even in the narrow prison-cell, behind the very last bar, and it would be easier for me to die of a cold bullet than to spend the rest of my life not hearing the stroke of that forbidden clock."

7

The inhabitants of Homel were standing on the high banks of the Sosch, arguing for hours. Pfeifer had even become hoarse.

"I am telling you, this *Communist* has run aground, it is stuck and cannot move, and we can all go home to sleep."

(It was a good thing Citizen Pukke was not around! Afterwards one could have explained for a long time that the *Communist* was nothing but a plain "party-less" river boat, which was supposed to bring a load of eggs and some well-advertised actors from Kiev.)

"It is stuck!"

But Ossja Salkin wanted to know nothing of such revolting possibilities.

"May my enemies have such an easy life, if it is stuck! It is coming and will be here soon. If not in one hour, then in two, but it will arrive for sure, and you, Pfeifer, should be ashamed to deny science and these wonderful water-pumps. So what if sometimes the weather is dry. . . ."

Who knows how long they would have been standing on the hilly bank of the Sosch, had not a thin voice in the background attracted their attention:

"It is stuck and at the same time it is not stuck. What you don't understand, all of you, is the simplest kind of dialectics. One would think you were nitwits and that you read the timetable. Who does not know that the sun is burning, that the chain-pumps draw up water, that science is science, and that the *Communist* runs aground every day on a sandbank? Naturally afterwards it gets bored, and it comes down from the sandbank, and continues on its way home, to Homel. Then it whistles full of joy, perhaps a hundred times. If I owned a chimney, I would also whistle to my heart's desire, for I, too, got stuck once on a sandbank. I also came afloat, so I could swim back to these native shores. However, my heart, this heart of an unsocial small merchant, would burst into pieces any moment when looking at the free trees, at the whole organized mass of personalities so dear to me, and even when seeing your damned trousers, my unforgettable citizen Pfeifer."

When they saw Lasik, they stopped their dispute instantly. Was he released? So what if he was released. Nobody could be expected to embrace a man accused of offending the flag and coat of arms! And this in bright daylight! Pfeifer said only these words:

"The boat will always arrive, if, according to regulations, there are chain-pumps as well as a summer timetable. We know all that, without your inflammatory speeches."

Lasik burst into laughter.

"What has this got to do with the timetable? It seems to me it should have arrived early morning, but instead it is coming in late at night. But this is not the point. One can take a walk on Main Street and also get stuck on a sandbank: such are nature's laws. But why do you, Citizen Pfeifer, assume the role of a British diplomat, when I am trembling with happiness? Perhaps it was just because of your pair of trousers that I had a rough time, but I don't regret it a bit. I had tailored them beautifully, not like Zimach, who spoiled a wonderful piece of material for that scoundrel Raikin. Just look at this crease, doesn't it look like a smile? . . ."

"Without intending to make your closer acquaintance, my dear Roitschwantz, I must remark that you have obviously become completely blind in that well-deserved prison. It seems to me that I am wearing a pair of grey pants tailored by none other than Comrade Zimach, who cuts trousers in an honest fashion and who does not offend the flag. You have attempted to trap me into this dark conspiracy with these trousers, damn them, as though I knew nothing of your profane speech in court, where you used my unsullied name for no reason whatsoever. Six times they came to me because of that damned pair of trousers, and if anything saved me, it was only my pure Red past. I have thrown them away, those pants, may they be damned! Yes, I have gotten rid of them, like of a filthy slander, even though it cost me thirty-five rubles, which were not concealed by me, but by you. I can tell you one thing: the steamer will arrive in due time, you have been in jail for committing an offense, I am in line as a candidate to be admitted into the party, and so I am asking you, my from now on unknown Roitschwantz, to stop addressing me, at least in public places."

After having said these words, Pfeifer left in a hurry. The inhabitants of Homel did not wait for the arrival of the steamboat, but instead they toddled home. Lasik was left alone under the free trees.

"That fellow Pfeifer has simply gone crazy. Because of the heat, the Sosch gets shallow, and no chain pumps will be of any help. Zimach has made a horribly ridiculous suit for him. Anyone can see that the crease is not even in the right place. And as to becoming a candidate for membership in the party, I can do that, too. Besides I know more about the Chinese Question than Pfeifer. But meanwhile, one has to return home, to change at least the absolutely necessary underwear, and hurry breathless to Comrade Fenya Hershanowitch."

But when Lasik caught sight of his house, he felt as though something in him tightened and became numb. Was he seeing things? Had it not happened to an abnormal *Zadik*, that he was sleeping when he did not seem to be asleep, and then he used to cry in despair, "Pinch me hard, so I know whether I am asleep or not." Pinch the miserable Lasik! No, he is not asleep. This is the Klara Zetkin Street. Over here is the third house from the corner. This here is Lasik's heart, this restless heart filled with love for Fenitchka Hershanowitsch. Why then, under that left window where usually hung that handsome sign-board "*L. Roitschwantz, tailor of men's suits,*" why was there a quite different, ominous sign: "*Manufacturing of flags, according to regulations, as well as the best pioneer-drums, Moses Reichenholz?*"

At any rate, Lasik uncovered his head respectfully; he stood there for about five minutes, trembling and bowing; finally, he made up his mind and scratched softly at the door, like a dog with a guilty conscience. The door was opened by none other than Pfeifer:

"Oh, it is you, miserable Roitschwantz? Why did you come here? Don't you see that you are not here at all? Citizen Reichenholz lives here now. And he is not a tailor either. He makes even . . ."

Lasik shook.

"In the name of all that's being ridiculed, do not say such punitive words in my presence! I am not offending anyone, as you can see. All I wanted is to ask you, where in such a case are my wretched belongings, at least one shirt, that I need so badly right now?"

"I am sure Reichenholz is wearing it. Is that perhaps a reason not to need any shirt, because he manufactures flags according to regulations? And to be quite honest with you, there is no greater brute than he, and his connections are fantastic. What significance can your shirt have for him, when he, entering my home and seeing five hard-boiled eggs on the table, gobbled them all up in one moment. He did not even find it worth his while to tell me he enjoyed them. He has taken hold of all your miserable belongings, and all he has left for you, are two bitter mementos: this sign-board and the portrait of the Portuguese hostage."

Lasik did not shed any tears over his lost shirt. He did not even bewail the cruelty of his fate:

"Well then, good-bye Pfeifer! You used to be a wonderful official country-surveyor, and you must not hold it against me for having used your blameless name in court. This was only an outbreak of unexpected remorse, and I am sorry now. But you are wrong in one thing: you have thrown them away for no good reason. They were really an exceptional pair of pants. They were certainly the last pair I will ever make, or as Fenitchka Hershanowitch would say, they were my swan song. It appears that now I'm not a tailor any more, but only an undefinable nonentity. If, within the next quarter hour, I should find the happiness I dreamed about, I shall live on the high banks of the Sosch amidst the trees, feeding on rare berries. Then I will be happier than this Reichenholz, with all his doubtless connections. On the other hand, if I do not find anything within the next quarter hour, I shall travel far away—perhaps to Mosyr or to that criminal country, Palestine."

Lasik knocked for a long time at the door of the synagogue-employe. Nobody opened. At last, Hershanowitch's grey, old beard fluttered out the window:

"With your permission, what right have you to make such a scandal here? Haven't they taught you enough in jail yet? If the door is not being opened, that means that one does not wish to open it for you. I may be a backward citizen, but I am not a bandit. I am praying, so that our great confederacy may grow and flourish, and I do not have the slightest wish to converse with an infamous scoundrel."

"Excuse me, Citizen Hershanowitsch, if I have not knocked properly, but ardent feelings are stronger than common sense, and I have been waiting for this moment exactly six endless weeks. I am only asking you to push back this cruel bolt, so I may behold the heavenly eyes of your dear daughter."

"I assume that my daughter does not wish to associate with such a horrible criminal either. She sings international airs, and furthermore, she spends all her time with the respectable Comrade Schatzman."

In spite of his small stature and his thin voice, Lasik was jealous. As soon as he heard the name Schatzman, he began to knock harder at the door. And he whimpered:

"Open up! If the iron door of a prison could open up for me, surely this ridiculous grating will not stop me. Fenitchka cannot possibly amuse herself with Schatzman, for Fenitchka has a swan-white soul, and Schatzman is dumb like an Indian turkey. Open the door, or I shall commit a crime! I shall insult that Schatzman, and who knows, maybe he is the same as a flag or a coat of arms. . . ."

Scared, Hershanowitch opened the door. He hastened to calm Lasik down:

"Why did you have to pick just my Fenya? Can't you marry some other girl? And why all that scandal, if she is already one-third married to him? I say, one-third—because I am a backward synagogue servant. For, according to the Talmud, a woman to become a married woman, the man has to slip a ring on her finger in the presence of two good Jews. That would be the first third. And naturally Schatzman has not done that. He has to sign a marriage-contract. That would be the second third. He has not done that either. But, instead he has signed a certificate that I am an invalid and must not be deported into the swamps in the north. But there is yet the last third as the Talmud prescribes. He must have spent one night with her to make her his real wife. That indeed he has done. He has not only spent one night with her, but perhaps twenty such nights. Thus, she is one-third his wife, in my opinion. However from his point of view, she is his wife all three thirds."

Lasik lost his senses. His downy tuft of hair trembled violently on his tiny tiny head. He whimpered:

"I shall stick a knife into him, like they did two hundred years ago."

The shouting attracted Fenitchka's attention. She came out, wearing a violet-colored bonnet. At the sight of her lovely white throat, Lasik fell to his knees. He stretched his quivering little arms out to her:

"You are like the most beautiful lilac and the most heavenly swan from your songs. You cannot be Schatzman's wife. Schatzman has only a high position, but a shameless heart. I have never said it to you, but now I must make a terrible confession—I love you with the most backward love, and I could die instantly of these exaggerated emotions."

As a reply, Fenitchka burst into laughter:

"What an . . . admirer! You had better change your shirt, it is as black as though you had come to a funeral."

"I cannot do that, since my shirts are not my shirts any more. A Citizen, who manfactures unmentionable objects, has taken them from me. However, I did not come to a funeral. If you wish, you may say I came to a wedding, for even though I have contempt for the cheap opium of your respectable father, nevertheless I am ready to fulfill all three thirds of the Talmud on the spot, for a single kiss from you . . ."

"Do you really think I could kiss a miserable dwarf like you? I have chosen Comrade Schatzman, and you are nothing but a ridiculous figure to me. If anyone wishes to enter into a free relationship with me, he must have sex to begin with. And you have no sex whatsoever. Ten times you were walking in the park with me and not once did it occur to you to kiss me boldly. You do not need a woman; what you need is a lady-bug. Second, one has to have money. What have you given me all this time? One portion of ice-cream from the itinerant ice-cream vendor and some stupid conversation. Thirdly, one has to have a position. What a noticeable personality—a former tailor who was in jail. Fourthly, I need mental delight. Can you claim to be as clever as Trotzky? Can you dance the foxtrot? You have not even taken me to the American movies. All you have done was to walk around me sighing, like a freight-locomotive. A charming lover, indeed! Why don't you say anything?"

She was not laughing any more—she was furious. Her voice sounded harsh and cruel, like the speech of the Citizen District Attorney. Lasik deliberated for a moment, then he answered:

"You are absolutely right, Comrade Hershanowitsch, and I shall promptly vanish into the deep night. I only wish to explain why I did not kiss you boldly during our walk in the park, and why I have not given you precious dresses and other gifts. Let us put it under the title 'Funny tale of a cow.' Perhaps I read it somewhere in the Talmud, or maybe Lewka, the barber, told it to me—he loves such vile anecdotes.

"A Jew needed candles for Sabbath, and he had no money to buy them. So he took his cow and sold her. But hardly a day or two had passed when his neighbor shouted furiously:

"'Your cow does not give any milk . . .'

"However, the Jew answered him quite calmly:

"'Why do you get so excited? The cow does not give milk not because she does not want to, but because she is not able to. You know what—I am sure she has no milk.'

"That is all, Comrade Fenya Hershanowitsch. Indeed, I was filled with ardent love and other such stale feelings, but that is nobody's business now. I wish you a wonderful happiness at the side of that unmentionable Schatzman, and I beg you not to be angry at this laughable dwarf."

Lasik spent the night on the hilly bank of the Sosch. The following day he went back to his former house. He did not even bother Pfeifer any more, but turned directly to Citizen Reichenholz:

"I am not coming to you because of the shirts. You may wear them with complete ease of mind. Why should I talk to you about the shirts, when you will not want to talk about them anyway? I know that you have fabulous connections. But I beg you, give me four miserable rubles for this beautiful signboard. I am sure it will be of good use to you. Maybe you will get the idea to become a tailor. That is a much more peaceful occupation. Nobody is ever brought to court for offending a pair of pants. But even if you should not become a tailor, you might get the notion to change you name, perhaps. I assure you that 'Roitschwantz' is in a much closer relationship to the present times than such a capitalistic-sounding 'Reichenholz.' In that case, you just have to paste over the upper line, and you have a splendid signboard. And besides, you may cover everything and then print the most unusual things. It is of good quality from before the war, and it has survived eight different governments. It used to have the funny orthography from long ago, it even had a flourish from Petljura's times. Pay me four rubles for it, and I will immediately swim away to unknown lands. All I shall take with me is the portrait of the Portuguese hostage and my misery. However, if you do not buy the signboard, I might drop dead right in front of my former home, and it would certainly not make you happy to wear the shirts of a man who committed suicide."

The steamer left according to the summer timetable. The whistle blew pertly, but after half an hour the boat ran onto a sandbank. Lasik was full of sympathy.

"It's all right. That can happen. It will pass. Let us blow the whistle once more, my dear little boat! I have lost my signboard and my happiness. I have lost even Fenitchka Hershanowitsch. It was purely an accident that I did not die. Therefore, I must go on living. Well, who knows, perhaps in another week or so I might be a proud party-candidate . . ."

8

Steamers go out into the high seas, and tailors from Homel become historical personalities. Compared to the river Dnieper, the navigable Sosch is but a miserable little stream. What would Fenitchka Hershanowitch have said, had she seen the crêpe de chine coats in the "Proletarian Park"! And Comrade Landau would pack up! And the buses roared by, the lights were shimmering, and inflammatory proclamations were being spread by the wireless telephone.

Lasik kept his promise. Immediately after his arrival in Kiev, he became a worthy party-candidate. Not only that: he also became a member of the club for employes, *Good Taste*. Now he was walking around on tiptoes all the time. And I will tell you secretly, despite his fragile body, he prepared himself, as befits a great boat, for a grand voyage.

However, hard tests were awaiting him here, too. Mischka Mintschik was also a party-candidate, besides he was a shrewd good-for-nothing. Lasik repeated it even in his sleep: "Tschang-kai-Schi, Tschang-Tso Lin, Sun-Tschung-Fang."

Mischka Mintschik, however, had no inclination to bother with such drilled stuff. No, he merely smiled enthusiastically when colliding with the powerful grotesque face of Comrade Serebrjakow, the secretary of the Control Commission.

In the evenings, the younger members of the employe's-club *Good Taste* would dance, and naturally there was nothing wrong with that. Lasik knew quite well that the leg movements of those notorious imperialists in Paris were nothing but the death rattle of a corpse that has already started to putrify. There they danced on a volcano, and under their windows, ghosts were waving their flags senselessly. Quite a different matter when young Communist people were moving their legs. That was only a short breathing space, indeed it was good for the development of their fighting energy for the disputes to come. Lasik's job at the club was to watch them, and as the young couples were dancing by, he murmured softly: "Dance, dance, you happy youth." He himself did not dance, because he could not forget Fenitchka Hershanowitsch's violet-colored bonnet, and also because none of the young maidens wanted to dance with him. They all said he was too short for them and besides he was too sentimental. All would have ended well, had Mischka Mintschik not meddled in:

"It would be interesting to know why the supervisor does not do his job here. No one minds when the young folks dance a real waltz or one of the dances of our great minorities. But in my opinion, there are several among our Comrades who dance the

shameless foxtrot, regardless of all the strict regulations. If this goes on much longer, I shall be forced to bring this matter to the attention of Comrade Serebrjakow."

Lasik lost his head.

"I can differentiate even in my dreams between the pink colored traitor, Tschang-Kai-Schi and the indubitable killer, Tschang-Tso-Lin, but I do not see the difference between the delinquent foxtrot and the absolutely permissible waltz, so I do not know what to do."

Mischka Mintschik replied intently:

"That is very simple, Comrade Roitschwantz. Naturally you could study the musical arias, but that won't help you, for the young people hear with their ears something quite different than what they do with their feet. Therefore you must take lessons in these prohibitive dances. You go to Number 6, Karl Marx Street. There, the young parasite, Paul Violon will teach you for five lousy rubles, on the spot, all that is necessary. Then you will be able to perform your duties in your position as supervisor."

Lasik had to give up many a dinner meal, to save up the necessary five rubles. But Paul Violon, alias, Ossip Katz, explained it proudly to Lasik:

"Indeed I could teach you the old-fashioned waltz for a lousy five rubles; however, the American foxtrot costs ten rubles, since it belongs to forbidden literature and therefore necessitates that we retreat into an isolated corner covered with valuable carpeting."

Thus, Lasik had to give up his noon meal too. Dancing was not easy for him. Ossip Katz whispered:

"I implore you, turn your foot this way, that is much more elegant!"

Lasik perspired, turned his foot, and to calm his conscience, he said to himself: "I am not doing this to impress anyone, but merely as with the Chinese Question, because I am a party-candidate, who must not make any mistakes."

After graduation from the dancing course, Lasik viewed the dancing youth with new eyes. This here—was all right. That over there—was somewhat suspicious. But this . . . oh, this! . . . And he ran over to the piano-player:

"What kind of provoking tune are you playing, my dear Comrade?"

"I am playing the waltz *Longing*."

"A nice waltz!"

Lasik pushed his way through the dancing crowd; bravely, he rushed over to a foxtrotting couple. He seized the tall man around his hips, not being able to grab him any higher:

"Come to your senses, you crazy Citizen! Do you realize what you are doing? You are committing a misdemeanor. Do you think I did not see where you were turning your left foot? He is playing a two-hundred year old waltz, and what do you do: you spit on him. Before the very eyes of our youth, you are beginning to rot, as though you were not at the *Good Taste* club, but on top of a volcano in New York. It cost me ten bloody rubles, to be able to judge these unlawful excesses. I will not let you go. I shall take you to Comrade Serebrjakow, for I am a faultless party candidate. I told myself: 'You have to crawl through, Lasik, and I am crawling through . . .' "

The tall man freed his leg and replied ominously:

"First of all, I am Serebrjakow. And secondly, we shall discuss right now what you spent the ten rubles for. Also I would like to know your interpretation of the duties of a club member. (Obviously, Mischka Mintschik had informed Comrade Serebrjakow in time.)

"A party-candidate spending his evenings in loathsome taverns amidst bourgeois scum! You should be ashamed, Comrade! Instead of being interested in the great problems of historical movement or in our economical build-up, you are spending your time with unwholesome pleasures, erotic excesses, the *Nep* with all its lust. Why are you wasting your time? . . ."

"Excuse me, Comrade Serebrjakow, I have spent ten rubles in this matter, and even though in the ideological sense, time is more precious than money, in my case money is worth more than time, because I have no money at all, while I had just recently in Homel six whole weeks of absolutely useless time on my hands. You are asking me what I have spent those ten hard-earned rubles for? I will tell you: for the treatise about an egg. That is a piece from the Talmud. When I was thirteen years old I studied that chapter day and night. Suppose a chicken had laid an egg on the Sabbath. Is one permitted to eat it or not? On the one hand, the chicken had obviously sinned, for thou shalt rest on the Sabbath; but on the other hand, the chicken bore this egg on all the other days, and on the Sabbath it has merely unburdened its heart. I must tell you, Comrade Serebrjakow, there are two factions among the Talmudic Jews. One group believes that an egg laid on Sabbath is pure, the other teaches that it is unclean. And so there were written at least a hundred impossible pages about this egg. I could never comprehend why they got so excited over an egg, which was surely eaten by some respectable fool. But now I understand the whole wisdom in this case. You are asking me, what I was doing at this young parasite, the dancing master. Once again, it involves the egg. For, if the foot is turned slightly to the left, it is a terrible scandal; however, if it is completely turned and the knee slightly bent, then it becomes the most decent occupation. I am afraid, Comrade Serebrjakow, I might offend your indubitable partisanship, but it seems to me, as though your foot did not even slide into the direction, though I will still reflect upon it. Perhaps one could interpret such a distinguished dance step in a different way. That will surely depend to what school one belongs, in reference to the egg. If to the one which . . ."

"This is enough! The devil knows what nonsense is crammed in your head! I am advising you to occupy yourself with . . ."

"Excuse me, I am already occupying myself. It all depends on

Hankow. All I have to do now . . ."

"Yes, yes, we should talk about that, indeed. Not enough that you are addicted to pleasure in the den of a certain Katz, not enough that you are introducing a hostile spirit into our comradely atmosphere with your foolish excesses, you are revealing a stupid sneaky cringing in your relationship to the party. What is the meaning of those words: 'Crawls through, Lasik?' "

"Very simple. I am devoted to our glorious idea with body and soul. And I am crawling towards it. As we in Homel say: 'If you can't jump over, you must crawl under.' Naturally, you are clever and a member of the party. It did not cost you a thing to jump. And you have jumped. But I? You yourself said that my head was full of nonsense. So, there is nothing left for me but to crawl. And so I crawl slowly and carefully. Please forgive me, if I grabbed you at your honorable leg. After all, I knew you only by name. I shall no longer dim your atmosphere. Now I understand, one may eat those eggs if only . . ."

Serebrjakow could not stand it any longer. He slammed his fist loudly on the oak table.

"You may go, Comrade. I have no more time . . ."

Lasik bowed politely and left the office. Meanwhile, he succeeded to add a few more words on his way to the door.

"No, you have no time to lose, but I can lose my ten miserable rubles . . ."

In the hall he met Mischka Mintschik:

"Well, what is your impression after the conference with comrade Serebrjakow? Are you pleased with your inexorable discipline?"

"All I can say is, that this is much more difficult than the Talmud. Nevertheless I shall try and crawl through. I am still a party-candidate, even though a slightly washed-up candidate."

9

Mischka Mintschik did not give up. He pushed Lasik into another mad adventure. The occasion came in the form of a circular, ordering the removal of all ideologically damaging books from the club libraries. Lasik was the club librarian, and when reading that order he got extremely upset. In the circular they had named no less than seventy-two books. However, the library of the club *Good Taste* owned no more than three: *Spiders and Flies, The Basic Arithmetic* by Ewtuschewsky, and a monograph about the poetic style of Demian Bednji.

None of the three above mentioned books were named in the circular.

"Now," said Lasik, "I see the Talmudists were the most ridiculous mongrels in the world. What did they think up?—A Jew must not eat sturgeon! Why? Because sturgeon is expensive? Not at all. Or because it does not taste good? Again no. The reason is, because the sturgeon swims along without scales, he must be unclean; and the Jews might dirty up their precious little stomachs if they ate it. Other ordinary people may eat it. I am tellling you, Comrade Mintschik, those mongrels surely could talk about food. Now however, in the genuine twentieth century, people have become smarter. So, what happens? Instead of the stupid sturgeon, we are faced with someone like Kant, for instance, and with him one thousand and seventy-one other offenses. May the French on their volcano, read all those dirty little tales; here, however, our minds are enlightened and we cannot afford to foul up our brain with shameless aberrations. Yes indeed, this is all quite beautifully thought out. Only one thing I do not understand: how can I do away with these books when they are not even here?"

"When you are ordered to do away, you must do away. I advise you, Comrade Roitschwantz, to search the whole house."

"Excuse me, Comrade Mintschik, but where am I to find such unworthy literature? I know myself that the whole house has to be searched. It is almost like before Passover. Then they also search the house for a crust of unclean bread, that might perhaps have fallen under the cupboard. But in my opinion there are no books whatsoever in this splendid house. I could look into the cupboard, but all I might find there would be low-quality beer and some absolute permissible sausage. To be sure, when there is no bread-crust under the cupboard, a good Jew will place a piece there, so he will find something to burn. The one Jew puts it under, and the other one finds it, and they both know that it is all a fake. But still they can go on praying most admirably, thus fulfilling the strict laws of their circular absolutely and completely. If I had the Talmud at home, I would bring it here, and destroy it, for I am sure, the Talmud must be mentioned in this annihilating list. However, I do not own a Talmud. I have the Talmud only in my head, and I cannot do away with my miserable head."

"Now, why do away with your head when all one has to do is to destroy some unlawful books? And that is quite simple. You just have to look for them in all possible corners. You might, for instance, find such contaminating literature in this unfamiliar briefcase, over there."

"It is indeed becoming increasingly difficult for me to keep crawling toward my glorious destination. It almost seems easier to drown in the foamy ocean, which for some odd reason is called 'Dnjepr,' than to grab a stranger's legs or to stick your hands in other people's briefcases. But I made up my mind to crawl toward my ideals, and I shall crawl until I've crawled through."

Comrade Serebrjakow found Lasik poring over an open book.

"In the first place, you are reading the devil knows what. In the second place, however . . . in the second place . . . in the second place you have had the nerve to search my briefcase!"

"I am not reading this ridiculous novel for the sake of reading it. I am just reading it in order to remove it, and I cannot understand why you are so upset, Comrade Serebrjakow. I should say you owe me some gratitude for having purged your formidable briefcase of this well-known contagious matter. And you must forgive my mistake about your left leg. To be sure, you were afraid I might get poisoned by that sturgeon, while you were carrying it in your own briefcase and you get poisoned by it, even though it is without any scales whatsoever. But why do I arouse your anger once again? Why do you keep shouting, 'in the first place' and 'in the second place'? I implore you, do not encumber my unresisting soul. For heaven's sakes, shout already 'in the third place,' so I will know what to do. Then I might perhaps start catching up admiring all the pretty flowers or gazing at all the stars wasted in vain."

However, Comrade Serebrjakow did not say any "in the third place." He merely laughed ominously.

10

Comrade Triwas gave instruction to the employes of *Good Taste* in accordance with the newest system. Instead of some tedious lectures, he scheduled an informal discussion. He started immediately with a friendly exchange of opinions or with the reply to some question he had never received.

And so this is how it was. Comrade Triwas looked at Lasik's small, enthusiastic face and said:

"Well! What are your questions?"

Lasik was shaking:

"It is not quite clear to me, yet, what I have to ask about:

whether it should deal with the sound reasoning of the ants or the disgraceful livery of a butcher in Amsterdam?"

"In that case, I would like to ask you an insignificant question. What, for instance, is your opinion, Comrade, about the sexual functions of a model member of a party cell in the light of ethics?"

"Excuse me, but I was not prepared for such a question. Perhaps you would prefer to ask me something else, as, for instance about Tschang-So-Lin or even about the Congress of Stockholm? I must admit I am not familiar with any sexual achievements. To be sure, in Homel I courted the daughter of a synagogue employe, the former Comrade Fenya Hershanowitsch. But we both did not belong to the party and had no functions whatsoever, apart from my purely pathological sighs. Certainly, now, a genuine member of a party cell has won Comrade Hershanowitsch over. Let us call him Comrade Schatzmann. But in my opinion this is a superfluous foxtrot, or even a blackmailed concession, for Fenya Herschanowitsch loves rustling dresses and sex, while Schatzman has no ethics whatsoever, only a very secure position and these are all absolutely naked functions, as with the uneducated parasites; however true love is missing, like the true proletarian lilac, which overcomes my devoted heart, compelling me to these public tears."

And remembering the lilac-colored bonnet of Fenya Hershanowitsch, Lasik burst into tears, much to the amusement of the employes of *Good Taste*.

And even though Lasik dampened his trousers with the most ordinary tears, Comrade Triwas called enthusiastically:

"Here we have it, the typical lemonade of bourgeois attitude. We must put an end to such shameful prejudice. Sex is fundamentally nothing but the naked means of propagation, and as long as the capitalism of Malthus or any other barriers do not meddle into that problem, we may look at so-called 'Love' as nothing but a direct process of production of two employees. The shorter it is, the more time remains for the proletariat to attend their trade union meeting, and their co-operatives. And as to the tears of our Comrade here, they are a characteristic leftover from the times of personal property, when a factory-owner regarded the female Comrades as his personal stock. It is high time to put an end to such mischief. Mind you, I am not criticizing the functions as such, as long as one is a strong, healthy, young comrade; but, such mushy love-making as we have just heard about, is a criminal distortion of facts, and we must get rid of any such black sheep, who might have the notion to replace iron materialism with such mush."

Lasik wiped his nose meekly. He admitted to Mintschik:

"This is ten times harder than the *Cheder*. There, we had to learn that there are many tasty things on earth which we are not allowed to eat. That is foolish, but at least it is clear. Here, however, they tell us 'You may eat those bananas that grow in Lewka's imagination, but you must pretend they are the most ordinary potatoes. You must not smile or even cry about such smuggled-in happiness. No indeed, you must put ordinary salt on them . . . I am afraid, I shall remain a miserable party-candidate as long as I live, for it would be easier for me to die amidst the prison cobwebs, than to forget the fragrance of the deluding lilac.'"

In the evening, Mintschik took the unhappy Lasik to the park. That was an extremely cruel way to ease his mind. Lasik saw the stars in the sky and the lovely flowers in bloom. And absolutely party-less couples kissed under the bushes. Suddenly Mintschik brought Lasik to a halt:

"Do you see that seditious girl over there? She is none other than Comrade Gorenko, a member of our club *Good Taste*. She attended Comrade Triwas' lecture today, but one may say quite safely that she was not there, for she behaves like the blackest of all sheep. I think it will be necessary for you to intervene, my dear Comrade Roitschwantz."

"I do not wish to be a black informer. I do not want to hurt this backward soul. She loves, like I do, the old-fashioned lilac."

"Who says you should do her any harm? You are here to save her from the dire consequences. You must save her, and that miserable man with her, from some unmerciful commission. Besides, I must ask you sternly: are you not a party-candidate above all, Comrade Roitschwantz, or are you, as you stand before me, already a liveried renegade?"

Lasik approached the couple shyly. He could not see their faces. All he could hear, was:

"I love you, Anja! . . . We shall take a trip to Crimea . . . Your lips . . . like a rose."

Lasik intervened:

"I implore you to put an end immediately to this unlawful demonstration. It could be that I, myself, once dreamed of such preambles, though my love does not concern roses, but rather lilacs or even the unrealistic orchid. But I cannot stand by and watch your cruel suicide. My dear employe, I am also an unsocial fellow-employe. I will explain it to you in a hurry. You must engage in sexual production; but instead of naked sex, you come with that long-done-away-with Crimea. In the name of the Control Commission, I must ask you to substitute immediately an absolutely permissible function in place of this angelic conversation."

This time, Comrade Serebrjakow did not even laugh. He only looked at Lasik. Suddenly Lasik understood everything. He started to run. Until the early hours of morning he ran through the deserted lanes of the park. In the morning, however, he frightened the barber "Georges," alias Simcha Zucker, with the following, mysterious request:

"Shave me thoroughly, Comrade Georges. Shave me down to the very bottom, once and for all, for six weeks or maybe

for the next six years! Of course, Tschang-So-Lin is ruined and we may smile. However, for me that certain unattainable function remains . . . Now, he will certainly say 'in the third place,' and with that, I, Lasik Roitschwantz, shall become silent amidst century-old spiderwebs."

II

"**You** have concealed your dark past and paragraph 87 of the Constitution. You have attempted to improve your situation with the assistance of stupid slander. You have revealed an ideology which is foreign to us: Antisemitism, Mysticism and morbid Eroticism. In your conversations with a younger Comrade, you have compared our sensible discipline with certain middle-aged obsolescence. Answer me!"

"May I perhaps, as Comrade Triwas does in his world-shaking lectures, not reply in a full chorus, but rather ask you a few insignificant questions? This will bring our present moment to exalted dialectics. I would like to ask you, for instance—why should I conceal paragraph 87, since it is not Pfeifer's pair of trousers? I have talked so much about my six endless weeks that even the sausage in the cupboard must be tired of it. If I as much as opened my mouth, the young people of *Good Taste* ran away from me as from a certain barrel in Homel, saying: 'This Roitschwantz is complaining again about his stay in prison.' Another question: whom am I supposed to have loudly slandered, if you'll forgive the expression? I have merely whispered a few words to an influential member, concerning his own leg. If, however, I have disturbed the functions of Comrade Miss Gorenko and her unmentionable escort-employe, I did it in a pure outburst of unconditional discipline. Third question, how can I be a senseless antisemite, if I myself am a one hundred per cent Jew from Homel? Fourth, and a very small question: what is morbid eroticism? If this expression implies several functions, I admit and swear by God, that I have not engaged in them, neither in a healthy nor unhealthy fashion—a matter for which Comrade Triwas has justifably scolded me in the presence of all the young people. I could ask you a hundred more questions; however, I do not wish to waste your well-known time. I will merely ask you, Comrade Serebrjakow, if you must stroll in the fragrant park at night, why don't you wear a tiny lantern on your honorable chest? Why didn't you seal your briefcase with a widely perceptible sign? Why, if you already have stepped in with your left foot, didn't you have it annuonced that it was you who did it, and not I—or some other Roitschwantz? Why have you embarrassed my unstable soul with your silent mysticism?"

Comrade Serebrjakow closed his eyes, ironically:

"Is that all?"

"No, not yet. I must tell another thing about your 'younger Comrade.' Of course, he is the one to thank for all this. And I say to him: a great, big thank you, in the name of the people,

Comrade Mintschik! Now you will naturally become a brave party member instead of being a quivering party-candidate, and I am advising you to marry a certain valuable person immediately. She does have an unfortunate last name, though this could hurt only a coloratura singer. But she is no singer at all. Instead she walks through the streets of Homel. If you would marry her, dear Comrade Mintschik, you could walk the streets together, and this would result in a genuine international melody!"

Comrade Serebrjakow made a gloomy face.

"Is this all, now?"

"No, this is not all yet. Since I have become so bold through my crashing failure, I will confide in you a thought as curly as this downy tuft of beard, which will obviously grow back some day. You know, of course, that the backward Jews believe in the Torah. The Torah is a set of laws that came down straight from Heaven, and the Jews spend their time studying it as you study your unconditional discipline. They thank God every morning for having given them that insufferable Torah. They keep reading it, making a thousand laws out of one; they are forbidden to smoke on the Sabbath, and they are forbidden to eat chopped cutlets with cream, and actually they are not permitted to do anything; they are one hundred per cent asses, and any Marxist could see that. However, once a year, they are sincere and frank with their invented God. Then they speak openly to him, the way they really feel, as I am speaking now to you. The Jews are obligated to be happy about their exodus from Egypt, though perhaps right now they would give anything to be back in Egypt; but they are joyful, because that is what the law commands; they eat crushed nuts and drink sweet wine. And on that day they talk to God without beating about the bush. To be sure, they do not call him names. They talk like diplomats. For, if one has to concede yesterday's politeness in the conversation with some Estonian ambassador, the Jews have to do even more. They must put each word into a ridiculous dinner jacket when saying certain unpleasant things to their chosen God. So they start from afar, not to arouse his anger. They bow and scrape to him, saying: 'If you had merely taken us out of Egypt, even that would have been kind.' Then they approach him from another side: 'Had you given us nothing but the mannah from Heaven, that alone would have been good, too.' Then they get tired of it all, and they burst out with shameless despair: 'But if you had not taken us out of Egypt, not given us mannah from Heaven, not given us the Torah, that would have been even better.' Naturally, one can say such things only once a year, when it becomes so unbearable that it chokes you right here in your throat. And that is why I told it to you, Comrade Serebrjakow."

Comrade Serebrjakow shouted threateningly:

"Is that finally all you have to say?"

"That is almost all, but not quite. I have contributed one ruble and eighty kopeks to the society *Hands off China*, though I am absolutely not interested in grabbing those three-syllabled Chinese with my bare hands; my weak head falls to pieces because of them, anyway. But still, I have given up with pleasure my one ruble and eighty kopeks. May no one touch them! Anyway, why should anyone stick their hands into such a big China? And so I understand that any employe of *Good Taste* has to greet enthusiastically the rebirth of the hindmost Far East. I am not opposing this at all. No, I am preoccupied with a fateful question: What would happen, if I were to establish a voluntary society—'Hands off the Unhappy Lasik Roitschwantz,' with all the necessary statutes and a clear, legible seal. You tell me, would that work or not? I would certainly not approach you for any contributions, Comrade Serebrjakow, as was the case with my mourned one ruble and eighty kopeks. No, right now, I am not interested in the money, but instead in the time, in other words, my imminent six weeks, or even six years. I would like to know how such a new Mintschik will behave in this new, powerful society, and whether they will grab me with unselfish hands, after all those enthusiastic slogans?"

At this point, Comrade Serebrjakow could not stand it any longer. Gasping for breath, he screamed:

"Is that all? Is that all?"

"Yes indeed, that is all. No, actually that is not all yet. I must inform you about another intimate piece of news: you don't have to fuss about me one bit, since I outwitted you this morning anyway. You were sitting here thinking, what to do with Roitschwantz? But I knew all along what you would do. So I had a real thorough shave before I came here."

12

Several weeks had passed. The trees in the *Proletarian Garden* had lost their leaves, Comrade Anja Gorenko had gone to a hospital instead of to the Crimea, Paul Violon had been deported somewhere to the East. Only the Dnieper went on foaming as usual below its steep bluff. One morning, Lasik, with a newly-grown, stately-looking red beard, knocked at Mischka Mintschik's door.

"So you have not married Pukke? What a pity! Now, at least, you have become a registered party member. But what about her? She has not gotten a thing out of this. Confidentially, I am afraid she will remain childless forever, this remarkable citizen. But such melodies should not be hopelessly lost. By the way, I have absolutely no wish to assault your free functions. I come to you, in quite another matter. I shall have to leave Kiev, just as I once had to leave my home town Homel. These are laws of nature, and I feel that another complete change is in store for me. Did the charitable Mottel Roitschwantz ever dream of the stirring life his over-a-grave-conceived son would have to go through? But I am not crying. I am gathering comfort from the words of an old *Zadik*. He said to move means to live, and to stay in one place is to die. The worst run-down mare is better than the most splendid castle. In my opinion, a Jew who is not on the move is almost indecent, he is like a broken-down steam-engine. So then, I am leaving Kiev. I have completely forgotten how to cut pants, and I can not become a very good expert, for I am not at all acquainted with the language of the state. It is true, I have memorized about a dozen words, not counting the names of our Great; but as it turns out, they are not even Ukrainian, but White Russian words. Jusja, the piano-tuner, taught them to me, and naturally, he has swindled me. I have made up my mind to travel to a small town where there are neither stormy streams, nor thundering foxtrots, nor any languages of the state, as, for instance, your language, my dear Mintschik. Do you think, perhaps I have come to say goodbye and to kiss your daily-shaven cheeks? But I must not keep you from your exalted problems with such nonsense! No, I came, first of all, to ask you—whether there will soon be real peace on earth: to be more specific, will it happen before we die, or after?"

Mischka Mintschik spit vigorously.

"There is no doubt about that. Naturally, before. It depends on one or two harvests, and on the complete annihilation of Tschang-So-Lin. It is a matter of a few, insignificant moments."

Lasik smiled happily:

"Very nice of you to think that way, Mintschik. Now tell me—will everybody have his share in this absolute peace, and will all those shares be equal? Yes or no?"

"Yes, naturally. With the exception of the parasites, who in that case would not exist any more."

"Now, listen to me, Mintschik. I am coming to you with a very favorable offer. I will sell you my share for ten miserable rubles. A mere pittance, right? Paul Violon, the dirty parasite, took ten rubles to teach me indecent body movements. He fleeced me of my unused share in this peaceful world to come, and I am willing to make out a formal receipt to you."

"You Roitschwantz, have you lost your senses after all these evil pranks of yours? How dare you play such mystical jokes with me, a proven Marxist?"

"Why are you so upset? This is an absolute natural barter of goods. Aha! You're thinking of Aaron Kagan! No, I will not lie to you. I did swindle Aaron Kagan. But I have no intention of cheating you. What Aaron Kagan purchased from me was quite a different thing. Like any backward product, he also believed in a life after death. He was not satisfied to have been a building supervisor in Homel and to have eaten fowl every day of his life. He wanted to make sure he would get chicken in Heaven. And since he is an awful glutton, he was afraid they would not give him enough, perhaps a chicken leg or even a wing only. Every Jew has his share awaiting him in the Hereafter, and so I sold my share to Aaron Kagan. True, him I even swindled in two ways. First, because I sold my share already once before, when I was a boy in *Cheder,* rather I had gambled it away, playing buttons with the other kids. Of course, I did not tell Kagan about it, for you cannot sell something you have sold before. In the second place, I knew I was smarter than he. He thought there were fancy meals in the Hereafter. I know there is only ordinary gas—or let's say, chewed up bones. But with you I am having an absolutely realistic conversation. I am offering you the most realistic share in a most realistic world. If you are a convinced party member and you believe in our glorious triumph, how can you afford not to give ten measly rubles for a happiness that should mean so much to you?"

"I have no time to listen to your ridiculous fantasies, Roitschwantz. You should go to the editor of a satirical magazine with such amazing talent. I'll give you one ruble, if you leave me alone immediately."

"No, besides the one, you will give me nine more rubles. The ticket costs one tscherwonetz, and I must leave this city. If I remain in Kiev, I shall have to stay with you, Mintschik. I might perhaps cut my throat with your proletarian knife, or I may hang myself with your honest suspenders. Then we shall see what you will have to say with your stately language! You will tremble like the tiniest grain of barley. Give me another nine rubles, and I shall go far away to start the quiet life of a former party-candidate, in some former park, amidst some ancient or not-so-ancient flowers."

Great is the power of human persuasion: two hours later, Lasik stepped proudly to the ticket office of the railway station. In his hand he held tightly the ten rubles.

13

In the train it was warm, smoky, and comfortable. Lasik chewed at a piece of sausage and was happy. Suddenly, one of Lasik's fellow-travelers stared at him and asked him:

"Excuse me, Citizen, aren't you Piskis from Belgorod?"

Lasik was shaking.

"What do you mean, Piskis? I must ask you, to stop such allegations. I am still none other than Roitschwantz, and besides not of Belgorod, but from Homel. I do not know this Piskis at all. Maybe he is the worst spendthrift? Perhaps he has shot somebody? What concern is that to me, when I have my ticket to Tula, plus my working-permit in my pocket?"

"Well, you don't have to be so upset. This Piskis is not a killer, he is a dentist. To be sure, he pulled four healthy teeth for my colleague Jegorow, and naturally Jegorow vowed he would beat him up. But that is Jegorow, and not me. I have merely asked out of curiosity. Such similarity! Strange are nature's ways . . ."

"Strange ways, indeed! In Homel, we had a shoemaker. Scheikewitsch was his name. All year round he drank vodka, the real strong, ninety per cent kind, and called his neighbor Wolf dirty names. So, what do you think happened? One fine day, the White Russians came and suddenly declared that Scheikewitsch was in reality the cavalry commandant, even though everyone in Homel knew that Scheikewitsch would have died of fear if they had put him on a live horse, even in peacetime. Nevertheless he was subsequently shot for being commandant of the cavalry. Is that not enough for you? Then I can tell you that Sacks, the contractor, was killed because of his resemblance to one of Denikin's generals, even though here again the whole world knew that Sacks liked shooting dice and was jealous of his wife, while the general must have shot with cannons or was galloping like crazy on the steaming battlefields. For, you must know that Sacks had a suspicious-looking chin. And, after all that, you are sitting across from me in this fine, I mean hard train-compartment, you are drinking tea, I am chewing my sausage, and you have the nerve to say I am not me, but instead some mysterious Piskis. You might ruin me, if not because of my chin, then because of my nose . . ."

"It can happen! How do we say—court errors. We also had a case in Belgorod, where our Doctor Rostowzew was mistaken for another Rostowzew by the *Cheka* in Sarapul. And that was his end! It just so happens *such* are the times we live in. And that is why one must not be full of reproaches. As the saying goes, when they clear the wood of timber, chips fly. As though not enough people had perished, you might say. But, therefore, everything has been welded together again. Without that you could not accomplish a thing."

The travelers yawned lazily. Lasik could not stand it any longer. He exhorted himself: shut up, Lasik. Indeed, he had been chewing silently all morning at his sausage. Therefore, he became quite passionate at this point.

"Naturally, if that doctor were as insignificant an animal as, for instance, Lasik Roitschwantz, he should lay down in a waiting grave in the first place. For when these fanatics and hundredpercenters walk down the street, there is nothing for an ordinary person to do but die politely—with an exalted look on his face. That's the Chinese multiplication table, and everybody knows it. But neither you nor I are somebody in world history. We are merely miserable fellow travelers in one of many hard train compartments. We may ask ourselves: "Why did that anonymous doctor have to pay so dearly for the 'noble phase'? Perhaps this doctor had children, too? Maybe he would have preferred to live another twenty-five years? I never saw him, but I know one thing: he was certainly a plain man, but surely not some banknote that one pushes under a ticket window. Then, tell me, why do you keep drinking your tea so unconcernedly, and do not want to understand such a simple tragedy. You think that when they kill a man and stamp a wailing seal on him, as though he were not a real corpse, but rather the multiplication table of a wonderful future, that then blood ceases to be blood? I would prefer to be down together with that finished-off doctor than to listen to such soulless multiplication. I am not very good at making a thundering speech out of my feelings, but I would like to tell you now a story of superstition.

"I heard it in my home town Homel from Berko, the old beggar. It is the story of a *Zadik* from Berditschew, but it could just as well be the story of Hersh, or even some doctor. You are under no obligation to believe these old-fashioned ideas. You may believe in your mind that God is as dark a prejudice as the Chinese multiplication table.

"Well then, in Berditschew there lived a far-famed *Zadik*. I should explain right now, that a *Zadik* is a pious God-fearing man, the true leader of his small community. The *Zadik* of Berditschew, besides, was revered as almost a saint, such was his kindness and his wisdom. Therefore he could talk to God, in a straightforward manner, without any use of diplomacy. He would not talk to Him in that insufferable language in which all the ancient books were written. No, he spoke to God in the plainest language, as one Jew would talk to another. He could reproach God and he could persuade Him; he could prove everything to Him sensibly; he could guess his thoughts easily; and he could make him laugh, yes, he made him laugh so hard that the whole world resounded with God's laughter and the window panes in Berditschew were ringing of heavenly laughter. In short, he also knew how to appeal to God's conscience when it meant saving some miserable human life. You can imagine how they revered the wise *Zadik* in Berditschew. He was respected and loved because, as I told you before, he was the kindest man on earth. He would almost hesitate to tread on plain ordinary grass, for fear of making it cry. Of course, Berditschew is a big town, and besides the *Zadik,* many other Jews lived there. For instance, there lived a Jew by the name of Meisel, I do not even know how to describe him. The closest I could come to any description is that he was a parasite. He was a profiteer, a scoundrel—and our Raikin in Homel is a blind, young puppy-dog compared to him. He scraped money together without regard to any lawful regulations. He gave loans against mortgages, and he took the shirts off those fools in Berditschew. He took over their houses, and who knows how many Jews were without a roof over their head. They did not even know where they would light their candles on Sabbath.

But even so, every insect has its peculiarity. This Meisel departed once a year from his black deeds. The Jews have the *Yom Kippur*—that is the day of the highest judgment. On that day they must confess their sins, and every year this infamous Meisel cried with genuine tears on *Yom Kippur*. And mind you, he did not just squeeze a few drops out of decorum. No indeed, his entire face was wet with tears, for he knew quite well that he was the worst evil-doer. On *Yom Kippur* he gave away all his money to the poor. He beat his chest with his fists and groaned most frightfully. On that day he was afraid to look the *Zadik* into his face, for the *Zadik's* eyes burned like hot coal, and he cringed under their look. But on the following day, he awoke in the morning as though nothing had happened. After the day of the fast, he devoured not one, but two chickens. He went on to rake the money. And if yesterday he had returned a hundred rubles to some poor devil from whom he had previously stolen them, today he hastened to deceive him anew. And when he met the *Zadik*, he no longer lowered his eyes. No indeed, he even thrust his hands insolently into his pockets and said:

" 'Today is not *Yom Kippur* anymore. It seems to me that when that day returns, I might confess again. Meanwhile, however, I have to think of my business. They say that the poor are not loved even by God. Then why should I love them? I only love good money, and I would appreciate if you left me alone with your questioning looks.'

"The wise *Zadik* could speak to God, but he could not penetrate Meisel's soul. Meisel remained the terrible scoundrel he always was, and all the people in Berditschew were afraid of him. They feared him and they hated him.

"At this point, I must add something about a third person, old Hersh. But I don't quite know what one could say about him. He was as old as the earth. He was as ugly as sorrow. He was as miserable as only a wretched Jew can be; he had neither wife nor child, no place to be, nor any money. He was about sixty, I believe. From his sick eyes, tears were running constantly. If he was not in a hurry to die, it was only because he had no money for a shroud. Maybe not even because of that. Perhaps he just wanted to live, as you and I, or that murdered doctor wanted to live. In one word, he was not in a hurry to die. He too, like my charitable father, washed other people's dirty wash. When the wash was so filthy that people were embarrassed to have their servants wash it, old Hersh appeared, and took the wash somewhere to the end of town.

"The *Zadik* was loved by everyone, Meisel was hated by all; old Hersh, however, was not noticed by anyone. He could have passed away and no one would have even sighed. The dirty wash would be given to some other old man—Leib or Eli. But he did not die. He went on living quietly, and only the *Zadik* would look sometimes into his eyes, which were always full of tears. Then, the *Zadik's* eyes glowed like hot coal.

"Now you know who lived in Berditschew. And I can inform you that Meisel died, after all. Of course, one could say, he died of God's anger, but in my opinion he died of a gluttonous stomach, for he alone it seems, ate up all of Berditschew's chickens. They buried him fittingly, which means, the poor smiled happily to themselves, but cried loudly with dutiful sorrow, because for their cries and sighs they would get his old clothes and even a piece of meat with gravy on top.

"And now, Meisel the rascal, had to appear before God. Of course, you know how that takes place in the imagination of old-fashioned, backward people. So we suppose God is sitting up there, in judgment over the dead person. He must decide where to send this desperate corpse—to paradise or to hell—as though man could not even lie in peace in his own grave after he dies. But what can you do, people love to sit in judgment upon one another. They brought me to court, too, in Homel, according to some crazy paragraph, because of an imaginary flag, and I know there is nothing more pleasing to people than to place themselves one foot higher than all others and to lecture about some impossible regulation. When people in some backward commission, have thought up God, they naturally made him in their own wonderful image. They did this, in gratitude: 'Thou shalt judge us, like the most intolerant judge.' And so, Meisel appeared before God, and it happened to be on *Yom Kippur*, the day of atonement. The Jews in Berditchew were fasting and confessing their sins, as they did each year. The *Zadik* sang his heart-rending prayer at the synagogue, and from the eyes of the old Hersh tears were flowing incessantly. Of course, they could not know that at the very moment the Lord was in judgment upon that scoundrel, Meisel. However, up there in Heaven, things were already proceeding at a fast pace. An enormous set of scales was being pushed in, and everybody began to talk to his heart's content. Too bad Comrade Landau of the court of Homel was not there—he could have really shown off with his eloquence. The first was naturally the Attorney General, I mean—and here I must implore you not to think that I am alluding to the present—it was the devil in person, and he brought out in great detail all the paragraphs of the code. He demanded the extradition of the deceased parasite into his realm. Afterwards it was the counsel's turn, and he talked and talked, stressing his origin, beating his chest with the wings, till finally it became too much, even for God to listen. He rang a bell, and all the Jews of Berditschew could hear it:

" 'Enough! It is time to weigh the deeds of the dead Meisel.'

"The angel hurriedly threw all of Meisel's wicked deeds onto one of the scales: there were the tears of the poor and the wails of the widows, cries of hungry children, and it was all true and genuine, so that the black scale knocked with a terrible crash against a cloud. Then, the angels began to place a few ridiculous tears on the other side of the scale. Yes indeed, they did not load it with Meisel's good deeds, even though he gave the poor some of his loot on *Yom Kippur.* No, they only placed those tiny tears on the scale. Meisel watched this and was quite dejected. Could there be any doubt? On the one side, the great, big mass of misdeeds, worth perhaps a hundred thousand rubles; on the other side however—nothing but a tiny jug with salty water. But what does he see? The lighter scale comes gradually lower. Of course, if those had been tears of formality only, they would have weighed very little; but as I told you before, those were real tears, that flowed from his heart; they weighed a half ton, or perhaps even a hundred tons. The scales stopped in the middle. The one side could not pull the other one down. And so it turned out, that the dead Meisel had done as many good deeds as he had committed wrongdoings. The angels and even God, were quite surprised. Nobody knew what was to happen. Meisel stood there, shaking. But he was already thinking of more outrageous mischief. This rascal, Meisel, waited a moment, and when God turned away to see, perhaps, what was happening in America, he grabbed one of the worst misdeeds from the black scale and let it disappear quickly in his pocket. But, of course, Meisel was not the first one to try such a thing, and God had adjusted the scale so that it would immediately point out any deceit. Meisel had hardly played his infamous trick when the black scale crashed twice against the cloud, and they all understood that Meisel had tried to deceive God Himself, after having swindled so many thousands of people, too. Now, even the counsel desisted from his eloquent rhetoric. He did not wish to defend such a crime. However, since the invented God has to be somewhat kinder than ordinary people are, He said to the angels:

" 'I do not intend to send Meisel to hell without a last word. Tell me, who among you will defend such an outrageous misdeed?'

"The angels, however, are known to be cowards, and they were afraid to violate the heavenly discipline.

" 'We do not wish to defend such a scoundrel, but if You insist on this formality, You may invite the *Zadik* from Berditschew up here. There has never yet been a case where he would deny the defense of even the most despicable man.'

"In the synagogue, the Jews noticed the *Zadik* suddenly falling asleep even before finishing his heart-rending prayer. Naturally, they were quite astonished, but they did not try to awaken him. If the wise *Zadik* had fallen asleep, it most likely had to be that way. And they went on praying.

"They believed the *Zadik* had simply fallen asleep. In reality, however, the *Zadik* had risen up to the skies. He appeared before God, and began at once, with the defense of the dead Meisel. He did not even take time to look around to see which angel was sitting where. He did not recount Meisel's good deeds; nor did he point at the little jug of salty water. No, he began to talk to God at once. With the very first word, he touched God at a most vulnerable spot:

" 'The question is, what are You judging him for? Is it because he has committed another misdeed right here? I think, one offense more or one less is of no interest to anyone. If he has swindled innocent children, it is a little worse than the ridiculous story with Your scales, for, he has really swindled them, while he has merely attempted to deceive You, and this, quite innocently, as a child would try to deceive his father. However, if You are judging him because he was evil on earth, I shall reply to You, that it was not his fault at all. It is Your fault, and no one else's. Had You shown man the paradise, all people would be as good as these invented angels; but You have first shown them hell—the real hell—for who can deny that life on earth is hell. Then why are you surprised that they act as they do, as though they were in hell? And now, you want to take this dead Meisel and send him once again to hell. Where is Your justice, and why do You claim judgment over men? It might be more truthful to say that You torture them, and You can do that without those scales, the same as people on earth are doing. Therefore, You must acquit the dead Meisel, at once.

"Naturally, God could not take exception to such words of wisdom. He was embarrassed. And he said:

" 'Very good. Take the dead Meisel to the richest paradise.'

"At this point, the *Zadik* from Berditschew could have returned home. But he noticed that God was in a good mood, and, somewhat impressed by his own fiery plea, the *Zadik* thought: I have to take advantage of this moment, I must prove to God that he had tried men's patience long enough; that the people in Berditschew and everywhere are very unhappy, and that it might be high time to send some invented Messiah on earth, to save the human race. And so, the *Zadik* did not leave. He went on to shame God, to convince and persuade Him. And God began to give in. Already, he smiled absently, setting the *Zadik's* mind at rest with these words:

" 'Why are you so upset? I never said I shall not send the Messiah. On the contrary, I said I will send him for sure. Perhaps you are right to think the time has come. Come over here, and we shall discuss this question. What year have we now on earth?'

"I am telling you, God was absolutely ready to give his consent. But at this point something happened. The Jews down there in their synagogue naturally could not see that the *Zadik* up in Heaven saw them quite clearly. He could see that because of his talk with God the prayer down there would not end, and therefore the fast could not end, either. One may fast easily at twenty, but not at sixty. And suddenly the *Zadik* sees the old Hersh fainting and falling to the ground. No wonder—he had not eaten, nor had he drunk anything since yesterday. The *Zadik* knew that old Hersh would die on the spot, if the prayer would not come to an end at once. And he said to God:

" 'Perhaps what I am doing now is very foolish. I should try to convince you that it is impossible to wait any longer. Then you might save all mankind. But at this moment I cannot spend any more time talking to you: if I were to stay just another hour in Heaven, old Hersch who washes dirty linen in Berditshew, will surely die. But where is it written that I have the right to pay for the happiness of all mankind with the life of old Hersh?'

"He descended from Heaven without completing the conversation. He hurried through his needless prayer, so as to bring the fast to an end. To be sure, perhaps Hersh passed away a year later, but he did not die that night. The *Zadik* had not treated him like some ticket that you push under a ticket window.

"This is what I wanted to tell you, my poor traveling companion. Of course, you may drink your tea, and try to justify the black soul of some glorified world history. I can tell you one thing only: that doctor is already lying in the hollow grave; and not just that one doctor. But you tell me, what have you been handed from your marvelous ticket window?"

14

Lasik was an outstanding cutter of men's trousers. Whatever people like Pfeifer or other jealous individuals may say, I maintain: Zimach, with his presumed English-fashion, could have waited a long time to achieve such style! However, in Tula there were plenty of other tailors. Whenever the citizens would pass by the glittering shop signs, they would merely turn away their melancholy eyes. Tula is famous for tea-kettles and gingerbread, but only in old women's tales. The truth was, that many people were fired from their jobs. If Lasik had to depend on his tailor's tools, he would not have survived a single day. He was saved by the famous dialectics: if people were fired, others had to be hired. That is a simple law of nature. If one is chased out of his room, another has to take his place. But still, the outcast has to eat, too. And if he was thrown out of one room, he will move into another one; for in spite of the foolish Talmud, the earth goes on turning, and with it all the tormented employes in the most plausible and implausible offices, including their various subdivisions.

Hardly a week had gone by, and Lasik had found the right door. He had found a position in the Department of Animal-breeding. His job was to supervise the increase of pure-bred rabbits in the entire Tula District. The main office had established that this could mean one of the most profitable breeding experiments in the frame of agricultural budgets. And so, Lasik stepped boldly through the open door before him, threw a glance over the field of his future activities, which consisted of one table with a smeary blotter, and addressed a question to Dunja, the girl messenger:

"Excuse me, Comrade, where are they . . . ?"

Dunja yawned.

"Where should they be? At home, having tea. Or at Maria Ignatjewna's."

"Ssst. I did not ask you about the Comrade Director. I had absolutely no wish to ask you about him. I had enough in Kiev, when I had to grab the superior's legs. No, I asked you merely about those pure and innocent rabbits."

"We have none here. However, if you wish to see Comrade Rabbitkow, he is not here, but in the bookkeeping department."

Lasik looked into the drawers, but all he found was an empty cigarette box. He sat down and waited dutifully until five o'clock. Then he went home. He had made up his mind not to start philosophizing. The next morning, nevertheless, he asked the Director:

"Excuse me, Comrade Petrow, I would like to ask you, where

are they, I mean, the rabbits I was entrusted with—are they here, or somewhere in the district?"

Petrow grumbled:

"The devil knows! Maybe in the cupboard. Look over there, in those papers."

Lasik worked all day. He rummaged through the drawers looking for rabbits like a long haired terrier, sneezing constantly from the pungent dust. Though he didn't find any, he did find a copy of a document, number 2178, which had to do with an account of the sad end that had befallen a pair of thoroughbred rabbits sent to Tula from the central office. Lasik's predecessor, a certain Rosechkow, who was now employed in the subdivision of the Music Department, communicated from Moscow: "In acknowledgment of receipt of the pure-bred cargo, we beg to inform you, that the remitted specimens did not arrive at the Tula receiving station due to the peculiarities of climate, difficulties in transport, as well as the ignorance of the native population in regard to rearing pure-bred rabbits. Inasmuch as a closer examination of the transport-car produced the dead specimens, and according to the certificate of the local Board of Veterinaries, death occurred either because of heavy frost or because of an inadequate supply of oxygen, or even because of the behavior of the citizens at the railroad station, who autocratically opened the box, thus permitting an unorganized hunt with heavy participation of all the stray dogs of the city of Tula."

Lasik read this sad document more than three times, and since the female messenger was not around, he took the opportunity and sighed audibly:

"Poor thoroughbred pair of rabbits—that is all that remains of your happy hopscotch somewhere under American palm trees; a copy of an act, number 2178! Meanwhile the question arises, what should I do? How can I, in the whole great district transmit this cruel reminder?"

And Lasik could not stand the irksome emptiness of his desk or of the whole District of Tula. Two days later he approached Comrade Petrow:

"What am I to do now that they are irrevocably dead and even attested to by this copy?"

"What do you mean what to do? Work, Comrade, work! Propagate! Produce! Intensify! Do you understand? Do you see this comparative chart? First—meat. Second—fur. Third—small expenses. Fourth—time-savers. At the end of the year we shall report no less than thirty thousand specimens."

"Excuse me, Comrade Petrow, but where will this rich fur or the meat come from when their silent ancestors have been dismembered by a bunch of unorganized dogs? All I can do is to propagate the sorrow stated in that circular; but that will not make a very nice chart, since they have, forgive the expression, dropped off to spite us."

"Dropped off? Haha! Sure, sure, they have dropped off. But now, just between you and me, what rabbits could there be here anyway? I could understand pigs perhaps. But Comrade, you can go on propagating, nevertheless. They will send us new ones from Moscow, and meanwhile one can at least work out the regulations for the agricultural enterprises. Or you may arrange a lecture with nebulous pictures. In short—don't make a tragedy of it. Do you understand? By the way, they sent us a questionnaire from the central office. As far as you are concerned, you have seventeen questions to answer."

Lasik remained by himself with his seventeen questions and some grave misgivings. What did he mean by "don't make a tragedy of it?" Should the rabbits be registered as rabbits? That would not be too bad. But in paragraph eleven he was asked the following question: "What influence did the raising of purebred rabbits have upon the economic condition of the farming population? Upon their cultural life? Upon their family relationships? Is there in connection with this a notable increase in the figures of birth production? Establish in round figures the relationship between the number of rabbits, and the consumption of soap per farm." If the rabbits had to be rabbits, then they did not exist at all. Of course, one can take it for granted that they are merely a symbol of some splendid electrifying power. In the Talmud they have many such crazy things. So, for instance, it is written of "Lambs tits," when really they are nothing but the holy receptacles of the Levites. And the great Raschi wants us to believe that the beautiful pair of breasts King Solomon sings about to his girl friend Shulamite, are, in reality, only a symbol for the two ancient Jewish leaders, Moses and Aaron. They might, by the same token, say "rabbits," and mean ordinary party cells. But still, Comrade Petrow had told him "not to make a tragedy" of it.

After a long deliberation, Lasik decided to stay away from any allegory. To the first question: What is the number of rabbits in the District of Tula on the day of filling out this questionnaire?—he replied, firmly: "One tombstone in the shape of a heart-breaking circular." And to the sixteen other questions, he added a true tragic note: neither soap, nor any increase in birth production, nor family relationships, nothing—absolute emptiness, sorrow, non-existence.

In any case, he showed the sheet to his superior. Comrade Petrow began to rage up and down the long corridor, cursing:

"Are you crazy? Do you know what that means? Firing of personnel!"

"You're telling me. It was I who had to sit in prison for six weeks, not the citizen Pukke."

"You don't understand a thing! You want to ruin us all! How can anyone fill out an official questionnaire with such answers? One has to give this thing special importance, stress the achievements. Charts, surveys, diagrams. If you would send in this nonsense, we would all go to prison. Change it all, at once. You have no understanding whatsoever of the needs of the state.

'A tombstone'—indeed! Is this supposed to be a joke?"

Days full of torment began for Lasik. Comrade Petrow went home at three o'clock; Dunja, the messenger, left at five. Only Lasik had no idea of time. Stooped over the table, he sat and figured and pondered, assembling his material.

At the end of the fifth day he had completed his work. All seventeen questions were answered, and they read as follows:

"Since the late pair was dispatched to Tula on November 18, 1924, the population of rabbits for the entire district may be set at 11,726 and a ½ heads. In regard to the normal occurring functions and the lack of lemonade, the number as of January 1, 1930 in this entire district, is 260,784. Parasites, such as ground-squirrels or phylloxera vastatrix were not noticed. As to other diseases, aside from the tragic end of the first pair, and the possibility of an insignificant runny nose, thanks to the heroic attitude of the District Board of Health, we have no complaints. The rabbits are being kept in plantations and in other cupboards. The birth increase in the population swells enormously. In relation to this, the soap production can therefore barely keep in step, since, even when a small, miserable piece, half used up is being added per farm, one can nevertheless say in round figures, that this is a bare zero compared with the richly feathered wings of our, into the thousands spreading, rabbits."

After completion of his work, Lasik decided not to disturb Comrade Petrow, who was busy anyway with Maria Ignatjevna, and he sent the document to Moscow. For two long weeks he enjoyed peace and tranquillity. Dunja, the messenger, yawned, the tea was lonesome cooling in its glass; Comrade Petrow shone through his fruitful absence; and the manager of the breeding of rabbits had nothing else to do, but to draw the ears of his unforgettable grandparents on the blotting-paper. But, one day, the corridor resounded with the noise of crashing boots. A commission from Moscow had arrived to study the model rabbit breeding enterprise of Tula.

"First of all, we would like to congratulate you, Comrade. The number of rabbits in your district alone is greater than that of the entire Soviet Union. Obviously, you must have discovered a particularly favorable feed. In England they have achieved such results by using phosphor drugs. But we shall surpass them. What did you feed them?"

Lasik lowered his eyes meekly.

"Merely with the prescribed imagination, required in the office."

The gentlemen from Moscow did not understand. They said politely:

"Well, we want to convince ourselves, on the spot. Tomorrow we shall drive out to the agricultural, experimental stations. Tell us, please, in which region is the greatest number of rabbits to be found?"

"Where to find them? Not in the region, nor in the cupboard, but here."

And proudly, Lasik pointed at his small head.

The corridor resounded once more with the crashing of boots, but this time it was an ominous sound. Comrade Petrow forgot completely the presence of Maria Ignatjewna and raged:

"You have made fun of everybody! To jail! To court!"

"Why are you shouting at me, Comrade Petrow? When I wrote that one could hardly expect a great increase from dead rabbits, you were stamping the floor with your boots. Thereupon I tortured my weary brain with a multiplication chart and I have achieved a real administrative miracle: I have forced these dead rabbits to multiply. And now you are stamping your feet again, and I don't understand it at all. You remind me, and please forgive the indecent comparison, of certain Roman emperors; for, there was such a crazy emperor, when a Jew did not bow to him, he would call: 'Cut off his head! How could he, that impudent Jew dare not to greet the Roman Emperor!' But then, he saw another Jew, who naturally bowed very deeply to him; but he cried nevertheless 'Cut off the head of this Jew even faster. How dare this brazen fellow greet me.' I am asking you, Comrade Petrow, what should such a rabbit-breeder do, if he is not permitted to tell the truth, nor is he allowed to lie and be funny?"

"You are pretending to be a fool, but we shall see, what you will have to say, when they put you in prison."

"Nothing. I am used to it. And there, I either remain silent, or I tell improper stories. There is only one thing I dislike: when they come to pick me up. For then, my heart starts beating real fast. I would rather go by myself straight to the gates of the prison, and beg them to let me in, say, an hour earlier. Then the whole matter would be settled in a much calmer way. Goodbye, Comrade Petrow! Goodbye, you quiet desk; farewell, animal-breeding; goodbye, you tea in the glass of Dunja, the messenger; and goodbye, you sad shadows of two fallen ancestors. Day and night you were playing hopscotch in the stunted mind of an absolutely obliging expert."

15

Lasik was sitting on a bench on the Twerskoy Boulevard, thinking how good rabbit meat might taste. It was probably like the bananas of which Lewka had sung, or perhaps like orchids; but no, you do not eat orchids, you only smell them. However, Lasik felt very much like having a snack. He would not have insisted on rabbit roast; he would have been quite happy with a piece of old sausage. As though it were a joke, for the past three days he had to be content with sniffing spicy odors (worthy of the wonderful orchid) that filled the streets near various restaurants and taverns. He had neither money in his pocket, nor did he have any credentials, or even a dependable address. Moscow received Roitschwantz with a pomp that only made him more aware of his miserable self: "Yes, indeed, the statute of Pushkin; yes indeed, ten thousand little alleys; why certainly; a soviet consisting of all kinds of commissars! . . . But what now? . . . One cannot go on forever sniffing at the entrances of restaurant-kitchens."

Lasik started to look for shelter. Attentively, he began to observe his surroundings. Wherever he looked, he saw the edifying warning: "*Beware of automobiles!*"

"Listen to what one should beware of! First, there are as many automobiles here as there are orchids in Homel; and in the second place, they move much slower than for instance, the old Hershanowitsch when he returns home for dinner from the synagogue; in the third place however, if an automobile should run me down, it would at least be a real American ending, as befits the twentieth century. In any case, it would be a much more decent ending than death of starvation, as was the fashion in the old times. No, let me put on paper a small warning; I would like to write this: 'Beware of the deathly eyes of Fenitchka Hershanowitch! Beware of the perfume of rabbits! And, in general, beware of a strong appetite!' But who pays any attention to the words of the wise?"

Next to Lasik sat a strong, young fellow, dressed in nothing but a pair of breeches and boots that had acquired a reddish hue because of their age. He had a heavy growth of hair on his chest and legs. Under his arm he had a briefcase. And to himself, he was whistling a military march, beating time with his feet like a horse that had been standing too long on one spot. Lasik did not look at him. As though there were not enough people in Moscow to look at! The fact that he was naked? Let him be naked! After all, he was not Fenitchka Hershanowitch. On the other hand, however, the half-naked Citizen, while continuing to whistle, did not take his eyes off Lasik. What was he looking for, glancing at the roofs of houses, then at the sky, then again under the bench? . . . At last, his interest became so great, that he asked Lasik:

"Have you lost something? . . ."

Lasik looked suspiciously at the hairy shoulders of his neighbor, as though that other Mintschik could not have undressed just as quickly? . . .

"Lost something? No, I have nothing to lose, unless it were our hope in Homel. But I have not lost that either. Not yet. Of course, one could lose his wife, or money or even one's own name. But these are trifles. Today man loses his teeth,, tomorrow an American dentist will make him new ones. But one must never lose hope. That would be the same as if one were to die twenty years before one's death. What should I hope for when I have no connections and all Moscow smells as fragrant as a roast of non-existing rabbits. But I am hoping, nevertheless.

"Maybe in another moment, someone will pass by, on this Boulevard, and will give me a letter of recommendation. I might become the administrator of Moscow's pineapple plantations, or even the manager of the seminary for cross-breeding between sensible citizens and oppressed monkeys."

"Hang it all! So you are also interested in literature, Comrade? Permit me to introduce myself: Archip Stojkij. Have you read in the *Young People's Pravda,* the chapter from the novel *The Soapy Humming*? [illegible] Revolution, and no drivel whatsoever! And where have you been published? . . ."

Lasik became meditative. Indeed, why wasn't he a writer? If one had to take off his shirt, he could do that, too. The main thing was—imagination; and had Pfeifer not told him: "You, Roitschwantz, are lying, not like a human being, but like a real newspaper." But of course, in his soul, Lasik was a poet! That is why he had come to Moscow. Up to that moment, Lasik had thought very little about literary things, if we are to be honest. He merely knew that Pushkin was jealous of his wife, just like the contractor Scheekewitch; that Leo Tolstoy had a handsome beard just like Karl Marx, except that Marx's was shovel-shaped while Tolstoy's was like a spade. But now he knew, that he, Lasik Roitschwantz was not a men's tailor, not even an "Expert," but rather an exciting author. He winked, familiarly, at the jealous Pushkin.

"Published? Why, everywhere. And I had about forty different pen names. In Homel, for instance, they thought of me almost as Pushkin, but naturally without the property instinct, as that of a factory owner. You must have heard, of course, of our minstrel from Homel, Shurka Bezdomny? He writes poems about abnormal communistic cavalry, exclusively. And I have even given him advice. I told him: 'You should add a smile on their faces, my dear Shurka Bezdomny.' And he added it, too."

"This is old stuff, Comrade. Pushkin, as well as Shurka Bezdomny, it is all drivel. I will show you the way we write in Moscow now."

Archip Stojkij took a few sheets from his briefcase, jerked his naked leg, and thundered away:

"98th chapter. The soap was humming, like iron bees. Merrily, Senja Puwak nodded his head: 'This is right, Comrades, you have done well.' Dunja was smiling at his side. Proudly she looked at the assembly line, the red star on her breast, which seemed to swell with wholesome enthusiasm. The soap was sizzling. 'We shall supply the entire government,' Senja said. He looked at the girl's star: 'Well, Dunja, let us go. Ours is the glorious path of the young class to the sun. Let us forget the dirty diversions of those who were formerly the masters of this factory. Come now and let my calloused worker's hand press you to my heart!' And Dunja yielded to the beat of new life and whispered, blushing slightly: 'You see, we have surpassed pre-war production figures. Sizzle soap, sizzle! And if we will have a son, let us simply call him: 'Soapy Humming.' "

Archip Stojkij looked proudly around the Boulevard. Great pearls of perspiration glittered on his hairy chest.

"Nice, isn't it? This is how you should do it, too! You could, for instance, write about the silkworm . . . The main thing is to be amazing, nonplussed. Who writes in the magazines? Only degenerated bourgeois. We throw them out through the door, and they enter through the window. One has to pursue that gang to the very end! I have only had sixteen chapters printed so far. And all in all, there are two hundred fourteen. It is high time to put an end to this. I can advise you, Comrade, without hesitating any further, join our group *Watch*! We watch against carcasses sneaking into the publishing house. If you join our group, you will be published everywhere. Is it a deal?"

Lasik agreed readily.

"After the dead rabbits, I am afraid of nothing. If it is *Watch*, let it be *Watch*. But tell me, what do I have to do? Of course, to take off my shirt is a matter of only two minutes; however, I do not own, for instance, such a valuable briefcase."

"Trifles! That is not obligatory. I, personally, like sunbaths. It is good for the health, and distinguishes us already outwardly from the pale monsters of the compromising groups. I like to have a suntan. I prefer black bread and drink artesian fountain-water. I am simple, austere and stubborn. I am a real *Watcher*, and from now on, you are a *Watcher*, too."

At the mere mention of such not-so-choice foods as black bread, Lasik had to sigh sadly:

"Of course, it tastes better if there is a small slice of compromising sausage on that austere bread. However, if a *Watcher* can eat only dry bread, I will not contradict you. I am asking only one favor. Tell me, where can I find it at once—that inexorable bread—for the fresh air has made me a little hungry."

Archip Stojkij blinked cheerfully at Lasik and took him to a modest tavern. Chopped cutlets with onions and four bottles of beer soon appeared on the table. After the first glass of beer Lasik got tipsy and chirped merrily:

"If you call this austere water and artesian bread, one must ask, who am I and who are you? I think that in such case you are Leo Tolstoy and I am Pushkin himself, though I have no wife at all, unless it would be Fenitchka Hershanowitch, who is, however the wife of the cocky Schatzman, while you have no beard at all, or rather, your beard grows under your armpit. Tell me the name of this crazy dish? Cutlets? You are telling me, these are plain, ordinary chopped cutlets? No, after three days of strictest *Yom Kippur,* let me tell you that these are not cutlets, they are rabbits or, who knows, maybe bananas."

Archip Stojkij drank uninterruptedly. New bottles were brought, the cutlets were sizzling, the glasses resounded merrily.

"We shall smoke them out everywhere! . . . Long live the *Watchers.*"

Lasik felt quite heavy. He could hardly move his tongue, and he stammered:

"But of course, let them live long, when there are such rabbits on the table. You say, the carcasses come crawling in? Well, I must say, what kind of indecent carcasses are they? A carcass has to lie under some sentimental inscription. And to crawl through a window, that is quite improper for a corpse. That is not some soap, that can go on humming forever. I would like to make you just one offer. Ever since I was a child, I had weak eyes. Once, I have even grabbed the wrong leg, by mistake. I could, as they say in Homel, mistake a foreign elephant for Moshka, the cigaret vendor. And you are a very busy man. You take sunbaths, you drink artesian water, not to mention Dunja, who is probably humming all this time. In short, we will not achieve much with our own means. Therefore I make you an offer to accept one other person from Homel into our group. It is true, she has a horrible family name, but we could make her a gift in the form of a proud pen name. She could certainly be a poet. If she only saw your hairy chest, the purest poems would come from her lips."

Absorbed in such literary discussions, our friends did not notice the passage of time.

"Your bill is eight ruble twenty kopeks."

"Well, well, I will not deny it . . . All right, you pay this time. The next time I will be the host."

"I do not wish to deny it, either. Why argue? I should think I am not a carcass. But all I have in my pocket is the portrait of the Portuguese hostage and maybe another hole. I told you that I have fasted for three long days, and it seems quite clear to me that this is not opium, but iron materialism."

Archip Stojkij got up, belched and observed philosophically:

"The devil with it! I do not even have pockets to pretend with! Hey, Citizen! A joke, but unfortunately a fact: I have forgotten my coat with the wallet in it at home. That's it—all because of the modern sport. Well, goodbye . . ."

And he tottered out into the street. The manager of the tavern tried to shake Lasik, who had remained seated at the table; however, he found out soon, that besides a photograph, there was nothing to shake out of him, and so he contented himself with a blow of the fist. Lasik found himself on the Boulevard with a slightly swollen eye. But he did not lose hope. After all, he had a good dinner, and before him was the glory of Pushkin. Wait and you will see, they will yet place his statue in the Paskewitch Park! He will stand there in bronze trousers and smile down on all. And it will happen that Fenitchka Hershanowitch will come to his statue, crying: "Why did I have to give my love to that cocky Schatzman, who has no monument, and not to this hero, whose glory shines over all America?"

And even though Lasik will wear bronze trousers, he will jump down from the pedestal saying:

"I love you even after my death, and if you wish we can get married, all three thirds."

Thus dreaming, Lasik fell asleep.

16

The next evening, Lasik went to the *Literary Club.* Full of dignity, he registered in the guest book under the name "Roitschwantz—the Watcher." Somebody asked him: "Comrade, are you a poet or a critic?" Without losing his composure, Lasik replied:

"I am an inexorable critic of the control commission. But what is this hubbub here, tonight? Dances of the national minorities or is it a lecture about the sexual problem?"

When Lasik heard that he had happened to be in on an evening of literary debate discussing the theme: "Must one publish

—and whom?" he was delighted. Now, he could really show them!

The speaker was a *Watcher*. He spoke at great length that the "red mass vestments had to be white." The "fellow travelers," he said, were a superstructure above the foundation. As long as the reader was a greenhorn, they could foist all kinds of suspicious books upon him. But now, he has matured. He is asking for the protection of his brain from rotten publications. How could anyone publish the backward drivel of the various degenerates, in editions of twenty thousand books, after such epics as *The Soapy Humming*. "Down with the ostrich-policy, long live the writing youth!"

Lasik applauded wildly. He intended to speak up at once. He would make a motion for the erection of a double monument for Archip Stojkij and Lasik Roitschwantz—as, for instance, Minin and Posharsky. However the representative of one of the publishing houses interrupted:

"I merely wish to point out a few naked figures to this reporter. Comrades, as you know, we must adhere to the General Economic Plan. Unfortunately, the reading public does not yet buy the works of the *Watchers*. The novel, *The Great Brotherhood*, has sold only six copies, and the poetical fiction, *The Kiss of the Working People*, only four. One has to attempt to bring the grave economic condition to agree with the Marxist ideology. We publish into the twenty thousands the poison of some wayfarer so that we may have the possibility of issuing one splendid volume of the entire works of Comrade Archip Stojkij, as a proven antidote."

Archip Stojkij grumbled discontentedly.

"Nonsense! If you publish only our books, they will have nothing else to buy . . . Enough of such compromises!"

However the publisher's representative did not give up that easily. He proceeded to lull the audience to sleep with his figures. Lasik decided this was the time to speak up. He looked tenderly at the reporter and at Archip Stojkij, as well as at the representative.

"You are all very pleasant Marxists, and I will reconcile you at once with a small dose of dialectics. Archip Stojkij is an author like Leo Tolstoy, and his works must be published at once. Why all these long speeches, when he wishes to be published? It seems to me money is of no importance in such a matter. If we were treated to roast rabbit yesterday by a small tavern keeper who did not mind the expense, in my opinion, the state should immediately publish all parts of this *Soapy Humming*. If the state fails to do this, Comrade Archip Stojkij will have to stop taking sunbaths, and thus will have to become a crawling carcass. But there remains the second question in regard to those indecent wayfarers. On the one side, they must not be printed for they are not a healthy influence; on the other hand they have to be published, or else publishing houses will not only have a big gap, but they will also remain without any income. How, then, is one to solve such contradiction? Quite simple. Our Jews in Homel, who are still believing in God and who are denying the excellence of ham, are admittedly fools. But even they have found a way out. I will tell you, for instance, that a Jew must sell all his table utensils before Passover, and keep only the Passover dishes. This is how the experts of the Talmudic subdivision have figured it out. But to whom should they sell their utensils? And besides, you get only ten kopeks for a pot that cost one whole ruble. So, when Passover draws near, the Jew calls in a Russian, let's say the luggage-carrier or the doorkeeper, and he tells him: 'I am selling you all my table utensils for five kopeks.' And the Russian replies: 'Very well, I am buying it.' Of course, they both know that this is all a swindle, and the doorkeeper gets a half ruble to strengthen his soul with some vodka. You see, that is a practical way out of an unalterable situation! I can see you have not lived in Homel, and you do not quite understand these things. Therefore I shall tell you the story of the handkerchiefs. On Sabbath, a Jew is not allowed to carry anything, not even the necessary handkerchief, except on his own premises. However, a runny nose can occur even on a Sabbath. And, one cannot sit at home all day long. However, at the synagogue there is absolutely nothing to wipe one's nose with. Do you think for a moment that the Jews have to depend on their two fingers to wipe their noses? Not at all! They thought about it, and they found the solution. If they spanned a wire all around Homel, the entire town might be regarded as one's own backyard, and they could walk all through Homel, with a dozen handkerchiefs, if they wished. And so, they collected the money and bought a wire, and in ten minutes they had put the wire around the town. I am telling you, the main thing, is to understand one another. Perhaps, those wayfarers are one thing and the kerchiefs, the utensils, and the devil knows what else another. However, we are selling them to the doorkeeper, and we put a wire around them. We can say that they are on our premises, and then they may be published with some bewildering preamble. He may write, for instance, that Shurotchka has a great love, but we are pushing it like hotcakes in our blurb: 'Shurotchka is not Shurotchka, and love is not love, it is all a struggle of the social classes.' They will buy twenty thousand copies of the book, and there will be money in the cash register, and Archip Stojkij will receive a large sum of tcherwontzes for his *SoapyHumming*. . . ."

Archip Stojkij wrinkled his forehead suspiciously.

"Are you a *Watcher*, or not? You are flattering us as well as your own people. With whom did you talk in the meantime?"

But Lasik calmed him quickly.

"I said these things only to make that man with the glasses shut up, and to get them to give you, finally, a few tcherwontzes. Frankly, I am beginning to get hungry again, and I don't think our trick at the tavern would work a second time."

Even though Archip Stojkij wore a shirt with pockets, there was no money in them. Lasik could do nothing but dream how heavenly those rabbit bananas had smelled. Suddenly a well-fed citizen, with a very decent appearance, approached Lasik. With an apologetic smile he said to him:

"I beg your pardon, may I have a couple of words with you? You talk just like Trotzky. One brilliant thought after another. I think we two will understand each other. You see, I am looking for an understanding Marxist."

Lasik was touched.

"I know. I have also searched for an understanding maiden in Homel, but Fenya Hershanowitch has proved herself as inaccessible as two American castles. To be sure, later on she became considerate; but not to me—to Schatzman—and then she naturally ceased being a maiden. That is what is called happiness in Homel! But tell me, why do you need an indulgent Marxist? Did you possibly get the notion to improve Karl Marx himself?"

"Ssst. What are you saying? And here, of all places! . . . I have to discuss a very delicate matter with you. Can't we leave together? Permit me to introduce myself: Rurik Abramowitsch Solitair."

Lasik's nostrils swelled up. He felt a moisture in his mouth. He became giddy. He decided to skip all considerations:

"Do you know to whom you are addressing yourself, Rurik Abramowitsch? I am a great author. By tomorrow I might perhaps stand there in bronze trousers. I am a critic who knows no pity. Within me, rest a thousand investigations. But let us go out together. No, we will not only leave together, we will proceed together to some happy paradise. One can see that you have more than holes in your pockets. You may invite me to those rabbits, I mean, to tasty chopped cutlets with sour cream sauce."

Rurik Abramowitsch put his hand tenderly around Lasik's neck:

"Sure, sure. First we shall go to the restaurant 'Venetia.' There they serve pheasants and beer, as it says in the Book."

After he had finished the second pheasant, Lasik said:

"Merci. Thank you. After these rabbits I have become so understanding that I could cry right away. However, if you want me to improve Karl Marx, I will not do it under any circumstances. I like to shave every other day, and I don't care to spend my days in a house of correction."

"Well, how can you, how can you! . . . Am I perhaps a robber? I am only a Jew from Kryshopol. Would you like another little bird? Some more gravy? This is strictly a literary matter. We are almost compatriots and you will understand me. I have to sell my kitchen utensils to the porter. You are from Homel and I am from Kryshopol. No big difference, is there? But you are a Marxist, and I am an idle element, full of tears and sorrow. There is nothing I have not dealt in. I could even put it into poetry, like your Pushkin—saccharine and aspirin, English pounds and raisins, and the devil knows what else. I was deported eight times: I was sent to Narym in the north, to the Solovetski Islands, to Arctic places as though I were a Nansen on a mission to discover the North Pole. I have endured everything. But now—there is no business for me at all. One could go crazy with their price reduction policy! Just think, I have lost one hundred tcherwontzes on a single overcoat. I did not know what else to think up. There I was, standing at the Petrowka, like at Jerusalem's wailing wall. If the tears were not flowing from my eyes, it was only because of my fine upbringing. All of a sudden, that Fox jumps out and tells me: 'Publish books. I am publishing books too, and that is something!' Naturally, I grab him by the collar: 'Have you perhaps eaten foul fish? Am I perhaps a state committee that publishes books?' But he just laughs: 'You are not going to print any such propaganda. No, you will publish novels with Parisian niceties, and you will make money, in the hundreds.' Indeed, he was not such a fool, that Fox. I have figured it all out. I have a name for my business: *Red Divan Publishing*

House. I even have a manuscript ready. It is such a novel that I cannot read it without getting excited. I have read it eight times and I still cannot calm down. My eyes crawl up into my forehead. And I am telling you, what a city this Paris is! But you will read it yourself. First a boy sleeps with a girl. Well, that happens in Kryshopol, too. But then the boy sleeps with another boy, and the girl with another girl, and everyone by himself, and all of them together, and on page two hundred I lost it completely, because by that time it is not a bed in a family house any more, but instead it is some windmill. I do not know, it could be the translator had interpreted it all wrong, because he is a piano tuner from Estonia. Of ten words, he understood only five; and he himself told me that for forty rubles he did not have to understand all the words. I should be satisfied with half. But what do words matter anyway? This book will sell! Trust my instinct! I only hesitate to publish it so plainly. But for the time being I am a little tired of those excursions to the North Pole. I would like you to write a real Marxist preamble to it. I am ready to give you fifty ruble for it. After having heard your sensitive speech, I know that you will write a preface like a skilled diplomat. Do you agree? Here is some cash in advance. Another glass of beer? A cup of coffee, perhaps?"

Lasik spent no less time concentrating over the preamble than over the questionnaire regarding the raising of defunct rabbits. He read the manuscript eleven times without understanding anything.

"As Valentin entered the streetcar, he saw Angelica dancing between the limousines. And his passion for the shadows arose, and almost mechanically he took his neighbor's tennis racket. He said to her: 'You want to lie with me at the *Beuf sur le Toit,* in the midst of the Bois de Boulogne, or even in the cabin of the deaf *concièrge*?' "

Lasik groaned quietly. Wow! this was surely one who had eaten foul fish. Well, let them lie on the roof or even in the deaf cabin: that was their own family business. But what part did the tennis racket play in all this? No, it was indeed easier to make dead rabbits multiply. However, Roitschwantz was a man of iron will. He had made up his mind to work toward those bronze trousers, and he slaved like an ox. After several days he had put together a short, but meaningful, preface.

"The French author, Alfonse Curose, whose book we hasten to present to the proletarian reader, is not as simple as it might appear on a first superficial glance. Under the pretext of conflict between the different sexes, he criticizes severely the French bourgeoisie, which dances madly among the chandeliers and limousines. Valentin, the typical degenerate, who certainly desires our petroleum, is momentarily busy exploiting the miserable female *concièrge*. The condition of the oppressed class is expressed in the following words of this vote-entitled slave: 'Master, will you kindly wipe your shoes, please,' she said. What servile devotion is hidden under the mask of a false freedom! To be sure, Alfonse Curose vacillates between two opposing camps, and he does not succeed to put his feet on safe ground. We know, from the standpoint of inexorable Marxism, that he is a completely de-classed type, teetering on the crossroads. But it is his talent that whispers to him: soon there will be no more phenomenons, and tennis balls will get into the calloused hands of new pioneers. When the massive wash-basin falls to the floor of the boudoir, he is symbolically startled; he proceeds to hide the dirty wash of his past in the cupboard, calling out insufferably: 'He is approaching, he is approaching!' Our proletarian reader will not be able to suppress a smile: yes, indeed, he is approaching, the new master of life, and it is high time for all you, unprincipled Curoses, to step under the glorious flag and its well-established appearance!"

One can easily understand how shaky Lasik was when he finished writing this preamble. He remembered Paragraph 87 quite well. However, enlightenment won over fear. Rurik Abramowitsch read the preamble out loud. He read full of pathos, spitting and gesticulating at the same time. "This is first-rate, that is all I can say. I can just imagine how envious that beast, Fox, will be . . ."

When Lasik received his fee, he swelled with pride. He betook himself to the "Venetia," emptied a small bottle of vodka and began to extol:

"I can cut up anything from the standpoint of Marxism, even a chicken stomach. I am a public genius, and I can only smile when thinking that before me will be real people, and not merely eternal glory. Well, Fenitchka, have you not made a mistake? I am opening your lilac-colored bonnet, scientifically of course, and I say—this is vacillation between two platforms. Hey, you, Beethoven, play something nice! And who are you? The waiter? No, I don't know you. No, we are not acquainted. Perhaps you are Maxim Gorky? Anyway, will you kindly help me to get up. My legs are stiff. Surely they must have changed into bronze already."

They took Lasik to the bathroom. He forgot his glory and stiffened wretchedly over the toilet seat. Why deny it—he had never drunk that much.

17

Two weeks later, all of literary Moscow knew Lasik. He visited all the newspaper editors, like one of the guild, talked to them and made himself at home. He demanded money in advance from the editors for various writings he was going to do and even appeared at public meetings as a lecturer. They all got used to his unbelievably short figure, as well as to his thin, little voice, which sounded like the squeak of a mouse. Naturally, no one knew what his fame and popularity consisted of, but, at any rate, it was always: "We must invite that fellow Roitschwantz, too. . . ." When Lasik was asked: "Do you work?"

he would reply arrogantly:

"I should say so! I am just about to finish the sixth volume of a Marxist criticism of phenomena."

Some people reacted to this with dramatic reverence, others simply with jealousy. One day Lasik was sitting at the *Litterary Club* waiting for things to happen. Who knows, mayby a new Solitair might show up from nowhere. And indeed, he was soon approached by a bespectacled type, who was yawning incessantly:

"What a boring lecture today. . . ."

"When is it not boring? In this place you can search a long time for a 'Venetia' with its music. . . ."

The bespectacled person laughed out loud.

"Are you a lyricist? Or do you write prose?"

"Me? I am a Marxist up to the seventh volume. Yes, indeed, not one who sneaks around, but a real honest-to-goodness critic. And who, may I ask, are you?"

"I am—a Learned Secretary of the Academy."

Lasik was impressed. This was quite a fellow! He certainly gets his hundred rubles for a preamble, and probably all the honors one can imagine. And how, for instance, is such an academic bigshot being fed? Certainly with the finest orchids. Why could Lasik not be a Secretary of the Academy, too? That was most probably an ordinary house, if not on the Lubjanka, then on the Petrowka Street. And as to higher learning, there could really be no objection to him. To imagine anyone more learned would indeed be very hard. As if he, not to mention the *Cheder*, had not learned enough from Comrade Serebrjakow!"

At the next event, which was a debate about "Today's Language," Lasik began his speech as follows:

"I am not speaking merely as an inexorable critic, but also as a very erudite secretary of our great Academy. I know your great language in and out, and I claim it is only a death-ride, for when the ocean of classes will fly into a rage . . ."

He never finished his speech.

One misfortune followed another. Rurik Abramowitsch was absent once again on a trip to discover the North Pole. The *Red Divan* publishing house came under investigation, and they were so rude as to take a closer look at the author of the pathetic preface. After the scandal at the meeting, the *Watchers* hastened to deny any relationship with Roitschwantz, and Lasik's literary career ended with the following, not very literary conversation:

"Your name? Year of birth? Are you registered in any party lists? Fine. Now tell me who you are?"

"Me? I am a superstructure."

"What did you say?"

"Very simple. If you represent the foundation, then I am a superstructure. I speak to you as an old Marxist."

"You know what? Stop that nonsense! You are not going to fool me. I know your kind. Answer me, without pretending, what kind of a bird are you?"

"If I have to be a bird, I would like to be an owl. What? You do not know that infamous story? The whole town of Homel knows it! Well, I must tell it to you. Two Jews were talking to each other. 'What is an owl?' 'A fish.' 'Then why does it sit on a branch?' 'Because it is crazy.' Therefore, I am most likely a bird or a fish, in short, some such crazy animal."

"I see! . . . So you insist on pretending! . . . By the way, I am an expert on all shirkers. There was once a rascal here who dealt with dollars on the black market. He tried to be funny, just like you. He claimed he was a dog. Crawled around on all fours, barked, he even lifted his hindleg. So I said to him: 'If you are a dog, we do not have to fuss a great deal: a dog should die like a dog!' Well he jumped as though hit by lightning and cried, 'I am not a dog any more, I am—Ossip Beitschik; please treat me like a human being!' And so, what are you—a fish?"

"No, I am no fish. I have no intention whatsoever of swimming in cold water. I have tried to speak to you loftily, as one does at important meetings. But if you do not like it, I can talk plainly to you. Who I am? I am a former tailor of men's clothes. It all started with Pfeifer's trousers, and it all ended with these bronze pants. I have been crushed under the weight of history. For instance, I was fasting three long days, and then I met Comrade Archip Stojkij. His beard was not where it should have grown, and he read such nonsense to me that even the worst idiot in Homel would have died of sarcasm listening to him. So I said to myself, if this Archip Stojkij is such a famous poet, why should I not crawl onto such a ready-made pedestal too? It is not my fault if I did not understand Citizen Curose's novel. You would not have understood it either, and I give you my word of honor, not even the Chinese generals could understand it. And if I had a good time once at the Venetia, you certainly cannot call it an offense against the state. As we say in Homel: 'Man was created from dust, and to dust he shall return.' That is quite simple. But during the time between his birth from dust and his re-entrance into the earth, it cannot be a crime to have a drink of vodka. I do not remember what I have said in that noisy Venetia, for I became quite sick. And now I am dethroned like a non-existent God. What is there to do? I will not contradict you. You do not wish for me to be the new Pushkin, so I will not be. I shall take off the bronze trousers, and I shall say goodbye to the tasty orchids. I promise you, I shall be more silent than grass that is cut too short. But please, do not send me to Rurik Abramowitsch! I do not own any fur coat and I am sure he is not in any mood to order another preamble. Do not torture the wretched Roitschwantz! No, please, let him run in fifteen different directions!"

18

It was fall and Lasik had found himself a nook once again. He could eat cutlets once more. His new job was not very exciting. But there were too many unhappy experiences behind him and he was not longer dreaming of world-resounding glory. A certain Boris Samoilowitsch Chaifetz received smuggled cloth from Minsk and it was Lasik's job to take the merchandise to the homes of the various private tailors. For this he was paid six tscherwontzes monthly. Though Moscow was much warmer than the North Pole, Lasik, nevertheless, shivered all the time. He carried the cloth like a poor mother who wants to rid herself of her baby, frightened by every chirping sparrow. He even envied Rurik Abramowitsch, who was now probably out of danger; and, used to his surrounding, perhaps had even grown a heavy fur like the polar bears. While for him, Lasik, one dangerous trip after another lay ahead.

His only comfort were his two female neighbors. He sometimes met them in the hallway or on the stairs. Then he would stop and sigh devoutedly, letting his piece of cloth fall to the ground. Time won out—in his soul he deceived Fenya Hershanowitsch. After all, by now Fenitschka was an apple of backward origin, while Lasik's neighbors worked in the "Linen Trust"; they went to the theater to see plays where people shot one another, and in general, they expressed themselves in an educated manner. One of them, bumping into Lasik at the door, said to him: "Such Arabs should not be permitted into decent living quarters. . . ." Lasik fell in love with both, and he was somewhat embarrassed. He knew the one who was rosy and plump was "Comrade Nussja"; the other, a brunette with a pointed nose, was "Comrade Lilli." Which of the two was he in love with, Lilli or Nussja? Moreover, this question interested him only in an abstract way, and he would have rather agreed to visit the ice surrounded Rurik Abramowitsch, than dare to address one of his charming neighbors.

One evening, Lasik coming home from a day of strenuous work (Chaifetz had received another big load of textiles), noticed Comrade Nussja standing at his door. She was the first one to speak:

"Why do you stare at me all the time without greeting me?"

Lasik was speechless.

"Have you lost your speech?"

He made a heroic effort and forced himself to speak:

"No, I have not lost my speech. Pukke is the one who lost her speech. And, besides my name is Roitschwantz. But how can I dare to speak to you? If I had only met you some time earlier, when I was going to become a new Pushkin or even when I was only a party-candidate! But what am I now? Nothing but a faded messenger-boy in a strictly private enterprise,—I mean, at Boris Samoilowitch. You, on the other hand, are a bronze goddess."

Nussja burst into laughter.

"I am no goddess, only a manager. But your room is really beautiful. You do live alone, don't you? How did you do it, to get such a marvelous room all to yourself?"

"That I owe to Boris Samoilowitsch. He has wonderful connections. But why talk about this stupid room, when you yourself are one of the most respected fighters, one might almost say, a bronze, imaginary dream."

"What is the matter with you and that bronze? I am not of bronze. I am . . ."

Nussja did not finish. Instead, she proceeded to show off her not-so-bronze shape. Lasik blinked his eyes. He could hardly murmur:

"What nocturnal fireworks!"

Nussja stepped to the window. She inspected the modest furniture carefully. Lasik could not take his eyes off her: a dream, a heavenly vision! One must admit that Lasik distinguished himself through exaggerated enthusiasm. Though she was an imposing looking female, Nussja was by no means beautiful: a potato-nose, instead of eyebrows a whitish, fuzzy down, also a short, fat neck. The only thing she could boast of was an opulence of flesh. Standing next to Lasik, she resembled a stormy ocean in width, a skyscraper in height.

There was a long silence. Finally Nussja said:

"Are you still staring at me? Do you like me?"

"Oh! . . . Oh!"

Lasik could not find the right words. He fidgeted with his tiny arms, breathing fitfully.

"Do I like you? What a poor way to describe it! Why am I

not Pushkin? Why am I not at least Shurka Bezdomny? I must laugh when I think of my latest doubts. Can you hear my shocking laughter?"

Nussja shrugged her shoulders. Lasik was not even laughing.

"Can't you hear it?"

And he cried out loud: "Haha!"

"Did you hear it now? I am laughing because of my doubts regarding Comrade Lilli. But she really has nothing to offer aside from her nose. She does not even deserve to sleep in the same room with you. When I look at you from all four directions, my eyes become loaded with electricity. Right now, you are reigning over the world, like a bronze . . ."

"Ugh! Not bronze again! Come over here and feel me, I am really not as cold as that. . . ."

All kinds of disconnected thoughts whirled through Lasik's head: Fenya Hershanowitsch, Schatzman, cow, dwarf. . . . Now, it really means to be brave! But I do belong to the class of the brave! However, how shall I kiss her when she is standing up? Shall I climb on the stool? Courage! . . . How many times had Lasik spurred himself on, with the beloved exhortation: "Crawl, Lasik!" And he jumped onto the stool. All of a sudden he was tall and courageous! He embraced Nussja's massive neck with his thin, frail hands and kissed her smack on her lips, just like the bold Valentin had kissed his Angelica in Paris. But at this point, something unexpected happened. He lost his balance, and accompanied by Nussja's laughter, he fell to the floor.

He knew he should get up. But she was laughing. . . . It was not his fault. He had gone into the battle bravely, and if he was wounded, that could have happened to the greatest of heroes. However, she would not understand. Thus it was better not to get up. Rather, he preferred to lie on the floor as if he had died of overwhelming happiness.

"Haha . . . Why are you not getting up? Have you hurt yourself?"

"No, I was not hurt, but perhaps I have died—irrevocably—of my ardent emotions. Maybe, you see before you the cold body of a toreador or even that of Eugene Onegin."

When Nussja had her fill of laughter, she ordered Lasik to get up. In a calm voice she said:

"I have also had enough of Lilli, sticking her nose into other people's business. One cannot invite anybody without having her alienating his affection. Though you are not quite as handsome, and rather short in stature, it will be all right with me. In short—we will get married. First thing, tomorrow morning we will go to the 'ZAGS,' and when I return from my job in the evening, I will bring my things to your room. Then we shall stay together."

Inste[illegible]swer, Lasik fell on his knees. He cried incoherently:

"You are sweeter than a banana! You are foaming like a hundred Dniepers! If I can get six tcherwontzes from Boris Samoilowitsch, I will buy you a tennis racket. I love you like an excavated god."

Nussja, petting him on the head, said:

"Well then, until tomorrow." And, like a sensible bride of olden times, she left and went to sleep in her own room. But Lasik could not think of sleep. He forgot the strict regulations of communal living, and ran through the room like a tiger, full of fear, passion and happiness. He said to himself: "Lasik, do you know what has happened? Here you have been living for thirty-two years like a stupid mole. Who, beside aunt Chassja, ever had the idea to embrace you? And now, all of a sudden, you have become a lover! You can go to all the theaters. Tomorrow you shall enter paradise. Why should such a room be worse than the cabin of a deaf *concièrge*? They will yet write Parisian novels about you. Shout, Lasik! Laugh and dance! Now you are not a messenger-boy for Boris Samoilowitsch any more. You are a steer, ready to jump!"

The next morning Lasik pushed away the package with the overcoat contemptuously. He explained to Boris Samoilowitsch:

"I am not going to work today! I have discovered a very special plan for myself. Tomorrow I may take the merchandise over to Suchatschewsky on the wild Schabalowka street. Today I do not even wish to talk to you; for you live on earth with your miserable overcoats, while I am fluttering among miraculous mirages."

"What is the matter with you? Are you drunk so early in the morning, or do you have a complicated case of grippe?"

"I have a case of complicated love-attack. Tomorrow I shall come back to you, but today I am getting married, and not just to an ordinary woman, but a dream of unreality."

At the registrar's office, Lasik behaved with great dignity. The only thing that bothered him was that no matter how hard he tried, he did not succeed, holding Nussja by the arm. To climb on a chair at the registrar's office would not be dignified, while Nussja did not have the slightest intention of bending her knees. I shall not dwell too long on how Lasik became a triumphant lover at the age of thirty-two. It was almost dawn when he woke Nussja. With overflowing emotions, he began:

"You know, in Homel we performed the tragedy of Comrade Lunatscharsky. At that time, I did not understand anything. I was as blind as a bronze-colored rat. I was supposed to bite the duchess, but all I could do was groan like an imbecile. Only now do I see what a wonderful tragedy it was! If I were a real count of rank, I would bite you at once, in long-forgotten anger. However, I am not a count, and I would like to embrace this not-bronze you."

Nussja argued:

"Go to hell! I want to sleep."

In the morning she got up, dressed, yawning all the time, drank her tea and said to Lasik:

"All right, now let us go to the 'ZAGS.'"

"But we were there yesterday. . . ."

"Yesterday! Yesterday we got married, and today we are getting divorced!" Lasik sat on the little stool on which he had experienced love's first bliss. He began to cry silently.

"Nussja! My dream! Why do you wish to disintegrate? I do not understand. . . . Why must we get divorced, when we could live together until our death? The old, backward Jews have a rule whereby newly married people have to get a divorce if they have not slept together on their wedding night. Of course this is a violation of freedom, but it is understandable. Why do people get married anyway? But there is no law which says that young people who have slept together must get divorced the next morning!"

"I am sick and tired of you! You pipsqueak! So what if we slept together! We also got up together! And that is all! I am not going to spend my nights with such a bedbug. Now we have freedom. One can choose whomever one wants. And if you are not coming with me to the 'ZAGS,' I will go by myself—it is on my way. Wait, let us discuss the room problem. We cannot divide it into two halves. And I am not going back to Lilli. We had an argument because of you. And besides, she said she was also going to the 'ZAGS,' today, with Garin. They will live in her room. So, since you are the man, it will be easier for you to find another place. I am keeping this room. Take your stuff out of here, and all at once, so you don't go back and forth. I do not like that. And don't get any ideas to visit me. I was fourteen times at the 'ZAGS.' If all my former husbands would come to visit me—where would I find any place for them?"

Lasik wiped his nose, meekly.

"I know, I am being haunted by misfortune. My late aunt Chassja used to say I had bumped my head into a heavy pot. For me a dream is coming to an end and you are talking about a room problem. If I owned an Academy, I would give it all to you. Forgive me, if I woke you at night with my theatrical applause. I will disappear at once to roam the whole, wide world. This is the curse of destiny for the miserable Roitschwantz. On this earth there are square meters and 'ZAGSES,' and even something that is not made of bronze. But there is no such thing as happiness on earth. That is only an old-fashioned word from a great language."

When Boris Samoilowitsch caught sight of Lasik, he laughed.

"Married? Congratulations!"

"Give me the overcoat for Suchatschewsky and do not touch my sore spot. I am not only married, I am also divorced. And it was all your fault. Why did you have to give me that terrible room? I might have been better off on a bench on the boulevard! I could kill one and all like an insane rabbit. I am protesting against your organized world! All you want is money, tscherwontzes! All that woman wanted was floor space! I wanted something else, but I shall not speak of it now. However, I will ask you—is there anyone who wants nothing? Just love after death and a few drops of happy tears over someone else's happiness? . . ."

19

Lasik found shelter in Chaifetz's kitchen, together with the old servant, Dascha, who was known as Boris Samoilowitsch's aunt. Lasik became known as his nephew. At night, Lasik cried over his lost happiness. During the day, however, he went on delivering merchandise, collecting overdue bills, or repairing Boris Samoilowitsch's trousers. You might perhaps ask why Boris Samoilowitsch could not afford some new ones, made of the best English cloth, and not as if a pair of trousers was nothing more than a pin! Lasik knew quite well what a pair of trousers meant! . . . Boris Samoilowitsch spent his days in great concentration, as befits a man devoted to a great ideal. He liked, for instance, turkey or pheasants. But Citizen Titschenko shared the apartment, and he might have smelled the suspicious aroma. Therefore Boris Samoilowitsch had to content himself with boiled beef. And that is why he also walked around in old trousers, patched up by Lasik.

"Well, Roitschwantz, you were at least married one night, while I must live on wrinkled memories of two years ago. To bring one here is quite impossible. Titschenko would find out: 'Who, what, why such indulgent living?' And outside the house it is also dangerous. One can fall directly into the hands of the police. Marjantschik told me that at Nikolsk there are three naked Danish girls, impersonating an undersea cable, and a telegram costs no more than one tscherwonetz. That is almost like giving it for free! I got so excited, it affected even my heartbeat. But I am out of there already. And I am back home. If they catch me, it is the end."

One night, Boris Samoilowitsch took Lasik into his room, checked to see if Titschenko wasn't lurking in the corridor, and locked the door. Then, from under some dirty wash, he brought out a small portrait in a very valuable frame. Lasik recognized a hound, tearing at a peasant woman's skirt. Boris Samoilowitsch whispered piously:

"Can you see? Sapelow sold it to me for ten tscherwontzes. Sapelow was not only the owner of a museum of firearms, he also owned a stud-farm. He told me: 'The risk of having it confiscated, is great. But if you can hold on to it, until the very end, it will represent a fortune. Foreigners might pay you as much as one hundred thousand or more, for this is the work of a great master. This is either a Rjepin or a Raphael, or both together.' And so, I took a chance. I am not even thinking about the money. I am admiring it gently by night, and it gladdens my heart. Look at the expression of the skirt! That is real art! You, Roitschwantz, do not appreciate anything in this world, but I must tell you, my friend, there is marvelous beauty in it."

The days passed by, and one always had to expect some dangers. Lasik went from one tailor to another. Sometimes, seeing the scissors and the steam-iron, he became remorseful: "Why did I exchange this for such incomprehensible wandering? . . . But what was I supposed to do? It was not my fault that I have lost my sign-board and my happiness. It is a little late to complain! Now I am drifting like a miserable leaf, chased by a hundred-year old storm."

Boris Samoilowitsch exchanged the tscherwontzes for English pounds, and from time to time he would count his money. And Lasik had to sit on the latrine, rustling desperately with the paper, to divert Titschenko's attention.

After having counted the money, Boris Samoilowitsch would sigh sadly. Then he would tiptoe to the kitchen and say to the servant:

"Aunt Dascha, how about a simple, proletarian cup of tea for me?"

"No girls, not a decent eating place in the 'City of Moscow,' unadvisable to visit an operetta," he complained to Lasik. "I am really suffering! A martyr! A saint! After my death, I will surely not rot. No, that is when I will really start to smell heavenly! But how should I amuse myself in the meantime?"

"You could, for instance, pretend to have died already and you can start emanating sweet fragrances right now, if this is any comfort to you." But Boris Samoilowitsch could not be tranquilized that easily. He whispered:

"Don't you understand, you fool, that their whole communism is nothing but a lot of nonsense?"

Lasik replied, evasively:

"In Homel, we say: one herring can do even for ten people; however, a big chicken can be gobbled up by two. This is very true. You like chicken, so do I, so does everybody. A herring in your mouth—that is a different story.

"Taken altogether, it is not your personal anger when you rustle with those little papers, but strictly arithmetic. I understand this, without any basic, political instruction; we both represent two embittered camps. Everyone will admit that you are the soft-cushioned train compartment, while I am the very hard one. Right now, it is true, we are being pulled by the same crazy engine. But no one knows what can happen tomorrow."

Coming home one evening, Lasik noticed Boris Samoilowitsch wrapped in a cape. He looked as though he were limping:

"Where did you fall, Boris Samoilowitsch? On the Boulevard of Enthusiasts? It is really slippery there . . ."

"Shut up! I am not Boris Samoilowitsch any longer. Now I am Oskar Zacharjewitsch and I've limped since early childhood. First, hold this package. But be careful—my entire future depends on it. In the second place, they have arrested Titschenko, and it turned out that he was not even a party member, but had been working together with Marjantschik. This means that it all goes by way of Minsk, and they are going to get me today. If I could be sure they will send me again only to Northern Narym, I might reconsider it. But this smells like a real trial. Roitschwantz, I have decided to escape to Lodz. I have a nephew there. Not one like you—I mean, a real one. If it is God's will, I could manage to get this little package over the border. And now the question arises, what will you do?"

"Me? Nothing. I am used to it. The only thing I can do under the circumstances is to get a shave."

"You are a fool, Roitschwantz! If I escape, they will certainly arrest you. Then you can try for a long time to prove to them that you are not my nephew. And, furthermore, who did they see going around with the merchandise? You. Do you want to get ten years in prison? Do you? You idiot! And what if they shoot you?"

"Why should I look ahead into my bloody future? In any case, I want to go and change my clothes."

"Wait a minute! . . . I tell you what. I am going to take you with me. You will carry this small package across the border. The rest will be easy. Feigelson from Minsk will smuggle us across. Do you have any doubts? You are an idiot, a fool! I will take care of you in Lodz."

"I do not understand why I should run. Naturally, you want to save your Raphael and the white banknotes. But what have I got to save? If only myself, it really does not pay to go all the way to Lodz. I can just as well find a grave on the cemetery at Dorogomilowo. And if not for myself, then for whom, may I ask? My former wife, or Titschenko, or is it perhaps to save your precious little package? Very well, you have a nephew there. But I don't. And I have as much confidence in you as in the snow of two years ago. I used to have an aunt in Gluchow, but she is dead. So, why should I run away, or even step up my pace? But nevertheless I will agree, and flee to Lodz with you. Anyway, I am not an upright citizen anymore, but one who runs to and fro, full of uncertainty. I cannot even stand still any longer. Let us run, Oskar or Boris, or even Rjepin with the palette, but let us run! We are nothing but leaves, and all around us rages the storm. But wait a moment, please—I have to shed a few bitter tears. I must say goodbye to my lost youth. I say goodbye to Homel and to my thimble. Goodbye to Ivan The Great and to the stool belonging to my former wife. Here I stand, struck, rooted to the spot, and I cry, 'What can I do against such an earthquake—but run, run, run . . .' "

20

"**Let** us be honest, Roitschwantz. You are a great philosopher, not afraid for your life. You were ready to lie down and sink into a grave in the cemetery of Dorogomilowo. You have no relatives in the whole world. I, however, do have a nephew in Lodz. I do not feel like dying yet. I even get upset when I see a funeral procession in the street. Therefore, you should take the package. If they catch you, well then, at least you will have died in an interesting way. However, if you get this little package across the border, I will wrap you in gold, just as you are. And I am sure you will get it across. You are such a little fellow no one will notice you. Besides, you are my employe, and it is one of your duties to carry my packages for me."

"I am not saying, no, but I might as well tune in my own funeral march, for I would also much rather live, at least for another year; and I, too, am feeling funny in my stomach, as though I were attending my own funeral."

The fugitives came safely across the border. When Boris Samoilowitsch caught sight of the cap of the Polish gendarme, he said to Lasik:

"Well, now you can give me the package."

Lasik unbuttoned his trousers and took out the package. He handed it over and asked:

"And when will you start wrapping me in gold?"

But Boris Samoilowitsch did not answer him. He smiled confidently at the gendarme, pressing a white banknote into his hand:

"Here, Pan, is the passport."

The gendarme tried to bargain: it was not enough. It might suffice for one person, but not for two. Thereupon Boris Samoilowitsch shrugged his shoulders: "He does not belong to me. I do not know him at all. He must surely be a Bolshevik. You can see on his mug what a brute he is."

Lasik was arrested. He did not argue or even defend himself. He only whispered softly to Boris Samoilowitsch:

"I told you already in Moscow that I trust you as much as the snow of two years ago. You may give my regards to your dear nephew, and then you may wrap yourself in gold. You will become such a handsome gentleman that all the Polish beauties will contrive one single wireless telegraph. For you, Roitschwantz, however, will sit in various foreign prisons and think that in this world there is not even justice among thieves."

Before beginning the investigation of the prisoner, the captain decided on a little tonic: he ate a piece of Polish sausage and emptied a bottle of vodka. Though his legs became heavy, his head was light, and he greeted Lasik with childish contentment, smacking his tongue:

"Good day, you tramp! What are you, a Red spy?"

"Me? No. I am most likely the poor devil Roitschwantz."

"Do not pretend. What secret plans were you about to steal, for instance? From Warsaw or from Wilno? Or did you even intend to finish off our little grandfather Pilsudsky?"

"He is not my grandfather, and I have no intention to finish off anyone. I did not even think of finishing off Boris Samoilowitsch, though he had promised to wrap me in gold, only to take off as soon as he could. Neither do I need any plans. I am no artist, and I do not own Rjepin's paint brush. It is true I spent one night on a grandiose plan with my former wife, but that matter came to an end with an ordinary housing question."

"Is this a man? No, this is the cholera in person! Here you are not in your rotten Soviet Union, to produce such nonsense! Answer me, why did you cross the Polish border?"

Lasik became thoughtful. To answer this sensible question, was indeed not easy.

"Most likely," he replied, "because the wind was blowing in my back. If you have one or two hours at your disposal, I could, of course, tell you the whole story. It all started with the deaf-and-dumb Pukke. I was in love with Fenitchka Hershanowitsch at the time, and you surely know that love is not just any ordinary vegetable . . ."

"You scoundrel! How dare you talk like that to a Polish officer? Here we are not in your Asia any more. Here, we are almost in Paris. We have the League of Nations. We have Wilno—a magnificent university. We have produced Copernicus. We have precious cocottes in our cafés. I will knock your teeth out. Answer me: who are you?"

"I am a former tailor."

"Aha! And where do you come from?"

"I told you before, from the famous city of Homel."

The officer became tired and dozed off. The steps of his orderly woke him. He had hardly come to, when he was shouting:

"Another bottle! . . . From where are you, you son of a bitch! From Homel? Well, what do you know! That means you are Polish. The Homel countryside falls under our claim. Stand upright before an officer, you old screw! Though you are a dirty Jew, you are still a Pole of Hebrew faith, for we shall take away the Homel country from you at the next opportunity. All you inhabitants of Homel, you are really Poles."

The captain was sipping his vodka from a tea-glass. Lasik looked thoughtfully and tenderly at him:

"If you drink so much, you will experience what I went through at the Venetia, only here you do not even have a washbasin. You say I am Polish. It can be. I have not yet thought about it. But I was a learned candidate of the Academy. Why should I not be able to become a Pole? Now, with Pfeifer you might have a much harder time, for he is stubborn like a mule, and besides, he is at the moment in the Polish Homel, while you are still here. He could, for instance, maintain that he is not a Pole, but a convinced member of a party cell. However, I am here, and I am not arguing. Let us proceed, and suppose I am a full-blooded Pole . . ."

The captain did not listen to him any more. He groaned:

"Stand up, you bum!" (Even though Lasik had been standing upright all the time.)

"Stand up and sing our gallant hymn: 'Poland is not lost yet!' "

Lasik wanted to say something.

"Shut up, you carcass! You should rejoice, beat the drums, blow the trumpet, walk on your head; and here you whine and whimper. I shall make stewed fruit out of you! I will throw you out through the window! You should get to know the Great Poland! This is not some Red dung-heap!"

"I have gotten to know it already. I think it is time for me to enter a great Polish jail; and it would not hurt you to find a comfortable washbasin, otherwise you will dirty up my valuable confession, which you have written down on this precious sheet of paper. I can see for myself already that I am not back home in Homel, but in the marvelous country of Poland. It is true, there they kept asking me for the cubic meter of my charitable father, while here it appears you want to make a dessert out of me. As far as I am concerned, you can go on making your rich desserts and rid me of a hundred Pfeifers, but let us finish now this harmonious monologue."

At this point, the cavalry captain stood up with some difficulty, gave him another shove, and began his search for the latrine. Obviously, Lasik's eloquence had overwhelmed him. Lasik was taken to the prison cell. After several days, he was brought to Grodno. There, he had to undergo a new investigation. The officer who questioned him, was very polite, he even addressed him as "Pan Orthodox" (Mister Orthodox). Lasik was touched, and he exclaimed:

"Would it not be possible always to be questioned in the morning, when the gentlemen officers have their coffee with milk instead of vodka."

The Captain did not give him an answer. He merely covered his mouth with his hand. Well, yes—so what if he occasionally enjoyed a small glass of slivovitz on an empty stomach.

"So, you yourself have confessed to having crossed the border illegally for the purpose of criminal propaganda among the so-called White Russian peasantry."

"I am sure he did not find a washbasin, that first captain. He dirtied up the paper, and therefore you are reading words that are not there at all. All I have confessed to is that my name is Roitschwantz and that I am a pure Pole. There was no talk whatsoever about any propaganda among peasants or any such thing. We discussed various matters, like, for instance, that one could come and do away with dear grandfather Pilsudsky, or steal the entire city of Wilno with all its plans. However, the first mister captain had said nothing at all about the peasants."

"In other words, you are denying your own statements? Now you claim to be Polish?"

"To be quite truthful, I am not the one who said it. You and your colleague said it. It was he who told me that Homel is in Poland, and that I was nothing but a lousy Moses of Polish denomination."

"Yes, indeed. Homel is a Polish city. We were there, and legally it belongs to us."

Lasik cheered up.

"Pan Captain, you have been in Homel? It is a first-rate town, is it not? The Paskewitsch Park alone is lovelier than anything Raphael had ever put on canvas. And what is wrong with the theater? And the river Sosch, is it not a real sea? I have never seen such trees as grow in Homel, nor have I encountered such women! For, if I compare Fenitschka Hershanowitch with Nussja, temporary Roitschwantz, now from a historical distance, they are beyond comparison. But why am I telling you all this when you yourself have been in Homel? It might be interesting to know, where did you live? If you stayed at the first State Hotel, the location is quite exceptional, because one can watch the people passing by from the balcony, but on the other hand, it is full of bedbugs."

"You did not quite understand. Personally, I have never been in Homel. But we, we Poles were there, consequently it morally belongs to us."

"You are so friendly, Pan Captain, I would give you a bouquet of flowers if I had one. You are not shouting at me, not calling me an old piece of furniture, and you are keeping your hands in your pockets, where they belong. Now listen to me. I have raised defunct rabbits in Tula. That is a beautiful city with an extensive elimination of personnel. Well, in Tula there was also a Pole, I give you my word of honor. He was employed by the city administration, in charge of supervising smelly barrels. He used to visit our messenger Dunja, saying such nice things as, 'What a heavenly perfume you have, dear Comrade! . . .' So you see, my dear Pan Captain, there is another city for you! I am not joking. In five minutes you have become unbelievably rich. You have the Homel country, and now you also have the Tula region. And if you write a postal card to Rurik Abramowitsch, I am sure he will present you with the entire Narym region. Then you will become a whole hemisphere. I am asking you just for one favor: please let me go! I might find a way to make a suit for some Polish Moses, from his own material. After all, I am a little weary of sitting on a prison bed. On my backside, I am not Roitschwantz any more, but rather a sieve."

"Unfortunately, I cannot let you go. You are a Russian spy and you may be blamed for any incident, as for instance the conspiracy in Lwow, the bombing in Wilno, the proclamation in Grodno, the counterfeit-stamps in Lodz, the attempt on the Marshal's life in Krakow, the munitions-camp in Lublin . . ."

"I implore you to stop! I know you have many cities indeed. At this rate, you will soon be in Tula. But I do not wish that any such thing be attached to me. I have already attached myself to you, and I am a pure-blooded Pole. If you wish, I will even create a brand new Copernicus. It is time for me, at last, to see those cocottes of the cafés!"

Lasik stayed four months in prison. He was transferred from Grodno to Wilno, from Wilno to Lomscha, from Lomscha to Lwow. Not without pride, did he say to his fellow-prisoners:

"You are all dirt! But I am a Pan Learned Secretary. I have discovered Poland, like a new Nansen. My insides do not consist of intestines any more, but of one general plan with a detailed menu of all alcoholic drinks. But I do not lose hope. I already noticed that you have even less space than we. Of course, it is not so easy since you have the League of Nations and each bunk-bed has to be occupied by ten Poles of the purest kind.

True, I am only a Moses, and of not too stately growth, but I can still dispose of my own square meters, while the Pan captains have nothing better to do than contrive plots and conspiracies. Consequently, the day will come when they will set me free, and then I shall beat the drums valiantly."

21

At last, Lasik arrived in Warsaw. The twelfth cavalry captain said to him in a friendly voice: "Soon you will be expelled from Poland."

Lasik sighed and was relieved.

"Thank God! Not in vain have you produced a Copernicus! But what do you intend to penalize with your expulsion: the aspersion against Pan Pilsudsky, or merely the riot of several hundred Galicians from Wilno? By the way, I am only asking out of pure curiosity. Merci, Pan Captain, merci! After all, I have nothing to do than lie on the prison bed and think about the amazing freedom that exists here! In my travels, I have been through ten prisons, and I may safely say, this is not a country, it is a children's paradise. I understand that you call Pan Pilsudsky your little grandpa. This foolish family designation is of no significance. I, too, have an uncle, Boris Samoilowitsch, but he could never stand up to Pan Pilsudsky! One breathes freedom here, indeed! All one has to do is to say something which is misunderstood by some fool, and at once the error is being corrected at the expense of the state. And what abundant border regions you have! In other places one finds only dust and dirt near the borders. That crook Archip told me that near our borders lived a nation, called the Mordweens, and they even shout in their mordweenish tongue. Here, however, and in Homel, there are only Poles. And naturally, they all sing, so as not to rot. I know that it was worth it, as the seventh Pan Captain had told me, to die for two hundred years in order to obtain such freedom!"

The cavalry captain made a friendly face.

"It is nice to hear that you have learned to appreciate our freedom. Poland understands, as it did even at the time of our great Mickiewicz, how to conquer the most stubborn hearts. Now then, in one month we shall expel you. You shall be free to run around in one of those un-free states. There you shall remember the Polish 'defensive.' You will be touched, and you will say: 'The state of Poland is not only a protector of freedom, it is also a pillar of justice.' "

After this impressive speech, the captain closed his eyes wearily, yielding to a pleasant slumber. Lasik, however, was in no hurry to return to his prison cell, and so he decided to continue the conversation:

"I would like to tell you quickly a story that has to do with small cattle. Though I do not smell your noble breath, Pan Captain, I can imagine that you are not a friend of alcohol, be it new or old vodka, or of any slivovitz. I am sure your thoughts

man or no. There is nothing more beautiful on earth than such a day! . . . I am very pleased to meet you. To be truthful, you are not my first love, you are my thirteenth, therefore it is special, a lucky number, the devil's dozen."

"You Moscovite criminal! You shall cry, and not make jokes. I have just signed the order for your expulsion, and tomorrow you will leave our great Poland."

At this point something unbelievable happened to Lasik. He lost his senses for sheer happiness. He skipped from corner to corner, humming like a bee, clapping his hands on the most unmentionable of places. Then he remembered the dancing course he had taken from that parasite in Kiev, and he began to dance a real foxtrot before the very eyes of the amazed captain.

"Have you gone crazy?"

But Lasik could not utter a word. He went on blowing his imaginary trumpet. The captain in his confusion, ordered a doctor.

"The prisoner is suffering from emotional shock. He has horrible convulsions. Is it perhaps St. Vitus Dance, or a fit of apoplexy? How depressing to see a human being suffer, even if he is a Bolshevist scoundrel!"

The good captain produced a big silken kerchief and proceeded to wipe his nose in a truly tragic manner. The doctor examined Lasik.

"Show me your tongue. Say: thirty-three. Breathe. Don't breathe. I do not think it is anything serious, Pan Captain. I shall prescribe castor oil and a water-cure for six months."

As soon as Lasik heard those words, he became as quiet as can be.

"If you wish, I can drink a gallon of castor oil, Pan doctor, but kindly permit me to go abroad for my cure. I give you my word of honor, I shall find water in other countries too, it is not such a rarity."

The captain could not take it any longer. He started to cry.

"Is it not terrible? He has an opportunity to spend another six months in a Polish prison, and now he must leave tomorrow. How much sorrow there is on earth! I look at him and my heart goes to pieces. Give him at least the castor oil, Pan doctor, or else he might die of a heart attack on his trip. Why don't you cry, you tramp? Relieve yourself, crying. Just think, tomorrow the sun will rise, lovely ladies will walk in the streets, the colors of the rainbow will play on the bottles of our world-famous 'Perluwka,' our beautiful language will resound and rustle even behind prison doors and you will leave for some unknown destination . . ."

Lasik became restless.

"What are you calling 'unknown destination'? The North Pole or Rumania?"

"You will be expelled across the nearest border. Drink your castor oil! Pray to God! Cry! Tomorrow morning . . ."

"Morning . . ."

Lasik heaved another improper sigh.

"Are you getting your convulsions again?"

"No, no, Pan Captain. As your oldest ancestor said, I am only blowing the trumpet. If I had any money, I would at once celebrate with a bottle of the famous 'Perluwka.' "

"Foolish creature! What have you got to celebrate? If I had a heart of stone, I would be glad: another Asiatic barbarian forced to leave our holy ground! Getting rid of another Bolshevist, a Moscovite, a Tartar, a criminal, a henchman, a barbarian! Do not forget that you were wiping your nose with two fingers when we had the great Sienkiewicz already. Yes, I could be happy indeed! But you should beat your chest from sorrow and pain. Or else you are insane, and in such case you will have to undergo a medical examination."

"No, not that. I shall gladly drink the castor oil. I am also willing to beat my chest. I could even explain to you why I am blowing, but I am afraid in case you do exercises in the morning. No, you don't? You spend the mornings writing reports? Then everything is perfect, and I can tell you what this is all about. As soon as I have to pack my belongings, my tongue has a way of loosening up. Let us begin with Pharaoh. He was a high official, who sat on the very top, while somewhere down below, the Jews were building the pyramids. He lashed the whip and they had to build. Let us say, they were all Moses's of *Pharaohnic* faith, even though Moses did not yet exist at the time. However, when Moses made his appearance, they decided among themselves, how much can one go on building? Were ten pyramids not enough? And so they left Egypt by foot. Here the argument began. Some said the Jews were happy to have fled from Egypt, though they were forced to eat certain trifles from heaven; others, however, were sure that the Pharaoh was happy, because, as you yourself know, everyone had trouble with the Jews. They are being chased or hung or fed in prison with big words. And so it happened at the time that there was a wise man, who changed it all to the good. This is what he said: If a fat, heavy man rides on a little, weak donkey, he is not comfortable and neither is the donkey. And when they finally reach their destination, they are both happy. However, now comes the question: Whose joy is bigger, the rider's or the donkey's? . . . Therefore we may both be happy. Put your handkerchief and your tears away, and stop breathing like Sienkiewicz. You had better dance the foxtrot. Is it perhaps not a pleasure to get rid of such a Roitschwantz? Now, as far as I am concerned, I still think that the donkey was happier . . ."

At this point the conversation between Lasik and the officer from Poznan came to an end. I do not wish to describe what followed. Suffice it to say that the thirteenth cavalry captain had deceived Lasik. He spent his mornings not merely writing his reports.

23

At first Lasik was delighted: it seemed to him as though everyone around him spoke Yiddish, even though in a slightly imperfect way. In his enthusiasm, he even whispered to the stationmaster in Yiddish: "How is a Jew?" But the man growled ominously, and Lasik disappeared quickly. He walked around town, looking attentively at the people's faces.

"Surely there must be some Moses of German descent around here."

And sure enough, very soon an unmistakable Jewish face appeared. Full of joy, he ran towards him.

"At last I found you! Good day, good day, how are you and may God send you twelve sons, so you will be sure to have a nice *Kaddish* over your grave! You must help me. You are a Jew and I am a Jew, and let us hope that in another year we shall meet again in Jerusalem. All I need is a few lousy marks to get to Berlin and to have a bite of food. In Poland I was starving. Imagine! I am sure you had parents once, and they are probably dead now. I shall pray for them for the rest of my life. But if you find that my pious tears do not suffice, I can also make you a coat of grey cloth. I can even . . ."

Mister Rosenblum interrupted Lasik, harshly:

"I understand your language only because I do not live far from the border. However, I am not a Hebrew, but a pure-blooded German. Naturally I adhere to the Jewish faith, but this is a personal matter. As to the prayers for the dead, I have already engaged someone, and I am not so rich as to be able to afford two people to pray for my deceased parents. Also I am not in the habit of wearing just any coat. I order all my clothes from the tailor Spiegel. He works for all the distinguished financiers, not to mention the great Herr von Krinkenbauer. However, if you will shorten my winter coat, make alterations on one of my suits, and press my entire wardrobe, as well as repair all my children's clothes, I shall give you five mark, even though you are an Eastern Jew, and even though you might infect us with cholera, typhus and Bolshevism. Yes, I will give you five mark, only because you are also of the Jewish faith."

"You see, I knew we would agree! And the way I put my patches on, people notice them a hundred kilometers away. However, as to your parents, it seems that for a man of your standing, you should have at least two men praying for them. I bet you your parents were two people, and not just one. I, for instance, have chosen your mother already. And, in general, we will understand each other. The main thing is that in private you are Jewish. Everything else is unimportant, just trifles, no more than a child's dress. . . ."

Clothes have to be repaired: that takes time. Lasik spent ten days in town; making alterations, shortening, patching, mending. Without much ado, he knocked at another door: "Oh, so you are also of our faith? . . . What have you got to have shortened?" In the end, all trousers were shortened or repaired.

Lasik succeeded in getting as far as Koenigsberg. There he saw Kant's monument, and he became sad.

"Dear God of Homel! What shall I do with him? I cannot shorten him! If I had only found him when I needed him at the club *Good Taste*! What joy for Comrade Serebrjakow if I had been able to do away with such a stony sturgeon. But what good is all that talk? I must find a piece of bread, or else I will die on the spot."

He stopped in front of a delicatessen window and whispered longingly:

"What a beautiful picture! Such a painting!"

But the store owner chased him away:

"Do not block the traffic! This is the taxi-stand for the ladies who come shopping here."

He wanted to cross the street but a policeman called out harshly to him:

"You might have been run over by an automobile. True, today there are no cars, but last night two cars passed by. You have no right to play with your life."

He sat down on a bench in the park, but in a matter of minutes a guard approached him:

"This is only for attendants and for blind or half-blind soldiers."

Lasik sighed dejectedly:

"I think I am losing my mind."

"Wednesdays and Fridays from nine-forty-five until ten-thirty—medical examinations free of charge at the Municipal Hospital."

He espied a gentleman with a Jewish face in the crowd:

"Wait a minute, you there, with your face! I am Jewish too, and I have not eaten yet!"

The gentleman with the face pushed Lasik aside:

"The synagogue is on Victoria Street number 7, the kosher butcher shop is on Schiller Street number 11. Begging is forbidden by a regulation of the police authorities since June 16, 1889."

Lasik exclaimed: "I am ready to die at once! . . ."

No sooner had he uttered these words when a character came out of the crowd and handed him a business card, saying:

"Sale of burial grounds of all faiths at favorable installment rates."

In conclusion, Lasik fainted and fell to the ground. A tall man, with melancholy opal-blue eyes and a short moustache was bending over him:

"Hey you! . . . What is the matter? . . . You are blocking traffic. Are you an acrobat or are you having an epileptic fit?"

When he did not get an answer, he nudged Lasik with his foot.

He could hear a barely audible squeak:

"What have acrobats to do with this? I merely have a terrific appetite after all these speeches. If I had the money for these favorable installment rates, I would lie right down into a grave."

The tall man scrutinized Lasik attentively.

"It is forbidden to lie on the sidewalk. Here, take these ten pfennig. Go over there to the bakery across the street and buy yourself some bread. You can eat it afterwards in some quiet sidestreet. I shall wait for you at the streetcar stop. It is forbidden to stand here,–it blocks the traffic. Quick now! . . ."

The last remark was quite unnecessary. Despite his weakened condition, Lasik galloped off to the bakery.

"Well," his friend asked, "where is the bread? In your pocket, perhaps?"

"Oh no! In my pocket is nothing but a big hole. The bread

however, is nearby—in my stomach.."

"What nerve! The ten pfennig belong to me. Now you must do as I tell you. I have your interests at heart. I can insure your future. What can you do?"

"Anything you wish. I know, for instance, how to patch old clothes, most terrifically. When I put patches on Soloweitchik's trousers in Homel, everybody recognized him merely by my patchwork. And when he was walking in the marketplace, you could hear them shout all the way from the railroad station: 'There goes Roitschwantz's patchwork!' "

"What nonsense! Good patchwork should not be noticeable. We have six such shops in Koenigsberg. Can't you do anything else?"

"What do you mean, can't I? I just told you I can do everything, including the propagation of dead rabbits."

"Double nonsense! Nobody eats rabbits around here. Only pork and veal. Talk of venison perhaps, or roast hares and fawns."

The bread had been diminutive. Lasik began his lamentations:

"For heaven's sake, stand still, if you don't want to block the traffic! If you are starting to raise hares right here and now, I can do that, too. But please, before anything, just give me a little tail or a wing of a goat."

"I am no rabbit-breeder! I am the owner of the finest drugstore in the city of Koenigsberg, as well as of all East Prussia. Supplier of His Former Highness. Pull in your stomach when I mention the name! I supply the finest families. You may call me simply, Doctor Dreckendorf. You will not achieve a great deal with breeding experiments. Around here, we are breeding only Germans. The future soldiers of His Former Highness. With democrats and other such traitors, two for each married couple. With nationally-minded, six to eight. In the event of twelve, they get a medal. Unfortunately, I must practice restraint. As a patriot, I would like it very much, but as a drugstore-owner I am bound by spiritual obligations. I have to present a living example for the excellence of my merchandise. Well then, so you cannot do anything else? Who are you, anyway?"

"I am—a Learned Secretary."

"Learned? Chemistry? Gases? Anilin? Engineer? Road-building? Bridge-building? Architecture? Iron concrete? Toilets?"

"No, I am a scientist in a different way. You see, I am a small expert in regard to a great language."

"A linguist? Sanskrit, of course? Wrong for the third time. Do you know the Malayan language? Aztec? Zulu? Then you must go to Hamburg. They are negotiating trade agreements there. Give us another five years and we shall have colonies once again."

"My dear Doctor Dreckenkopf, don't think for a minute that they gave me a piece of, say, crisp pork roast in that bakery. It was merely a small roll, not bigger than your father's watch. I did not even have time to inhale its fragrance. And after such a hungry introduction, you are speaking of 'Aztecs.' That is torture of the worst kind. And why should I understand an unfamiliar Malayan language when I myself am from Homel? Languages? Of course, I know a great many. I know, for instance the language of the Jews in Homel, in Gluchow, and even in Moscow. To be sure, this is no Sanskrit, but nevertheless they are three important dialects in one confederation. Furthermore I understand the Polish language. 'Pan Dreckenkopf, you'r verry stupid ass.' That is not just an ordinary language, it is pure music! Finally, I also understand the German language; and if I do not speak it as well as you do, or Mister Hindenburg himself, it is only because, even as a child, I have always been a character. Just listen, doesn't this sound extraordinary: "Herr Doctor, Ihr sond a ausserordentlicher 'Chochem' (Herr Doctor, you are a wise guy!). I do not think Hindenburg could say it any better."

Herr Dreckendorf was silent. His spiritual struggle was evident on his face—his opal-colored eyes shone with a great illumination, while his moustache wriggled convulsively. After a long pause, he began to reflect out loud:

"Split personality. Interesting for its pure intellect. Not Cold-cream, but psychoanalysis. While I make business, I also serve my country. His Highness would understand. After all, His Highness bought suppositories and rhubarb. Pull in your stomach, by the way! You are—a Jew. Consequently one should chase you away—notify the police—insist on your expulsion. You have deserted the black-white-red for the black-red-yellow! That is unheard of! That is sabotage! That is an attempt on our race! Certainly you must be related to Wirth, Wilson, Heine. A cousin, maybe? Give me back the ten pfennigs. I better give you a laxative in my drugstore. Takes only a few minutes. Stop! Where are you running? I am not giving you anything yet. I am only thinking out loud. Like Kant—or His Highness. Take off . . . ! That was only the first half. The second half however: I have a plan. You are a lucky find. In all of Koenigsberg there is no such misfit. I am sure you don't weigh more than forty kilos. No, not more. You could be taken for an eight-year-old child. Matured before his time. You are a unique character. I hesitate. My soul is torn in two different directions."

Lasik was shaking fearfully: what a horrible man this doctor was! Even if he offered a hare's tail, what good would that do when just a moment ago he was planning to get back that miserable piece of bread! How should I know Wirth? So what if his heart is torn, as long as he does not tear me to pieces! . . .

"Well then, it is settled. I shall forgive you your damned origin. I will accept you. Twenty marks a week. The money will be deposited in your name at the bank every week. You get a contract for one month. After that, the bank will pay you the whole amount. I shall provide you with food. I am calling your attention to the fact that you will have to be on a strict diet. A piece of zwieback and two glasses of milk during the day. We must prevent a gain in weight at all cost. You must also preserve the dullness in your eyes. Occasionally you will have to faint. For this you will get eighty marks after one month. Then you may eat even a hundred pork cutlets as far as I am concerned—with cabbage or potatoes, or even with eggs, with zwieback. . . . All right? Do you agree?"

"No!—yes!" cried Lasik. "But this with the zwieback, will not be until another month! . . ."

"If you sign the contract, I will agree to digress from your diet, for today. You will get a piece of sausage and apple sauce."

"Fine. I am ready to sign. Why should my soul go to pieces in advance. I would have gone into debt anyway. Of course, with only one piece of zwieback, it will not be so easy, but I am dying to eat the sausage and the apple sauce, come what may. Just tell me, Doctor Dreckenkopf, of what disease do you intend to cure me, and what is your usual procedure?"

"Cure you? I have no intention of curing you. I am a doctor of philosophy. I am a businessman. Germany is the first and foremost country of Europe. However, it is still behind America. We must improve. Develop our will power and mind. The basis of every business is advertisement. This, unfortunately, is not being used in drugstores yet. Kant wrote about absolute reason and judgment. His Highness has sent a letter to all the disabled war veterans saying; an icebag, a syringe, even a modest mustard plaster are no less than a new silver tablet or a fountain pen. The meaning of these things is in themselves. One can extol them to the very absolute limit. The only thing necessary for that is advertising. Last spring I advertised enemas. I put a pile of stones into the display-window: our nourishment. A precise chart: so much meat, so much bread, etc. etc. We swallow stones. People get sluggish, the guts get sluggish, the bowels get sluggish. Long live the enema! I had electric bulbs lighting the entire procedure, from the first mouthful down to the final elimination. The water was rippling through glass tubes. Anything that blocks the motion must be eliminated. A microphone was blasting: *I take an enema, you take an enema, His Highness takes an enema!* Do you understand? And now I would like to advertise cod liver oil. You are a child that was fed only surrogates. Willi, however, has been given the Icelandic cod liver oil that I produce. Furthermore, because of the great expense, I am combining with this the advertising of several other products. Quite unobtrusively, you understand, so as not to make the respectable mothers suspicious. Airtight wrapping—I am the first one in Eastern Prussia. Even surpassing America! We, Germans, do not stop halfway. If it is to be common sense, then it will be common sense. If Bagdad—it will be Bagdad. If America—America it shall be. The main thing is to enlighten the spirit. The water runs through the tubes. In airtight wrapping nothing can spoil. The stars in the sky gladden our hearts. Cod liver oil of the finest cod . . ."

Lasik did not hear what the Herr Doctor was saying. What good would it do to listen to him, when this was absolute Sanskrit? However, it was quite another matter what he understood of a piece of sausage and apple sauce. Did he mean the tail-end, or perhaps a quarter of a pound? . . .

The German took Lasik into the dining room. A fair-haired blonde of about forty stared at them with the dull look of a dead cod. Beside her sat an extremely fat boy in short pants and a sailor's blouse. Herr Dreckendorf addressed his wife:

"This is my new patient. Strict diet. One zwieback, a quarter liter of milk. Now and then he has to faint. Today I am permitting a deviation. Give him a piece of sausage and some apple sauce. Two slices of zwieback. No more than six hours sleep. Do you understand? Now get me the stamped paper. We shall sign the contract."

Lasik's hand was shaking. He could hardly sign "Roitschwantz." He drew a little cross next to his name, explaining to the doctor who did not understand:

"Just a symbol, even though I am of Jewish faith; nevertheless I will soon have to start paying off."

Before eating the tiny piece of sausage, Lasik sniffed at it. Mrs. Dreckendorf was offended:

"We have only fresh merchandise."

Herr Dreckendorf added:

"The freshest in all of Eastern Prussia."

But Lasik explained, full of guilt:

"I am sniffing at it only for the sake of remembering. I do not want to forget the heartwarming aroma when going on the zwieback diet."

The real test, however, began when the servant brought in the dinner for the fat boy. The host explained to Lasik:

"This is Willi. A rare specimen. Twenty-seven years old. The face of a child. Weighs ninety-two kilogram. Height: one meter, eighty-one. Do you observe the radiant complexion? Cod liver oil from Iceland. Four mark ninety-five the liter."

Willi ate one enormous loaf of bread, corned beef with potatoes, mannah dumplings with bacon, pork cutlets with beans, and rice pudding for dessert. He emptied one jug of beer after another, breathing heavily. Groaning, he tried to leave one dumpling on his plate, covering it with the spoon, but Herr Dreckendorf said strictly: "Willi!"

"I cannot eat any more. I am bursting. It will not do you any good if I break the window."

"Willi! . . ."

Lasik tried to intervene:

"Herr Doctor, may I eat the dumpling? You can be sure, I won't burst."

The host did not deign to give him an answer. He merely looked at him and Lasik lowered his eyes at once.

The next morning people were crowding in front of Herr Dreckendorf's drugstore. Two boys were sitting in the display-window. One was rosy and fat, smiling happily. On his chest he bore a sign which said, *I am being fed with genuine cod liver oil extracted from cod of Iceland. For sale only here; 4.95 the liter.* The second boy sighed miserably. The crowd stared in amazement:

"One would think he's forty years old."

"Where did they find such a misfit?"

"Perhaps he's a dwarf? . . ."

"How could that be! Just look at the way he's drooling from the mouth. And furthermore, it says: *I am eleven years old.* This is simply an abnormal child."

Besides the information about the age, it also said: *I was fed with imitation cod liver oil. I suffer from rickets, anemia, have white blood corpuscles, paralysis, hysteria and seventeen other diseases. Protect your children from my tragic fate! And, if you never want to have children like me, buy only "NEVER," absolutely guaranteed, one-ninety per package.*

Herr Dreckendorf watched the behavior of the two boys through a crack. Every now and then, he would whisper to them: "Willi, smile! Send the lady a kiss! Raise your hands! Sing of joy!" "Hey, you Jew! Groan! Beat your chest! Pull your hair! Try to faint!"

The boys talked softly to each other. It turned out that the rosy-cheeked Willi was not as happy as he looked!

"That butcher has been torturing me for three weeks now. I just cannot eat so much any more. I am so stuffed—God knows, I am ready to burst. He even forbids me to walk. What's more, I have to live like a monk. He is doing fine, everybody knows he is crazy. He can sleep with night-slippers—he does not know the difference. But I, I itch all over. And now he wants me to smile at a lady! If this keeps up I am going to break the window and jump at her . . . !"

Lasik could not understand his companion at all:

"Why do you want to jump when you are going to get another ten dumplings in an hour? And what will I get? Just a slice of zwieback. Maybe these fools think I had been drinking some stupid surrogates in Homel? Let me just tell you what I ate at Drawkin's wedding. Two years ago, I made a coat for Drawkin, and he was so overwhelmed that he said without thinking: 'Roitschwantz, you come to my wedding!' And I went. And I ate. I had, for instance, chopped liver. That would be one thing. And I had stuffed derman with kasha. That would be number two. And I had greaven and dumpling with sauce. That could be already number five. Anyway, what good is it to count? I ate a hundred dishes. What chickens! But I am really an idiot, how could I forget the stuffed fish? It was prepared with red horse radish, and then I had kugel with raisins, tsimmes with plums and radishes with ginger. But why the hurry? A lot could be said about the goose-necks. They were so nicely roasted that one could hear the crack of the crisp crust all over Homel, and the stuffing was made with onions and mushrooms . . ."

At this point Herr Dreckendorf whispered ominously:

"Hey, Jew, stop smiling at once! The nerve! Think of something exalting! For instance—remember that you live in *Exile.*"

"Very well, Herr Doctor. I am thinking already: You, miserable Roitschwantz, are living in exile. No more talk about any goose-necks, and in another hour you are getting half of a hardly visible piece of zwieback. You see, I am groaning already. I am crying. I am descending down into your island. I think I am going to faint. . ."

24

Whatever happened afterwards was Herr Drekkendorf's fault. Even in Koenigsberg it is not permitted to live only by the stars and by one's wit. Since he was a patriot, he had a son and a daughter. But there he stopped. His wife was amazed, but he explained it quite simply:

"At this point, the drugstore business begins."

And Mrs. Dreckendorf sat there with her boiled potatoes and profuse tenderness in her lustreless eyes. Herr Doctor had no time for her. He had to tend to his business. He was meditating about the absolute. On Sundays he met with his political friends, blowing patriotic marches on the trumpet. He improved Germany's borders on all school maps. He cleaned his helmet with chalk. He drank beer. He embraced concubines from the colonies in his dreams. In short, he had to perform a great many important civic duties. Besides, certain innocent amusements were not unfamiliar to him either. Once a week he would become his own double. On the signboard of his drugstore he would remain the respectable Herr Doctor, as well as in the minds of all his honorable customers. His body, however, would repair to a house on Kaiserstrasse, number six. There his mustache would bristle up in ecstasy. Willi had been telling the truth: the Herr Doctor Dreckendorf loved footwear—exclusively. In the house on Kaiserstrasse, number six, he would spend the evening biting an old slipper, warbling:

"I shall eat you up, oh eternal Gretchen! . . . Hurrah! . . ."

Of course, this was perfectly all right and nobody's business, except perhaps Mrs. Dreckendorf's. Every year she became heavier from eating potatoes, and yet, somewhere underneath the masses of fat, there beat a yearning heart. When she found out about her husband's secret passion, she made an attempt to wear a slipper on her head when going to bed, instead of the usual nightcap. But it was not easy to deceive the Herr Doctor! . . .

Anyone who knew Mrs. Dreckendorf would certainly say that she was anything but frivolous. And so it happened one day, when some pretty girls were crowding around the drugstore window, Willi became so desperate that he made an attempt to lay his hands on her well-matured, fatty curves. But Frau Dreckendorf scolded him harshly:

"Willi, no nonsense! Finish your dumplings! Don't think I have not seen you hide three of them. I am going to tell the Herr Doctor."

Willi provoked Mrs. Dreckendorf's displeasure. He breathed heavily like a wild boar, while Frau Dreckendorf's desires turned toward some pale youth with flaming eyes.

One evening she was alone with Lasik. Herr Dreckendorf was chewing his slippers at the Kaiserstrasse, and Willi was asleep, his stomach trying to digest a mass of dumplings. Lasik looked at her, and she froze. What fire! What passion! Overcome, she murmured softly;

"You are like Lohengrin . . . Can such ardent desire be rejected? . . ."

Lasik, full of hope, fell on his knees and cried:

"Just once! One time only! He shall never know. We can call it an imaginary dream. Oh please, let me have two or three dumplings!"

Frau Dreckendorf's heavy curves were striking against the cupboard wall like ocean waves hitting a rock. She gave Lasik not just three, but four dumplings. Let all virtue wither, yes, even the cod liver oil of the finest cod of all Eastern Prussia! . . . She pulled out the nightcap from its pearl-embroidered covering: "Immerse in my love! . . ."

Lasik remembered what he had learned in *Cheder*—that you had to earn your bread by the sweat of your brow. Well, it applied all the more to such first-rate dumplings.

It was fifteen minutes before Lasik could speak again, but when he did he said:

"You see—I was immersed, and I have risen again. I am from top to bottom covered with the sweat of my brow. I implore you, give me quickly a pork cutlet with beans! While that fat blockhead was gorging himself, I inhaled an aroma . . ."

And Lasik ate an enormous cutlet.

"More!" he moaned, in expectation of rice pudding.

"More yet!" groaned Frau Dreckendorf, expecting something else.

Anyway, they understood each other. Willi was snoring morosely. Somewhere on the Kaiserstrasse, the Herr Doctor was squeezing the obedient slipper lovingly; the happy lovers, however, were cooing tenderly:

"You are so tiny, that I am afraid—you might get lost, like a pin . . ."

"Do not worry. I shall not get lost. I am always noticed by everybody. As soon as I passed the threshold into the great Poland, everyone took notice of me. But I want to ask you something else. The Herr Doctor told me something about roast goat. Would you prepare a tender piece with cabbage for me tomorrow? . . ."

About three days later, Herr Dreckendorf noticed a change. Lasik's cheeks were slightly rosy. He did not groan any more. He even whistled boldly Lewka's song: *Yes, we have no bananas!* and answered himself smilingly: "Surely, with cabbage!" In short, he behaved as though he had been living on Prussian cod liver oil, 4.95 a liter all his life.

"Jew, you have gone crazy! Why are you smiling? How dare you have rosy cheeks?"

"It must be your diet, Herr Doctor Dreckenkopf. After all, I am living on wonderful air, the purest in all of Eastern Prussia. Why do I have rosy cheeks? Well, don't you know, this is the beginning of the end. Just as the sky gets rosy when the sun goes down, not only in Homel, but even in your famous Iceland. Furthermore, you have dressed me in a children's jacket, making me exactly twenty-one years younger, thus forcing my organism to develop in that direction, so that I am not eleven years any more, but rather eleven months. Therefore my cheeks are rosy like those of a baby in its crib, and I sing and whistle, even though the contract is in your hands. I'll probably wither because I am the sun before the sunset, or a newly-born fact."

On top of everything, Willi became sick. His stomach could not take it any longer. He sat morosely in the display-window, and the passersby said:

"It almost looks as though the little one is the healthier of the two. His short body doesn't mean a thing. Just look at his cheeks . . . See, the effect of the cod liver oil. . . ."

Herr Dreckendorf was furious:

"My careful plan was in vain! His Highness has lost everything. Eastern Prussia is losing its finest drugstore."

He became so despondent that one evening on his way to the Kaiserstrasse, he suddenly changed his mind and returned home: "I am not up to having fun right now. At worst, I can always chew my wife's slipper."

And when the Herr Doctor caught sight of the diminutive pants of the eleven-year old, next to his wife's nightcap, he cried in despair:

"Where are you?"

Lasik did not quite know what was going on—he had just finished eating two goose-livers and a mountain of fried potatoes. He chirped:

"I am here! Do not worry, I am not a pin in a haystack. I will not get lost."

And while the angry Herr Dreckendorf was shaking him at his collar, he went on murmuring quietly:

"Why are you getting so upset? I have absolutely no intention of getting married. I had enough of my experience in Moscow. I am not taking away any of your living space. Neither do I have a plan to increase the German population. Yours is the finest and foremost business in all of Eastern Prussia, so you should be quite satisfied. Will you stop shaking me; after all, you are not a Polish cavalry captain. You are always talking about absolute common sense, so why don't you use it for a couple of minutes? Furthermore, I am not doing anything wrong. I'm adhering to my Jewish faith, which orders me to earn my food by the sweat of my brow. Did you really think I could go on living on one impressive piece of zwieback?"

Herr Dreckendorf was in a rage.

"We shall see, you robber! . . . I shall have you thrown in prison! I am taking you to the police at once! You thief! You

Bolshevik! There they will show you what it means to insult the wife of Herr Doctor Dreckendorf!"

Lasik took the opportunity to use the open door, which Herr Dreckendorf had forgotten to close, and ran into the street. He went as far as the first crossroad, obeyed the regulation regarding pedestrians, and approached a policeman cautiously:

"Please tell me, Herr Doctor of Police Philosophy, what do you think? If I choose to go to the penitentiary right now, will they accept me or not? I admit I have probably insulted her, and she is certainly the best of all in Eastern Prussia."

The policeman meditated conscientiously:

"That I do not know. They will probably require three photographs and a vaccination certificate from you."

Lasik sighed heavily:

"Well, then, in such a case, there is one thing left for me only. You can see, Herr Police-Doctor, I am going to faint in a minute, thus blocking the busy traffic. So why don't you take me there at once, without any further photographic vaccination."

25

Lasik was lucky. He did not only get to Berlin, but he also found a new patron. And once again it was his dwarf-like figure that helped him out of trouble. It almost seemed as though fate was trying to make up for all the hurts and insults Fenitschka Hershanowitsch as well as Comrade Nussja had inflicted upon the amorous shrimp. Who knows, maybe Lasik, like a midget-cactus, would have found another greenhouse in the soul of a new Frau Dreckendorf. After all, wasn't that the year when small umbrellas and short-legged scotch terriers were fashionable? But new horizons opened up for him. He was picked up by a man of the free arts, the director of a great movie enterprise, Herr Alfred Kuemmel.

"What a discovery! One senses immediately that you are a Russian, and a *Bolshevik* at that. You were the leader of many hordes. There is something mysterious in your look . . . it tells of the wide steppes, of creaking peasant-carts . . . and that Mongolian profile. Only an Ataman can wave his hands like that. And these pitch-black eyelashes! You shall get five thousand marks. You are going to play the lead in my new picture *The Song of Lips and Cannons.*"

Lasik became frightened:

"My dear Herr Doctor of Arts, though five thousand marks are quite an amount, which surely does not even exist, like orchids, for instance, I will nevertheless control my feelings and not embrace you with my wavy Mongolian Ataman-hands. First, you say I am a Bolshevik, even though we are not such close friends, let us not become so familiar with each other. It is true, in Homel, Lewka always shouted 'I am an old Bolshevik' whenever there was music in the park and he wanted to get in for free; but you, I should say, are not from Homel—quite the contrary, and to have a man constantly beaten up—I am afraid, not even the lost Roitschwantz would agree. Therefore let us leave such designations until we meet at a more intimate conference. Of course, I can act. I have already appeared in a public performance of a tragedy, in the part of a duke with gnawing teeth and real class-oppression. But I certainly do not like the title of your film. I have nothing against the lips. That can happen to anyone, and even if Fenya Hershanowitch should have the notion to deny it, I can get a real certificate of maturity at any time from Frau Dreckenkopf. But you also want to squeeze the cannons into the title. Well, I, as an absolute opponent of imperialism, do not like such subjects. They tried to draft me eight times, and eight times they had to send me home. I had a heart-liver and a navel disease, and a few other illnesses. I could hardly find the time to make the suits for all those artistic doctors free of charge. Once they even cut out a healthy part of my intestine when I gave them a jacket, made out of my own material, only to make sure I would not be drafted and die because of some incidental hetman. Now you tell me—was it worth while to lie under the knife in order to get to Berlin and lose my life through your precautionary invention? . . ."

The director murmured full of enthusiasm:

"What eastern passion! A midget, and yet such lively spirit in a fragile body! He sets fire to the ocean, he leads the masses of sailors and nomads who are following him . . . No, my dear friend, I shall never let you go! Hello, driver! Take us straight to the studios."

Alfred Kuemmel showed Lasik around the studio.

"You see—everything is ready for shooting. You were the only one I was looking for. You will play the part of *Sascha Zemalonkow, the Phantom of the Steppe.* We have invested enormous amounts of money. Here—these are the cannons. Where are you going? No, no, I am not letting you go! This here is your partner in *The Soul of the Loreley.* She is a famous actress. Get to know each other. Tomorrow the cossacks are arriving. Are you running off again? Doorkeeper, bring him back!

"The shot of the thirty-eighth scene: You are embracing the 'Soul of the Loreley' amidst a wild lance-attack of four squadrons. You understand—this is not an ordinary movie picture, this is an epic of world struggle. You catch sight of the Red Square—over there in the corner. Let your emotions play—you are back home in your beloved Moscow."

Lasik had not been too often in the Red Square. He was afraid the guard in front of Lenin's Tomb would start shooting —he always avoided passing that guard—"What has he got to lose. His finger gets stuck on the trigger, and the bullet lands in my body." However, he had seen the Red Square. And he said politely:

"It is my opinion that this looks rather like the opposite, and if you would put a nightcap next to that onion-shaped cupola, you will have a perfect drugstore."

The Director smiled in a friendly way:

"I know what you mean. You want to say the proper atmosphere is missing? But wait, you will see how differently these backdrops will look when you start galloping around on a wild Arabian stallion."

"Goodbye, Herr Film Doctor! Good night! I am already galloping somewhere far from here. Find yourself an Arab, so he can gallop in your raging imagination for I still treasure my life, even though it is in the phase before the last."

"Wait! I told you I would not let you go. Do you want to be insured? We will agree to that, too. How much do you think you are worth?"

"What has insurance got to do with this? Am I perhaps a combustible house, would I set myself on fire? Maybe I am worth only ten pfennig, and even that is doubtful, since I cannot do my patchwork any more. But if I die and they pay me one hundred thousand afterwards, that would be absolute humbug. As though I could shed precious tears over my beautiful grave!"

"But you are not going to die. You are not running the slightest risk. I only mentioned the insurance because you are so nervous. To be sure, a few accidents belong to the shooting of a good movie picture. We have surpassed America, we are not afraid of anything. And as far as advertising, no one can equal us. But we shall be satisfied with two or three doubles. We shall pamper you like a star. Well then, we will start tomorrow morning. And I am going to tell you the story of the movie.

"Steppe. Croaking Raven. Drifting clouds. The people are oppressed. Rasputin, the monk, is dancing the foxtrot with a young lady of the court. He is carefree. The land is being taken away from the nomads. They sigh at their campfire, and then go wandering ahead. A monumental scene! The sailors are sighing, too. Oh yes, I forgot to mention: you see the fleet approaching. The sailors start the mutiny. They want fresh water, crystal-clear water, and all they get is colored lemonade. One of the sailors dies aboard—he dies of sorrow for his people. Now the nomads appear, gnashing their teeth. The maid of honor beats the serfs with her spurs. The clouds are gathering, a storm is in the making. Quick succession of shots: clouds, spurs, nomads, tears. Storm. You, I mean the 'Phantom of the Steppe,' crawls out from a grave.

"He is small, but powerful. You grab an ikon, stirring up the sailors. They buckle on their cartridge belts. The castle is in flames. This scene is the most expensive. Nine hundred people. End of the first part. Second part. The Rhine is gently flowing. Vineyards. Castles. The forester's daughter—she is the Soul of the Loreley. She feeds the freezing birds and teaches singing to poor children. No one understands her. The Rhine flows gently. She feels she was chosen by destiny. She is high up on the mountain. Her white robe contrasts with the smoke-screen. Double-shot. She dreams of the East. You are flying over the Square. You are flying over Russia, through Europe, over the whole world. Do not interrupt me! The clouds cover the horizon. The sailors have become nomads. At the cabaret *Alkazar,* the ladies are gaily dancing the foxtrot. The ladies' legs. The nomads are swimming. The sailors are riding by with their spears. Europe on the eve of destruction. And now, your meeting with the 'Soul of Loreley.' She sings to you the song of the finch. Embrace. Close-up. Everybody embraces each other. The nomads decorate their carts with wreaths. Sunrise. The sailors are swimming in the Rhine. The forester blesses you and dies. He leaves everything to you. You open up a cigar shop. Your picture with a pipe in your mouth. The 'Soul of Loreley' bending over a cradle. The nomads return to the steppe. The sailors present Hindenburg with a bouquet of pansies. The pansies—

close up. The cradle. The baby boy smiles bravely. Text: 'The future German soldier.' Well, isn't that terrific? Love. Mysticism. Revolution. Fatherland. For export we shall have to cut only the last hundred meters. Guaranteed success in America, Russia, Australia, China. Your name—Roitschwantz—will travel all over the world. Why are you so quiet? Admit it, the story has impressed you."

"I am impressed all right. It is in the vein of Alfonse Curose's novel. You could even have taken one or the other thing from there. For instance, why do they have to put on those cartridge belts? They are not so glamorous, and besides, one of them could really fire a shot, accidentally. In my opinion, each and every one of them should have a tennis racket in his hand. Then the contours will show more clearly. But, of course, you have better eyes for those things. I just want to ask you one favor. If I have to gallop through the whole world for twenty-four hours, would it not be possible to do it without the assistance of the Arabian stallion? Let the sailors gallop on whatever they like, since they have agreed to go to war anyway. But I will gallop on my own feet."

However, Alfred Kuemmel remained stubborn, and the next morning he put the shaky Lasik on a horse:

"Get up there!"

A military band was blaring to preserve the heroic spirit. Everywhere, the cossacks were moving around their horses. Lasik was dressed in the long caftan of a rich boyar, with the cartridge belt buckled on. He had to close his eyes because of the unbearable bright lights, and he blinked miserably.

Alfred Kuemmel brought an enormous microphone to his ear, shouting furiously:

"Don't delay! Mount the horse, quick! Each wasted minute costs us a hundred marks."

"My dear Herr Artist! . . . I am ready to forego my five thousand."

"Mount the horse!"

"How can I mount a horse when the highest seat I ever sat on was the bench of the accused? Furthermore, when they were shooting cannons in Homel, I could always hide behind the viaduct at the edge of town. But now where can I hide? You've put around me that stupid cartridge belt—what if it suddenly gets a notion to shoot?"

"Enough of that nonsense! You are the 'Phantom of the Steppe'! You are storming about boldly and with a devil-may-care expression. Do you get it? All right, get on! Do not be afraid. It is a tame horse. An old mare. Almost an ass. Are you up? Now—look boldly. Ready! Full light! Karl, rouse the mare! Operators! 'Phantom of the Steppe,' more boldness!"

Lasik could only call:

"Goodbye, Pfeifer! . . . Prrr! . . . Prrr! . . . Horsey, what got into you?"

The microphone was thundering in vain: "Sit up straight! Smile!" Lasik did not hear a thing. At first he was holding on to the mane, but with the very first jolt he fell backwards. He clutched the horse's buttocks, whimpering with fear. When the 'Soul of the Loreley' appeared, he was supposed to send her an etheral kiss, but he was hanging from the horse's tail like a rag. The horse sadly wagged its posterior. Lasik fell to the ground. He bumped his nose. After having wiped off the blood with the boyar's caftan, he said proudly to the director:

"Well? . . . How did you like it, I was storming about like a real phantom."

Herr Kuemmel did not take refuge in the microphone. He was shouting wildly: "Get lost," and Lasik was glad to oblige him this time. He ran so fast, he got all tangled up in the flaps of the long caftan. But before the exit, he stopped:

"Have you calmed down, after all this excitement? Then, listen to me. I was not the one who wanted to gallop about. I always told you, I was not a 'Phantom of the Steppe,' but only a miserable little tailor from Homel. You yourself have put me on that bloody scaffold. Here, take your abnormal suit and these deliberate cartridges, and you may give me some money, because, even though I did not sign that unfortunate stamped sheet, you were talking yesterday of some insurance covering various houses. For how much, then, did you insure my bloody nose. I would like to get at least ten marks for it, because I am as hungry as a real amazon . . ."

"Hey, Karl! Show him the exit! . . ."

And so, Roitschwantz, the poor devil, had to start wandering anew, across the yard, through the streets, through Berlin, through the whole, wide world.

26

For several days Lasik was busy distributing leaflets for an Institute for Combatting Venereal Diseases. He was then set upon by an old lady, who beat him with her umbrella, and took off with the remaining leaflets lest they corrupt the young. After that, he found a job as a cat's nurse, at the clinic of the famous veterinarian, Doctor Keller. He had to hold the cats, while they were submitted to ultra-violet rays. It was obvious the cats did not believe in these treatments, for they fought and scratched frightfully. Lasik had to give up this job too, after his face was scratched to a bloody pulp by a wild Siamese cat. Doctor Keller was afraid that Lasik's sad appearance with his face in bandages would scare away certain sensitive clients. And so, Lasik got into a wandering circus. His job was to substitute for the monkey, "Jigo," who had bronchitis. He had to climb around on trapezes, covered with fur, with an ape-like expression on his face. So he climbed. He had to crack nuts. So he cracked nuts. However, when they told him to jump across a barrier during a performance, he could not stand it any longer.

"In the first place, you have not told me anything about such a suicide; and second, if I must cover myself with my own blood, be so kind and take off my tail, because as far as I know, no man jumps around with a tail."

Lasik just could not find a quiet nook. He tried in vain to seduce the passersby with his famous patchwork. He offered to sew anything: frock-coats and elegant suits, even steel helmets. He tried to move the hearts of the people in Berlin in all possible ways. He tried to remind them that he adhered to the Jewish faith, that the "Soul of Loreley" had been in love with him, and finally, that he could not be made responsible for an artificial tail. But he was to hear only angry, abusive words. At last, a policeman, feeling sorry for him, took him along.

At the police-station, he was accused according to several paragraphs, relating to loitering, shady business dealings and indecent assault.

In jail, Lasik felt at home at once. He hung the portrait of the Portuguese hostage over his bed, and began to boast:

"This is already the eleventh. And I could write a magnificent guide book. To be sure, the air here is much better than in Lomscha; however, in Kiev they served a marvelous borscht."

Next to Lasik slept a man by the name of Kotz, who was accused of stealing a sausage. At night, he would complain in a soft voice:

"I was looking for work, six days in a row. Then I could not stand it any more. It happened in the market. There it was lying, and I just grabbed it and swallowed it."

Lasik patted the enormous Kotz on his shoulder:

"Do not be so unhappy! You will certainly go free. I can understand you very well. There should be a law against displaying sausages in general: they just smell too good. In my opinion, no man can resist that aroma, not even Herr Hindenburg himself, though all they could think of was to present him with a bouquet of pansies. You know what, Comrade Kotz, there is no justice on earth! If you had stolen pansies, they might have had some reason to arrest you. Because why should anyone steal such offerings? However, a piece of sausage is a vital necessity for anyone. So, who needs this stupid court? And about work, you don't have to tell me anything, either. You could not find any work? You were lucky. You see, you are in jail, and I am in jail, but at least your nose is undamaged. I had to gallop about on a wild Arab, and so I jumped over my own tail; I had to molest various doctors' wives in the streets; and I had to hold genuine Siamese tigers in my own hands. This is called 'the sweat of your brow,' and then the people go to the synagogue and even to church, and they pray to God for these things. In general, I belong to the spiritual avant-garde, and I know up there is nothing but gas, that no one wants, anyway. But suppose there is a God up there, then He is the greatest cheat, and we should change places with Him. He should lie among the hundred paragraphs of the penal code, and you and I should rest in Heaven. You think I am not familiar with all these tricks? I know them as I know the five fingers of my hand. And if you insist there must be a beginning, then it is only—an absolute incoherent cry. All right—so it was forbidden to eat the apple. God has funny ideas, too. But you tell me, why this historical hullabaloo merely because of a small fruit? Isn't it just like your sausage? But I would like to

kinds of stupid fools kiss his old slipper, and there were plenty of pretty girls in Rome. So there was constant kissing to be heard in his castle. It was carnival time in Rome. What a wonderful holiday! I remember at home, in Homel, the telegraph clerk Sacharow once treated me to such pancakes that I almost became converted to his opium with sweet cream. But of course, people celebrate their holidays in every country in a different way. In Rome, they almost lost their senses. Without getting paid for it, they clad themselves in monkey-furs with tails. They promenaded from morning till late at night in bandits' costumes. If one looked about, Rome no longer resembled a city, but rather a civic operetta. One person claimed he was an elephant, wagging his trunk indecently; another one swore he was a real duke who liked to eat his duchess; and everybody skipped around, and they all danced the dances of the Roman national minorities. I do not even want to start talking of the women! Who knows what kind of mechanism functions in your body. Maybe you are going to break the window, like the fat Willi? I will only tell you this much, that these women had the chubbiest curves. What bananas they were! At this point we had better stop.

"They skipped, and sang, they kissed, but the main thing had not happened yet. As I told you before, there were also Jews in Rome. Naturally, that is an impudence: how dare they live in the same city with the Pope? But what can you do? Look at the ants, for instance! Is there a place where they don't crawl in? Also the Pan Captains, who are really strict, what good does it do them? You step over one Jew, right away another one follows to be stepped over. The Pope cursed, threatened with his slipper, and then became tired of it and decided to let them stay. How can you throw a runny nose into prison? Since the Pope was a great believer in the carnival, he came up with a terrific joke: at least, let the Jews produce a jester for everyone's entertainment. This unfortunate joker shall run around the city three times, completely naked. The Pope would sit with his elephants and his ladies on golden chairs, and they would laugh and have a wonderful time.

"As the saying goes: one gets the carnival, the other one gets the naked run. So, the Jews met for a conference: who should be the tortured horse? There are all kinds of Jews: some wear their carats even on their stomachs, others have only cheap tears to offer. I, for instance, am lying on the eleventh prison-bed, while some Rothschild is probably gobbling up a whole goat. In Rome, too, there were business people of the first guild, as well as cemetery-beggars, who are ready to shed a few tears each evening on any grave for a piece of bread. Well, who will run three times around the city? Of course, not the rabbi—he is a learned man, and without him they will all become ignorant. And naturally, neither will it be the Roman Rothschild—for, without him, no one would be able to feed the beggars once a year with leftovers.

"Each Jew gave a gold coin, just so he did not have to run, and even the poorest devils gave something, for it was worth it to pawn the Sabbath-candlesticks or a coat or even a pillow, just not to die naked in front of the crazy elephants. They found a miserable tailor, who owned neither a coat nor a candlestick, nor a pillow, not even a silken *Talles*. All he had was a wife and six children, and his creeping sorrow. But for that he could not get a gold piece. Let us call him Leiser. I suppose he was my grandfather's grandfather, for our outstanding tribe of Roitschwantzes could have originated only from such an unhappy shadow. The hour of the run approached. The Pope made the cross, emptied another quart of wine and mounted his throne. Seated at his side were the various clergymen and lovely ladies with their exhibits, and also some dressed-up rascals. They were all God-fearing people, and since the Pope himself was among them, they had displayed the pictures of their charitable God everywhere. He was shown in gold, silver and even in diamonds worth one million rubles, so all would know how generous they were and what a magnificent God they had. And so, the Pope sits there, all dressed in velvet, and above him floats an enormous cross, just delivered from the jeweler's, and on the cross is Christ, not just gilded or hollow, but made of real gold, as no one has ever seen it. Very nice! But where is the runner, the one of flesh and blood? The Pope becomes impatient. He rings his bell: 'Get the horse, it is time to start.'

"They brought Leiser, whose wife and six children were following him, crying deplorably. Even a little child understands that you cannot run around Rome three times without pausing for breath. But if you stop for a moment, the Pope's horse jacks will chase you with their whip. Consequently, it is the same thing like dying. Leiser began to take off his patched trousers. The Pope laughed so hard, it even hurt his stomach; the other bandits lost their trunks and tails: one should not laugh so hard! The show was quite funny. Such a wretched creature is a joke even with his pants on. Well, without his pants, you can be sure they split their sides with laughter.

"The Pope was laughing, but not Leiser. The latter embraced his wife and children:

" 'All right, I shall run and die, but who will feed you tomorrow? The rabbi, perhaps? Yes, indeed! He will eat a big goose, but he will not even give you the bones to lick. He will feed you only learned words. Perhaps the Roman Rothschild? Oh yes, indeed! He will say: I am a Jew and you are Jews and may God bless you, but I cannot talk to you rigtht now. I ate so many geese, ducks and chickens, the doctor has to apply leeches. I am a real martyr, and you are the fortunate people and you can all kiss me on the ass! Yes, this is what Rothschild will say to you. And there will be no one who will feed you, for the poor have nothing but their naked heart, and the rich have everything, but no heart at all; and that is why you will die too. I shall die today from so much running about and you will die in a week or in a month also from running around. You will roam the city, begging for a crumb of bread, and finally you will die.'

"His wife was screaming frightfully. She could be heard all over Rome.

"'Oh, woe! How will you run, Leiser? When you cannot even run! Tell them you are a miserable tailor, not a horse. You will die, upon my word, you will die! And who will take care of me? And who will protect your children that will become orphans?'

"The Pope put cotton into his ears. He did not even raise his eyes. The first servant tickled Leiser with the whip: 'Come on, start running!'

"'Keep well, my wife! Goodbye, my children! Goodbye, my life!' Leiser sat down on a rock, clasping his naked knees; he sighed deeply for the last time. He sighed and a wind blew all over Rome: that was his farewell from life. Then, quite understandably, he got up and started running like an old mare. It was a hot day, not like the usual carnival weather, but rather like a real summer day. For you must know, in Rome the calendar is not normal, and one can always go around in a plain cotton shirt. But of course, running is much hotter yet than just sitting. And so, Leiser was soon covered with perspiration like a horse. He stumbled, groaned and wiggled his beard and the horse jacks kept lashing their whips at him. Rome is not Homel. Rome is more like Berlin. To run all the way around it can take perhaps two hours. Everywhere were those horse jacks. They saw to it that the human horse should not rest for a moment. Besides the jacks, there were also onlookers: who was not interested to see such a race on two legs? They all stood there, apes and tigers, dukes and ladies, and they all laughed:

"'Get going, run, you old horse! . . .'

"And Leiser answered them all, in a gentle voice:

" 'I am running.'

"And so he had run once around Rome. He could hardly lift his feet, and the jacks were lashing out at him more and more with their whips. The blood ran over his entire body. And he had to run two more times. He knew he could not do it. When he saw his unhappy wife and the six children and the golden throne with the Roman Pope, he lost all hope. Suddenly he paused. The Pope shouted: 'Run, you old horse, or else my servants will whip you without mercy.'

"Leiser became angry:

" 'Why, I would like to know, do I have to suffer like this? Perhaps so Rothschild may eat his ducks? Or so the Pope may embrace his insolent ladies? Or so his diamond-studded God can shine and show off his gold? . . .'

"However, a hundred horse-drivers ran after him, lashing out with their whips. Leiser threw another glance at his future orphans and started running once again. He had hardly run a hundred or two hundred yards, when it became clear to him that he could not run any further. He fell to the ground, waiting for death to save him. And that is when one of those stories full of prejudice occurred.

"Namely, all of a sudden, he sees another Jew running naked in the street and he realizes that it was not he, Leiser, but someone else. Why these hallucinations? All the Jews had paid their way out of the race. He looks closer at the other Jew, and his amazement grows steadily: Why, he looks just like me, nothing but skin and bones, and covered with perspiration, and bloody all over, and the beard wiggles up and down! Anyone can see it: he is not going to last much longer! His eyes, however, do not look like mine, and his nose is also different. Therefore, this is not I, but some other Jew. But who can he be? Leiser knew all the Jews in Rome. This was neither Elias, the ragman, nor was it Nathan, the shoemaker.

"Well, then it must be a stranger. And Leiser asked him:

" 'Where are you from? Your face looks familiar, as though I had seen you before, but I could not have seen you because I was never away from Rome. Could it be that I am dead already, and I am dreaming all this? What is your name? And tell me, why are you running, when it is I who is supposed to run?'

"The other Jew answered Leiser:

" 'My name is Jehoshua, and you cannot know me, for I have been dead a long time. However, you are still alive. I look familiar to you—probably because you must have seen my picture. They are giving me all kinds of ridiculous names, but I will tell you who I really am—I am a poor Jew. Of course, you are a tailor, and I used to be a carpenter, and we will get along fine. I wanted the absolute truth to reign on earth. What poor devil does not want it? Naturally, I have seen that the rabbi knows how to make great speeches and that Rothschild eats ducks, and that there is neither justice, nor love, nor even the humblest happiness on earth. And I was with the poor against the rich. I have seen machine guns, while the others had only their naked chests, and that it is a small matter for an iron bullet to pierce a heart. And I was on the side of the weak against the powerful. I used to love it when the sun would shine warmly, when children were laughing and everybody was happy, when all were drinking wine, smiling at each other . . . when the sabbath candles were burning and the freshly baked bread would be on the table. But what poor man does not love these things? A long time ago they killed me, and now they do not let me rest in peace. They rob the poor, calling my miserable name at the same time, and I am turning over in my grave. They put some wretched people into dungeons and sing songs about my age-old sorrow, and then they proceed to cut off their heads, and they make me jump again in my coffin. They chase stupid fools away, driving them to kill each other, and they carry my sad picture on their flags, and

I rise from my grave full of disgust. How is it that they do not laugh over my dead body? They make my image in gold and diamonds, exhibiting it everywhere. They display it in front of hungry children and even before the gallows! And I used to love the fresh bread on the poor man's table! Have pity on me, tailor Leiser! You will die, and they will bury you, and they will leave you in peace, but I must run feverishly all through the world. I am lying in the earth, and suddenly I see that Pope. He sits and laughs with those well-dressed scoundrels; he plans an amusing death for you; and floating above him is my picture in gold. Through the earth of my grave I see what is being done to me. For my dream of a perfect happiness, you must die—or so they think. So I came running. Woe is me! Woe is me! You say I am omnipotent. Have you ever seen a poor Jew who could do everything? If I knew only half of everything, would I not call out to you: 'Enough?' Would Rothschild eat all the ducks, would the Pope sit on a golden throne, and would you run around Rome? But I cannot find my peace. Day and night I am roaming like a bloody shadow, just the way you were running today.'

"Leiser raised himself and embraced the other Jew.

"'I feel sorry for you, carpenter Jehoshua, for I know now what it is to run. But I will tell you one thing: today you may rest, have peace in your grave. Why should we both run? Today I am running for you and me.'

"But the dead Jew replied:

"'No, you will go on living. You have six children—that is not so simple. I think we are going to outwit them. They will not look merely at my nose, and from a distance, we do resemble each other. You stay right here in this ditch, while I will run twice around Rome. Don't contradict me: I must run anyway, if not here, it will have to be in another town, for surely they are killing someone at this moment, while calling my name, so I may have no peace.'

"After these words, he ran around the city, and the jacks beat him, and the elephants laughed at him. But when he arrived in front of the Pope, the latter was laughing shamelessly in his pillow, calling out:

" 'Hey, you old horse! Paw your hoofs! I will show you, what a Pope is! He is the legal representative of the charitable Christ, and you are getting another hundred straps, so you will know in advance what it means to crucify our God!'

"This is the entire story, Comrade Kotz. Of course, you may make the sign of the cross once more, if your hand is healthy and your head not quite right. Just think—you are lying side by side with Roitschwantz. Maybe it was just this Roitschwantz who had crucified your God? . . ."

Kotz became angry.

"Your whole story is nonsense. And I advise you, do not come again with such foolishness. It might be bad for you. You might be accused of blasphemy."

"Well, you really found a ghost to scare me! As though it would not be the same to me whether it is three or four paragraphs that get me before the judge. That is only a matter of statistics. However, Leiser's story you have not understood at all. You cannot understand such a thing with your hands. I already told you, you probably have a hole in your head. You think I did not see you making the cross all the time while I was telling you that story? I would like to ask you now, even though you are a five-ton heavy hole, whom do you give your respect to in your city of Wurzburg? If to an old Jew—he does not demand it. If, however, you give it to an omnipotent God, then why are you here because of a mere piece of sausage? . . . You know, Kotz, we are arguing; but we will make peace again. At the moment we are both decent people, for we are two poor devils, sitting in an infamous prison. But tomorrow you could became the Pope, and I might become a Rothschild. And then, we will surely forget all the many tears, and we will become most ordinary pigs. As long as the poor carpenter was dreaming of the truth, he stood as high as the invented God; but when they made him a God in a golden frame, you see, he became nothing but an ordinary piece of furniture. Rothschild could crucify a poor devil who said he loved the poor instead of the rich. That is perfectly understandable and Roitschwantz has nothing to do with it. I think a hundred Roitschwantzes are crucified every single day, and no one protests. But what about the children's laugh? And what about the fresh bread on the poor man's table? Well, those are ridiculous dreams. Shut up, you foolish Roitschwantz! You need a shave! You are not here to philosophize! All they want from you, is—to gallop about, without pants."

27

Lasik sat through his prison term faithfully. Then his wandering began anew. He sold newspapers in Magdeburg, he cleaned windows in Stuttgart. Finally, he came to Mainz, where he found a job in the butcher shop of Otto Worms. There, quite contentedly, he sold sausages, until one day he was caught stealing. It happened that he had noticed a warm ham on the counter. In no time, he grabbed a knife, cut off an enormous slice, and swallowed it quickly. After this prank, Lasik had to leave the city of Mainz immediately, since the butcher swore he would show that rascal!

Lasik arrived in Frankfurt with only three marks. He decided, first of all, to have a shave, so as to be safe against any possibility of philosophical occurrences. His astonishment was great when the young barber asked him the following question:

"Excuse me, Herr Doctor, how would you like to be shaved —plainly or according to the Laws of Moses?"

Lasik stared in amazement.

"According to the Laws of Moses, it seems to me, one may not shave at all, so that this religion does not apply to your shaving brush at all. But if I already came to you, it is proof enough that I think nothing of those ridiculous paragraphs. Maybe you are afraid I will not pay you? Look here, you will not find a more genuine mark anywhere."

"Herr Doctor, you are offended without any reason. Here in Frankfurt one can get a shave without violating the Laws of Moses. The Jews are merely forbidden to scrape off their hair with the edge of a knife; that is why we shave our honorable customers without the unholy razor. See here—this is a patented invention. In five minutes all the hair is removed, without irritating the skin or any religious feelings. It is an invention of Doctor Klemke who made a fortune with it. . . ."

But Lasik did not listen to him any more. He took advantage of the fact that the barber had not yet started to shave him, and became deeply absorbed in thought. At last he said:

"Please shave me without all those tricks. However, you have to sharpen the razor as good as you can, since my skin is much more sensitive than my religious feelings. And here is one mark, a tip for you, if you give me the address of some respectable citizen!"

"Well, whom should I recommend you? Perhaps Herr Wolfgang Schenkelsohn? He is one of the most respected business people. But he has not come here for a long time, I think he is ill. . . ."

"Ill? This is just what I want. Well, have you finally scraped off everything with your dull stuff? Now give me quickly Herr Schenkelsohn's address."

We must admit Lasik's heart beat with excitement as he approached the magnificent mansion of Herr Schenkelsohn. He rang the bell. A maid opened the door:

"Well, how are things? Is Herr Schenkelsohn still in bed? Not dead yet? Excellent. Then I will go right in to see him. Forbidden? What does that mean—forbidden? You think I am perhaps a hoodlum. Anyway, I did not come here to have a conversation with you. Go, get his wife or his mother, or his daughter, or even his aunt."

A crying woman came out into the hallway.

"You must be Frau Schenkelsohn? Well, may God be praised, how is your dear husband? I must see him quickly. Who I am? I am the *Zadik* from Homel, and I arrived in Frankfurt, and heard that a Jew was sick. Naturally, I came to visit him right away. I know your husband is a good, law-abiding Jew."

Frau Schenkelsohn stood there undecided. But Lasik did not give in:

"When I was visiting the famous Rabbi Josche. . . . You know, of course, the *Zadik* from Dwinsk? We went together to see a sick man. He was in bed, like your husband, and was ready to die. However, Rabbi Josche noticed that the sick man's bones were grown together, and he commanded the bones to obey God's will and at once the bones were growing in the right places. Thereupon, the sick man wanted to eat a whole chicken immediately. It's all very simple. A human being has two hundred forty-eight joints and three hundred sixty-five bones, so that if added together, he has six hundred and thirteen of those things. In other words as many as there are good deeds. You are looking at me, how is it possible that I know so much, when I am still quite young? But I am really not as young as I look. I have passed my fiftieth year. You see, the

Lord gives me two years for each one. He does not only know how to punish, he also knows when to reward somebody. I can assure you that your husband will jump out of bed like a trapeze artist, tomorrow or the day after."

Mrs. Schenkelsohn burst into tears:

"All the doctors say there is no hope whatsoever . . . I have already ordered the synagogues to read prayers in the name of 'Wolf.' You see, his Hebrew name is Zeff. But he gets weaker every day."

Lasik said with dignity:

"You are a woman, and God will forgive you such foolish talk. The doctors see only skin-deep. They cannot look inside everything."

The woman took Lasik into the patient's room. Amidst precious furniture, gold-bronze chandeliers, paintings and carpets lay, on an enormous wooden bed, a shriveled-up, old man. He was already unconscious. Lasik asked:

"How old is he?"

"Eighty-four."

"That's just what I thought. Well then, it is all clear to me, and I am telling you: the sick man lacks a joint inside. He has surely forgotten to do one good deed. Naturally he has prayed to God, he has observed the *Yom Kippur* and he has even given contributions to the synagogue. But I do not think he has ever treated one single *Zadik* to a good meal. However, since he is not in a position at this moment to go down into the kitchen, you should do it, in his place, and very quickly at that, instead of hollering unnecessarily. Then you will see, he will be well tomorrow, or after tomorrow, and jump around happily."

Lasik was taken into the next room, where all the sick man's relatives had congregated. Some were crying, others were discussing the quotations of the Hamburg stock exchange, more specifically, the navigation shares Herr Schenkelsohn had purchased. The sick man's sister hearing that Lasik was a learned

Rabbi, if not from Galizia, at least from Lithuania, became quite cheerful:

"It is so difficult to find a real Rabbi in Frankfurt, one that knows all the Laws. And when man gets sick, it is time to think of God."

"I know the rules as I know the fingers of my hand. I was only thirteen years old when the ten most famous Rabbis placed the *Smiche* into my hands, thus ordaining me and I became a full-fledged Rabbi. And after that I spent ten years with the famous *Zadik* in Vinnitsa. My name? Rabbi Leser."

"Please, tell me, Rabbi Leser, what do you think, should a change of name be undertaken for our patient? Our Rabbi here thinks it might help. If it is written in the Book of Fate that a man called Wolf has to die, well then it just applies to Wolf."

"Your Rabbi seems to have some knowledge. Maybe he has picked up something with one ear. However, I will take care of it right now and here. Indeed, we will outsmart the approaching angel. So his name is Wolf? All right. It is all taken care of. His name is Mendel from now on. And if it is written up there that Wolf has to die tomorrow, your beloved Mendel will eat chicken, because that piloting angel will look around for Wolf. You see how simple it is? Your Rabbi would have wasted two hours and most certainly a good deal of your money. I am staying here, and if he does not get better during the night, I shall make him a 'Chaim' instead of a 'Mendel,' and it will all be at reduced rates."

When Lasik woke up after a good sleep, he inquired cheerfully:

"Well, how is our dear Mendel?"

"He is dead."

"Dead? I figured he would die. I merely wanted to save you the pain and sorrow. It is always early enough to cry. But I knew it right away, when a Jewish woman in Mainz could not give birth to her child because God did not have a soul available. I understood at once: God is reaching out for the soul of your beloved, let's call him, Mendel. Well, what can one do? So then let us bury him."

Now Lasik really knew what to do. A Jew has to be buried according to all kinds of rules and regulations, so that he may be able to rise with ease when the *Messiah* blows his trumpet. And for this Rabbi Leser really knew the prescribed rules.

"What about the earth?" his widow was crying. "Should they not place Palestinian earth under his head so the worms will not touch him?"

Lasik comforted her:

"I will get you earth from Palestine in half an hour. It is the best brand. It comes straight from Rachel's grave; the *Zadik* from Rowno gave it to me as a present. I was keeping it for myself. But now I am traveling to Palestine to die. And when the trumpet sounds, I will be right there, so I will not have to run again. Therefore I can let you have my earth. We can talk about the price after the eight mourning days are over. I am a *Zadik*, and not a highway robber, after all."

Lasik went out into the street. He went to the park, put a handful of earth into his handkerchief and became sentimental:

"Who knows, where will Roitschwantz die? Into what latrine will they throw his infamous body? . . ."

The relatives wanted to pile up wreaths on the dead man's grave, but his pious sister protested:

"That is forbidden. Is that not so, Rabbi Leser? It might do him harm."

"But, of course, wreaths are forbidden. However, you may put straw on the grave. Well, what is straw? Nothing but withered flowers. And as soon as a flower is plucked, it is withered already. Therefore, I, the strictest of all the *Zadiks*, give you permission to place as many wreaths as you wish on his grave."

One of the sons of the deceased, a very cautious man, got

quite upset:

"And what about the suit? They say it has to be torn to pieces—of sorrow."

"That is all very simple. You can put on my suit. It will be a little too small on you, but with such sorrow, who has time to look in a mirror? You may tear it to pieces; it is torn anyway, and besides you can use it again at another funeral! And you will give me your suit, and we may even put it on the bill of the necessary *Kaddishes*."

All the children and grandchildren of the deceased were furious when they were served hard-boiled eggs. Lasik saved the situation once more:

"You have had enough misfortune. I shall eat the hard-boiled eggs, and you may take the chicken bouillon, for the *Zadik* from Glukhov has said already that the chicken comes from the egg, and the bouillon from the chicken."

The wisdom and ingenuity of Rabbi Leser made a great impression on all the Jews of Frankfurt, who came to the Schenkelsohns to express their sympathy. The chief of the Jewish community, Herr Moiser, a well-known stockbroker and philanthropist, hearing that hard-boiled eggs can be substituted by the more hygienic bouillon, exclaimed enthusiastically:

"That is what I call a man who studies the Torah day and night! In his hands, the hardest Law becomes soft as camel's hair. Tell me, Rabbi Leser, if your presence gives such happiness to the Jews, how come they have not kept you from leaving your home-town?"

"I already said I am on my way to Palestine, to die there. If you will ask me such questions, I will leave tomorrow. Besides, I am also capable of doing just the opposite. In Homel there was also a Jew, who would not leave me alone with his insolent questions. He would, all of a sudden, ask me: 'It might be interesting to know where you hail from, and what you have in your pockets and where your diploma is?' And what do you think became of him? One day, I stepped forward in the synagogue to bless the crowd. I am of noble blood. You see, we Roitschwantzes are *Cohenites.* And so, I raised my hand as the leader of the *Cohenites.* Naturally, everyone closed their eyes, for it is forbidden to look at a *Cohenite* when he blesses the people. But that insolent rascal wanted to satisfy his curiosity even then. He looked at me. Perhaps he wanted to find out whether I was holding my fingers correctly? Ridiculous! I know my fingers as I know the Talmud. And what do you think happened to that, let us say, curious Jew? In no more than ten seconds, he became blind."

Lasik's story made a great impression on all. Naturally, Herr Moiser did not get the moral. For, as soon as he had heard that the *Zadik* from Homel was a *Cohenite,* he was thinking of one thing only: how could he be prevailed upon to remain in Frankfurt? He approached the matter from afar:

"You are still young and the Lord will grant you all your ninety years, if not all hundred and twenty; so I really do not see why you are in such a hurry to get to Palestine? Take a rest before such a long journey. You will find respect and peace in our community. You will pray in our synagogue. We have a magnificent Synagogue, you know. I have contributed quite a bit to it, and you will marvel at those doors, its seven-armed chandeliers and its magnificent Torah. But alas, we are lacking one thing—we do not have a *Cohenite.* If you would consent to pray with us, you would surely not refuse to bless us. Believe me, my honorable Rabbi Leser, here you will not find such ungodly people as in your home town. None of us has the slightest desire to become blind. On the other hand, mere belief does not suffice to travel as far as the Holy Land. There, you need Egyptian pounds, and I happen to know how high they are. . . . So I beg you to accept our offer."

For decency's sake Lasik waited a moment before answering:

"I feel very sorry for you, and since I am a good Jew, I shall not travel to Palestine right now. Well then, you may start taking care of me."

The next day, a man called Schwarzberg came into Lasik's room, bowing humbly:

"I would like to ask you, honorable Rabbi, to take over the protectorate of my Kosher restaurant. I want to be able to write on the menu—*under the supervision of the Rabbi.* Without this no self-respecting Jew will come to my place. I have already heard from Herr Moiser that you understand how to adapt the harsh laws to the demands of our time. I do not dare offer you a remuneration in money, no, between you and me, you will be my partner with twenty per cent of all net profits."

Lasik consented gladly. He merely added: "And three full meals every day."

Schwarzberg, full of courage because of his quick success, proceeded to the main point without further ado.

"As you know, Rabbi, we fulfill all the rules of hygiene, but the meat spoils slightly because of that. According to the Law it has to lie in salt for a full hour. One can easily imagine what kind of a beefsteak or rib roast that would make. But who gets all the complaints of the guests? Not Moses, but the restaurant-keeper. The same Herr Moiser who demands that all rules be fulfilled, wants to be served a juicy roast beef at the same time. And so I venture to ask you whether it would not be possible to leave the meat only a half hour in salt? Then my beefsteaks will taste much better than those at Rosen's and I can beat the competition without difficulty."

"What is an hour? If a man is hungry and before him is a rib roast, every minute is like an hour. That is what the wise *Zadik* from Balta always said. However, everybody is hungry before dinner, therefore I give you permission, according to the law, to salt the meat exactly one minute. Only do not salt it ten minutes, or else, instead of beefsteak for dinner, I might get an almost Babylonian complaint."

Schwarzberg winked tenderly at Lasik. The next morning he came again to ask for more advice.

"I will come straight to the point, honorable Rabbi. My guests like neither coconut-butter nor melted fat. I am convinced the ungodly Rosen fries his cutlets in pure butter. Please tell me, what I, the God-fearing Schwarzberg, can do?"

"It is written in the Book of Laws: 'Thou shalt not eat the calf in its mother's milk.' Butter is made from milk. But who is to know which cow was the mother of what calf or even of any full-grown bull? Therefore it is not permitted to fry meat in butter."

Schwarzberg sighed dejectedly.

"Wait a minute. It is too early to sigh! You may serve pork roast. I, for instance, love pork cutlets. Of course a pig cannot be the daughter of a cow, and so you may fry pork cutlets in cow's butter and crisp potatoes to boot. This is absolutely within the Law, and you will see, when Herr Moiser will eat a pork cutlet, he will exclaim full of delight: what a juicy veal roast you serve!"

"But according to the Law, pork is absolutely forbidden. . . ."

Lasik interrupted him:

"If, according to the Law, a pig does not have two toes on its feet, so that it may be eaten, you do not count them. Why should you waste your time with pigs' toes? And furthermore, if you are speaking to a learned Rabbi, you do not have to philosophize. Period."

Schwarzberg could not contain himself, tears came into his eyes:

"Indeed, God must have rewarded me for having given that beggar forty pfennigs! . . . And you are not merely an ingenious Rabbi, but a blessing sent by God."

A week later Lasik heard more flattering words. It was the eve of the *Yom Kippur* fast, and Herr Moiser was sighing unhappily: how was he going to starve a whole day long? He went to Rabbi Leser for advice.

"You see Rabbi, I suffer from gout. And besides I am not used to it . . . I might pass away . . . But according to the Law, I must not beg you to release me of fasting. Otherwise some misfortune will be entered into my Book of Fate, and all my stocks will fall at once. The same thing happened to Weissman."

Lasik was full of dignity:

"We shall take care of that right away. Of course for this it is necessary to have three Rabbis. However, a *Zadik* like I am is as good as three. Put on your elegant top hat and sigh. I am commanding you to eat everything tomorrow. Answer me: 'I shall not violate the *Yom Kippur.*' Yes, that is right. Now, sigh. And I am ordering you once again, in the name of God and in agreement with the Law, to eat tomorrow, for the fast threatens your weak heart, which might result in a fatal end. That is all. Now you may smile again. Tomorrow you will eat chicken, and in your Book of Fate, your stocks will rise to the uppermost floor."

Herr Moiser asked enthusiastically:

"Couldn't you do the same thing for my brother, too? He does not have gout, but I am sure he will find something. For instance, he has a polyp in his nose. He could also die of weakness."

"Send him at once. . . ."

Lasik released not only Herr Moiser's brother from fasting, but thirty other Jews from Frankfurt. He went from house to house and for a certain, modest fee, he conciliated the stomachs of the Jews with their conscience. After that, Rabbi Leser's authority was completely established. Lasik blessed the praying men at the synagogue. He could not quite remember how to do that, but the Jews closed their eyes faithfully—and he could have even danced foxtrot.

He gave advice for family life. In Schwarzberg's restaurant

he gobbled up juicy cutlets. In short, he lived well and happy.

One day, having completed another heavy meal, he was walking with Herr Moiser on one of Frankfurt's narrow streets. Herr Moiser was asking Lasik whether there was any divergence in the Law regarding umbrellas.

"I do not understand why it is forbidden to carry an umbrella on the Sabbath. After all, it also rains on Sabbaths. I walk to the synagogue and I get wet. Have you ever spoken about it to the *Zadik* of Dwinsk?"

"But of course. And we have also found an excellent solution. When it rains, it begins to be dangerous. The rain is not better than any machine gun bullet, for you can catch a cold in the rain and die. According to the Law you may defend yourself when being attacked, and in such a case you are permitted to take a stick in your hand, even on the Sabbath. Well, the rain attacks you, and you have to defend yourself. In the interpretations of the Rabbis. . . ."

Lasik could not finish—a big, husky man had grabbed him by the hand:

"At last I have caught you! You scoundrel! Just look at the way he is all dressed up—with stolen things, eh? I will teach you to steal ham! . . ."

Herr Moiser made an attempt to intervene.

"You must be mistaken. This is a personality honored and revered by everybody. It is our Rabbi."

No, Lasik had no doubts: before him stood Otto Worms, in person. Well, of course, Mainz is no more than an arm's length from Frankfurt! . . . However, he had gotten so accustomed to his new part that he shouted at the angry butcher:

"Can't you hear—I am a Rabbi! And not merely a Rabbi, but even a *Cohenite*. Have you any idea, what a *Cohenite* is? That is the noblest tribe of all. I do not even have the right to visit a cemetery, so as not to make myself unhappy, and you dare bother me with your unclean ham! . . ."

Otto Worms burst into sarcastic laughter:

"Oh, so now, all of a sudden, it has become unclean? But when you swallowed it before my very eyes, it was quite clean, was it not? You dirty dog! Excuse me, sir, I do not know you, but I am sure you are an honest man. How can you be acquainted with such a tramp? I picked him up from the street out of sheer pity, and he tried to rob me of my property. I noticed it for a long time, that he was quietly busy around my liver sausages. But I have a soft heart, and I kept still. But when he tore off a piece of ham, right before my eyes, I could not stand it any longer. He got away, but now I am going to teach him a lesson with this stick."

Lasik did not deny it any longer. He merely said, with a guilty smile:

"You did not give me much to eat, Herr Worms, and the ham was nice and warm, anyone would understand that I could not resist."

Since all this did not occur on a Sabbath, Herr Moiser had an umbrella in his hand, and he took the lead, even before the butcher. By the way, Otto Worms did not hesitate either. They beat Lasik—one with the umbrella, the other with the stick, one from the left, the other from the right, until he rolled down the sidewalk.

28

Lewka, the barber, used to hum whenever he got a soapy brush into somebody's ear: "Yes, Paris! Yes, Paris! Where on earth is another such paradise!" and Lasik remembered it, now that he was standing on the square in front of the Opera.

"Well, I am standing on this corner. But how shall I get across to the other side? This is the most unexpected suicide! Sooner or later, I will have to cross the street. One cannot stand forever on the same corner. One car, ten cars, a hundred cars, but where is a passage for the little Roitschwantz?"

Finally, Lasik tried to step down from the sidewalk into the busy street, but he immediately retracted his foot as though it had touched boiling water.

"This is even worse than that raging Arabian stallion!"

Suddenly he noticed a policeman with a sign on his sleeve: "Speaks German." Lasik approached him meekly:

"Herr Learned Secretary! Don't you think these vehicles are blocking the traffic a little? For instance, I have to cross the street for some reason. However, my not yet expired life is still worth something to me."

"Wait a moment. When I raise my stick, the red light will go on, and a bell will ring. Then you may cross."

Lasik waited. Indeed, a few moments later things happened just as promised. The automobiles froze on the spot. The square was deserted at once, and the pedestrians ran, like a startled herd, from one side to the other. Lasik liked it very much. He repeated this interesting procedure several times. After that, he was so impressed, he approached the policeman once again:

"May I touch your magic wand? It is forbidden? Aren't you, dear sir, the Moses of the Parisian Laws? Because Moses played such tricks too, when the Jews were crossing the sea. What? I have to move along? All right, I shall go, but please just raise your baton once more, so the waves will ebb away from me."

Lasik began to deliberate. What now? To be sure, here in Paris they had learned secretaries and Arabian horses and bananas and such a tower of science that one could scatter about all the opium, for it surely went up to the sky; and it was already proven that up there is—no God—only a wireless telephone. But what should the lonely Roitschwantz do? To begin with, they spoke an altogether different language. Of all the words used in Homel, the only one they understood here was *merci;* but there also has to be something for which one says *merci.*

While meditating, Lasik suddenly thought he heard someone speaking Russian. He did not miss the opportunity:

"Very pleased to hear this exalted language in the midst of these Arabs. Are you perhaps also from Homel?"

The tall gentleman examined Lasik with a critical look:

"Get lost! You did not come upon the right person!"

"Aha, I understand. You are not from Homel, but quite the opposite. But why be angry right away? I am merely a harmless Moscovite soul, and I am not yet acquainted with the ceremonies around here. If you wish, I can sew magnificent Tolstoy blouses for you, so you will look not like one, but two deceased dukes! All right, so you are not interested. Period. I do not even want to mention the rabbits. But, among other things, I can dance the delinquent foxtrot, especially since there is such an Arabian life around. Why are you shouting? I am not deaf-and-dumb. And you are wrong if you think you can simply run away and leave me here to die. I will catch up with you, anyway. Besides, I know how to jump. You wish to know what I want from you? Very simple—I want to live. That is, what we call the 'Maximal Program' in our basic political course. Until then, however, some foreign credit, I mean fifty Parisian kopeks to buy a portion of wretched cutlets will do. You are asking, what the basic political course has to do with it? Everything. Here, you are the foundation, and I would like to be the superstructure . . ."

"Go to your Bolsheviks! . . ."

"This is exactly what I cannot do, because I am coming from them. I had a position with Boris Samoilowitsch, and when they came to arrest him, there was nothing left for me to do but disappear with the speed of a bullet. Do you think I have not been a party-candidate? Ridiculous! I could have become an imposing Commissar, but the whole thing was messed up because of the leg of Comrade Serebrjakow, and they threw me out in a jiffy."

By now, the Russians did not try to get rid of Lasik. No indeed, they slowed down their steps. They began to question him: how long since he had left Russia, how long had he been in the party, what positions had he held there, whom had he seen? Lasik lied, saying what came into his head.

"The devil knows what they are up to. Either they are related to that horrible female, Pukke, or there is something Polish about it."

When Lasik told them he had been on intimate terms with Comrade Serebrjakow, that he had smuggled machine-gun belts across the border, that he had been elected to become the "Learned Secretary of the Communist Academy" in Moscow, and that it all ran afoul because of his feelings, since he, Lasik, after a great deal of thinking and deliberation, had broken into the Kremlin one night (well, what do you know!), offending a thousand flags—the tall gentleman whispered to his companion:

"This talkative Hebrew could be of good use to us . . ."

Lasik sensed a change. He became bolder:

"Well yes, I have also talked to Trotzky, about that Chinese manslaughter, without mincing words. . . . But now, I would like to ask you something else: when do people eat dinner around here? The last dinner I ate was exactly four days ago. After that there were only jumpy border-crossings, and a new horizon. By the way, I smell a wonderful aroma, coming out of this café. Do you know how it smells? Maybe you think it smells of coffee or cheap lemonade? No, I bet, it smells of calf's liver in cream sauce with onions, yet."

"Listen to us. If you are really a repentant Bolshevik, we are ready to assist you in restoring your good name."

"I can be as penitent as no other man. I have started to repent already two years ago, because of Pfeifer's trousers, and since that time that is all I am doing. As to my good name, you do not have to worry either: in the worst case, if the fashion is different here, I can always cut out the 'Roit.' Then I am a plain 'Schwantz' without any party designation."

"You will give a public lecture. That is very simple. We shall instruct you what to say. And the admission price flows straight into your pocket. First of all, we would like to acquaint you with our National position."

At this point, Lasik became harsh and implacable.

"No! Before anything, you will acquaint me with this aroma. We shall go into the café and there we can effect your national change of position."

"Well, why not? We can have an appetizer. Waiter, three 'Bitter-picons.' "

Lasik got excited:

"Gentlemen, please no Arabian tricks. You want me to give a thundering lecture, and here you treat me to nothing but damp anecdotes!"

Ignat Alexandrowitsch Blagowerow, the tall gentleman, editor of the nationalistic newspaper *Russian Beacon,* smiled condescendingly.

"Everybody drinks that here. It's good for the appetite."

Lasik jumped up, stamping his feet furiously:

"*Good* for the appetite? That is good for a criminal offense! I am ready to kill someone as is, but after this drink, I will kill him for sure. Kindly order liver in cream sauce or at least a big roll, or else I will drink this provoking concoction and wind up slaughtering the whole city of Paris!"

After having gobbled up a piece of bread and butter, Lasik remarked sensitively:

"You will go bankrupt, since my appetite is continuing. If I were not hungry, do you think I would even talk to you? I would rather cross the streets from morning till night on that famous square. Sausages? Excellent! Now you may proceed with your dislocation of troops."

Ignat Alexandrowitsch cleared his throat significantly:

"First of all you do not have to worry . . . how shall I put it . . . I mean, about your origin. In this organization we already have another Jew in our employ. When he saw what happened to the so-called freedoms, he himself came to us, begging forgiveness. He was crying: 'I shake like Judas. The Jews have sold out our Mother Russia. Where are the remains of the Saint Pitirim? Where is the sound of bells of the forty-four . . .' We have forgiven him. He is now working on our newspaper, in the ad department. Thus, you need not have the slightest worry. We shall treat you as a lucky exception. The leader of our great movement is His Highness, the Emperor . . ."

At this point Lasik interrupted Ignat Alexandrowitsch:

"Do I have to pull in my stomach, or does it suffice if I do it in my thoughts? For, after all these sausages, it will not be too easy . . ."

But Ignat Alexandrowitsch did not listen to him. Full of pathos, he was reciting the latest article from *The Russian Beacon*: "Tremble in your dungeons, you henchmen of Miljukow! The whole civilized world and forty eons of great Russian history are on our side. The Romanoffs have created Russia, and the people of our entire orthodox country hold their breath awaiting the majestic step of our illustrious Highness! Right?"

"Of course. Pfeifer can hardly wait. All day long he looks out the window. And also in regard to the breathing, you are quite right. Who will dare breathe over there when the illustrious steps will be heard here?"

After two more drinks of "Picon," Ignat Alexandrowitsch patted Lasik benevolently on the shoulder:

"Nice Jew! Good thing you landed with us without any detours, instead of joining the *Free Voice*. There they have nothing but Tcheka people. One Jew abuses the other. Besides they pay only a fiver per line. With us, however, you will fare well. First thing, tomorrow we shall publish an interview. Wassilij Andrejewitsch please make a note: Fat Print: Confession of a Tchekist. Start as follows: 'Yesterday a henchman with a tear-stained face forced his way into our editor's office' . . . What is your name? . . . Oh yes, the henchman 'Schwantz.' He cried: 'I am begging forgiveness of all innocent widows and orphans.

All of oppressed Russia listens to the beat of your *Beacon.* In Kargopol a desperate crowd has practically torn to pieces the Jewish Commissar.' Well, from there you can go on . . . Just do not forget to mention the *Free Voice*: (In Pensa everyone is shocked about Miljukow's provocation.) Give it to them. Listen, you little Jew! I will pay you again tomorrow for the interview. You will get twenty francs, my word of honor!"

Ignat Alexandrowitsch's companion, who had kept still like a fish up to then, suddenly opened his mouth:

"Ignat Alexandrowitsch, you have not paid me my salary for two months. Winter is almost here, and I am still walking around in my summer coat . . ."

"Little brother, we shall talk about that later. Now we have to discuss important business. Now listen, Schwantz, you will get one or another hundred for your lecture. But that is only a one-time thing. You understand, of course, you cannot give lectures every day. And you could earn a good bit of money. You have your connections over there, and we need reliable people everywhere. You should engage in organizational work."

"Sure, why not. I could do that quite well. I have raised dead rabbits in Tula, and I can also make the best harvest out of you. Let us suppose you are two, if we don't count that other step. Now all we need is a pencil. Next fall you may increase to 612,438 head. It is only a matter of multiplication and a monthly salary."

After the fourth "picon", Ignat Alexandrowitsch's legs became heavy. Quite sentimentally, he whispered:

"You are quite a guy, Schwantz! Though a Hebrew, you love your little Mother Russia. I will make you into something. In the *Beacon*, yes, you will be salaried per line. And for the organizational work—a fixed salary, commission, daily expenses and traveling money. Then I will introduce you to the Rumanians. Nice fellows! They receive you politely, not like the Englishmen who let you wait in a waiting-room. No, they shake your hand, offer you cigarettes. And what's more, they pay promptly and in dollars. You have to tell them about Kargopol. And also the story of the machine guns. However, if they start to talk about Bessarabia, you just smile. How do you think I won them over? With a smile, of course. I told them, 'What do we need your Bessarabia? I used to have a little estate near Kaluga, and I am crying day and night that you did not march as far as Kaluga.' You understand? We have learned diplomacy around here. I and Wassiliji Andrejewitch here, that is our entire army-corps, haha!"

"A Parisian merci to you! Of course, to travel to Rumania is not for me. I have had enough of the Polish music. However, here we shall understand each other perfectly. After all, I am also one of your army corps. I have already given Tula to the Poles. So why should I not give Kaluga to the Rumanians?"

The four "picons" had at last roused Ignat Alexandrowitsch's appetite, and he decided it was time to eat. The silent Wassiliji Andrejewitsch took Lasik to the restaurant "Boyar's Harem." Lasik remembered the summer coat and he asked cautiously:

"Perhaps you resemble Archip Stoikij, I mean, you are in the habit of forgetting your wallet at home? In such case I must tell you that I have a hole in my pocket."

"Do not worry!"

Wassiliji Andrejewitsch beat his chest tenderly: "I stayed behind to warn you. This Blagowerow is a shrewd beast. He will squeeze everything out of you—and then he will grab you by the neck. He always does that. But soon he himself will be out. And then I will become chief. Well, what do you expect? He is busy with one thing only: he found a Hebrew whom he is using as a cover and through him he sells certain manure to the Bolsheviks. A fine patriot, indeed! And as to the Rumanians, he is lying too. Look, I liked you from the first moment I saw you. But those Rumanians—they are nothing but cheats. You won't get ten francs out of them. I tell you what. I will offer you something else. But first come—let us have a bite to eat."

"I have already chosen you, and not that Rumanian from Kaluga. I also liked you, if not at first glance, then at least from the first word. One can see right away that you are the better patriot, you don't begin with some dung, but with a real bite. But what are they serving here? Well, even Frau Drekkenkopf would not have dreamed of it! . . ."

"Oh yes, one does not eat badly here. Now, try this caviar—it is just like from home, from Astrachan. I supply this restaurant with it. I get it from a Bolshevik rascal and sell it here. After all, one has to live. Now let us talk business. You will hardly be satisfied with the *Beacon*. I shall introduce you to decent people. Not just people—but pure golden people. Check from Reval. Do you know Reval?"

Lasik was thinking.

"Did you say Reval? Aren't those sprats?"

"My friend, they are not just sprats. They are also English pounds—that is, it's a state unto itself! All you have to do is tell them three words about Trotzky, and you have the check in your pocket. Agreed? Another drink? Here's to you! To our national movement! To His . . ."

"Have pity on my stomach! I cannot keep pulling it in all the time. Let us rather drink to the sprats."

"Hurrah!"

At first Lasik took it bravely. He drank vodka, ate Beef Stroganoff, and carried on a friendly conversation with Wasiliji Andrejewitsch.

"Here it is just the same like at the 'Venetia.' By the way, please tell me, where is the exit?"

"Yes indeed, this here is still a little corner of old Russia. The traditions of a nation are a great thing. Do you know who is waiting on us? A colonel. Yes, by God! And those ladies! . . . Tatjana Larina! I love you, why all these words . . . Simple, like turpentine. Yes, we will show this rascal, Blagowerow! . . .

Here, meet our agent of the ad department, Mr. Grinstock."

Lasik became more cheerful:

"In Homel, we also have a Grinstock. He is the chief of the Nursery for Exceptional Children. Aren't you related to him?"

Mr. Grinstock fenced Lasik off:

"I have no relations whatsoever among those bloody henchmen."

And he bent down to Lasik, whispering to him:

"And even if it is my own brother, why these questions? Don't you see I have to collect ads for them? Today I got three: two neighbors and one from a doctor of venereal diseases. Now I have money for supper."

In the meantime, Wassiliji Andrejewitsch plied him with so many questions that thinking became difficult for Lasik.

"Give me at least ten names of famous bolsheviks. You see, we are preparing lists, so we will know who is to be liquidated, when the time comes.

"Ten names? And how many drinks were there? Well then, write: Trotzky, Roitschwantz, Boris Samoilowitsch . . . More? All right. Rabbits—that is a party-nickname. Hindenburg. Drekkenkopf. Sprats. No, I am not drunk at all, that is also a name, and now enough of that torture. What do you think I am—an address book? I know, you want to give it all to the Estonians, and they will give you a check for it. But what do I get out of it?"

He was completely drunk, and he went on shouting:

"I am a Rumanian guard! I am an intimate friend of Trotzky! I want nothing but machine guns."

They beat him. They shook him. He could not remember a thing.

As Wassilij Andrejewitch testified afterwards, he seized a can of sprats and tried to put a sprat into everyone's mouth. He then began shouting:

"The check is ready! . . . Let's give them Paris with all its

Arabian horses! . . . Long live the Steppe! . . ."

Glasses, bottles, tables were flying. At last they got Lasik out into the street. A policeman appeared. Wassiliji Andrejewitsch defended his boon-companion:

"It is nothing, he just had a little too much to drink! He was a henchman, and he repents. He is looking for comfort. A Slav soul!"

The policeman listened and then took Lasik by the hand. He took him to the nearest toilet. In Lasik's dim consciousness, a tiny glow of awareness appeared. Full of enthusiasm, he bellowed at the officer:

"You are the only one who understands me. Merci! and once again, merci!"

29

Directly before the lecture, Lasik was suddenly overcome by sadness. He had to make an effort to climb up onto the high bed of the cheap, little room Wassilij Andrejewitsch had found for him. He yielded to despondent thoughts:

"I used to be an honest tailor. On the Great Holiday, the First of May, I would march with all the other tailors, and above us fluttered the not-yet-offended flag, with its silver thimble. And now I have sunk as low as those crazy sprats. Ah, Madam Pukke—you see, I am talking Parisian to you, not any other way, but Madam—ah, Madam Pukke, what have you done to the miserable Roitschwantz? Now I must run with my very own feet to that full-fledged pogrom, as though I was not familiar with their Swedish gymnastics."

In a melancholy mood, Lasik opened his shirt collar, closed one eye and proceeded to examine his body, which was black and blue from top to bottom.

"This one here is still a Polish one . . . Those two, however, are from the time of the cod liver oil . . . This one? I cannot remember . . . Perhaps after the conversation about the ham, but it might also have been because of the monkey tail . . . Well, and these over here are Parisian. . . . It might be interesting to ask a philosophical doctor how much an ordinary Jewish skin can take. I, for instance, have the impression that I am not capable of taking it any longer. But the whole misery comes from the fact that one blue spot lies on top of another, and so it becomes an eternal earth rotation. It is time to leave! In my stomach the melodies are starting up again, and Karl Marx did not grow a beard in vain. He understood a few things up to the very end. Instead of all the learned words, one might say: 'The appetite moves the many-shaped human race ahead.'"

When Lasik came to this point, he closed his eyes, and out of nowhere chopped cutlets with potatoes appeared before him. He tried to recall how they smelled? . . . He lay there for a long time, thinking once again of Frau Dreckendorf's dumplings, the greaven at Drawkin's wedding and the aroma of sausages. Only the fury in Wassilij Andrejewitsch's voice brought him back to reality:

"Have you lost your senses? . . . Everybody is waiting out there, and you are dozing! . . ."

Indeed, there were about thirty people in the audience. Old men, who could have been taken for valets, were sitting in the first row. They chewed liquorice sticks and snored every now and then. In the background, young people were humming gaily, showing off their new tight fitting jackets. Ignat Alexandrowitsch came out on stage. He was the permanent chairman of the society "Cross and Scepter."

"I am giving the floor to the penitent Bolshevik, Lazar Matwejewitsch Schwantz. He will inform us about the national movement in our homeland. I am asking all widows and widowers present to preserve absolute calm. Though Schwantz has many a dark spot on his conscience, nevertheless he has confessed honestly and is ready to return to the homeland, to clear his earlier disgrace through active warfare against the oppressors."

Lasik threw a dejected glance at the audience, the chandelier, the table with the green cloth, the jug of water and the bell. Then he looked at himself. Too late! Nothing could be changed now. . . . He got up, bowing politely in all directions. He smiled.

"Comrades . . ."

As an answer, the young people began to shout threats. Lasik was worried.

"Excuse me, every now and then a Homel idiom escapes my lips. Of course, I know that there are no Comrades here, but since we are talking about it, can you tell me how I should address you? My Herr Police Doctors or Pane Cavalry Captains?"

Ignat Alexandrowitsch rang his bell.

"You should address the audience: *My very honorable ladies and gentlemen.*"

"Very well. Ladies and gentlemen, though I must admit I do not see any ladies here, except for one in the second row. I shall start with the national minorities since that blond young man over there is already calling me a Hebrew. Well, I am not a Hebrew, but merely a humble Moses under the laws of his Highness. Let us make a historical cut. Of course, there are Hebrews. They sew trousers shamelessly or even lead the bloody nursery for little children in Homel. They laugh impudently because they have sold out Christ and also our little Mother

Russia, altogether for perhaps thirty silver rubles. However, the very respected Mr. Grinstock over there certainly does not sell out our Little Mother—on the contrary, he moves ahead in a national spirit. He collects venereal ads for the *Russian Beacon.* Thus he is not a Hebrew but rather a nice, respectable Moses. Therefore I request the fair-haired young man to calm down, for I do not like it when people shout. At the moment I am just like Mr. Grinstock, and you must listen to me with the fullest respect."

Voices in the background could be heard:

"Tschekist! Henchman! What, isn't he going to confess? . . . Such a disgrace! . . ."

Ignat Alexandrowitsch had to ring the bell.

"This place is at our disposal until twelve o'clock. Besides we have to keep in mind the subway. I am requesting the honored audience to be sober-minded. And I am also asking you, Lazar Matwejewitsch, in view of the late hour, to begin with your confession."

"As if that was easy! I have forgotten what you told me to say, and I do not know what to confess to? Of course, I could confess to the case of the sprats, but then why did they have to give me one drink after another? Furthermore, even though I had thrown the little fish all over the place, another man threw a great, big kitchen table at me! And you will admit, it was much heavier! . . ."

The fair-haired young man would not be quiet.

"How many people have you shot, you Tschekist dog?!"

"Mister chairman, this respectable blond young man has to stop interrupting my train of thought, or else I will not continue with my speech. I was just going to explain the conditions in our homeland, and he has decreed already that I am a dog. Furthermore, it is unfair to be needled with foolish questions. What has this got to do with shooting? I am not a sharpshooter. I am a tailor. However, if this young man threatens to hit me in my mouth, I am ready to say that I have shot all seven thousand. I stood there shooting with the machine gun, and, of course, they fell and the most terrible bullets went through them, and they were crying: 'What kind of tricks are these, you Tschekist dog? If you do not stop shooting at us with your cannons, we will call the Militia.' However, I remained deaf to the pleas of those orphans. I shot Pfeifer who was wearing the trousers I had tailored so artistically. Now are you satisfied? And now, I shall proceed to discuss the current matters. About the events in Kargopol, you have read enough in the papers, and besides, I have never really studied much geography. Why insist on details when we have to keep in mind a certain subway? Suffice it to say that the whole Mother Russia is holding her breath, waiting for you. You are being expected so impatiently that if, for instance, the mailman rings, or what is worse, the washerwoman comes to pick up the dirty wash, everybody meets him or her with pansies, and afterwards they cry because it was not the white horse, but merely the dirty underwear . . .

"And what about *steppe*? Indeed it is hard to mention it without breaking into tears. Let us suppose, Titschenko is coming up the stairs; right away Boris Samoilowitsch whispers to me: 'Did you hear that step?' I just do not understand one thing: why aren't you coming? It is cruel to play around with human patience! I, for instance, was faithful to Fenia Hershanowitsch, even though she was warbling with Schatzman. But how long could I wait, with my build? I waited and waited, but then I discovered Nussja, and everything fell off the chair, and goodbye! In my opinion it is time for you to get started, first to that relentless subway, and after that to the Little Mother herself."

The young people had left their seats, crowding around the stage.

"What a disgrace! . . . Such nonsense! . . . How dare he, that scoundrel! . . . We shall teach him a lesson! . . ."

"Please! You must give the speaker a chance to finish his lecture," the chairman shouted.

"Down with him! To hell with him! . . ."

The bell rang desperately. Lasik covered his face with his hands.

"You want me to finish? I am all finished. What? I must go on? All right, I shall try. I would like to speak about the national change of position. It goes without saying, the Bolsheviks are traitors, and such an opportunity must not be passed by. They do not get foreign credits? That is because they do not know what language to speak. However, right here is your fabulous army corps, and I know now how to proceed. It is possible to have two factions in one party, why, even ten. That happens in Homel, too. The main thing is that all raise their hands at the same time. Then, and only then, an iron discipline can be achieved.

"What is the difference, for instance, between Ignat Alexandrowitsch and Wassilij Andrejewitsch. One goes to the Rumanians and gives them Bessarabia, while the other receives checks from the sprats. One can go to the Rumanians as well as to the sprats. It is only a question of legs. However, as far as I can see, one cannot live in Paris on thirty silver pieces, when they serve hot Beef Stroganoff in this harem. I implore you, take away your fists! I am making a very concrete proposal: how would it be, for instance, to pack Moscow into a tiny bundle and take it away . . . What have your hands got to do with that? And if you insist on beating me, will you please do it on my posterior, so I do not have to see the bloody traces: Help! You will be late for the subway! . . ."

All of a sudden, Lasik had a lucky idea. He grabbed the jug from the table and poured the water on his audience. When there was no water left, he threw the jug, then the glass and finally the bell. Hearing the noise, the janitor appeared.

"Ladies and gentlemen, this hall is rented until midnight. Will you kindly disperse at once!"

Lasik was the first one to obey. Swiftly he disappeared through the door. However, his head turned up again:

"Honorable chairman, where is the net profit for two or three empty sandwiches?"

30

A thin, small Jew approached Lasik in the street, saying in a friendly voice:

"Oh, here you are! . . . Perhaps you need a band-aid? I always carry one with me. I am the reporter from the *Free Voice.* It is part of my job to attend all the refugee meetings."

"Band-aid? You are joking! What I need is an ambulance-dressing; in the meantime, however, I could do with five francs for a bite."

"Come with me to the *Rotonde*—there you will fortify yourself. Well, have you seen for yourself what a despicable bunch that is? You should have come to us. We may perhaps believe in a Patriarch, but we certainly do not arrange any pogroms. After all, you have not been here for too long. Having just arrived, fresh from Russia, you surely know what they are really waiting for. The Grand Duke has certainly nothing to do with it. Over there they are only waiting for the elections to Parliament. You have not noticed that? Well, of course you are still intimidated. If you stay here another year or so, you will notice it. We understand that there are some conscientious people working over there, too. After all, one has to be able to separate the wheat from the chaff. We are not the kind who condemn everyone without discrimination. Take, for instance, the writers. They have sold themselves, of course. But yet, there are exceptions. Who among us does not respect Pushkin or even Aiwasowsky? Well, I can tell you, we will have no difficulty understanding each other. You will give a short lecture."

Lasik interrupted him:

"Not for the finest bananas! I would rather jump around with a tail!"

"No, no! Do not get upset! Here, take a few sandwiches to refresh you. Afterwards we can go directly to the editor's office. I shall introduce you to the chief of the trade paper. He is a clever man, with a brilliant mind, a famous social thinker. He is known all over Europe. He will explain everything to you much better than I. You see, I am not a politician, I am really a business agent. For instance, if you should need a small apartment for a very low rent or genuine ladies' stockings, twenty-seven francs a pair, just remember Suesskind."

The chief of the trade paper, Sergej Michailowitsch Agramow received Lasik very politely. He questioned him in detail about the harvest conditions, about the progress of the opposition inside the Red Army, about prices for rubber articles, even about the number of abortions, whereby, as a matter of fact, he would answer his own questions. He made Lasik curious:

"You really are a European mind! I look and I cannot stop marveling: How can you talk and write at the same time? That must really be a difficult trick! But may I ask you, what kind of dictionary you are writing?"

"I am merely writing down what you told me."

What *I* told you? Well, these are two tricks already. I have not opened my mouth at all."

"Here, listen carefully: 'A conversation with an outstanding Soviet expert. To our first question, as to the atmosphere in Moscow, X answered promptly: The *Russian Beacon* does not rate at all. The population is waiting impatiently . . .' "

"You do not have to read any further. The fellow with the ladies' stockings has already explained to me what the abundant population expects."

Agramow looked compassionately at Lasik:

"I can see you are completely contaminated by the Bolshevik disease. That is terrible! . . . Pioneers! . . . October children . . . corruption and perversion of the young minds . . ."

"Excuse me, Mr. Sociologist, but I am already thirty-three, and I was even married one and a half times, if I may count the matter with the dumplings for half a marriage."

"You are thirty-three? Well, you are half as young as I. Politically, you are a baby! How terrible, that such a great country is being ruled by children! I know, you will quote Marx. But are you acquainted with the basic material? A country with a backward economy can have no claim to world supremacy. Those dogs think they have discovered America. They came to power by sheer accident. They have robbed me of my professor's desk and position. They will be annihilated. And I can prove it to you in figures."

"No, please do not prove anything to me. I am very poor with numbers. I spent all of three days counting rabbits. Furthermore, why should you, at such a respectable age, bother with a certain arithmetic? Do you think, I am not sorry for you? Very much so. You, such a European arithmetician, are going bankrupt with ladies' stockings. I understand your learned sorrow. Naturally, I cannot argue with you, since you have surely completed four foreign universities, while I was merely fed opium for thirty years. All I really know of the entire Marx is the fact and his beard. However, I do understand a few things. Marx was not the only one who had a beard. I could, for instance, enlighten your belated situation with a story from the Talmud. Now, you certainly cannot say the Talmud is a Bolshevik invention. No indeed! They even wanted to suppress the Talmud at the *Good Taste* and it is older than you. It tells also about Moses' death.

"I do not think I need dwell upon that personality too long. As you are the chief of a department, there are about ten or twenty people with good brains working here with you. But, you see, Moses was all of you put together: a sociologist like you, a general and even a writer. In short, a European mind! But since the Jews were lost for twenty years in the desert—a small matter, you know!—he could not help getting older, and the time came, when he, and please do not take it personally, had to die. God said to him very calmly: 'Moses, you shall die!' But he replied: 'No, I do not want to.' Well, you know, that is understandable! . . . And so they argued day and night. When I read that in *Cheder*, my hair was standing on end. Finally, God became tired of it. He said: 'You were the recognized leader of my people, but now you are old and you must die. I already have a candidate waiting. His name is Joshua. He is younger than you and he will become the official leader.' Moses shook with anger, all over his body. He said: 'But I do not want to die. All right, so I will not be the leader. I will merely be a shepherd. Only, please let me live a while longer.' Now, God was really embarrassed. You see, at that time, there were very few people on earth, and he was probably not used to people dying. And so it was decided: the old Moses should drive the sheep to pasture, the young Joshua, however, would be the official leader. Can you imagine the humbling and insult?! That was worse than your professor's lecture desk! And so the miserable Moses was herding sheep on the pasture all day long. In the evening, they all gathered around the fire, discussing many wise and baffling problems. Naturally, they all wait for Moses to begin his lecture, but he remains silent. He is pale like the wall, and tears are running down his cheeks. And he says: 'I am old, and not wanted any more. Here is your Joshua. He knows everything from now on—how to leave the desert, which way to go, how to get mannah, how to live, rejoice and how to cry.' The people, well—are just people. They sigh a little, as a matter of form, and then turn to Joshua. At that time, however, Joshua was already busy discussing with God the current affairs. Moses was so used to those conversations that he tried to listen in. But no, he cannot hear a thing. He becomes impatient, and calls out to Joshua: 'Well, what did God say?' Joshua is still young, therefore he is eager to quarrel. He is not interested in an old man's tears. And so he replies: 'Whatever he said, he said. When you were the official leader, I did not ask you either what you were saying to God. No, indeed! I have only obeyed you, and now it is your turn to obey me.' And Joshua began his first lecture. Moses notices that Joshua is still young—that he does not know certain things, forgets others—and he tries to meddle. However, the old fire in him is gone, he cannot find the old wisdom, nor the right words. He speaks, but the people do not understand him any longer. Only yesterday, they had carried him on their shoulders, and today they say: 'Old man, your place is with the sheep.' Well, Moses could not take that. Who knows how much he loved life, how little he wanted to die! And yet, he could not survive the time allotted to him. He shouted so loudly, it pierced all the clouds. 'All right, I shall argue no more. I shall die.' Of course, Mr. Sociologist, you are not Moses, and I certainly do not wish for you to die before your time. No, I know every human being wants to live, even I, notwithstanding the fact that I am a miserable dwarf. But you must not be angry at some insolent pioneer. It is not his fault that he is only fifteen years old. He is young, a loudmouth, and he does not give a damn for the whole world. Maybe he is organizing ethnological dances on your professor's desk! What can you do—there is no justice on earth. But if you are such a clever man, why are you calling to him: 'Away with you!' You know, he will not leave. You are the one who is left, and you are with the sheep, period. You had better order a bottle of wine, and let us drink to our dead youth."

Agramow closed his eyes ironically:

"Your comparison does not stand any criticism. Parallels are generally very dangerous in history. In the case before us, it was an evolution, a change of generation, progress. In our own case, however it was a violent overthrow. The revolution is a crime, communism a childish venture. Only very uneducated people can believe in Utopia. The contemporary sociology . . ."

"Hold it! You want to kill me once again with your oaken professor's desk? After all, I am no celebrity. I am talking to you in all sincerity, and you are making a whole discussion of it. Do you think I do not know what a revolution is? You had better ask me how many times I was in prison. If not for these historical events, I would still be peacefully pressing the trousers of my dear friend Pfeifer. I am certainly not in raptures about this revolution. It is neither my sister, nor Fenitschka Hershanowitsch. But I cannot go around shouting: 'Forbid the clouds!—because I, Roitschwantz, am afraid of a storm, and I even hide my head under the pillow!' Of course, a storm is a great annoyance, but they say it is necessary for certain atmospheric conditions, not to mention the rain, which waters all the vegetable gardens. You are asking me in vain about the heretic tendencies among the officers or the revolts in Buchara. I know nothing about it, and besides you will describe it in your own way regardless. I would much rather tell you another story of that same Moses. It may fit our argument. Moses was a young man, at that time. He was not yet a leader, but surely a candidate. All of a sudden, God said to him: 'Go and tell him to set the Jews free.' Moses hurried to the Egyptian castle, pushed all the guards aside and said to the Pharaoh:

" 'Set the Jews free, at once, or else!' "

"The Pharaoh blinked his eyes, just like you are doing now:

" 'What kind of rude Utopia is that? Who are you anyway?'

" 'I am ambassador of the Jewish God Jehovah.'

" 'Jehovah?'

"The Pharaoh wrinkled his forehead.

" 'Je-ho-vah? I do not know such a God. Hey, you learned secretaries, get me the complete list of all gods!'

"The secretaries brought him a whole library, for in those times there were more gods than are wise heads nowadays, as for instance, your own. Day and night, all the Egyptian scholars were looking through the lists.

"There was a god with a dog's mouth, and one with a fish tail, but no trace of one 'Jehovah.' The Pharaoh laughed heartily:

" 'Well, what did I tell you? There is no such god, or he would be listed in our books, and you are a shameless rascal! Out with you!'

"But of course, my dear Mr. Sociologist, you know that Pharaoh had a very bad end. What are you writing again? The fact about the Pharaoh?"

"No. I have no time for historical anecdotes. I shall finish the interview with you, as follows: 'X. also reported that the higher schools exist under conditions impossible to describe. The new universities are examples of negligence, ignorance, and rowdyism. The old desks, where professors used to lecture, are now occupied by half-ignoramuses.' I believe I have expressed your thoughts correctly. Now you may go."

Lasik sighed.

"May those be my thoughts! You have completed four universities, and I cannot change your mind anyway. At least, please count all the lines, or to make it simpler, just give me a twenty franc note."

Agramow looked at Lasik in surprise:

"What francs? What lines? You have nothing to do with it, after all. This is *my article*. Will you kindly remove yourself at once from these premises."

31

"**Where** to go? Cross the square back and forth, until I am run over by some absent-minded Arabian? Or shall I climb that high tower of wisdom and then hurl myself down? It does not matter, sooner or later one has to die anyway. Well yes, but there is a difference. It is easier to die after one has had good food and drinks, and a good conversation. Then you cannot even call it death, but rather an interesting slumber on a divan. However, to die on an empty stomach is uninteresting. Just now I am really not prepared for such musical moments. Of course, everyone will see a sad little man flying down from the tower, and they will take off their hats: there he goes, thinking of mountain peaks. But I, as a wretched ne'er-do-well, will think at that very moment of yesterday's sandwiches at the Rotonde. If you lift the uppermost layer—what an exciting surprise—for instance, cheese or even a liver paste. . . . No, I am not ready to die as yet, and the best thing to do is to go to the Rotonde. Perhaps I will find that fellow Suesskind there, with his stockings. I will see whether or not I can extort from him, if not the entire surprise, at least the uppermost layer."

Lasik entered the Rotonde timidly. As soon as he had looked around, he became cheerful. To be sure, Suesskind was not there. However, he noticed several other guests, who might be of use. They distinguished themselves from other Parisians by their dirty shirts and melancholy eyes.

"They must surely hail from Homel or its surroundings."

Lasik approached the first table.

"Are you, by any chance, from Homel?"

"Not at all. I happen to be from Kremenchug."

"Well, the apple does not grow too far from there. I thought you must be from that area. But, tell me, in what directions do your interest go hereabouts? Ladies' stockings or is it interior decoration?"

"You really are backward in Homel! Who deals in stockings any more, or even with cupboards? Are you going to say, perhaps, that I am still using apples—or bottles? As though last year's fashion would still be possible today! When I need a still-life, I do not have to think long. I take a piece of meat, or a bird, or even a rabbit."

Lasik became excited, he tried to embrace the melancholy stranger.

"Me too! Me too! We have the same kind of soul!"

The stranger wrinkled his forehead suspiciously:

"Do you intend, perhaps, to imitate me? That trick will not

succeed! I am being robbed aplenty as it is, even without you. I will not show you my paintings anyway. But even if I would, you could not do a thing regardless. This is the end of bare dabbling! Now every decent picture dealer demands feelings in the paintings. See, over there at the other table—that is Lentschuk. He always copies me. And over there, the man in the reddish-brown hat—that is Monkin. He has stolen my piece of roast and simply moved it to one side. But, thank goodness, the dealers know. They have a nose and they can smell the difference. They can see my meat trembling as though it were real. They are not stupid if they still pay me for my fifteenth piece a thousand two hundred."

The others at the table nodded consent.

"Yes, his meat tinkles . . . At the autumn exhibition there was such a crowd in front of his paintings, they had to post a policeman."

"You do not seem to know who you are talking to? This is Rosenpupp, his name is on all the fences and billboards. There is so much written about him that one cannot even read it all. This is what the critic Cuibon said publicly about him:

" 'Rosenpupp is a son of Renoir, and he will soon wipe out his father just like Zeus swallowed Chronos.' Beautiful, isn't it?"

"And all these untalented Monkins are trying to compete with him! But they sit in the Rotonde, drinking their miserable coffee, while even the Americans are interested in Rosenpupp."

Rosenpupp was in a mellow mood.

"Today one ought to have a drink. I have sold two pieces of meat, and I shall treat you. But with what shall we start? Beer or cognac?"

Lasik was not invited. Miserably he stood on the side. Finally he could not stand it, and he said:

"I beg your pardon, but please grant me the good fortune, permit me to sit next to you. I will just sit, and not drink anything. I would like to tell you that I idolize you. When I read your name on the billboard, tears came into my eyes, and I sobbed wildly. I will not even mention the meat. What does that idiot, Monkin, do anyway? He merely steals the leftovers. Yours, however, is a nice big, fat piece of meat. You think, we have not heard of you in Homel? There they always say, Kremenchug has surpassed all others. I, personally, have given a lecture about you. I said: 'This son of Zeus will swallow anything he wishes.' By the way, I am getting thirsty. I am sure you will invite me? I would like some coffee and those little pieces with the surprises; inside, they have liver paste or ham, and please, three coffees and five of those things. You do not have to be surprised—I am not a beggar. I have already eaten dinner today, and my name will also be on posters. It is just a habit of mine to swallow a whole bread in one gulp. You see, I am quite a character!"

After having gobbled up sandwiches and coffee, he decided it was time for an open discussion:

"Life here is extraordinarily pleasant. That is much more agreeable than to have to confess and repent before taking a certain step. But tell me, Monsur Rosenpupp, have you perhaps a butcher shop, including venison, or are you just a famous cook, because I did not quite understand two or three Parisian idioms you used."

In his rage, Rosenpupp broke all the glasses:

"How dare he make jokes, this nincompoop! And mind you, after five sandwiches! I had a feeling right away that he must be in cohort with Monkin and Lentschuk. If you are talking to the world's foremost artist, you must keep your mouth shut! I know you want to rob me! Steal my green rabbit or even the bull's pizzle. But you will not succeed! I will not let you across my threshold! Go packing, together with Lentschuk, and go on bribing the critics so they will ignore me! As though I do not know who is responsible for the silence following my exhibition!

Lentschuk and you! Who has alienated all the picture dealers from me so I cannot sell anything? Monkin and you. Go or else . . ."

Lasik preferred not to hear the threats to the very end. Why should he get into a bad mood after such delicious surprises? He got up quickly, said merci, and made his way over to Monkin.

"Monsur Monkin, we know each other. How? You do not know whom you have the pleasure of talking to? That is strange. I, for instance, know everything about you. I have already proclaimed in Moscow: 'Monkin has swallowed the Zeus.' We stood there, marveling at how your meat hums. Ridiculous, when this nitwit, Rosenpupp, tries to imitate you. You must surely be the owner of an American castle already, while he is a mere lack of talent. I was just sitting over there with him, telling him the whole truth frankly to his face, and he got so angry, he broke four glasses. With you, however, I am speaking as to an absolute equal. You want to know who I am? My name is Lasik Roitschwantz, and I am the second greatest artist in the world, if we assume you to be the first. We could organize a powerful union. To be sure, my name is not yet on the billboards, but that is merely because I am in hiding for the present. You see, I am being followed by real Americans. I am a secret celebrity. You want to know where my paintings are? At a dealer's. No, I am sorry, I cannot divulge his address. This is a terrible secret. I will tell it to you in a few days though. I will even take you along to that great store. But now, let us discuss the current affairs. No more drinking for me, but I must ask you to let me stay over night with you; for I have not yet found an adequate shelter in Paris. Don't be afraid, I will not rob you. I am not a worthless creature like Rosenpupp."

Monkin became cheerful:

"You really gave him the right name. Indeed, a worthless creature, that's what he is! And he even dares tell the critics that I am a dauber. He knows nothing of painting. He is so backward, it is even ridiculous to look at him. Indeed, nowadays one has to daub, the paint has to be applied in such manner that one can feel the meat. But he does not paint, he scribbles. He is a ridiculous upstart. He has alienated a dealer from me, saying: 'Just look, Monkin does not think about anything in his paintings.' But when you ask the same dealer, he will be the first one to tell you: 'Nowadays it is not necessary to think at all. It is only important that the meat trembles.' "

Lasik agreed wholeheartedly:

"It really is not worth while talking about Rosenpupp. He is an empty centimeter. I have been a follower of your thesis since my childhood. And we shall never get into an argument. In my opinion, it is possible to divide the world among two celebrities. I am not talking of empty bottles or apple sauce. Let us leave that to the Dreckenkopfs. But you will take the meat and cabbage and the dishes, and everything else you want, while I will put down only rabbit bananas, being an absolute specialist in that. And now, let us retire—I am a little tired from so many feelings."

The next morning, Monkin showed Lasik his work.

"Here! Look at that canvas! One simply flows from the other!"

Lasik closed one eye, then the other and said with the tone of an expert:

"Nice painting. I mean to say, it is full of genius, like Zeus. It trembles so that it is difficult to look at it on an empty stomach. Every single bite just crawls into your mouth. Tell me, please, where did you get such beautiful cutlets for models?"

Monkin was surprised:

"But these are not cutlets. This is my self-portrait. Besides, is resemblance really so important? Resemblance is out of style. I am just taking small parts and I enliven them. Do you understand? At the moment I have started a still-life with a duck. Just marvel at this juicy impression it gives: the duck, the carrots, on a background of olive-green velvet. I am only afraid the duck came out slightly dry."

Lasik glanced at the painting and asked quickly:

"But where is the live original?"

"Over there, on the table. Well, I've got to hurry. I don't have a single sou in my pocket, and I get absolutely no inspiration on an empty stomach. I have to go to all the dealers and try to sell this self-portrait—for at least fifty francs. That nitwit Rosenpupp has all the galleries full of his dung. You can stay here. If you should leave, put the key under the door."

Lasik stayed. He waited faithfully, two or three hours, for Monkin to return. Monkin, however, came back late in the evening. He found the key, as agreed, under the door. A letter was on the table:

"Dear Monsur Monkin! My word of honor, it was not my fault. You yourself were saying that there is no inspiration on an empty stomach. I repent, as I have not even repented at my lecture. But I am asking you: why did you leave me alone with her? I struggled for a very long while. How many times did I approach her, only to withdraw quickly! . . . Then I saw the alcohol-stove and the casserole-dish. You must forgive me. After all, you have started it already, and the details you will probably remember. You are not a pitiful Rosenpupp! I have also eaten the carrots, because it really does not taste as good without a vegetable. However, I have left the olive-green background absolutely intact. I know, I am a perjurer, worthy to be spat upon. But one must not joke with the appetite. Some day I will pay it back to you with interest. I shall give you all the world's dealers for a present. Meanwhile, however, may you blossom as the foremost celebrity, and do not think too badly of me. I am, your partner, Lasik Roitschwantz. P.S. You slandered her without reason. She was not overdone, or dry. She had lovely fat on her behind, I am even now licking my lips."

32

Two weeks had gone by, and everyone at the Rotonde knew our friend Lasik. When American tourists came to see how the "Parisian bohème" lived, he invited them to treat him with sandwiches or sausages. He was quite independent:

"You may tell them afterwards in America how you were at the side of the famous Roitschwantz. You have not seen my green rabbits, and you will not see them either, because I live like a monk—for my art only. What do you know of juicy centimeters? You think I don't see you staring at me with absolutely untalented eyes?"

The Americans said timidly:

"We were at the Louvre . . . We have seen the Gioconda . . ."

"I should be ashamed of myself to sit with you. The Gioconda, indeed! . . . That is nothing but an empty bottle that my latest pupil painted."

Lasik acquired the prevailing customs and habits of the Rotonde rather quickly. He knew now how to scare newcomers, how to extort a franc, how to push an empty plate under a sleepy neighbor. To be sure, Rosenpupp and Monkin were lost for good. But he did make friends with Lentschuk. He knew how to anticipate Monkin:

"Soon that thief who steals everything from Lentschuk will show up. And he will say that I, an innocent lamb, have stolen his picturesque duck. But he himself does not believe it, and it is he alone who steals his own portrait from the first best person he meets."

The artists could not make head nor tail of it: where did he come from, this Roitschwantz? What did he do? Lasik was evasive: the address—has to be kept secret, soon everything would be clarified, he was not worried about the future. Some said: "He is just a swindler," others objected: "One must not be jealous of other people's successes." They were sure someone had seen Lasik's paintings and had been wildly enthusiastic—that it was true art, of the highest order! Monkin or Rosenpupp could go packing! Lasik's fame spread. Meanwhile, he nearly starved. But once, when he succeeded in getting twenty francs out of an enthusiastic Dane, he ordered business cards immediately: "Lazar Chvance, free-lance artist."

Chvance—that sounded quite Parisian, it was short and polite. For example: "Merci, Monsur Chvance." It was so beautiful, one could cry. The business cards together with his proud behavior had the desired effect. One day, a very elegant man approached Lasik in the Rotonde. Raising his hat, he said:

"You are Monsur Chvance, aren't you? I have heard a great deal about you. I visit the Rotonde quite frequently for my aperitif. I live next door. My store, dealing in chamberpots, is right around the corner. I would like to have a talk with you. The situation is such that there is a crisis in our line of merchandise. On the other hand, I keep hearing how rich the art-dealers are getting. I have been told that an art dealer paid an artist twenty francs per painting, the artist died, and now each painting is worth about one hundred thousand. This is what I call circulating capital. Furthermore, I have heard that all artists here die young, which is, of course, a great advantage for the dealers. And so, I have decided to get into art a bit. I am looking for a young talent to start this adventure. There is a great deal of talk about you. They say you are an enigma. I like that. Furthermore, you have, and please forgive me for saying it, not exactly the appearance of a great hero, so that I could depend quite safely, that you, God forbid, will have an early death."

Lasik interjected:

"Yes, I think so too. Roitschwantz, or Chvance as they call me here, is a fireworks that will burn in and out in an instant. There is really very little left of me already—just the appetite, the philosophy and two or three dirty jokes. But what is your offer?"

"I am offering you a contract for the rest of your life. You shall paint five pictures per month and you will give them to me. I shall pay you fifty francs per picture. But first I must see your work."

"I do not understand. You mean to say you have never heard of the famous palette of Chvance? Just read the posters! They cannot even be described as billboards any more; they are pure sentimentality, and all the women of Paris cry like at the wailing wall in Jerusalem, whether it is a green rabbit hanging before them or their self-portrait. Resemblance—that was merely a scandalous invention of yesteryear. I do not think at all when painting. It just flows out of me. And I daub like the most genial dauber. Take a millimeter—there is no such thing, only in arithmetic, but it is alive in me, it lives, it is already a part of a golden frame. And now, just imagine, at this very moment, my last cough resounds before the end. You are crying, you are giving me a laxative. You are calling: 'Chvance, do not die!' I, however, am a polite character. I do not take your advice, I die. And in your hands is an entire factory of painted canvases. You would become a Rothschild over night. After all, those are not some stupid mundane pictures!"

"I understand you do not wish to show your work to the other artists, but you certainly can show them to me. Really, you may trust me. I have had my store here for seventeen years. Here is my business card: 'Achille Honbuisson.'"

"Monsur Achille, if you are that stubborn, I must confess to you that I have had some difficulties. I had money. I ate roast duck every day and traveled in an automobile through the square. And I ordered all kinds of business cards, just like yours. But then the money was accidentally gone. My heart moaned. I gnashed my teeth, put all my valuable paintings in a sack and took them to a cod liver oil dealer and pawned them for fifty miserable francs. That can happen to anyone, to Monkin, or even to the Gioconda! You are willing to give me fifty francs for a single piece so you can sell it after my irrevocable death for a hundred thousand. Well, there are a hundred paintings of mine, and if I bring the fish creditor his fifty francs, you will be able to cry in front of all my masterpieces."

Achille Honbuisson growled a little, breathed deeply and finally gave Lasik fifty francs.

"Here, give me a receipt. What can one do—nothing ventured, nothing won!"

In the evening, Lasik looked up Monkin at the Rotonde.

"As you remember, I told you in my suicidal letter that I

would repay you a hundred-fold. First of all, here is the address of a wonderful dealer. Do not pay any attention to the white obscenities in his display window. In his soul there is nothing but picturesque enthusiasm. You can sell him even your self-portrayed cutlet, for I have not seen such a fool in a long time. And second, I am taking you now to a magnificent restaurant where you may order any duck with the complete trimmings."

After emptying a glass of wine in the restaurant, Lasik began to cry:

"I am crying because of the beauty! If there are such things in this world, like the Gioconda for instance, or the son of Zeus, or you with your portrait, how can one not cry? For in my soul, I am a real artist. How often have I painted mentally Fenitchka Hershanowitsch's eyes with the lilac from Homel as a background! If one wants to talk of feelings, I certainly have them. Today at the café I saw such a girl that I was almost run over by one of those Arabian cars. Her eyes reached up to her ears, and her lips were like the flag I used to carry bravely in happier days. Do you happen to know who she is? For I have just decided to kiss her or—to die. You can see the abundance of feelings I am capable of. I am sketching her hastily and she is already tinkling in my head. Well, that is all fine, but what will the next day bring? . . . It is great to die of love, but not of Swedish gymnastics; and this chamberpot manufacturer has machine guns instead of hands."

The next morning Lasik decided to stay at home, and not to go anywhere near the Rotonde. But then he remembered the eyes of that lady, and he could not resist any longer:

"I shall go there on my tiptoes and hide near the entrance. I may die, but I must see her first."

But alas, he did not see her. He did see, however, Mr. Honbuisson.

"You have swindled me! . . ."

"Please put your machine guns away! Why is it my fault when

they got lost? I have lost more than you. Take a pencil and figure it out. You have lost fifty—multiplied by one, that makes still only fifty. I, however, have lost a hundred, and that—multiplied by fifty—makes five thousand! So you see? And even so, I did not kill him. And now you put those machine guns nicely in your inside pockets. I've been crying all night long and my eyes are swollen. Maybe, before the end, I'll begin to feel better; then I will certainly paint you ten masterpieces on the spot. But of course, I have neither a canvas nor paint, nor do I have any rabbits that could pose for me. If you would risk it once more . . ."

"That is what you think! . . . You think if your business card reads 'artist' and mine 'chamberpot salesman,' that gives you the right to cheat me? I could have you arrested immediately. I could smash you to pieces. Do you see these hands? But, I will give you one more chance. I shall give you a canvas, paint, and a model . . . You will work in my place. Behind locked doors. Do you understand?"

After these words, Achille Honbuisson took Lasik, who was shaking frightfully, to his apartment.

"Whom would you like to paint? A man? A woman?"

"No. That is old stuff. I paint only meat. In short, I will paint a rabbit, and not in its stupid fur, but only when it is well roasted."

After a while Achille Honbuisson brought the canvas, paint, brushes and a huge, fat rabbit. He growled:

"The ideas artists have these days! Rabbits! . . . What a time I had getting one from the butcher's. Do you know what he charged me!—eighteen francs!"

Achille Honbuisson locked Lasik in and left. Lasik looked through the window: no, he could not jump from there, this was almost as high as the tower of science.

He remembered Monkin's edifying explanations and began to besmear the canvas with paint, but it was mostly his hands that got smeared. The brushes broke. And nothing came out—neither a self-portrait nor a rabbit.

"Now he is going to kill me. These are the last minutes of the doomed Roitschwantz. Well then, if I have to die such an untimely death, I shall at least have a good meal enjoying this roasted banana."

And he yielded to an indescribable delight. Upon Achille Honbuisson's return there was nothing left of the rabbit but dry bones. He yelled:

"Where is the painting?"

"Oh, woe is me! Goodbye, my country! Adieu, my motherly Homel! You want to know where the painting is? It is not yet here. To begin with, it would not have come out. We used to have a photographer in Homel who for a mere sixty kopeks would take a picture of not just one, but two people—in their wedding garments, mind you—and even he would fail quite frequently. It is just like on a wild boar hunt, you know, anyone can miss."

"Ignoramus! Swindler! Take the brushes and get started! Look at the model!"

Softly and tenderly it came from Lasik's lips: "It is not there any more. Why are you shaking me like that? You know, you cannot shake out my hundred masterpieces . . . Go back to your chamberpots, but leave me alone! Oh, how it hurts! After all, I am not an artist, I am a tailor, and I would not dream of messing up such beautiful material. But please, don't start a fight! I will be glad to repair your trousers. Oh, I am dying. You think you could have squeezed a painting out of me? A scoundrel—Lasik? This was the only rabbit in my entire tormented life! . . ."

33

The *Rotonde* was deserted like a meadow after a nomad invasion. Even the Americans stopped turning around when Lasik appeared. As soon as he approached, the regular guests would whisper to each other: "Not a single franc for him —remember now!" The waiters demanded money in advance, even for a cup of coffee. Lasik swore in vain—the bruise on his forehead had occurred at a sports event:

"I have taken part in a race, five hundred millimeter per hour, and the little horse had luckily fallen on his back."

The story of the rabbit he had gobbled up at Achille Honbuisson's gradually became known in the area. Monkin's friend, Spritz, drew a caricature: "The Birth of Venus." He pictured Lasik naked, with black and blue marks, covered with bloody weals, in the midst of a foaming sea. He was standing on one of Achille Honbuisson's masterworks, a chamberpot, to be precise, bashfully covering up his nakedness, and, from up above, came such earthly blessings as chickens, ducks and rabbits. Lasik did not pretend to be offended, he merely tried to straighten out the facts:

"The things looked quite different. Anyway, resemblance is of no importance." The cartoon was hung up at the Rotonde and an American bought it from Spritz for one hundred francs: in remembrance of the most typical customer of the Rotonde. Lasik attempted once more to get into the act, hoping to obtain a sandwich, but he was thrown out in disgrace. When all opportunities had been lost, and death of starvation was awaiting him at one of those fences that should have been embellished with the names of Rosenpupp or Monkin, salvation came unexpectedly. Louis Kohn, who was notorious in café circles as a snob, gourmand, and playboy, noticed Lasik standing in front of a delicatessen store and felt sorry for him. More than that, he made the dirty little rake his private secretary. Now Lasik walked around proudly in very wide trousers, and the only complaint he had was:

"This material could have been enough for three."

He ate at the most elegant restaurants and rode around in a 40 HP limousine. His photograph appeared in "Adam," the magazine for men's fashions, with the following inscription: "M. Lazarious Chvance, our young visitor, a prince of Polessia, a friend of M. Louis Kohn." Lasik cut out the picture and put it carefully in his pocket where it joined the counterfeit of the Portuguese hostage.

Before reporting more of Lasik's new position, however, I must linger for a moment upon an unfamiliar person with radiant lips.

It was because of her, that he, Lasik had come to know the heavy hand of Achille Honbuisson. Every night she sat at a small café opposite the Rotonde, and every night Lasik would stand at the entrance of the Rotonde to get a glimpse of her big, magnificent eyes. Of course, Mademoiselle Chique did not notice him. Once, when after a great many cocktails, she left the café somewhat unsteady on her feet, she even believed him to be the doorman:

"Call a taxi!" she said.

Charmed by her heavenly voice, Lasik did not move. She gave him a shove with her umbrella, and when he finally called a taxi, she gave him a franc. Lasik threw the coin into the window of the car:

"For this great amount of money you may buy yourself an orchid, for I love you more than I ever loved Fenitschka Hershanowitsch!"

After Lasik's fate had taken such an unexpected turn to the good, the first thing he did was to ask Louis Kohn for a free evening; and without losing time, he repaired to the promising café. He sat at a table next to Mademoiselle Chique and ordered a bottle of champagne. For the rest of the evening he did not take his eyes off her. Finally, the girl could not stand it any longer:

"Why are you staring at me, like a cat at the cream?"

"No! No cat, male or female, can look like that. Even I, in the days when I was blessed with a good appetite, have never looked like that at any cream, regardless of whether it was with liver or rabbits. Don't you recognize me? For three long weeks I used to stand breathlessly at this door. Don't you remember, I even gave you your own coin to buy yourself an orchid? It might be interesting to know what kind of flower you bought? Naturally, for one franc one cannot expect a whole bouquet of flowers. However, two days ago, I came into a lot of money because some fool discovered I had temperament; and tomorrow

I am going to buy you pansies for one thousand francs, if you will only permit me to look at you for another ten minutes. I am in despair."

Mademoiselle Chique became alive.

"You are a funny fellow! . . . Would you like to dance?"

"Absolutely not! I know all this jumping around by heart, but at the moment I have not a learned approach to it. I am afraid I could not succeed as Comrade Serebrjakow did."

"Well, as you wish. May I sit at your table? What are you drinking? Champagne?"

They drank to each other. Lasik emptied his glass with one gulp. His head was spinning from wine and happiness. Mademoiselle Chique tickled him with her elbow:

"You are an absolute baby!"

"I, a baby? You are trying to demoralize me with your sarcasm! Even though I am already thirty-three years old, I am not an old man yet. You will not find the real passion in those young zealots with their gleaming eyes. No, at twenty, men are afire, anyway. They burn with love, or class ideals, or simply because they have a fever. But the question is, what about their feelings? A handful, maybe another handful, and they are completely burned out. And what is left? Nothing but a spark. The years go by, and the tiny spark comes to life. Then it really can put the whole world on fire, and there is hardly time to cry for help before the heart is consumed by the flames."

"I really much prefer the more mature men. To be sure, they are more demanding, but they also know how to appreciate what they get. I am convinced you have good taste. So, let us pay and leave."

Lasik did not know what was happening to him. He should take her to her place! But where were the orchids? He felt like dancing with happiness. But, alone!—right then and there. Why not? Her name is Margot. What a name! She is surely the Venus that ran away from the American Louvre at night. Why did he have to drink that champagne with the bubbling sparks when he is losing his senses, anyway? Little horsey, do not shake so hard! What is she doing? She is kissing him on his ear! Do you understand? Roitschwantz being kissed on the ear, that miserable ear from Homel, carressed by a mad goddess! The stairway? All right, he is coming up! He will bellow with happiness, like an antelope. What? It is forbidden to bellow? Everybody is asleep? Who can sleep at an earthquake?

In the room, Margot fell on the divan and began to laugh hysterically:

"I think I am going to die of laughter! . . . I have not seen such a funny chap in my whole life! . . ."

And Lasik responded full of enchantment:

"In this paradise, I will walk only on tiptoes."

When Margot was through laughing, she became businesslike:

"As to the picturesque bouquet that you offered to buy me tomorrow—you are going to get it right now. This way it is much safer. After all, we have had champagne. Don't you understand? But you yourself have told me . . . One thousand! Yes, yes. After all, I do not know you. You don't want to? Then go—get lost! I do not know how you usually do it, but with me it is always in advance. Do you understand?"

"Why this inexorable proclamation? Naturally, when you think up a hundred ceremonies, one might as well give up living. I have to tell you, a pious Jew must wash his hands before and after he has slept with a woman. Before, because he is about to undertake a genuine, God-pleasing deed, and afterwards, because, though he had completed a God-pleasing deed, nevertheless he had touched something that might not be pleasing to God, as, for example, an absolutely naked stomach. That is nicely figured out, isn't it? But what is the result? Instead of the most wonderful ecstasy, all that is left is just a miserable washbasin. But you do not have to follow such regulations. Then, why are you tormenting me with all these 'befores' and 'afters'? All right, I shall give you those paper-made orchids, but just do not tear my wild heart to pieces with all that horrible accounting!"

Margot took the money and began to undress.

"Well, little fellow, let us go to bed."

Lasik sobered up.

"There are two possibilities: either you are the escaped Venus, or you are a one hundred per cent Marxist, and have attended Comrade Triwas' lectures. What do you mean, 'let's go to bed,' when my heart is full with rose-colored preambles? I woud like to flutter back and forth with you, warbling and speaking of love, singing lullabys to you and carrying you in my arms like a tender fairy tale; and I would like to die, for that would be better than living. It would be paradise. And what are you doing? You are offering me nothing but the bare, familiar functions! After all, you are not Frau Dreckenkopf! Your name alone has an aroma so fragrant, not to mention your lips. But if you want to sleep, go right ahead. And I will sit in this chair protecting you from the wind with my own hands, so my almost last ideal will not be swept away."

Margot shrugged her shoulders.

"Go to the devil!—sit, if you like to! As though I needed you! —you flea!"

Wine and lassitude had made her sleepy. She took a hot bath, went to bed and fell asleep at once.

Lasik sat there, sighing heavily. There was no justice on earth. Nussja had called him a bedbug. Margot had degraded him to a flea. Was size of such importance? His love was as big as the tower of science. But they could not understand that.

"When such a Venus is exhibited at the Louvre, do the Americans touch her with their hands? They pay an entrance fee, they cry of ecstasy just to have the privilege to be in one room with such a marvelous piece of stone. All right, so I am a flea!

But I will not just simply crawl into the heavenly landscape with my small business. I would rather like to feel that I can sit near her. I shall gaze at these fireworks . . ."

And Lasik was gazing at the sleeping Margot. Suddenly, a desperate squeak was heard:

"I implore you, wake up quickly! You have been robbed. That must be some mystic phenomenon! Where are your great, big eyes? Your dewy lips of May? Where are your eyebrows that were as black as my fears? Or could it be that I have become blind from sheer expectation? Answer me quickly, or I shall call everybody in the house to take me to an insane asylum."

Margot rubbed her eyes and looked startled at Lasik. When she finally comprehended what it was all about, she began to abuse him:

"You wretch! You highwayman! Not in vain have you sponged people out of their francs. Do you think just because you have swindled a thousand from somebody that it gives you the right to do as you please? What do you think I am, a model? Or shall I sing children's songs to you? You idiot! Did you think I would go to bed with my makeup on? And what would become of my complexion? You imbecile! Do you want me to become disfigured forever, for a lousy thousand francs? You rascal!"

"Ssst. Just make a little pause in your list! I understand everything, already. In other words, you are a juicy canvas, with every centimeter uttering a sound. Surely it must be Monkin who is besmearing you, since he has the most complete palette. At night, however, you are like Mrs. Dreckenkopf. The whole difference is that I am now in full possession of the dumplings. How terrible! You are just like my aunt. At least she used to sell eggs in Glukhov. What about you? A women at your respectable age, just standing in a frame and having somebody hit her with a paintbrush, so she can dance at a café like a schoolgirl! Just for the sake of a swindle! That cannot even be compared with the pension the invalids are getting in Homel. This is merely the empty laughter of Mephistopheles!"

Lasik had hardly finished his moving speech when all kinds of things came flying into his face: the furious Margot did not take time to select the missiles. A chip of a pot injured Lasik's nose. When Lasik went down the stairs, he tried not to sigh. Everybody was asleep amidst the earthquake. But it was daylight by now, and the *concierge* stopped him:

"Where are you coming from? Why is your face so bloody?"

Lasik tried to explain what had happened. "Lately I am being pursued by the handiwork of one Achille Honbuisson. What can you do—nobody escapes his destiny. Now Mr. Louis Kohn will scold me—I have ruined his triple trousers, not to mention my nose. But since you are not sleeping, I can sigh loudly. I will not sigh because of the nose. My nose is used to it. I shall sigh like a philosopher because a complete split in my personality has occurred, and I do not know which memories to live with. On the one side, Venus; on the other, the incapacitated working woman, and all added together, it results in my love, fifth floor to the left, there she lives and trembles. And, Madam, you look just like my cursed destiny, even the broom in your hands is ready to strike. Just tell me, what is life, and love, and what are the dim stars?"

But alas, instead of all sublime philosophy, the doorkeeper put the ominously-mentioned broom in action.

34

Monsieur Kohn was twenty-eight years old, but he distinguished himself through wisdom and scope. He had inherited a sizable fortune from his father, who was the owner of a vegetable canning factory. He did his best to get rid of it, in a pleasant, happy-go-lucky way. As a matter of fact, he rather enjoyed seeing the big newspapers mention some of his oddities in their local news. Lasik took over the job of the unfortunate lobster whom Kohn had liked to take walking on a leash along the Champs Élysées.

"Oh, so you are Russian? Naturally, you are Bolshevik. That

is nice. We are suffocating in our academism. I knew Racine already in my cradle. The Third Republic is the government of the shopkeepers. To me you will be the battle cry from the East. Your eyes are glowing with revolutionary mysticism. Oh, how I would love to see your Red Square when the Chinese swear allegiance to Karl Marx, and the women dance the Polowetzian Dances in wide trousers! I am a great admirer of the unexpected—the jazz bands, the revolution, the syncopations. The other night I had dinner with the Viscountess Picetreaux, and after the pheasant, quite unexpectedly, I pulled a red flag out of my pocket and unfolded it right in front of all those academicians there. They were dumbfounded. Even the *Figaro* wrote about it, saying it was a grim joke. But that is no joke at all. The Parliament is afraid of me, for I, Louis Kohn, am a Communist."

Lasik did not know what to say:

"It is very difficult to travel, when one is not familiar with the standing rules. Of course, rain is the same everywhere. But in politics, it is quite a different matter. Judging from your appearance, I would rather say that you were—quite the opposite. But if there is such discipline here, so much the better. I was a party-candidate in Kiev and did not do too well, but I am sure, here, I will be able to crawl through. As though I could not pull out a flag, after eating a pheasant! So, tell me please, there is no Control Commission here, is there? And you are not forced to fill out questionnaires all day long? Well, in that case, will you please register me at once in this excellent party cell?"

"Phooey! How can anyone belong to a party! That would mean rubbing elbows with the dirty masses. It would be the same as riding the streetcar. I am a—spiritual Bolshevik. I love everything that comes from the East. By the way, aren't you a Buddhist? What a pity! I have a Buddha from the fifth century in my living room. You could have prayed before him. You see, I have never yet seen a real Buddhist pray. That must be quite exciting. Oh, you are Jewish? That is dull. That is the religion of the little shopkeepers. You know, you should really become a Catholic. I am a great admirer of the cult of the Holy Rose. To be sure, the idea of one God is good enough for those who ride the streetcars. But there is still the symbol of the immaculate conception, the mystic prophecies, the dark. And, after all, what can one do—that is the fashion today. Just as I would not dream of running around in narrow trousers or a long coat, nowadays! Anyway, next Sunday I shall be your godfather and the Viscountess Picetreaux, your godmother."

"If this is all my job requires, all right, then. I am of the genuine twentieth century; and after a partridge dinner, I can even pray in front of your Buddha, if you just write the words out for me. So, you are asking me to crawl into that sinless dark? I shall crawl. I imagine this will not require a special operation and I know, it will be easier for my godmother, the Viscountess, to bathe me in mystic water than for you to be circumcised by the little shopkeepers. Period. I am already a Bolshevist Catholic. And now, tell me, exactly, what do I have to do, as your Learned Secretary?"

"Do not speak so loud and fast, or I will get a headache. It is the fashion, when you speak, to make everyone feel you are ready to die of indifference and boredom between any two words. It sounds much more polite. Only, now and then, when I nod my head you may let your Eastern temperament go. Among your duties, one of the most outstanding will be to have lunch with me regularly."

Lasik's face lit up, but since Louis Kohn did not nod at him, he controlled his feelings. They rode to a restaurant. The headwaiter, who obviously knew Louis Kohn quite well, wrote down the order without waiting—noodles in water and apple sauce. Then he asked:

"What will the gentleman have?"

"We will discuss that right now."

Louis Kohn studied the menu a full hour. Lasik tried his best to hold back his saliva. Finally, the lunch was ordered.

"My friend, now you shall be introduced to a sublime art. I am not going to give you a long philosophical explanation of Savarin's system. But what is the meaning of esthetics, poetry, morals, the Charleston? What is a syncopation, the second reality, Count Lautremond, what is my smile? All these are merely the achievements of the chefs. Four years ago, at the Restaurant *Paix des Nonnes*, they served me a chicken dinner prepared by the master chef Emile. It was stuffed with venison liver, truffles, and orange slices and prepared with a sauce of Cheres wine, vintage sixty-three. It was garnished with Artichokes à la Toulouse, which means, in hot wine and beaten eggs. I remember that day as vividly as the Epic of the Revolution, as Stravinsky's first chord, as the consecrated wafer of the Holy Supper. I have studied all the dishes of France, and I could have become, for instance, the best expert on Perigord Pâtés. But, alas, we of the Kohn tribe, distinguish ourselves by a very delicate constitution. I became ill of gastritis, enteritis, nephritis, arthritis, and gout. I can only eat noodles boiled in water, and apple sauce. Instead of wine—mineral water. I suffer like a painter who has lost his sight, for I well remember the taste of that sauce, and I could never be mistaken in guessing the vintage of a Lafitte. Well, I have decided to deepen my suffering even more. I will order the most delicious foods for you and relish watching a neophyte like you become entranced with the aroma of a lobster or a camembert, and I shall explain to you the solemnity of every single moment. I will turn your meals into a divine service. What do you have on the plate? Marenne oysters? Do not swallow them! At this moment, the Atlantic Ocean is conversing with your Heaven! One sip of Chablis! It is full of autumnal dryness and freshness. A lovely morning breathed upon the grape. Can you taste the slight metallic aroma? Next, you will get a stream trout and with it, a dry Vouvray, vintage twenty-one. It is still young, but filled with the blossoms of the Loire, the laughter of Rabelais, the . . ."

Lasik was not listening any more. He conscientiously swallowed everything the waiters served. But after the sixth course, he could not take it any longer. He pushed away the plate with the pheasant, thanking the headwaiter, as well as Mr. Kohn, profusely.

"Merci. It is strange, but even the appetite has its limits. Now we can talk about something interesting and exalting, as for instance, the Polowetzian Syncopation. I did not quite understand it. Why is it first the Red Square and then the immaculate conception? In Homel, where I come from, they would not pat your little head for that."

"Fashion, my friend, fashion! The real freedom consists of submission. The people riding the streetcars submit to a miserable moral standard, while we, the chosen, submit to the fashion of the day. Nowadays, one has to be part Bolshevik, part Catholic. Those are incomprehensible nuances, like the pepper, the honey, the cucumber slices, the maraschino in the claridge sauce. I would certainly not dance the one-step or play croquet when it is fashionable to dance blackbottom and play golf. However, it won't help you to push the plate away. I have only started to enjoy this, and there are nine more courses coming up. This pheasant has the aroma of Nostradamus' prophecies. It smells of the sickly-sweetening decay of the entire Latin culture. I bet they did not have it hanging in a warm place longer than a week. It has only gradually attained that 'bouquet.' Just smell it! Can you feel the breath of death, the mythological mushrooms, the Roquefort, the thousand year old sleep?"

Lasik inhaled the aroma of venison, cautiously. He remonstrated angrily:

"Now I understand why you pulled out all those flags after

eating the pheasant! Such a smell can even kill a man! With me, at least, I feel that Polowetzian Syncopation acting up. Do you know what it smells like? In my home town Homel, they drive a stinking barrel through the streets and . . ."

"Do not speak! Take one leg. It is your duty. Do not forget: you are my private secretary. Now, a sip of Chambertin. That is vintage ninety-one, it wraps you in misty twilight—do you notice? It embraces your soul gingerly. It makes you warm. It is the soil of Burgundy, not south, not north, the heart of culture, twenty centuries, then falling apart, darkness, abysses, syncopations, and in the very last instant, two or three dust-covered bottles."

Lasik could hardly breathe. His face became purple, then violet. The waiters, however, kept bringing new plates and glasses, torturing him on and on. Lasik ate and drank dutifully: what could he do, he had agreed to it, hadn't he? He could not differentiate any longer. He seemed to see Buddhas on the pâtés, syncopations and twenty Latin centuries. Suddenly something hit his nose. It felt like ammonia. Kohn whispered happily:

"This is 'livarot' cheese. It is kept for several years in a golden yellow dung. There it can ferment like mad. Just smell it! The aroma tightens your heart. Here, smell it quickly!"

Things were swimming before Lasik's eyes. The cheese, it seemed, was whirling around. He looked at the bottles—they were bowing to him. And Kohn? Kohn nodded his head. Well, what do you know? That meant—he was free! . . . Lasik jumped up and yelled happily:

"Take that barrel away, right now!"

Louis Kohn tried to calm him down, but in vain.

"Everyone is looking at you. . . . That is indecent."

"Let them look. Why did you have to pour all that stuff into me? And, anyway, what kind of ideas do you have? Instead of one decent cutlet, you make a person eat thirty syncopations with all kinds of smells! If he will not remove that Homel barrel from the region of my nose, I shall throw it into the face of the first Viscountess I see! So, I am drunk! What did you think? How should one not be drunk with such methods? And furthermore, I was sitting quietly; but you decided to nod your head and my temperament got the better of me. You say you didn't nod? Then it must have been the Chambertin nodding. Anyway, take me, and I mean fast—to my destination! . . ."

The first test was a failure, but Louis Kohn did not give up hope: this midget certainly had a marvelous temperament. Two days later, he took Lasik to the "Beauty Salon." When Lasik saw the revolving chair, the lancets, tiny jars and bottles, electrical apparatus, he fell to his knees right in front of the masseuse:

"For, let us say, Buddha's sake, have pity on Roitschwantz! What will you do to me? Cut out half of my stomach or kill me on the spot with that little lamp, like they do in America?"

"Do not be afraid. First we shall smooth a few wrinkles. That will not hurt at all. We have four thousand letters of appreciation. Sit right over here. Lean back. Relax!"

Lasik sat down. He tried to relax, not to think about anything. But how could he? They were changing him, like making alterations on an old, insensitive suit of clothes! All right, so most likely they will smooth away his wrinkles with some iron. We shall see what will happen—as though one could smooth away one's entire misfortune, starting with a Madame Pukke to the moment of his need for a toilet at the restaurant *Paix des Nonnes!* Just keep polishing, keep smoothing the wrinkles, and yet pain and sorrow will remain the same forever, and Roitschwantz will remain Roitschwantz! You will not succeed in changing him into a Buddha, nor even a Chambertin! . . .

Suddenly, Lasik was startled by an unpleasant and quite familiar pain. The masseuse was squeezing his nose together.

"What do you want with my nose? After all, you are not Achille Honbuisson! And it has no wrinkles at all. The wrinkles are on my forehead. Stop it, will you? It is not made of gutta-percha!"

"Just keep your shirt on! It is a very simple operation. I shall begin with shortening your nose, slightly."

Lasik slid down the chair. He rolled around on the floor in his patient's gown, moaning:

"You will pay for that! My nose is not a pair of trousers, and forthwith I am declaring a general strike! It does not bother anyone, why should it be cut off? I have not pushed you nor any other person with my nose, have I? I am the one who is being pushed around. And after all, maybe I like it to stay long! To be sure, I cut off part of my name, but that was only an external superstructure. And anyway, how do you know, maybe some day I would like to return to my home town! Nobody would recognize me with a short nose, neither Pfeifer, nor Fenitschka Herschanowitsch. Not even Pukke! No, I cannot give you my personality! . . . Just cut off some of that indecent head-covering and goodbye, never to see you again!"

In the evening, Louis Kohn said harshly: "My friend, it has been five days since you came to live with me, and I am not at all satisfied with you. You have not made the slightest progress in the field of gastronomy. At the *Select* you tried to embrace the bartender after one single cocktail even though I had asked you to court me, since that is the fashion now. And at the beauty salon you behaved like a wild man . . ."

"But you yourself wanted me to do these Polewetzian things."

"Do not interrupt me! . . . You are neglectful in your duties as a private secretary. Right now I am going to give you one last test. Look over there . . ."

Louis Kohn took Lasik to a door that was ajar. A young woman was sitting in the adjoining room. She was completely naked. She yawned lazily and smoked a cigarette. Lasik closed his eyes, sensitively.

"A very lovely person. But I advise you to watch her carefully, or she may steal your very eyes or lips. Two days ago I learned how such tricks can happen. But naturally, you are an experienced expert, and I am sure, in your case things will happen exactly as in the novel of Curose. I wish you a perfectly restless night."

"You are beginning to annoy me. I have a headache. Give me a powder. Do you think I am showing her to you for your own pleasure? It is time for you to fulfill your most important duty as a private secretary. As you know—we Kohns are of fragile bodily constitution. There was a time when I was famous for my conquests. But alas, now I am condemned to eternal dieting. . . . In short, you are going to play with my new girl friend, and I shall watch you and relive every moment through you. I long for these painful emotions. Do you understand?"

"I think I do."

Lasik greeted the lady politely:

"My name is—Chvance. Private secretary. Please, there is no reason to be bashful. Archip Stoikij, for example, was not at all bashful. Let us assume you are going to get a suntan right away. And furthermore, I am not even looking at you, I am watching the ceiling. Tell me, please, are you also some kind of private secretary? Do you have to smell that horrible cheese every day, too? I will whisper something to you, because, you know, he is sitting by the door: the main thing is—not to let them shorten your nose. That is pure torture. But we should not talk so much, we have to go to work! The only thing is, I just do not know what games they play here. In Homel we used to play poker or sixty-six. By the way, I do not see any cards . . ."

Lasik ran out of the room and asked Kohn in a matter of fact voice:

"Why are there no cards in there?"

It was the first time Kohn could not control himself:

"You are going to be responsible for my death! . . . Headaches . . . Not even the powder helps. I think I was mistaken in choosing you . . . Where is your temperament? . . . Here, drink this cocktail to give you courage . . . Now go to her, quickly! . . . I cannot wait any longer! . . . How can you remain so calm when a naked girl sits at your side? You must fool around with her!"

Lasik became meditative.

"I must say—this is a problem! Now it turns out, it has nothing to do with cards, and you, sitting around without your fur coat! Of course, you must be cold to sit like that in one spot. Well, what do you say, shall we do some exercises to warm you up? I cannot quite remember how to do it, but I think we could play 'cat and mouse.' You have to jump and then I will jump, but you must also mew, and I shall crawl under the divan and play the scared little mouse."

Lasik crawled under the sofa, and began to squeak softly. Louis Kohn could not take it any longer. He came rushing into the room:

"You idiot! . . . Is this what you call temperament? . . . Oh, if I only could! Come out from under there! Drink another cocktail! All right, did you drink it? Fine! Now, go to work! Whenever it is not necessary, you show your barbarian inclinations. . . . But now I am ordering you . . . Go on, show the kind of wild, free barbarian you really are!! Do anything you please! Oh, I am dying! . . . I yearn for pain! . . ."

"Well, then, if you nod your head, I can also become fresh after two such intoxicating attempts. First of all, my dear madam, I implore you, put on at least a bathing suit—you are neither Venus, nor are we at the American Louvre. To tell the truth, I am in love with Margot Chique, even though she is an incapacitated worker and my heart is broken. But I am sure you appreciate multi-colored gifts, and so I am handing you now a briefcase full of syncopations, and you may go home. That would be number one. And as for you, first and foremost syncopation, lie on the divan with your Polowetzian face down, and you can even behave as though you were not at home—that is, you can take off your trousers and I with my excellent suspenders can produce—one, two, three— such terrific pain of ecstacy, that you will begin to pray before any Buddha. What? You do not want to? But I should be a wild man? Fine. Here is one for you—right into your face! We shall start with the ashtray. And now, please receive these orchids together with their pot. Afterwards I can use the Buddha, provided he is five centuries heavy!"

A white-haired, dignified butler answered the bell.

"Jacques, you will have to fulfill the duties of my private secretary—temporarily. You are staying here with this lady. First, however, throw this scoundrel out into the fresh air and give him a good lesson for his farewell . . ."

35

These were dark days once again for Lasik. He took a job washing dishes in a tavern, then he became a barker at a county fair, he was an organ grinder, he sold Chinese nuts. Every now and then he was arrested, beaten up and then released again.

Once he was also expelled. When he arrived at the Belgian border, he heaved a melancholy sigh: "How many times do I have to go through this. . . ." He took the train coming towards him and tried returning to Paris without a ticket. On the way he was thrown out. He sold Louis Kohn's suit and managed to get back to Paris.

The following nights, lying under some bridge, he kept reproaching himself: "You idiot, why couldn't you finish that stinking pheasant? . . ." Quite frequently, he would stroll along the Rue des Rosiers, to the Jewish quarter. If he only had money, he would drink some tea, eat chopped herring and discuss philosophical problems . . . the Talmud, Mrs. Dreckenkopf, the Bolsheviks . . . One day it happened that he met there an old inhabitant of Homel. When Jankelewitsch heard the story of Lasik's adventures in Frankfurt, he exclaimed:

"Why, you don't need to live under wet bridges and be ruined! You could live like Chamberlain! I was in London and I know. It seems to me, you have a real head on your shoulders! You should travel to London at once and see Mr. Bottomgolow. He is the biggest fool in England. You will leave his place a respectable missionary. Why, Monjka Schmerkin lived four long years on preaching! . . ."

Well, that thought was not so bad. But how was he to get to London? One really did not need too much money for that. One could be a barker once again, or play the part of a monkey, or even that of the devil. Anyway, he could also declare a whole week of *Yom Kippur* and fast. In short, some way or other he could get hold of the money. But what about the passport?

"You can get a passport from the League of Nations."

Lasik remembered the unforgettable Pan Captain and he felt uneasy:

"Isn't that the League where one gets beaten up?"

"Nothing of the kind. You put a hundred francs on the table, and you become a member of the League, like the most respectable nation. But perhaps it is better for you to become Rumanian, because those Chamberlains just adore the Rumanians. For the same hundred francs you could become an enthusiastistic Bessarabian and get a Rumanian passport with the queen herself on its behind."

Less than two months had passed when Lasik was standing in front of Mr. Bottomgolow.

"What do you wish, brother in Christ?"

"I wish to have a small fortification. But once again, I am not coming to the point. That is because of my mystical shyness. On the contrary, I would like to take a solemn mission upon myself. I am not yet clear as to how that is being done, for Jankelewitsch talked more about passports, but I hope you will explain it all to me, and I shall leave your room with a mission in my pocket. Why shouldn't I be as good as some Schmerkin?"

Mister Bottomgolow smiled sweetly, and Lasik relaxed. No, Jankelowitsch had really not fooled him! Not even the one-eyed Natik had such a smile, and he was really dumb!

"Tell your brethren that Israel has gone mad! It gave the world the Old Testament, but later it stoned its Apostles. Our church is the daughter of the synagogue. It is time for the Prodigal Son to return to his fold! We accept enlightened Jews with open arms! We press them to our heart. Our house shall be their house. The Holy Scripture is already translated into six hundred seventy-eight languages, and we spread the Word everywhere. The Hebrews may come to us like greatly honored guests to a feast. You are familiar with their customs and habits. You must try carefully to win their confidence, and guide them to the Feast of Christ. Our rules are quite simple: Holy Baptism, love, abstinence from alcoholic drinks, chastity, observance of the Sabbath. Tell them to make haste."

Lasik replied readily:

"I shall tell them! For sure, I will tell them! And now let us talk business. I do not know how to address you, for 'Brother' is a bit too intimate, isn't it? And besides, you know, we really do not resemble each other. Would it suffice if I just called you 'Cousin?' "

"Just call me Mr. Bottomgolow."

"Well, I can always skip certain syllables. And as far as I am concerned, just call me Mr. 'Roitshwanch.' Well then, Mr. Bottomgolow, I shall proclaim everything, because we have just met, and they will listen to me, as though I were Moses himself, because, you see, I am the Chief Rabbi of Frankfort. But there is yet something else. Namely, I have been in London for four days now, and have not yet eaten dinner. And I would like to go at once to your feasting banquet. If you do not serve any wine, it does not matter too much—first, because one can always stop at a bar on the way, and second, I am quite satisfied with a weaker drink, such as tea with milk. The mere sound of that word makes my mouth water! Just press me quickly to your heart, and take me to that house!"

"My child, you are confusing the heavenly riches with the earthly ones. I own four houses and two factories, I have a small amount of capital. However, in my soul, I might be poorer than you. But it is written: 'Blessed are those who are poor in their mind.' So, do not forget, my Brother, the heavenly part! That is why I, for one, am at peace. Go hurry to your erring brethren and tell them the Messiah has come! They just did not notice him. How terrible! . . ."

And Mister Bottomgolow began to cry. Lasik comforted him:

"Do not shed so many tears! It can happen. They just did not notice anything because they are so absentminded. At that moment they most likely were eating fish with bones, or maybe they were asleep. But I will tell them. He has come already. And now, answer me, without any chaste allusions: will you give me an advance or not? It is true, I may be rich in spirit but I don't have the smallest factory. And anyway, it might be interesting to hear how you pay; per month, or per piece—I mean for every lost grandchild?"

"You shall receive sixteen shillings per week. Here, take one pound, and get yourself some decent clothes. And now you may go."

Lasik bowed politely. But while leaving, he remembered the main thing:

"Where is the fold?"

"What fold?"

"You said yourself, they have to be brought back to a certain fold. So please, give me the correct address."

Mister Bottomgolow shrugged his shoulders sadly.

Lasik began immediately carrying out the prescribed orders. He went to Whitechapel. Misery? As though he had not seen misery in his life! And yet, his heart froze when he saw those dreary pubs, the tramps and the starved faces of the inhabitants of that quarter. He even forgot all caution and sighed audibly:

"Well, one must say, a fine country, Great Britain. Now I can see what a fine thing our town of Homel was."

By the way, no one heard those suspicious opinions. The women crowding around were busy hanging up wet diapers, gathering potato peels and arguing with one another. Without difficulty, Lasik found a dozen hungry Jews.

"Let us begin at the beginning: which means, let us go into this lovely smelling tavern. What do people eat here? Fine. Twelve portions of meat with potato pudding and twelve bottles of beer! Well, now we can talk about our plans. After all, I am not a monster, to have all the good things just for myself. Jankelewitsch told me everything, and I am proposing here and now a decent organization for you. The fool owns four factories and books in six hundred seventy-eight languages. Nobody knows what he really wants, and besides it is quite uninteresting, for, as I told you, he is a blockhead. A valuable one, to be sure. But he has his fancy, and he seems mostly preoccupied with problems of relationships. To him, I am a brother and a lost son and a first-rate guest, and the synagogue he calls the mother of the church. And of course, the people at the synagogue are his church children. In short, he cannot even differentiate between the father and the son. But I will take you to him into a fold, and you must cry that you had been lost and now you want nothing but pure chastity. Then he will surely press you to his heart, and you must not push him away, for he is such a melancholy character, that if you push him away, he will burst into tears. Do you understand? Afterwards, however, he will give you something, and besides I am paying for the whole music right now. Agreed?"

Needless to say, Lasik's proposal was accepted unanimously. Smiling proudly, Lasik took the entire group to Mr. Bottomgolow:

"I have told them everything. Do you see how fast it went? I do not only have a voice, mine is a regular Jericho trumpet from Sinai. But that is quite understandable, for they were starved. They are all rich in spirit without any happiness. Please, press them quickly to your heart, and then you must give them something, for I have spent your one whole pound on ten portions for them."

However, Lasik's hopes did not come true. Mr. Bottomgolow sighed:

"You did not tell them the main thing: that man does not live by bread alone. My brother, I can see, you are not yet ready for your high mission. Here, take a few books with spiritual advice. Before anything, I advise you to read them carefully. After that, you may preach and explain the texts in fat print. Next Saturday night, we shall make a small hall available to you. You will gather these enlightened lambs around you and blind them with the word of God. And now you may go, my children! I am expected by some Chinese who can barely wait to become enlightened."

Lasik made another attempt, stammering:

"But what about the deceased pound? After all, it went for these half-blind sheep!"

But Mr. Bottomgolow gave him merely another piece of

advice:

"By the way, you must not forget, dear brother, that beer is also an alcoholic drink."

In the street, Lasik glanced triumphantly over his flock of sheep:

"Well, what did I tell you? Can you say that you have ever seen such a fool before? I just do not understand why he has such a nervous nose. Of all things, he smelled the beer! That he knew! But with the relationships, he made such a mish-mash. I am his brother, you are his children. In that case, you would be my nephews. He does not know himself what he wants. First, he wants me to blind you, like a scoundrel; then, suddenly he wants you to become enlightened. But we shall outwit him. On Saturday night, you get everyone there who has an orchestra humming in his stomach. I shall give such a thundering sermon that even the walls will bleat like sheep. Then we shall get the whole hundred pounds out of him. Meanwhile, however, let us buy some bread for a spiritual supper, since there is a little bit left of the pound."

On Saturday night, the auditorium was packed with a newly-founded society—"Israel Saved." The memories of the potato pudding and the reports about Mister Bottomgolow's four houses had put Whitechapel on its feet. Lasik climbed the stage, cheerfully:

"Ssst! Third bell! I can see the group is favored by a fabulous success! Not even the Moscow Operetta Theater in Homel can attract such an audience. Well, let me begin. My dear sheep! And you, dear redeemed Israel Mowsched, famous matchmaker of our golden town of Homel, greetings! I will immediately explain the fat print. But first, I would like to ask you a favor. In the interest of my appetite and yours, do not sit here like sticks of wood. If I say the words 'get blind,' you must close your eyes at once, for otherwise the healing words will get into your noses; however, when I say: 'be enlightened,' you must look at me with both eyes, even if they crawl up into your forehead, for it is from the second word that the entire surgical operation starts. Do you understand? Anyone who did not understand shall raise his hand. Fine, put those three erring hands down, and listen to me with overwhelming majority. Fat print, number one: Israel, look up—the Messiah, whom your prophets have proclaimed and whom you are waiting for, He has long since appeared. Period! And now you may be blinded, and I shall explain. Naturally, the prophets have expressed their opinions. Had they lived in our time, they would have surely been arrested. Well, what did they say, those crazy agitators? After all, we learned their tricks in *Cheder*. They have, for instance, made a lot of noise that all was not as it should be on earth, that the strong offend the weak, that truth has to be hidden deep in one's pockets, as though it were a newspaper, that some have too much, others too little, and that it is all just a Babylonian pigsty. Naturally, they intimated cautiously, the very opposite could happen. All of a sudden, Messiah will appear, and then a wonderful justice will prevail. Rothschild will come out of his house and graze on the pastures together with you, and he will have his pudding, and you will have yours, the Pan Captains or let us say, Madam Pukke, will stop striking Roitschwantz at his vulnerable spots, and instead of border guards, there will be only the most wonderfully blossoming orchids. Of course, Messiah is a shrewd pseudonym. And what is the result: as it turns out, He has appeared already. Strange to think that we did not notice Him. Make haste, and be enlightened, including the trinity of the minority! Can't you see that there is an absolute one hundred per cent justice on earth? Mister Bottomgolow, for example, owns four houses and he does not need them, for he lives on spiritual clouds—because you see, he is a poor man, in spirit. You will ask, why does he not give those houses to you? That is because he feels pity for you. For as soon as you have a bed with a blanket, you would become spiritually poor, while now you are only poor. But I beg you, just once take a walk through London, and you will see that the Messiah has already appeared. You might protest that Rothschild is not yet grazing with you? You see, he is not a sheep. He eats chicken. And if you could get hold of a few pounds, you could eat chicken too. But even though you do not have any money, what you have is more important: a promissory note for the paradise after death, it is written in the ninth scripture, and you can cancel that letter of credit at any bank. Furthermore, you all have freedom of speech. You may say, for instance: 'I would like to eat something,' and no one will protest. However, one must not get into prison and one must respect strangers. In Homel we had a broker, Gurtschik. Once he was sitting and eating roast goose with groats, and a beggar came to his window, begging for a piece of bread. Gurtschik showed him a poster on which was written: 'These tramps do not eat themselves and do not let others eat either.' I, for instance, have made a mistake too. I grabbed the wrong leg in Kiev. In short, everywhere on earth there is absolute justice, and Mister Bottomgolow is pressing everyone to his heart, and I make the unanimously approved motion—that the Messiah has appeared already. However, for those elements that are still doubtful, I shall read from the seventh text, which says that He will appear again, which is called 'Return to the Last Judgment.' If He can show such good results, I am of the opinion that He can appear infinitely. And so, may He appear forever, but we shall repair to our banquet. I will just warn you quickly, if you do not hurry, that fool will give everything to the ardent Chinese, for they also know the way to his fold. Let us, then, make a resolution and sign it. We shall state that we are his brethren, his children and his grandchildren, yes, even his fathers, if he will only give us a few golden bricks off his factory. For it is written in fat print, in scripture number four, that the hungry should be fed and even given the last shirt, and I am sure he has another shirt under the last. And so, let him feed us and clothe us, when we are all unanimously so hungry, that my sermon is drowned out by the noisy opera of your hundred stomachs. And therefore . . ."

Lasik did not succeed in completing his speech. Someone made his way through the crowd and approached him. He was shabbily dressed and did not distinguish himself in any way from the others in the audience. He said in a strict voice:

"Follow me."

"Where? If you mean the fold, I know my way, and besides they pay the salary only on Mondays."

The stubborn stranger showed Lasik a small card. Lasik looked at it and exclaimed unwillingly:

"I am not Chamberlain, to be able to read all the amiabilities of Great Britain at once! But I am beginning to guess. Just tell me, where to follow you—there or not there?"

Of course, the detective had no idea of Lasik's vast experience, and he merely replied in an official tone:

"I am a representative of Scotland Yard. You are being arrested as a Communist agitator."

36

Mister Rottenton bewildered Lasik with his very first word.

"You—are a Bolshevik courier. You were on the way from Archangelsk to Liverpool. You were carrying secret funds—money of the international Communist organization as well as a letter from Trotzky—to two unworthy Englishmen. When arrested, you got rid of the money, giving it to members of a criminal group, and you swallowed the letter."

That last accusation seemed absolutely ridiculous to Lasik. And even though Mr. Rottenton's trimmed moustache was bristling, Lasik could not control himself: he had to laugh out loud.

"I understand quite well what you are aiming at! . . . You want to accuse me of swallowing important documents. Not even the Polish Pan Cavalry Captains went that far. That is so funny, it gives me a pressure right here in my stomach, though perhaps those are just my fatal noises. Can you really think up such diabolical schemes? Then you must be a first-rate comedian, guest appearances absolutely guaranteed. Lasik Roitschwantz, men's tailor from the most ordinary city of Homel, where everyone eats cutlets or if you wish, pigeons feed on scribbled pieces of paper! No, mister . . . what is your name, even though I substituted two days for an ailing monkey, I am still not capable of doing that."

"You are lying in vain. I request you to state where the secret funds are at present, and also to write down, word for word, the contents of the document swallowed by you."

"Listen! Could it be that 'documents' are after all, just a pseudonym, as for instance, the kind of rich meal for the sinful sheep? What do we know what kind of Scottish tricks you are up to? It is quite true that I did swallow a big piece of meat with potato pudding on Thursday. That I will not deny. But how much saliva has flown under the bridge since then? And thus, I am absolutely not in the position to bring it back with the gravy. Don't you think I am not sorry? If I could bring back something I have swallowed, I would certainly become a Mister, just like you. I would grow a mustache to scare people, and that would be all. Let them all get excited, I would sit at my table and call: 'Hello, hello! Goose liver from Drawkin's wedding, return to the light, if you please!' That would not be just living, it would be paradise."

"Your attempt to outsmart me is in vain. If you confess, we shall let you go. If you continue to be stubborn, we shall also have to proceed in firmer terms. In such case, you might have to stay longer in England than anticipated."

"When I was still a yellow-beaked owl, I used to be afraid of such sojourns. In those times, I tried to go free as fast as possible. But now I am used to it. Besides, it is nice and dry in your prison, not like the one in Grodno. The food is average, to be sure, but at least there is running water, and not some paper to swallow. Also, I am not in any particular hurry. One or two months—I can take it."

Mr. Rottenton's mustache quivered convulsively: "You are a party fanatic."

And he decided to stagger this fearless sectarian by sheer logic. He told Lasik a great deal about the power of the British Empire, of the flower of its industry, of the loyalty of the Hindus, of the love of peace of the Irish, and even of the opening of four new coffee houses and a high school for pearl embroidery somewhere in the Solomon Islands, where they had a certain kind of cannibal who just adored and idolized King George, Mister Chamberlain and English pipes. Lasik listened with great interest. He nodded his head:

"A marvelous lecture! We were also taught at our political courses that maladministration has fallen by two hundred per cent, and that now they do not blow their noses with two fingers, but more. I congratulate you, Mister—what was your name again? . . . But, will you kindly tell me, how do those cannibals swallow the little pipes? Perhaps with pearl-embroidered documents, because, in that case, you must have surely confused it all: Homel is not situated on an island, it does not swim around, it stays put in one place, and down in the valley rush the majestic waves of the river Sosch."

Mister Rottenton did not fully appreciate Lasik's geographical knowledge, and he proceeded with his patriotic speech. Now he began to ridicule Russia's weakness and impotence: red tape, breakdown of its industry, empty state treasury, miserable army, riots in the borderlands.

"Just compare your fleet with ours, if you please: a dreadnought and a ridiculously small boat. Your laws, compared to ours: one hundred heavy volumes, and the little slip of paper you swallowed. Our finances, and yours: the Bank of England, and a few stolen pence that you have hidden away in time. And finally, our intelligence, and yours: you and I! All we have to do is blow and you flutter away like feathers. How dare you remain stubborn after all that? And is it possible or even thinkable that there could be such base creatures among Englishmen who believe in your stupid dogma! If not for the abovementioned one hundred volumes, I would simply have you hanged. But as it is, I must wait until Mister Chamberlain will have completed his hundred and eleventh tome, which will be an amendment to the first one hundred. But then we will really show you! . . ."

Mister Rottenton's moustache was wiggling like mad, and Lasik decided to cheer up his amusing friend, with a story from Homel.

"This is the very same situation as with the invented God. One day he just decided he did not like the fact that the Jews were bowing to a certain Baal. And he began to shout: Why such unnecessary expenses! That Baal cannot do anything. He is nothing but a bad piece of wood, and certainly not a god with any authority. If I wish to, I can send upon you bloody rains, locusts, cholera, in one word, anything that comes to my mind. But what can he do? Nothing at all. And the dear Lord was grumbling so, day and night, that all the Jews got sick and tired of it. And one of the very clever Jews decided to bring this all-too-long scene to an end. He said to the Lord:

" 'I am going to ask Baal to make me a present of two hundred thousand, while granting Zipperowitsch an execution, Egyptian style.'

"God laughed—he pretended to think it was funny.

" 'Well, we shall see what kind of Egyptian execution he

will think up to fulfill your wish.'

" 'Do you mean to say Baal cannot do anything?'

" 'Of course not. He is nothing but a telegraph pole.'

" 'If that is so, then why are you jealous of him? Is there a Jew who would be jealous if his wife loved a piece of wood?'

"At that, the invented Lord became embarrassed, and he tiptoed quietly home. I heard this story a long, long time ago, in Homel, and most likely this was only the first part, for I am sure, Baal became upset, too. However, I know from a learned doctor, that one can break out into boils because of excitement and nervous upsets. Therefore, I beg you not to lose your temper. If you have nothing but your abysmal stupidity, why get so excited? You may blow, and they shall fly away, and your respectable coffee houses will remain intact."

Lasik was mistaken—his story did not pacify Mr. Rottenton.

"Criminal! Spy! Shameless individual! How dare you make fun of the Empire's Constitution! I do not wish to speak to you any longer. Just kindly answer my questions. And without subterfuge. Or you will have trouble. You are a Bolshevik courier. You are coming from Archangelsk! Here, sign the confession."

"All right. I am taking the pen. That is still better than seeing your mustache wiggle. Who knows what kind of custom you have here! Well, are you satisfied, now that I have signed? And now, will you tell me, where it swims around, that town of Archangelsk, because I have not yet been there. Perhaps one could appear there as a Rabbi or as a monkey?"

"Do not pretend! You have swallowed the letter. It is too late for subterfuge—I have your signature now. You are well acquainted with the contents of the document. It was from Trotzky, who informed the world how rotten conditions are under the Bolshevik clique, and he insisted on an upheaval in Liverpool. Here, take this pen and paper. You are going to write the text down once more. If . . ."

Lasik interrupted him:

"Not if, but rather already. . . ."

And a fleeting smile came over Lasik's face, showing creative effort. After several minutes, he handed Mr. Rottenton the written sheet.

"Honorable Comrade for the entire Great British numbers! Our clique amuses itself like the most insolent rabble. We are living high with the stolen money from the empty state treasury, eating our potato pudding with sauce, while all the border regions are collapsing in a great crash. Everywhere one looks there are Chinese generals and liver pâté with cabbage. That cannot be called living any longer, but a ridiculous orgy. But why are you sitting here, catching flies, wasting all that valuable time? I am calling out to you: The time for a revolt has come! Here, take twenty pence, wind yourself around with cartridges from top to toe. Our plan is very simple: Blasting of the Solomonic coffee houses, then the cannibals are left only with their pipes, and you can send that moustachioed Mister, who just yelled at me, to them. I don't know his name exactly, yet. Afterwards, all the loyal Hindus must be invited to a banquet at the castle, and of Liverpool nothing will remain but four or five bare rocks. But I am imploring you on my knees—do not delay! When I command: one-two-three, you must begin. And if you do away with every single one of them, I shall treat you to such a delicious pork roast with groats, that you will lick all your red-spy-and-henchmen fingers! And now, goodbye, I am tired, and give my regards to your wife. By the way, how are the little children? Yours, even past my grave, Trotzky."

"Bravo! That is what I call a document! How natural! . . . And that sentence about the mustachioed Englishman is also first-rate: the eye of Moscow. I congratulate you. And now you may go to prison."

"If it is 'bravo,' then why to prison? I agreed to remain here for a while, in order not to offend my hosts, but naturally, I do prefer to gallop away on the open road."

However, Mister Rottenton did not listen to Lasik any more. In prison, Lasik had plenty of time, and to soften Mr. Rottenton's heart, he wrote a few more letters: from Trotzky to Zinoviev, from Zinoviev to Mister Bottomgolow, even from Missis Pukke to Mister Rottenton. (The latter was flowing over with comradely advice.) Despite all that, Lasik was not released. He liked his new occupation so much, he decided to write someone a real letter. But to whom? To Fenya Hershanowitch? Out of the question—Schatzman could intercept it. To Mintschik? But why get him and oneself upset? Perhaps to Pfeifer? After all, Pfeifer was an official surveyor.

Lasik handed that letter also to the warden.

"Will you kindly mail this one too, since you are not a state but merely a post-office. But please do not confuse them. This letter is neither to Zinoviev nor to Chamberlain. It is addressed to no one else, but a mere anonymous."

"My dearest Pfeifer. I am writing you from the eighteenth prison, and it is only the beginning that is difficult. I do not think I am losing hope, even though my life is nothing but one big anecdote from Lewka's repertoire. As you very well put it: man is weaker than a fly, and stronger than iron. What occupations did I not have? If I had to fill out a statistical questionnaire, I would use at least a half a ton of official paper. I am sending you my portrait of one short moment, when I was urged to eat evil-smelling bouquets of flowers; but do not pay any attention to it. Even though I look like a playboy from the theater on that photograph, I am still only an ordinary Jew who has his share of small troubles in life. Please do not show the picture to Fenya, born Hershanowitch—I do not know to which Schatzman she now belongs. She should not see that gorgeous tie because she will say: 'That midget is acting like a big shot.' Just give her greetings from the justifiably offended Roitschwantz. At this point, an impertinent tear has fallen on the sheet, so please forgive the horrible blot. Write how you and your dear wife are getting along, also about your diamond, little Rosa, the clever child Leibtschik, and the dear heart, little Solomon. Whose trousers are you wearing now, my dearest Pfeifer? Do you remember? Whenever a button comes loose or the posterior busts open, do you think of the funny Roitschwantz who was always there with a needle in his hand? My heart is full of longing, and I am jittery like a tiger. Will I ever see Homel again, with its lovely trees on the banks of the Sosch, and all my friends and even the smelly barrel, or must I die among these hundred volumes? But I must not say any more, because of the complete censorship. I am even shouting 'hurrah' for their royal dreadnought. Farewell, my dear Pfeifer! I shall probably die soon. For one thing, lately I have been dreaming quite often—I was already resting under the earth, but that might just be a dream. The main thing is, and that is number two, that they want to publish certain letters, and thus it is time for the author to go into the next world, particularly if he is a great poet, like Pushkin, for instance. Please do not be angry if this letter has turned out to be an illusion. You know how it is when everyone around you is interested in you, as though they were your mother or brother . . . A thousand periods. If I should die, I do not wish the flag at our club of the small merchants to be put on half-mast. Those jokes are much too risky. No, I would rather they played a funeral march, because I have been an honest worker, and following me is a new heroic generation. Grow up and be happy, Rosele, Leibtschik and little Solomontschik! This is the wish from the grave of the half-deceased Roitschwantz."

Lasik wrote this beautiful letter in vain. Pfeifer never received it. But three days had hardly passed, when Mister Rottenton had Lasik summoned once again to his office. As soon as he entered, Lasik asked eagerly:

"Should I write some more? The rhythms are already beginning to dry up."

"I have read your letter to an unknown Eastern agitator. Is it possible that you might wish to return to Homel?"

"Aha! So now you finally understand that I am from Homel and not as you said, from Archangelsk! Whether I wish to return? I would have to think it over. I think I might. Though I am sure they would not waste any time in throwing me into a dungeon. After all, in Paris I voted for the latest step, so it is really quite possible they will shoot me altogether. Here I have a coffin cover over my head, and so the only question is, where will my curiosity be better satisfied. At least, in Homel I will learn before the end what turn the affection to Schatzman has taken."

"No, I am not going to let you, poor Roitschwantz, get into that trap! Soon your hour will come. I am putting all my cards on the table: we have sounded the trumpet. Now the delay is only on your part. To be sure, you are not yet flying, but tomorrow or after tomorrow you will certainly fly, like down feathers."

"Of course! That is why you are so cheerful today. Even your moustache does not wiggle. You see, when the atmosphere is so heavenly peaceful, I just love to have a good talk. But why are you constantly preoccupied with them? It really is not worth while. You see, already there is a blister on your nose. You know, you are like an old cook I used to know. She was very religious, and lived at a flour mill near Homel, and the old Jew Serkin lived there, too. And he ate only *kosher* cooking. He was so backward that he could get a runny nose—by just looking at a pig. Every day he would cook his own soup in a special pot. And what do you think? One day, Shurka from the party cell notices the pot boiling, Serkin counting the flour-sacks, and the cook drops secretly a piece of pork into the soup. And the same thing happens day after day. She did not even economize with her ration. Naturally, Shurka could not contain his curiosity and he asked:

" 'Why these ingredients?'

"But she answers quietly: 'Well, you know, it is only because otherwise the old Jew will not get into Heaven.'

"And now you are doing the same thing to me. By the way, I am sitting here for two months already, which means you have published everything I have swallowed a long time ago, and now you might as well throw me out."

"No, we are not simply throwing you out. Now you are obligated to us. I am going to make you an advantageous offer. You will give us information about the Jews in London and the Bolshevik agitators. Eleven pounds per month."

Lasik could not suppress a sigh:

"So you really do not want any lard! . . . What can one do in such a case. A small advance would be absolutely necessary . . ."

In possession of his newly found freedom, Lasik went to Whitechapel. There he had a snack, bought himself a second-hand suit, as well as a Lithuanian passport, and without any further thoughts about the future, he went to the nearest railroad station. At the ticket window his eyes caught sight of a familiar name, and so he bought a ticket to Liverpool. Arriving there, he strolled along the bank watching the steamers. Where should he travel? Well, it really did not matter . . . as long as it was not to Rumania or the Solomon Islands! All of a sudden, he noticed a group of Jews on deck of a steamboat. Homel, in flesh and blood!

"Where are you all going, in such complete chorus?"

"Where? What a question! Of course we are traveling to our homeland, we are going directly to Palestine."

Lasik thought: why should he not go along with them? Perhaps the Jews would be more polite than those powerful British. All right! So now he was a good Zionist too, and he was traveling on a reduced rate to his beloved country.

Just before the steamer's departure, Lasik became uneasy. It just goes to show what habit means! He quickly bought a post card, showing the picture of a dreadnought, and wrote:

"My dear Mister Rottenton! I became used to writing, and so I am writing to you. You are really a Scottish blockhead. Perhaps you are even related to Mister Bottomgolow? But this is not why I am writing you. I forgot to tell you, that I am really a courier, that I really swallowed a paper with a real secret written on it. Now it arrived in Liverpool, and I have recovered everything with one blow. So, be careful with your pipes! And now I am going back home, and not to Homel, but to Archangelsk, because you just happened to point your finger at the wrong spot. We have emptied several bottles of wine with your money, and now I cannot stop laughing, like a humble Hindu. You may write me, c/o General Delivery, or not, as you wish. But, please, shave off your moustache, because all the cats that see you will laugh at you. Yours, until the grave, Mister Lasik Roitschwanch."

37

He did not have enough money. However, Lasik got on the boat. He polished the shoes of the first-class passengers. When he had nothing to do, he would go over to the helm which sheltered the third-class passengers. Everyone was there! The unemployed from Whitechapel, Lithuanian refugees, old *Zadiks* (traveling to Palestine, to die there), and ardent Zionists, singing nationalist hymns from morning till night. Also, characters with *Peyes* curls from long-forgotten times who would pray with *Talles* and *Twillem,* and next to them, Communists. Upstarts from New York, changing dollars, *Chassidim* from Galizia sighing unhappily and pulling out their miserable zlotys from underneath their caftans, and a constantly frightened butcher, hiding a lonely tscherwonetz, like a secret document, from the eyes of his companions.

It was quiet up in first class, respectable and boring. A rich Jewess from Chicago was on a pleasure trip to the Holy Land. In the expectation of the great mercy that God was going to grant her, she gave Him, in the meantime, her obviously useless soul, praying day and night near the porcelain wash-basin. British officials, amusing each other with all kinds of tricks, were drinking port and promenading on deck. Their legs, sticking out of long, checquered trousers, did not take a single unnecessary step. Here, there was neither an anathema, nor a prayer, neither pogrom-reports, nor arguments between Communists, and Poale-Zionists, not even one interesting biography. Here, Lasik did nothing but polish shoes. At the helm, however, he was listening, talking and sighing.

Sometimes he would sit down on a barrel and meditate in complete solitude. He had not lied in his letter to Pfeifer; in all these years of wandering, he had indeed become thinner and older. One might have thought he was over forty. He was sickly, he groaned and coughed, he complained—he had a pain in his chest, another in his hips. At the slightest effort, his forehead would be covered with cold perspiration. Perhaps he had caught a cold, or maybe the butcher from Mainz had overdone it—I do not know. But at the mere sight of his feverish eyes, anyone would have exclaimed: Hey, you dear inhabitants of Homel, you live marvelously and happily among your finance inpectors, operettas and goose *greaven,* but take a look at our poor Lasik Roitschwantz who is falling apart! He has seen a great deal, he has come to know love and sorrow, he has experienced everything. Now he is sitting in a corner, coughing, cringing, he does not even have the strength to tell the god-fearing *Zadik* how that rascal, Lewka, had gobbled up a whole sausage on *Yom Kippur* right in front of the synagogue, toasting the health of all the fasting Jews, while Kogan's mouth was watering and his indecent saliva was drooling down into the street. No, he just sits in a corner, wrapped in an old sack, looking out into the ocean.

"Why don't you say something?" Lasik was asked by one of the New York Jews.

"I am here to polish boots, not to talk. I should say I have done enough talking in my life. If you saw me without my shirt, your mouth would fall wide open. There is not the smallest spot that is not bruised. You would think my miserable body were a passport. As soon as I uttered two words, they started to hit me. Why do you think I am traveling to Palestine and not to America or to the North Pole? I should say because the Jews are not organized in giving beatings, and there is a small chance for me to survive. I can imagine the electrical gadgets they have in America for thrashing people! And at the North Pole, they probably have a police doctor with no less than two heavy fists. The Jews, however, have not beaten me too much. To be sure, in Frankfurt, Herr Moiser broke his umbrella over my body, but how can you compare an umbrella with a butcher's club. I hope, in the Jewish Palestine, they will finally stop jumping on me. Then you will be quite right, for it will be a Holy Land. Why don't I give lectures? I am tired. That can happen to anyone. And besides—how do you know, perhaps at this very moment I am talking to the crazy water out there. The old Berko in Homel used to say that anything can sing. You think this sack here is dumb? No, it merely transforms its way of singing. Naturally, blockheads can hear only the ready-made words; the wise men, however, can understand the tune too. That is why two fools sitting together cannot be quiet, they are bored, and so they start wagging their tongues. I certainly do not think of myself as belonging to the wisest people, but I can hear some tunes. I can hear, for instance, the singing of the ocean, and not merely the ripple of the water, but also all kinds of imagined fantasies: of the great life without any shores, where ocean and sky flow together, and then they are—the real world; those three classes, however, with all their whistling, are nothing but one sour note. I have heard in my lifetime how these various things can sing. When I would cut a pair of trousers and cut them well, they would sing, and be happy. Every object would like to be better than you and I, only it seems people are ashamed of the beautiful songs. The trousers, however, open their hearts to the very bottom.

"Berko used to say: The wiser a man was, the more melodies he could hear. But Berko himself was an old fashioned *Chassid*, and he could only hear the souls of the pious Jews singing at his synagogue. If one may believe him, Moses must have heard the hearts of all the Jews of this world sing. Of course, I am not sure how much opium is in that. I, for one, hear once in a while a little sound and then I smile of happiness. After that, however, the same dreary life starts once again. It might be interesting to know whether there was any man who could hear all the melodies at the same time: the Jews and those powerful Britishers and the cats and the suits and even the hard rocks? I imagine the heart of such a wise man must move into his head—to be nearer the ears so as to hear better, for, with the brain one can indeed figure out a wireless tower like the one in Paris and start angling for all kinds of words, but to catch a real melody in one of those tubes, that is not possible, is it? Only the heart can hear that.

"Now you have seen that I can talk sometimes. It is a good thing that I am not traveling to your country, America! There they know how to take the Jewish language and transform it into a numbered dollar bill with the head of their married president."

The sea was tranquil, and Lasik looked admiringly at the

blossoming shores of Portugal.

"What inmost perfect beauty! Now I can see with my very own eyes the invented paradise. I am sure they have so many orchids here that they make ridiculous hay out of them, and nobody even notices the bananas, just like we do not notice the sunflower seeds in Homel! Just the uneducated Portuguese will chew them. And those castles! Do you see the castles? But if one really thinks about it, this is no paradise, either. I have in my pocket the portrait of the Portuguese hostage. I managed to save it through all my trials and tribulation. Well, my dear hostage, take a good look at your fatherland! Most likely, this hostage is perishing somewhere in a Portuguese prison. Of course, to have this marvelous sun means already a good deal of happiness. And it shines for everyone. But still, the Portuguese want to eat too. After all, one cannot smell orchids all day long. And so, if we take a closer look, Portugal is no better than Homel. What do you think, Homel seen from the distance is quite attractive! It is quite easy to sigh of admiration for it. From the distance you can see the mountainous shores and the tall trees and the Paskewitsch Park with all its beautiful arcades. Yes, one can see happiness at a distance of a hundred kilometers; misfortune however, one smells only when it is quite near. That is all. We can go on and continue our meditation. But I don't know why. If a nice upheaval of the masses should help this hostage to regain his freedom, they would only throw someone else into prison, for the earth is everywhere the same—it scratches. Man, however, is made of the same dough: either he is an insolent scoundrel with Swedish gymnastics, or he is a slaughtered rabbit. No, it is much better to look out into the sea that shelters the poor, miserable fish.

"I have heard a very good story in Homel, about King David. It is indeed an understatement to say that he was just a king; he was, besides, a marvelous poet, and he had everything:

wine as good as musical drums, and his dinner at the first ring of the bell, just like the first-class passengers on this boat, and as much paper as he wanted, so that he could make up one nice poem every single day. One day, he was really lucky. He was sitting and sweating, and could not figure out how to praise this invented God. He could not find the right words. Having thought up a thing like such a great God, they also thought up ways to behave with him, and King David kept using the same old words over and over again, none of which were any good; they were all so small and insignificant that God appeared in them almost as though he had been wearing a child's dress. And all of a sudden, two or three absolutely fabulous words come to his mind. He makes some poems, real first-class. Naturally he was deliriously happy, took the sheet under his arm, read it aloud to everyone, and was widely complimented: 'King David, you are the new Pushkin, a recognized genius.' Of course as you know, all poets love to be flattered. Shurka Bezdomny wanted the cigarettes to be named after him, instead of 'Tscherwonetz.' And of course, you can easily imagine how the singing king felt about being praised. He was nearly bursting with glory. Already he had read his verses to one and all: to his wife and his children, to his court and the critics, and generally to all the Jews he knew. Now he had almost no one left to read to. He went for a stroll in the garden and he was radiant with happiness, like a polished tea-kettle. Suddenly he saw a toad, and the toad asked him with an impudent smile: 'Why are you shining, David, as though you had been rubbed with chalk?' King David did not have to answer at all. He was a king, a genius, this and that, why did he have to even talk to an unknown toad? No one stops to have a conversation with a toad anyway. You kick them aside so they will not get under your feet. But after all, King David was not a mere Shurka Bezdomny. He knew a little more than just a few compliments. And he replied to the toad:

" 'Yes, indeed, I am shining. I have written some wonderful poetry. Just listen to it!'

"And he began to read his enthusiastic words. However, the toad was not easily moved. It asked:

" 'Is that all?'

" 'This was only one poem. I have thousands of them, for every morning when I awake, I am glad to be alive and that is when I write my beautiful hymns.'

"At this point, the toad burst into laughter. To be sure, a toad does not laugh like a person, but if something is funny, it still laughs. 'I just cannot understand why you make such a fuss about it, David. I, for example, am the most miserable toad, but I sing just as you do. Have you not heard me croaking? No one compliments me. What would you say makes your words better than my anonymous croaking?

"King David actually blushed of embarrassment. He no longer shone. No, he strolled humbly around the garden, listening to the singing of each blade of grass. That miserable toad taught him to become a wise man.

"Just look at the ocean! And those clouds! Is it not much better than all our talks?"

But alas! Lasik did not rejoice too long with the beauties of nature. A west wind started blowing. The ship began to sway. With great difficulty Lasik crawled to the edge of the boat.

"What kind of deadly foxtrot is this? Ocean, I have just praised you so glowingly, and now it turns out that you too are against the miserable Roitschwantz! Enough now! . . . I have seen that you know all the little tricks, but do not let me die! Oh, Fenitschka Hershanowitch, how good it is that you cannot see me now! . . ."

A bell rang. A maid called angrily:

"The slippers for cabin forty-three! Quick! Why did you not

clean them?"

"In a minute, I may dirty them worse than they are. Don't talk to me about slippers when I am ready to die. What kind of a 'Holy Land' is this anyway, if it gives a little Jew such a hard time to get there! It is almost better to wander for forty years through a definite desert! Take these slippers away, or there will be trouble! . . ."

The sun came out again, the sea calmed down and became blue once more, the boat "Victoria" pursued its course calmly. The first-class passengers changed their clothes for dinner. Bells were ringing, constantly. But neither the English major's boots, nor the slippers of the two gay tourists, nor even the tiny shoes of the rich Jewess were anywhere to be seen. A small shadow was moving along the helm. Lasik was bending over the railing, as before. At last a steward found him:

"Everyone is searching for you? And where are you, catching fish, perhaps? Where are the shoes?"

"I . . . I cannot . . ."

"Don't pretend! It does not sway any longer!"

"But what if it starts up again? You know the bell does not have to ring for that? So, I found a comfortable spot."

To be sure, that was a clever idea. However, the steward was obviously not a lover of philosophy. He beat Lasik with the major's boots. They were strong, heavy boots—with spurs.

38

On his arrival in Tel-Aviv, Lasik noticed a dozen Jews who were standing at the railroad station, gesticulating vigorously.

When Lasik came closer, he heard old Hebrew words. He was seriously surprised:

"Why do you meet on the street to pray. Don't they have any synagogues for your old-fashioned services?"

"You nincompoop! Who said we were praying? As a matter of fact, we are discussing the rate of exchange of the Egyptian pound. Here everyone speaks the language of the Bible. This is our land and we would advise you to forget your idiotic jargon at once."

Lasik could only scratch himself. As though he did not know those singing languages! They wanted to organize a stock market in the biblical manner? Fine. Who does not have his whims and fancy? The main thing, where could one get something to eat?

Miserably he walked past the new houses, gardens and shops. On the signboards of the bakeries they had real Hebrew letters. No kidding! But rolls are rolls, and in order to be able to buy them, one has to put some wretched money on the table. . . .

Lasik sat down on a bench on the square. He was so hungry his eyes became dim.

"The land looks like any other land. I, for example, do not feel that it is mine, for it certainly does not belong to me, but probably to Rothschild or maybe even to Chamberlain, and I do not even have the feeling that it is Holy. It scratches the same like any other place. But what do my eyes see? . . . Abramtschik, how did you get here? How many years since you have left our beloved Homel? Three years already? Well, what do you know! Tell me, have you also been seasick on that wet swing? . . ."

Abramtschik sighed miserably:

"I cannot remember very well. I have been shaken so much since then that the boat just seems like a cradle to me. I tried to do work in the fields, but I got a sunburn and I had to lie half a year in the hospital. Afterwards, I was beaten up one night by some Arabs, so I had to return once more to the hospital. Then, when I was trying to sell newspapers in Yiddish, it was not the Arabs who beat me up—but the Jews. And then they did not even admit me to the hospital any more. Fine. So I decided to become a beggar in Jerusalem. That is a pretty profitable business. You remember how the orthodox Jewish women in Homel used to drop five, sometimes ten kopeks into a small metal box, and then came a man from Palestine and took the whole money with him. Now, it turns out that those little metal boxes are everywhere, and the result is a great many juicy zeros, so that it pays to stand at the Wailing Wall and wail, and you get a fixed monthly salary. I was wailing as though I was being cut in four. But it all collapsed because of a cigarette butt. I forgot I was not in Homel any more, but in Jerusalem; and without thinking, I began to smoke a nice cigarette butt that an Englishman had dropped. Well, what do you think happened? It turned out to be Saturday—that is what I call luck from Homel—and I was given such a thrashing that I could hardly crawl away. I yelled at them: 'If it is Sabbath, you must not do any work either, and you are working when you beat me!' But they did not even want to listen to me. And now I have returned once again to this wonderful city of Tel-Aviv, and I am sure I will die here. The old *Zadiks* who traveled to Palestine to die were really not such idiots. This is the most acceptable profession here. Why did I believe their beautiful words, why did I come running here? Simply because I was a fool, and when you used to tell me during the preliminary political course: 'Abramtschik, you are a little slow in catching on,' you were absolutely right. But what about you, Roitschwantz, you are almost a Marxist, how did you get here?"

"That I shall tell you some other time, after I have eaten and not before. You do not know anything, When you left for Odessa, I was still sewing my tail-coats. In those times, the streets of Homel were full of real people and a few dirty pieces of paper, but not with citizens like that female, Pukke. I got caught up in some historical whirlwind. I came here, for instance, from some intentional Liverpool. It seemed to me they would stop beating me here. But after your bloody confession, I am beginning to tremble. You see, my body is so used up that my soul could leave me any moment. Anyway, whatever will be, will be! Before anything, I would like to eat something. Should I go perhaps to Jerusalem and start carrying on at the Wailing Wall?"

"You can carry on! But they do not pay you by the day. They pay you once a month, and now you will have to wait three weeks. Now I know all their inhuman excesses!"

"What shall I do? . . . I must eat. Is there anyone from Homel here?"

"Oh sure! Not just anybody, but David Goldbruch, in person. Do you remember, he used to have an office on the corner of Vladimir Street? Right at the beginning, when the Bolsheviks came, he disappeared in a suit he had borrowed from his servant. Yes, that is the one and he is here. You should know, he is sitting in your Palestinian Committee, and he is proclaiming to everyone that this is the paradise of oranges. I tried once to get in to see him, but he slammed the door right before my nose. Among other things, he owns three marvelous houses and such elegance inside that the Englishmen are paying a half a pound just for the privilege to look in."

"I have made up my mind. I am going to see Goldbruch. You just did not find the right tone how to talk to him. What? He is on the Committee and he should ignore Roitschwantz, when this same Roitschwantz came especially from the same home town, Homel, into his orange paradise? No, that is impossible! You will see, Abramtschik, I am going to invite you this evening to a leg of veal and potatoes, or perhaps jellied meat. I don't know which you prefer, I like them both."

Goldbruch lived well indeed. He supervised construction building. Sometimes he built for others, but most of the time he built for himself. And then took off for Europe on vacation. There he collected money, told about the orange export, had fun with the girls that had been left behind and fondly thought of Tel-Aviv: "If business is good, in the fall I am going to build another little country house."

Goldbruch received Lasik in the garden-house. He was resting and drinking ice cold lemonade. His bare chest was fanned by an electric ventilator. Even though Lasik could not remember what kind of bird this fellow Goldbruch was, he called enthusiastically:

"Dodja! You see, the world is not so big after all—here we meet again! Well, well, how have you been?"

And Lasik closed one eye, as Monkin would do when he was looking at a painting.

"A bit sunburnt, but otherwise, just the same. I would have even known you on the square in Paris! What? You do not know who I am? I am first and foremost, your neighbor. You used to live on the Vladimir Street. Now it has become, forgive the expression, the Red Flag Street. And I lived on the Clara Zetkin Street. That is a couple of steps away. It would be interesting to know who used to sew the trousers for you? Probably Zimach. Do you recognize me now? I am Roitschwantz, the tailor. What do you mean, it does not ring a bell? I am telling you! That should suffice! And how are your dear children? What? You do not have any children? So, for whom are you building all those houses? Well, don't take it to heart, the children will come yet. By the way, what are you drinking here? A plain lemonade? And when, may I ask, do you have your dinner?"

Instead of a reply, Goldbruch screamed so angrily that Lasik backed away at least ten steps.

"Why are you yelling as though you were in the desert?"

"Because you are a shameless man! Come to the point and tell me what you want from me, and leave me in peace!"

"What I want from you? Well, for example, a piece of homemade sausage on good Jewish bread."

"Go to work!"

"Oh, so you have something to be pressed? Just give me a thimble and I can alter any suit, or even shorten . . ."

"I have no work for you. Are you a tailor? In that case, you came to the wrong country. There are more tailors here than trousers."

"So what will I do tomorrow, if I am not dead by then?"

"Nothing. You will be like all the others—one of the unemployed."

"But do they get anything to eat? Because then I really do not mind."

"You want to know what they get? A long nose. We have here a regular state, but is there a state where there are no unemployed workers? You will sit still and wait until this crisis is over."

"How long will I have to sit without eating?

"Probably a year or two."

"A year or two?—You must be a clown. But let me ask you straightforward: what would happen if I took one of your blessed rolls from your buffet?"

"Very simple—you would be arrested on the spot. We here have a regular state, but is there a state without a prison? And I am already pressing this button to have you thrown out into the street, for I am much too hot for such a stupid conversation."

"I am going anyway. Goodbye, Dodja, and let us say, we'll see each other next year in Homel. You do not like it? So go and build yourself another little house! Oh my, how you grunt! You know what? I have not seen a single pig here yet. But of course, how can there be any pigs, when this is our Jewish homeland? You see, that could mean a minus for you. Because is there a state without pigs? But don't get excited, calm down. You really have a regular state, and you even have your own pigs, because you, for instance, seen from the profile . . ."

Lasik did not succeed in completing his comparison. At the sight of the broad-shouldered servant, he merely called: "It is starting already! And right away with the Goliath himself," whereupon he quickly disappeared through the gate. And so, Abramtschik got neither the leg of veal nor the jellied meat.

The same familiar misery began for Lasik once again. The daily job hunting, the heartrending kitchen aromas around dinner time, footsteps, philosophical talks, and, at night, sleeping on the bare ground. But it became more and more difficult to endure that life: his legs would not carry him any longer, the cough tore his chest to pieces, and at night he dreamed of the Sosch, of international melodies and of death.

He worked for about two weeks for Mohilewsky who had a clothier's shop in Jaffa. In Tel-Aviv there were many stores; in Jaffa, however, business was real good. Only one thing was bad: the Arabs kept beating the Jews. Each morning, when Mohilewsky went from Tel-Aviv to Jaffa, he put on a fez to look like an Arab. And Lasik, too, had to brighten his head with a red little hat. He liked that: after all, a fez was not a tail, and furthermore it was like playing in an opera. One evening, however, Mohilewsky had sensed the approach of a storm, and he had left with the profits for Tel-Aviv. Lasik stayed behind, watching the merchandise. The Arabs came. They shouted something, but Lasik did not understand. He tried in his best Homel language to appease the crowd.

"But certainly! I am a one hundred per cent pure Arab. I have at home a regular harem and the bust of Mohammed!"

However, it did not seem to make the slightest impression on the Arabs.

After he came back, Mohilewsky fired Lasik: "You do not know how to deal with them in a friendly manner."

Lasik scratched his back, grumbling sadly:

"You are just as wild as the real Arabs! Generally speaking, it is a good life for the Jews on this Jewish soil. But where will I have to die: at this fence or at the other?"

He begged around, helped a butcher slaughter chickens, stuffed pillows and slowly faded away. Once he succeeded to get into a night club with the assistance of the mechanic, Chishin. Girls with heavy makeup, not any worse than Margot Chique, were dancing, throwing their naked legs to the ceiling. They were singing dirty songs. Lasik could hardly understand them, for in Hebrew he could only pray. However, the girl's hips made an overwhelming impression upon him. Making his way through the honorable champagne-drinking audience, he jumped on stage and proclaimed:

"Indeed, here blossom the holy oranges! I am falling on my knees. I am in love with you all! How many are you? Eight? Good, I am in love with eight oranges and I would rather die here of heroic love than somewhere in the street of miserable appetite."

The girls seemed to enjoy it. They began to laugh. One of them even talked to Lasik in Russian:

"You are making the most charming compliments. One can see right away that you are from Odessa!"

"As a matter of fact, I am not. I am from Homel. But that is not important. Let us turn to the problem of the oranges . . ."

At this point, someone from the audience ran up to Lasik and shouted:

"Infamous scoundrel! How dare you bring your Slav accent into this rarified atmosphere! While they are talking the holy language of Sulamith, you come barging in, offending our honorable ears with your manure from Homel! You must be an avowed Bolshevik!"

Lasik looked at the ranter and froze: it was none other than David Goldbruch. Lasik asked him quickly:

"Dodja, is the Goliath with you?"

"Scoundrel! How dare you go on making jokes when all the committee members are seated at the table! Hey, doorman, free our valley of young palm trees from this squeaking rascal!"

The doorkeeper gave Lasik a good beating. Then he handed him over to two police officers:

"Mister Goldbruch said he is an avowed Bolshevik."

Thereupon the policemen began to hit Lasik with their fists.

"Hold it! What are you anyway? Jews or police-doctors?"

"Naturally we are Jews. But you will lose a few ribs today. Those Englishmen make a big fuss saying we do not know how to deal with Bolshevism. All right! Let them see how we are dealing with you!" Lasik was taken to prison, half-dead. There, he kissed the portrait of the Portuguese hostage most tenderly, said: "the nineteenth," and began to cry.

"They beat me no worse than the singing Pan Captains. How can there be any doubt—of course, this is a regular state! I do not know how many ribs I had and how many are left, I do not keep an inventory. One thing I do know—this is the end of Roitschwantz."

The next morning they questioned him. When Lasik saw the British uniform, he froze:

"What have the British to do with it? Are they, perhaps, also dissatisfied that I did not talk the language of Sulamith with those oranges?"

The Englishman asked sternly:

"Are you a Bolshevik?"

"What kind of great politics can this be when their legs have made me lose my senses? I think you are piercing me with your intelligent stare. Could it be that you received a postal card from Mister Rottenton? Then, you may as well begin to dig my grave."

"We are not going to tolerate any kind of Bolshevism here! We shall wipe it out completely! We shall purge our country of Moscow spies!"

Lasik became meditative:

"Interesting—am I sleeping or not? Have I perhaps lost my senses from those Goliaths? To be sure, they shook only my hips, over and over, but maybe my brains were shaken, accidentally, too. I don't understand, for instance, why you choose to remember your great country, with Trotsky's letters and even with the potato-pudding, when I am not in Liverpool, but in the Jewish Palestine?"

"You are revealing your entire black ungratefulness. We have returned your beloved homeland to you. We are protecting you. That is called 'Mandate.' Do you understand? We have built war bases for the great British fleet and an airport for flights from England to India. We are not economizing when it comes to spending money for you. However, we shall not tolerate any Bolshevik contamination."

Lasik thanked him, bowing deeply.

"Merci! Merci up to my grave! But tell me, perhaps you better take that mandate away from me when I am such a thankless Roitschwantz? I am going to die soon anyway, so please let me die in freedom, so I may yet get a glimpse of those orange fairy-tales, and the sun, and the thorny earth which has borne me for some mysterious reason! And then, after a month or two, you may protect my contaminated grave in its vast entirety. I can give you an absolutely unconditional mandate for that. You have already returned to me my homeland, with this splendid harbor and even with an airport. You are a Great Britisher and a golden soul. Just give me back a little bit of fresh air and the clouds that drift up there in the skies, so I may smile once more at the edge of my grave!"

39

For two long months Lasik had to sit in the prison of Jerusalem. When he was set free, the orange trees were blossoming, but he could not smile at them. He could barely make it to the Wailing Wall.”

“What shall I do? I can only stand here and cry. Maybe I am lucky, and tomorrow is pay day. Then I will really eat a whole ox! And if not, it does not matter either. At least it is interesting to die near a suitable object. Who would cry for me? Here, however, I will hear more heartrending sighs than any rich man has ever heard. Here, there must be at least three hundred pilgrims, howling from morn till night. Of course it makes no difference to them what they are crying about, and so they will bewail the dead Roitschwantz: 'Oh, why did you have to be ruined, our magnificent temple!' "

Lasik remembered his new duties. He began to beat his chest and cry. Next to him, a red-haired Jew was crying so hard, Lasik had to hold his ears:

"Couldn't you cry two tones lower, or my eardrums will burst! . . ."

The red-haired Jew looked up. Lasik was astounded: "What visions! Is it really you, Abramtschik? But how did you become red-haired, when you were always dark?"

"Ssst. I have simply dyed my beard, so they will not recognize me, you know, because of that event with the cigarette butt. All right, let us wail together!"

And they both began to cry. Lasik was bewailing the temple diligently, but his mind was busy with something else. When the wailers went home, he said to Abramtschik: "Listen to me, Abramtschik. I am going to make you a concrete proposition. What do you think, wouldn't it be high time for us to return to our home country?"

Abramtschik froze in amazement: "As though I had not heard such words often enough? It seems to me we have returned to our homeland already. What else do you want?"

"That is very simple. I am proposing that we return to our country. Of course, here we have the singing language, and the Holy Earth, and a Jewish police force, and even a mandate in British uniform. And naturally, there is no doubt, this is the paradise of the oranges, but I want to return to my home town. I do not know where you were born—perhaps under Arabian orange-trees. As far as I am concerned, I was born, by the way, in Homel, and it is time that I returned home. I have traveled around the world, have seen how people live, have experienced the various types of boxing in different countries. Now, all I yearn for is my unforgettable home town, Homel. I know my strength will come back all of a sudden, and I shall swim and get there alive! Once again I shall see the beautiful picture, when the Sosch shines at the foot of its steep banks, the trees and the crowds near the theater, and the market with its closed umbrellas. I shall see Pfeifer again. I will say to him: 'My dear Pfeifer, how could you get along without me? Who, for instance, made your trousers for you? Zimach, most likely. Here, just look at this crease, it is not even where it's supposed to be.' And Pfeifer will break out in tears. And his little son, Solomon, will jump around me: 'Uncle Jassja, please give me five kopeks for candy.' And I will give him my whole heart, of course. I shall see Fenitschka Hershanowitch once again. She will be strolling in the beautiful Paskewitsch Park with her little son. I will make absolutely no petty scandal. No, I will say to her: 'Good morning. Just go on taking your walk. May your little hero grow and blossom. I was away in twenty countries and just as many jails. I have crossed all the seas. I have seen the orchids in bloom. But I have always thought of you. Now of course, I have to die and you don't have to pay any attention to me, but I ask you just one thing, please put a flower from Homel on my grave. It should by no means be the indecent orchid, but rather the most miserable camomile that grows everywhere under your feet.' Yes, this is what I will say to Fenitschka Hershanowitsch, and then I will die with a wonderful feeling of happiness."

"You are speaking of death for no reason at all. You are still very young, and you might even get married yet. I just don't understand one thing. How do you propose to get from here to Homel? After all, it is not an arm's length from here."

"Well, I will just have to get on one of those swings again and close my eyes. So it will turn my stomach around! There are only two possibilities anyway: either I die or I get there."

"But you must have lost your senses. Who will take you along?"

"It is quite simple. Jankelewitsch in Paris explained it to me in detail. This is all I have to do: I take a sheet, and I establish on the spot a society with full authority, called 'Society for Return to the Home Country.' By the way, this will become a great federation: you see, you are absolutely not obligated to travel to Homel. You can return to Fastow, or even to Odessa. I shall collect a hundred signatures and send them by registered letter to all the Chief Commissars in Moscow, and they will send a real boat to pick us up. Don't you think there are enough of the same mind, right here? Will Juska not shout 'Hurrah'? Will the old Schenkel not fall around my neck? What is there to talk about? Everybody will go. I am not going to delay any longer. I am going right now and have the people fill out a questionnaire."

Indeed, Juska jumped with joy when he was told of the 'Society for Return to the Home Country.' He even treated Lasik to goat cheese. With Schenkel, however, it was not that easy. He did not begin by falling around Lasik's neck. He had his objections:

"Why do you want to return? Perhaps you are a Commissar? What a life they have there! Real honey! And maybe you think they are going to frame you in gold, because you came back?"

"No, I did not think about that. And I will tell you the truth, I think they will do just the opposite to me. After all, I will not be able to prove it to them, that Boris Samoilowitsch and I are different things altogether. You see, I played the part of being his real nephew, and they are naturally going to ask me, what had become of that valuable little package. Well, as long as the Citizen Pukke will not be there! But who knows, maybe she has remained forever in Homel? After all, it is a beautiful city, and she might have really liked it. And then they will shoot me, one-two-three. But does it matter? I would still like to die at home."

"You, Roitschwantz, are still young and foolish. Do you realize what you are doing? There they have cells and the Finance Inspector, and this is not allowed and that is forbidden too, and they arrest you for the smallest trifle. It is absolute hell! What fool with any common sense will hand himself over to such torture?"

"Of course you are older than I, but as to common sense, that is still a big question. All right. So there is hell, and here is paradise. Of course, I have not yet noticed that this is paradise. You yourself are not living like an angel, but rather on the barest dry crust. But it is entirely possible that I am shortsighted. In Homel, Lewka used to sing tunes of Paris that would make my mouth water. Well, I have been in Paris, and I must say, I have also not noticed that it was such a terrific paradise either. They beat me up there too. But let us say, the paradise is in America, for, thank God, I have not yet been there, and so I will not argue about it. Let it be the one hundred per cent paradise there, and in our land the purest hell. I accept this possibility, and I would still like to return. I am going to tell you a story from Homel, and then we shall see what you will say. You must have surely heard of the *Zadik* from Rovno. He was neither young nor foolish, as I am. He certainly represents absolute authority to you, once you believe in all that prescribed murmuring, as you do. Well then, one day a strict Talmudist came to see that *Zadik* with the most bitter reproaches: 'Listen to me, Rabbi! I do not understand you any more. Everybody says you are a pious Jew. I live next door, and it seems to me that yours is not a house, but a regular night club. I sit reading the Talmud, while your *Chassidim* do, the devil knows what—they dance and sing, they don't stop laughing, as though this was a Moscow operetta.'

"The *Zadik* replied calmly:

"'Indeed, they laugh like children, they sing like birds, and they skip around like young goats. For in their hearts, there is no room for any evil, only joy and overflowing love.'

"The Talmudist became so furious that he nearly swallowed the tip of his beard. You see, he used to chew his beard whenever he was trying to find the right word. And, indeed, he did not find it. He merely said: 'These are pretty indecent words for a Jew. As you know, Rabbi, when we study the Talmud for an hour, we are getting one step closer to paradise. Thus, if we do not study the Talmud, it is as though we were slipping right back into hell. Your *Chassidim* sing like idiotic birds, instead of sitting and pondering over the Holy Book. So where are you pushing them? To hell, naturally! In hell, however, there is fear and horror. There, some are being boiled, others fried, still others are being hung by their tongues. To be sure, if you like that, you may go on dancing an hour before being cooked. I, however, will study the Talmud, so I can go to Paradise. There, it is always warm, the temperature not too hot and not too cold, even good company—in a word, nothing but angels; everyone sits there with golden crowns reading the Torah. There, the roses have no thorns, the trees no caterpillars, and on the way there is not a single watch-dog. Could it be that you do not wish to get to Paradise?'

"The *Zadik* laughed out loud:

" 'No. Of course, I am grateful for your little pieces of advice, but I am not yearning for that perfect paradise. In my opinion, only angels can live there, for they are not people. They have neither hearts, nor livers, nor passions. And man should never be afraid, even if he falls to the very bottom. How can anyone rise who has never fallen? You have told me here of a strange paradise. That is not *my* paradise, and besides there is no paradise for me at all. I will not build one either. To stare at pretty pictures is not for me. If I will do a great deal of laughing and crying and loving, who knows, perhaps, on the edge of my grave, I will get to see my bloodstained paradise.'

"That is what the *Zadik* of Rowno replied to the learned Talmudist. I am requesting you to go. To be sure, everything is bad and difficult there. There is no even temperature, maybe even a deadly draft. However, there the people are searching for something. And I am sure they are wrong. Maybe they don't even fly up, but rather down instead; but they are flying somewhere and don't just yawn on their readymade pillows. Of course, you, Schenkel, are pretty old and you can stay here; but you, Broidek, and you, Selman,—you are young daredevils. Here, give me quickly your flaming signatures! . . ."

"What signatures? What is this gathering on a Holy Street? Are you, by the way, the chief agitator? Well, come over here and get your juicy signature!"

Lasik knew by now that the Jews could hit too. He began to run. At first they pursued him. He ran along the suburban boulevard, trying to get out of town. But his breadth would not hold out. He could not make it. Miserably, he thought to himself: "Just like that naked Jew, running around Rome . . ." He felt himself losing strength. He was sure now, he would not get back to his homeland! . . . He stopped. Nobody was behind him any longer. All around him the fields were dark—a few dimly lit farms, the stars, the quiet.

"Where is my paradise?"

And he tried to push on—without any strength.

40

Lasik was walking along the streets—where and why, he did not know. He could not walk, but he walked nevertheless. It seemed to him, he must have walked thousands of kilometers. Could it not be that Homel was already around the corner? However, the dark cupolas and minarets of Jerusalem contrasted as before with the white sky. Lasik kept walking. At last his legs gave up. He was now lying in the dust of the street.

"It seems as though this might be a good spot to write the last period."

But no, they were not going to leave Lasik in peace. A car honked. The driver, slamming on the brakes, cursed:

"Shameless tramp! How dare you lie in my way?"

Lasik smiled guiltily. All right, he would not lie there any longer. After all, he was a learned man, he knew that a crushed insect was not supposed to block the traffic.

But what kind of old garden-house was this? Surely, no one lived there. He would certainly not disturb anyone with his indecent appearance.

Lasik crawled up to the stony roof. Inside it was dark and cool. He saw a bearded Jew with a cap on his head and a fat lady. The lady was so full of diamonds, Lasik had to close his eyes. They shone like stars in the dim candlelight. And that rustling silk! And that feather on her hat! Gasping of pride and some asthma—small wonder, her fat was simply rolling on the floor. The lady spoke to the bearded Jew:

"You shall read the finest prayers, for, thank God, I have enough to pay for them. I came here all the way from New York and my husband has the finest restaurant there. I have come here to see the land of the forefathers. These patriarchs should know that not all Jews have become miserable beggars; no, indeed some of them have come up among people. I would like to make my fathers happy. It's no small matter to see the finest Jewish woman face to face."

The bearded watchman outdid himself in amiability:

"I am going to read ten such prayers, so that all the patriarchs in paradise will simply keep their mouths open with amazement. But, kindly tell me your honorable name and that of your unforgettable mother. I will put it on paper, and I will hide that paper behind this rock, so it will get straight to Rachel herself."

The lady opened her pocketbook.

"The only think I have is my visiting card," she said distressedly, as if she were making a great sacrifice. "The letters are not just printed, they are engraved. Here, right it on the back. It's the finest kind of visiting card, and my name is the latest —Victoria. My mother used to sell herrings. To tell you the truth, her name was just plain 'Chaja.' "

The watchman threw the paper behind the stone, leaned back and forward and began to say his prayers. The lady interrupted him:

"That is quite enough for the patriarchs! And besides it is dinnertime and my car is waiting already."

As soon as she had left, the watchman noticed Lasik lying on the ground. He looked contemptuously at his rags. To be sure, this one did not shine with diamonds.

"And what do you think you are doing here?"

"I? Well, I—already!"

"What means, already?"

"I am—dying—already."

The watchman began to yell:

"Dying!—What nerve! You scoundrel! Have you any idea where you are? This is not the place for beggars, this is Rachel's grave. Do you understand how holy this place is? Are you deaf and dumb? Nobody dies here. Everyone just puts money into my hand, and I lower the scribbled papers into the tomb and read a few prayers. Afterwards they leave. Do you understand? Why aren't you moving? Look, what's your name and your mother's name? Answer me quickly. While no one is here, I will give you a reduced rate."

Lasik smiled sadly:

"Your excitement is absolutely in vain. Suppose my name is 'Pain,' and that of my mother 'Sorrow.' What then? You don't have to move your lips. I am sure you have corns on your lips anyway. I am not deaf and dumb, that you should talk to nature for me. Also, I am not such an American pig and I don't have a single penny. So you better calm down. Within one hour I will surely be dead."

"Ingrate! Blasphemer! Dog! Go away from here, or I will tear you to pieces! Can you imagine what would happen if every beggar decided to die in this holy place? Go, die in some manure ditch! Rachel's grave was certainly not built for you! It was made for decent people.'"

Lasik did not budge.

"You may shout as much as you wish, I am not moving from here; if I told you I am going to die here, it will be so. When I could still be alive, the whole world shouted: 'Infamous Roitschwantz, how dare you live here?' And they tore me to pieces. Go ahead! Indeed, what a scandal that would be: Lasik Roitschwantz dares to pass away at such an outstanding place! But you might as well get used to the fact. During my lifetime I have not chosen the suitable spots for myself, either. No, the wind was simply blowing, and I sat down in the cruel train compartment. And now it is the same thing. I have crawled as long as I could, and this is how far I came. Do you think I knew that this here was Rachel's grave? No, I did not think anybody lived here. I was going to die in all humility, trying not to bother anyone with my last sigh. I know very well, indeed, it is forbidden to sigh aloud. And so I have been crawling up to this spot; and here I find you—screaming. Please, control yourself. Don't shout at me five minutes before the end! For once, be human, and tell me: 'Please, would you be kind enough . . .' You see, I have never heard such unexpected sounds!"

The watchman, however remained stubborn:

"It is absolutely against the custom for anyone to die here, and besides who will pay for your stupid funeral?"

To this Lasik replied in an unexpectedly stern manner:

"You know what, Jew, I must say, you bore me. You are disturbing me in the act of dying. Right now I am supposed to think about something exalted, sublime, and you keep talking about that dirty money. I have no money, and as far as I am concerned you may throw my body into the manure ditch. I really don't care. But at this moment, when everything in me is full of song, I wish to think only of the sublime."

The guard began to laugh.

"One might think, what a strange bird! . . . I can yet understand when learned *Zadiks* die—or ministers, or rich people—who have done many good deeds. They all have something to look back upon. A life full of glory lies behind them. But what can you philosophize about when you are such a sad beggar, a nitwit, a tramp off the streets?"

"Yes, I am no Learned Secretary, and no Rothschild, either. I am merely a tailor from Homel. Nevertheless, I must think quietly before I die. My whole stormy life is arising before my eyes. It sparkles down there, like our Sosch. It makes me laugh when I think of all the insignificant details. It hardly resembles real life, at this point. It looks much more like one of Lewka's obscene anecdotes. The memories are coming back and I must smile,—perhaps five minutes before my last sigh. I am sure, honorable people die quite differently. They count how many books they have written, the stormy upheavals they have caused, or the money they have made on certain merchandise. You are quite right, my honorable grave-watchman, I am dying an honest fool. You may bring your expensive candle closer, so you can see for yourself that my legs are not moving any more. You see, my death begins with the legs; on my face, however, there is still a smile. I am smiling because, in spite of everything, I am still thinking of the sublime. And even though you are a coarse brute, I shall tell you my very last story. It is the story of the little pipe.

"You know, of course, who *Bescht* was. He was the founder of all the *Chassidim*. These things are naturally as familar to you as the multiplication table, since you earn your living from the dead—while for me they are nothing but prejudice. I can see through your tricks quite easily. However, a clever man remains clever, even when he plays hide-and-seek. We won't lose any words about that—Bescht was an outstanding personality, and all the Jews respected him greatly. You merely had to speak to him, and right away you felt growing in wisdom and kindness! I am not even talking about the great heart this man had. In my opinion he was much more just than even his own invented God, for no one had ever experienced anything bad from Bescht, while of God, well . . . By the way, I do not want to make you too unhappy, since this is my farewell.

"Well, the city in which that man Bescht lived, was practically a chosen city, even though it had no bronze statues. It was a ridiculous little town between Homel and Berditschew, and it was neither Paris nor Berlin. But in it lived the most God-fearing Jews, and among them was just that *Bescht*. Fine. *Yom Kippur* came. The Jews gathered at the synagogue. They came to confess their sins. And sure enough, they confessed. But naturally, they had not committed any sins. How can such decent people even think of transgression? They obviously confess purely because it is the thing to do. Just take a look at the audience! Yes, there were all the *Zadiks* and all your charitable people. One knows the whole Talmud by heart, another has contributed three hundred rubles for a new Torah, this one fasts continuously, the other prays day and night. In short, they could not even be called Jews any more, but regular angels.

"But what happens? Up there, God opens the Book of Fate and weighs each and every sin. The pious Jews implore Him to be lenient. They beat their chest, they cry and shout. But they do not feel the slightest relief. Everyone of them feels a heavy rock weighing on his heart, and all tears are in vain. Nothing will help—too many transgressions in that just and fair-minded city. You cannot imagine the despair that came over them! At the synagogue there was such wailing that even the birds, flying over the roof, fell to the ground of distress.

But on that particular day in autumn, it was very warm. The clouds gathered and the thunder got ready to roll, but it just would not rain. The Jews were amazed and frightened: 'We are lost. God does not want to forgive us our sins. He is all set to take the pen and sign our death warrant. Maybe the cholera will come over us, or a new pogrom, and we shall be impaled, our women raped, our children trampled. Oh, woe, what pain and suffering will come upon us! There is no forgiveness for us! What did we do to deserve such punishment?'

"And all those learned book-people began to confess to all the various sins they could find in their books; however, they did not remember their own sins, and indeed how could they be reminded of such human trifles? Whoever knew the Talmud by heart, certainly did not know any plain, ordinary words. He did not know how to pacify the mourners, how to be merry with the poor and oppressed on holidays. And the one who had put down a thousand rubles for a new Torah, did not know what ordinary misery was. Indeed, he would give a couple of kopeks to the familiar beggars in the street; but he would never bring a poor tailor, who had no candle or a piece of bread for Sabbath, the smallest gift. He thought all people could live and be happy just with the beautiful Torah he had contributed. And the one who always prayed, did not know how to forgive. And the one who fasted, did not know how to feed the hungry. And their entire justice was only good for two hours. They put it on, like they did the silken *tallis*. But now the invented God was fed up with all this masquerading. And the Jews were crying, but there was no relief. And so, they went to see Bescht. When Bescht is with us, we will not be destroyed. After all, he is closer to God than any of us; he will beg forgiveness for us!"

"Bescht stood there, praying. But a terrible sorrow shows in his face. So much so, that it hurts to look at him. You see, he is not just one of those book-scholars. He can really look the Jews into their soul. He takes their sins into his hand, and his hands are dropping down: no one can hold such weight. He would like to burst into tears, but he has no tears. He is like that sky before the storm: heavy clouds are gathering, it is almost impossible to breathe, the rain must come down, the thunder must begin to rumble; but no, they cannot do it. It is still and sultry on such days on earth. The old Bescht feels unhappy and miserable. He implores the invented God: 'Grant me tears, so I can entreat you to forgive the Jews!' But God is deaf. He wants to be just. He closed his ears, so he would not change his mind. And Bescht tries in vain.

"The Jews get more and more desperate. They see Bescht's torment. They see, not even he can help them. They stop [illegible] Already they are all hoarse from so much crying. It is quiet at the synagogue, as quiet as before death, as still as it is in my soul right now. The Jews can almost hear the pages turn. Up there, God is turning a new leaf in the Book of Fate. Soon the thunder will break loose. Soon it will slam shut the heavy book, and all will be over, all will be over!

"All of a sudden, in the midst of this painful quiet, something very improper occurs. Really, those horrible beggar-folk have to come crawling everywhere! Of all places, I had to pick Rachel's grave!—and just into that synagogue, where all the rich and famous men were gathered, a little tailor came crawling in too. His name was Schulim. He had come with his little son who was three or four years old. Schulim had come to pray, but the child of course had no philosophical ideas in his head, only all kinds of childish tricks. He soon became bored at the synagogue. Everyone just stood there and prayed. An hour, two, but then the child had enough. He tugs at the father: 'I want to go to mother,' but Schulim has no time for the little boy. The poor Schulim just had to talk to God. The child does not know what to do. Then he remembers he has a little whistle in his pocket. His mother had bought it yesterday for him at the market for five kopeks. He pulls out the whistle and gets ready to blow, when his father sees it:

" 'Joska, put this away at once. Today is *Yom Kippur* and everybody must cry and not blow a whistle.'

"But the little Joska is stubborn. He does not want to cry. He just wants to blow his whistle. Everybody sees that this is going to be a scandal. As though they did not have enough scandal at the synagogue. Indeed, it was quite understandable why God was offended and angry. . . . For a moment they were even cheerful. Perhaps it had nothing to do with their guilt, but only with the sins of that infamous tailor. How did he get in here to begin with. And they chase Schulim out. But at this point, Bescht intervenes. To be sure, it is forbidden to talk during the prayer, but Bescht said nevertheless: 'Leave that child alone! If he wants to blow the whistle, let him!' Naturally Joska began to blow immediately. He blew with all the joy and happiness of a child. And what do you know, the thunder began to rumble, and from Bescht's eyes came real tears, and in one moment all the Jews felt relieved. They could hardly believe it, and before long, evening came, the stars shone in the sky, the fast was over. With tears of joy, they embraced each other: 'So, God has forgiven us our sins, after all! We have not prayed in vain, we have not fasted in vain! When Bescht is with us, how can God be angry?' And full of reverence they step in front of Bescht: 'Rabbi, your prayer has saved us.'

"But Bescht merely shakes his head:

" 'No. It was dark in the sky, and up there a fight over life and death was taking place. Your sins weighed so heavily, that even the most penitent tears could not have outweighed them. God had his ears stopped up. God had forbidden me to cry. God did not hear my prayers any more. And then, the child's cry resounded. The little boy blew his whistle, and God heard it. And God could not stand it any longer. He had to smile. It was such a foolish trick, bought with a mere five kopeks, and it was such impropriety on a high holiday like *Yom Kippur!* . . . But I am telling you one thing now, and I am saying this to all you clever Jews,—don't ever think that your reproaches or my prayers have saved our city. No—it was saved by this little whistle, one small ridiculous sound that came from a child's heart. . . . If you'll look quickly, you'll see little Joska smiling!' "

Lasik became silent. He had talked too much. He could hardly breathe. It was inconceivable how he could have finished the story of the whistle. His body was covered with perspiration.

The guard grumbled:

"And still I say, it is not right to do such things on *Yom Kippur!* You have just thought up this story to stop me from saying anything. And now, that you have had your say, you may leave these premises. Did you hear me?"

Lasik did not reply. He did not even sigh. Quietly and easily he passed away.

The watchman sniffed his tobacco, scratched his beard, could not understand what had happened to that shameless beggar. He took a light and brought it close to Lasik's face.

"Well, what kind of behavior is that"?

Lasik lay there, motionless. He did not breathe any more. A childish smile was on his face. It was the smile of little Joska, when he was permitted to blow his whistle. And when the watchman saw that smile on Lasik's face, he froze. He forgot completely about the money or the funeral. The usual prayers would not come over his lips. No, the candle fell out of his hand and onto the floor, and he sobbed violently.

Rest in peace, poor Roitschwantz! You will not dream any longer of justice, or of a piece of sausage.

Written in Paris,
April-October, 1927.